Roswell Rising - a Novel of Disclosure

Roswell Rising- a Novel of Disclosure
by Ben Emlyn-Jones

The Aldyth Press

Published by
The Aldyth Press

First published in 2016

ISBN: 978-0-9542229-4-9

"Sightings of UFO's are not restricted to just one or two parts of our planet. Reports come from all over the world today, and scientific analysis of these reports strongly suggests not only that a growing number of people believe that UFO's exist as a physical phenomenon but also that more and more countries believe that a more in-depth investigation into this phenomenon might make a significant contribution towards the well-being of the planet earth as well as towards man's better understanding of himself and his purpose on earth."

Sir Eric Gairy- first prime minister of Grenada in an address to the United Nations on the 12th of October 1978.

Chapter 1

The desert roiled and shimmered in the raging heat. The loose scrub seemed to glow from its own internal fire. Clane Quilley tore at his collar, tugging his sweat-soaked tie loose. He dried the steering wheel with his handkerchief where it had beaded on the dark purple leather rim. He had no idea where he was driving; he just knew he had to get out of town. He'd only been there three months so the urge didn't bode well. He'd seen a road sign a few miles back and knew he was on Route Seventy; but west or east of his new home, he wasn't sure. The landscape was featureless, yellowy-brown and almost flat to the horizon. Blue-black translucent mountains loomed in the distance ahead. His foot fumbled as he lifted it off the accelerator and the unfamiliar engine idled. The car slowed. He pulled over to the verge and cut the ignition, unaware of why he was doing this. His heartbeat thumped in his ears from the sudden silence. Without the breeze of motion, the car's interior became stifling. He opened the door and stepped out with a snap. The glare from the sun seemed to come at him from all angles, reverberating off the ground and even from the very air. He tipped his hat down over his eyes and walked away from the road. "The heat." he muttered to himself, his eyes stinging with sweat. Salt smarted an old cold sore on his lip. "The sun came down... That's how they died." He applied his mental brakes hard. He had promised himself he wouldn't think about that. The dusty gravel beneath his feet turned his new black brogues grey; his feet baked inside like potatoes in foil. He had been walking briskly for about five minutes; nothing lay ahead or at either side except the desert. Green bushes poked up out of the monotone scrub every few hundred yards. They coalesced in the distance into a verdant speckle. He stopped and focused his irritated eyes on the view. Transient quicksilver ponds of *fata morgana* flicked across the landscape. He sighed and then turned round to head back to his car. He froze in alarm; it was nowhere to be seen. The vista behind him was as featureless as that ahead; there was nothing at all to be seen of the road. His stomach clenched in fear and he began running. He pounded up to the crest of a gentle rise in anticipation of relief. "I'll see it in a moment." he gasped. But as the succeeding low ground came into view the road was still not there. He turned to his right and sprinted, realizing that he'd lost his sense of direction. The sun was near the zenith. After he'd cleared the next rise and still saw no road. He sank to his knees. "It's no good." In just a few minutes he'd moved from a state of security in a car seat on a modern paved highway to a dying man in a primeval landscape which God had intended only for lizards and crickets. It wasn't the first time a wave of mortality awareness had spread over him, but it was the funniest and calmest. He almost laughed with self-deprecating irony. He reached into his pocket for his rosary and whipped off a few Hail Mary's; then he lay down on a patch of grass and waited with his hat over his face. Would thirst and heat exhaustion claim him or would he live long enough to feel the teeth of a roaming coyote tear at his thigh? It didn't really matter. The sun went out. The sudden darkness and coolness gave him such a start that he sat up. A large cloud had just blotted out the sun. More of them gathered in a line of bruise coloured tumours across the sky. The sun fought back from behind its veil making the edge of the clouds fluoresce. Clane got to his feet, brushing the dust from his trousers. The shades of the landscape were totally transformed without the sun.

"Looks like there's some rain coming." said a voice from immediately behind him.

Clane yelped in shock and jumped round.

The man was small, barely five feet tall, and ancient. Little black dog-like eyes poked out from between the arroyos of wrinkles on his face. He wore a dirty Stetson hat and poncho. Through the accumulated desert dust and piñon twigs stuck to its fabric, Clane could see that the poncho had an intricate coloured weave, similar to Scottish tartan.

"Where the hell did you come from?" demanded Clane as soon as he'd got his breath back.

"I might ask you the same question, Mr Quilley." His voice was as cracked, hoarse and sun-bleached as his face.

"How do you know my name? Who are you?"

"It ain't safe to be out in the desert in the middle of the day. Grandfather Sun up there, he can roast you like a quail on a spit."

Clane realized that the man was an Indian, probably an Apache or Pueblo or something. He wasn't used to them; there were very few Indians in New York. The only one Clane had known was a filing clerk at the *Times* who drank Guinness and watched the Dodgers games just like he did.

"You should never leave the road."

"OK, well too late. I don't know where the road is now anyway."

The man slowly raised his arm and pointed without moving his head or taking his gaze off Clane's eyes.

Clane looked and saw that Route Seventy lay about a hundred yards away. His car was where he'd left it, parked on the verge. As he watched, a Shell gas tanker lumbered past leaving a contrail of dust behind it. He scratched his head. "That's odd; a minute ago I thought it was out of sight."

"It was!" said the man emphatically, opening new creases in his face as he raised his eyebrows and smiled. "Where do you live, Mr Quilley?"

"What?" he tittered. "You know my name, but don't know where I live?"

The man remained silent.

"Roswell."

"That way." The man jerked a thumb over his shoulder down the road. Then he abruptly turned and walked off. "You're an interesting young man, Mr Quilley." he called over his shoulder. "We'll meet again."

Clane returned to the car. When he reached it he looked back and saw the old Indian in the distance walking swiftly and purposively away from the road and out into the depths of the desert. "Where's he going? There's nothing out there. Didn't he just tell me that wasn't safe?" He got into the car, swung it round in an arc and sped off home.

....

Clane was beginning to daydream slightly in the mesmerizing heat haze of the highway. Shadows of clouds rolled across the landscape. The wind was rising too, heralding the approaching rain. Occasional gusts buffeted the car...

BOOM!

"Argh!" He exclaimed aloud as a heavy object struck the car. The windscreen was completely obscured by something large and grey. It flashed through his head that he might have crashed into a steer. Some ranchers let their cattle roam wild in that area. The car swerved from side to side as he instinctively slammed on the brakes. The tyres shrieked on the tar paving. As soon as the vehicle ground to a halt he leapt out. The front of the car was covered by a sheet of light grey textile. He grabbed it and tugged it off. He immediately recognized it. It was a weather balloon that had been deployed from the army air base south of Roswell. The meteorological unit sent them up regularly and anybody who lived in Roswell quickly got used to them coming down. In his three months in the city he had seen several lying around. This one had no instruments attached; it was just a torn and deflated nylon envelope with some radar targets fixed underneath by parachute cord. These were simple cardboard placards covered with tin foil and reinforced with balsawood frames. Its ripped ballast bag contained no sand. The only function of this one was to monitor the wind. He'd launched a few himself when he'd been briefly stationed at Guam. He dragged the balloon to the side of the road and threw it onto the verge. A gust of breeze caught the riven envelope and carried it away, rolling and tumbling across the desert. His second-hand Chevrolet Master was not his ideal car and he still hadn't quite got used to it. It was undamaged by the impact apart from a slightly bent windscreen wiper. "Shit!" he cursed. He'd have to drop into Gregg's Autos to get it fixed; luckily it was a new month and his salary had just gone through.

....

Clane couldn't get over the fact that Roswell was nominally a "city" when fewer people lived there than in an average Brooklyn block. New Mexicans didn't seem to have a clue about what a real city was. Roswell was a place that crept up on you slowly. It began with a couple of lonely ranch huts by the side of the highway separated out of sight from each other. Then there were a few isolated bars and diners; down-at-heel and rowdy joints; popular with visiting oil company workers, the local negroes and Indians. A legend said that the fugitive gangster John Dillinger used to call there, which Clane could well believe. At night there was usually a RPD squad car or two parked outside as the police broke up yet another drunken brawl. Then rows of houses began on both sides of the straight flat highway; right at the point where it became signed as West 2nd Street instead of Route Seventy. All these buildings had the traditional well in the side yard, as ubiquitous as doors and windows. Clane was reminded of a poem he had learnt at school by Samuel Coleridge, *The Rime of the Ancient Mariner* which contains the line: "Water, water everywhere, nor any drop to drink!" Roswell was the opposite. There was hardly any water in sight, but there was as much to drink as you wanted; however it was all out of sight underground. There were no sidewalks until you got close to mid-town Roswell. This looked strange to somebody like Clane who'd lived his life in the concrete canyons of New York City. Few buildings were more than two storeys high and the roads were calm enough to cross at any time of the day. Clane pulled up outside the offices of the *Roswell Daily Record* in dread. Sure enough, as soon as he was up the stairs and through the door the editor, Owen Mollett, rapped on the glass wall of his corner cubicle and beckoned him in. The boss swivelled on his chair back and forth, occasionally stopping to stoke his smouldering cigar with a match. The smoke in the unventilated room made Clane cough. "Quilley, I assume you have me the scoop of the century; why else would you be away all morning?"

"Sorry, Mr Mollett, but I don't. I was driving out of town and got lost." This wasn't a complete lie of course.

"After three months in Roswell you got lost?"

"I was out on the Seventy, sir."

Mollett paused. "You've not much experience for a reporter your age, have you?"

"I started when I was sixteen, sir. I made the coffee and swept the floor. I worked my way up, like Tristan does here. Sure I took some time out, but that was for the war. Surely I'm not the only one, am I?"

"What service were you in?"

"Navy. I enlisted in January '41. Submarines; then I was in Japan."

Mollett signed. "OK, Quilley, I'm going to cut you some slack; not because you were in the Pacific, but because... I know you've had some tough times since the war. I know the *RDR* is a bit of a comedown for a man who wrote for the *New York Times*, but..."

"No, sir!"

Mollett cut him off. "It is in the eyes of most people. We're not exactly... Bohemian here in Roswell. Reputation carries weight. If you want to be modest then people won't get it." He raised his eyebrows, "But even here we all respect punctuality."

"Mr Mollett, I'm very sorry I was late. I'll make up the time I lost."

Mollett nodded slowly. His face was puffed and sallow. He seemed to live in that office and maybe suffered from sunlight deficiency. "Alright, Quilley. Go sort out your in-tray."

"Thank you, Mr Mollett." smiled Clane. He got up to go.

As he was opening the door the editor called him back. "Quilley?"

"Sir?"

He grinned slyly. "I might still decide to give you some... er... punishment duties."

Clane felt edgy at his expression. "Sure, sir."

As Clane walked out into the office and took his place at his desk the others were all silent and looking nonchalantly in neutral directions, as they always did when somebody had just been chewed out by the boss. As soon as he sat down, young Tristan rushed to his side eagerly as always. "Hello, Mr Quilley. How are you?"

Clane looked up and met his enthusiastic smile. "Fine thanks, Tristan. How are you?"

"I'll make you a coffee."

"No need. Have you got my files?"

"Coming right up, Mr Quilley." The clerk scampered away and came back a few minutes later with a stack of folders, envelopes and loose papers. Then Clane lit a cigarette and loaded a sheet of paper into his typewriter. He began as always with today's date: *Thursday 3rd of July 1947*. He typed steadily and smoothly, using all his fingers like an expert. His latest story was about a situation in City Hall that all newsmen were born for. The previous year had marked the closure of a nearby prisoner-of-war camp. The inmates, mostly Germans and Italians, had been released and repatriated. They had been popular characters around town and did a lot of civic maintenance work, including a good job reinforcing the banks of the North Spring River, the only open watercourse for miles around. Even that was just a trickle until it rained. However after they had been sent home an aerial photograph had revealed that they'd arranged some of the paving slabs in the shape of a fascist cross. A parting gift of defiance for their former captors. Clane had done some investigation at the records office and found out that one of the mayor's staff got wind of the PoW's' plans in advance and had colluded with them. It turns out he was a shareholder in Patten Construction, the company brought in to concrete over the paving slabs, and in doing so made a hefty profit off the public purse. The net was closing, and Clane was the hunter.

"Quilley?"

The smell of cigar smoke and unwashed clothes told Clane that the editor was standing behind him. It took a moment for his eyes to refocus as he turned away from his typewriter. "Mr Mollett?"

"I have an assignment for you."

"I already have one, sir." He pointed at the typewriter.

"Put that aside and do this instead."

"Wh... What!?... But, sir! This is the Cochrane case! It's dynamite!"

The editor tossed an envelope into his lap and gave him a stern look indicating that his position was not negotiable.

Clane picked it up. It was already opened and smelled of perfume. He pulled out the letter and began reading its neat feminine handwriting: *Dear* Roswell Daily Record. *I'm a faithful reader of yours for over twenty years... never miss and issue... delivered every day...* He skipped to the next paragraph. *...was out on my porch last night and I saw a light in the sky. It got brighter and brighter until I saw that it was disk-shaped. Just like those ones we've been hearing about...* The author went on to describe her experience in more detail. It was signed: *Mrs Amelia Crewe. Picacho, Lincoln County.*

"Check it out, Quilley."

"But, Mr Mollett; this is a flying saucer story!"

"Correct."

"You can't be serious!"

"Quilley, for the next month you are *RDR*'s official flying saucer correspondent." Somebody on a neighbouring desk giggled.

....

"Well, I suppose I was lucky he didn't fire me." Clane took a sip of beer.

"Hey, Clane!" Stanley, always the office joker, walked into the bar and threw something onto the table in front of him. It was a copy of a magazine called *Amazing Stories*, a science fiction periodical. "I thought this might help." Everybody around the table dissolved into merriment. Clane felt his face burn, but he forced a smile at his own expense. "If they take me to Mars I'll let you know."

They were all having an after-work drink in *Browny's*, a bar on the corner of 5th and Main. This "inner Roswell" establishment was very different to the less reputable hangouts on the edge of town. It had a polished parquet floor and velvet curtains. A radio played music quietly in the corner. The tables were oval-shaped and the stools cushioned. Chrome, brass and red leather lined the bar top. In the corner was a raised dais and at nine PM the tables and chairs would be cleared away to make it a stage for the resident negro jazz band who would play until late in the night and everybody would jive until whenever their chosen bedtime was.

"Who did he give the Cochrane case to?" asked Clane dismally.

"Johnny." replied Marietta, a studious young woman who shared his desk.

"Johnny Ramirez?"

"From the sales column."

"Damn that old man Mollett! Ramirez is a fool! God, Mari; I was so close to publishing. I worked my ass off for that article and Mollett takes it away from me. Three weeks I've been on that story; all up in smoke. Ramirez' name will be under the title. And he'll screw it up first!"

"I'm sorry, Clane." Marietta put a supportive hand on his sleeve.

"I was only a bit late for Christ's sake!"

"Four hours late." Stanley qualified.

"So what? Does it warrant turning me into the *RDR*'s clown?"

"It's not that bad, Mr Quilley." said Tristan. He had only recently become old enough to imbibe liquor and he sipped his beer cautiously. "And anyway, it's only for a month."

"Flying saucers!" Clane hissed. At that moment the radio began playing a song by the Buchanan Brothers: "*You'd better pray to the Lord when you see those flying saucers...*" The others chuckled at the synchronicity. "The Lord is toying with you, Clane." laughed Stanley.

Clane shook his head ruefully.

"I don't get where all these flying saucer stories are coming from." said Tristan. "Everybody's talking about them, but it's all sprung up so recently."

"What's the name of that guy who kicked all this off?" asked Stanley.

"That pilot. Arnold, I think it was. Yes, Kenneth Arnold. He was flying up somewhere in the Northwest a couple of weeks ago and he saw a group of them. And since then the whole world and his brother is harping on about them. Nobody had heard of flying saucers before then."

"Bah!" scoffed Clane. "It's a stupid fad. It'll die off in a week or two; I've been doing this job long enough to know that's how the news works. Then I can get back to my normal job. Either that of the old man will just fire me." He chuckled. "'Redundant flying saucer correspondent'; that'll look good on my résumé."

"You know, Marietta; I don't think that's true." said Stanley. "There was talk of strange things in the sky before all that fuss with Arnold; it just didn't make the papers much. My brother saw one, way before the war. Of course nobody said a word about men from Mars in those days."

"Remember the thing that flew over Los Angeles?" piped up Tristan. "When was that? I was in high school. Only a few years ago."

"It was just a few weeks after Pearl Harbour." said Marietta. "January '42. I remember it well. This big flying saucer arrived late at night over LA Bay. Of course the triple-A opened up on it. Everybody was scared it was the Japs come back for more."

"The *LA Times* published a photograph of it." said Clane. "It was right in the searchlights and it did look like a flying saucer."

"We might get a flying saucer over Roswell, Clane." said Stanley. "Then the Pulitzer's yours."

"Huh!" Clane sipped his glass. "I think a report on Santa Claus would be more promising,"

Marietta remained serious. "It wasn't damaged, even though coastal defence fired fourteen hundred rounds; the shells just ricocheted right off. Five people on the ground were killed by falling fragments." There was a sober silence at the table for a moment.

"If our weapons can't hurt them..." began Tristan. "Those beasts from Mars can wipe us out real easy, like crushing a bug with your boot."

Stanley passed the comic book over to him. "You've been reading too many of these, son."

"No, Mr McWilliams. I never read things like that."

"Well, look of the bright side. If Mars attacks us we can stop worrying about the Russians." Stanley quipped.

Tristan didn't laugh.

"What do you think of this rumour that the Russians have the A-bomb?" asked Marietta. She appeared eager to change the subject, even if it meant moving on to another almost as grim.

"Phooey!" answered Stanley. "Only we have the A-bomb. That's why we won the war."

"If the Russians get the bomb we better hope there's never another war or it's the death of us all on both sides." said Marietta.

Tristan leaned forward and lowered his voice. "You know the guy who runs Dorsey's Grocers up on East 23rd? His kid's schoolteacher says they're doing some kind of experiment up at White Sands to check for Russian bomb tests."

"How does he know?"

"The teacher's brother's boss' barber saw this balloon. A huge one, a giant one! It has some kind of detector on it that can sense the Russian bombs being tested... And you know, I think I saw one of those balloons myself."

Clane got up and went to the bathroom. Talk of war bothered him and it was his drinking round. He stood at the bar, packing his unwelcome thoughts back into the locked cabinet where he normally kept them. Then Jesse Marcel walked in. He was dressed in his AAF khakis and carried a briefcase in his hand. *Browny's* was popular with men from the base so Clane knew he was always bound to bump into Jesse here again sooner or later, but it was still a shock. The feeling seemed to be mutual. Jesse pulled up short and gaped. He blushed visibly. "Hello, Clane." he said in an expressionless voice after a pause.

"Jesse." replied Clane in kind.

Jesse looked down at Clane's tray of beers. "Er... are you here with...?"

"Some guys from the office." Clane finished his sentence.

The two men grinned nervously at each other then parted with a nod. Clane returned to the table and shared out his round. As he chatted with his colleagues he occasionally looked over his shoulder and exchanged glances with Jesse. When he left *Browny's* to go home he felt his spirits rise. Some of the air between them had been cleared.

As he drove home he recalled his turbulent relationship with Jesse Marcel. They had met two years earlier on Tinian Island in the South Pacific. Clane's submarine, USS *Tunny*, had been forced to land at Tinian after suffering engine failure. The huge airbase on the island could easily accommodate the boat's crew for the fortnight until the necessary spare parts could be shipped out. Jesse and Clane had found a rapport and had exchanged a few letters after the war; and Jesse made sure to catch up with Clane when the latter moved to Roswell. Things had changed though since their first meeting. Major Jesse Marcel was head of the intelligence division for the 509th Very Heavy Bombardment Group; and Clane had been a Navy submariner and chief torpedoman who had later been posted to Japan. Therefore the two men had experienced the war very differently. This caused conflict between them, and to make matters worse their dispute had reached its endgame while Clane was a guest at Jesse's home and Jesse's wife was present. They'd had a few glasses of wine while eating dinner, followed by a couple of brandies which had lubricated their tongues. Jesse had been proudly regaling them with a monologue about the 509th and their bombing missions over Japan in the last weeks of the war, including the fire-storming of Tokyo and the atomic bomb attacks on Hiroshima and Nagasaki. "...so basically," he concluded, "the 509th are the boys who won the war."

"No you're not!" Clane's tone of voice came out even harsher than he intended.

Jesse sighed and rolled his eyes. He and Clane had had this debate before several times, albeit in a more light-hearted tone, and he didn't detect Clane's additional ire. Jesse's wife, Violet, was more astute; she glared nervously at the two men. "Hey, guys. Quit the inter-service rivalry clichés will you?" Clane spoke of how by 1945 the submarine war against Japanese shipping had been so successful that no vessel could stick its keel out of port without getting a torpedo in it. Japan was surrounded, isolated and depleted. It was moving towards a negotiated surrender, hoping the Soviets, neutral at the time with Japan, would broker a deal.

"Damn it, Clane," shot Jesse, "You're a real sucker if you buy that. The Jap is crafty; he was playing for time."

"Not a chance, Jesse." retorted Clane. "You need to realize something!" He jabbed a finger aggressively at Jesse with the word *You*. "The Jap needs to eat like everybody else! Downfall would never have happened anyway!" Operation Downfall was the proposed amphibious invasion of Japan's home islands. "One more month! That's all we needed!"

Jesse slammed his fist down on the table. "And how many Jap civilians would have to die to give you squid bubbleheads your month!? More than we killed with our bombs! Hirohito and his henchmen weren't starving; they had larders full of food and they made the decisions! Ordinary people suffered in that war, Clane, not the leaders! The Japs were too goddamn gutsy for their own good! They'd have fought on to the last man like they did at Iwo Jima, at Truk, at Okinawa! How much death do you want, Clane!?"

Clane cracked; Jesse had just tipped his trigger. Clane jumped to his feet and yelled: "You don't know what fucking death is!"

Violet flushed at the sound of the profanity.

Jesse gaped. "How dare you, Quilley!" In his rage he lapsed into the military style of an officer addressing an enlisted man by his surname alone, as he had done when the two had first met. "Get out of my house now!"

But as Jesse was speaking, Clane was already storming towards the front door. He slammed it so hard behind him that one of the viewing panes shattered. He calmed down somewhat as he drove home. Despite the antagonism that he still felt for Jesse, he chided himself over Violet. He felt guilty for using a cuss-word in front of a lady as if he were dived at a hundred and fifty feet with his pals in *Tunny*. It wasn't a slight to the submarine branch by a fly-boy that bothered him; that was just the camouflage for a much deeper conflict. He had last spoken to and seen Maj. Jesse Marcel on that night a few weeks before, but the memory, the guilt, the resentment, the embarrassment ate into him like acid. Greeting Jesse in the bar today had neutralized some of that.

Clane parked his car outside his home, a motel at the northern end of town. He had toyed with the idea of renting somewhere more settled, but hadn't got round to it yet. He was still not sure how long he'd be living in Roswell, but he sensed intuitively that it wouldn't be too long. He walked along the footpath under the awning that led to the row of rooms. His neighbour, Mrs Ray, was standing in front of her door. She grinned as she saw him approach, holding up her ubiquitous camera. She levelled it at him. "Smile, Mr Quilley." Clane obliged as she clicked the shutter. "Lovely shot."

"Another photograph, Mrs Ray? I swear I could sign you on part time with *RDR*."

"If I wasn't already a lawyer and pilot I think photojournalism would be my third choice of career. As it is I'm an enthusiastic amateur. I've got a darkroom set up in the bathroom; give me half an hour and I'll develop this for you. It's Kodachrome so it'll be in full colour. I can even make it into a slide if you prefer."

"Where do you get the money for colour film from, Mrs Ray?"

"Well, Bernard and I are hardly destitute."

"How is Bernard? Enjoying the oil business still?"

"Oh, he's camping out somewhere near Four Corners. He should be back on Monday."

"Good, well I'll see you both soon, Mrs Ray."

"Call me Hilda. We are neighbours after all."

Before he entered his room, Clane looked up at the sky. A B-29 Superfortress was passing overhead at about three thousand feet; its engine noise was an omnipresent roar of energy. Aircraft were a very common sight in the sky above Roswell because of the airbase, but for some reason he felt compelled to stare at this bomber as it banked over Roswell and shrunk to a speck against the burgeoning cloud cover.

Clane felt very lethargic when he entered his room. He dropped his hat on the sideboard and collapsed onto his bed feeling hungry, but too tired to get up and make any food. At least it was July the fourth tomorrow. He might not get the whole day off, but he should at least get a lie in before taking a cruise downtown to watch the parade. He reached under his bed and his hand brushed against his suitcase. He sat up and pulled it out. It still contained a lot of his belongings. He had never completely unpacked since he had moved to Roswell, another sign that he subconsciously did not intend to settle there. He opened it up, reached under his folded trousers and retrieved the leather satchel of his war memorabilia. Inside were photographs of him and his crewmates from *Tunny*, his honourable discharge papers and his silver submariners' dolphins; a badge that resembled a pilot's wings at first glance, but were actually made up of two piscine creatures facing inward towards a submarine's bow. Instinctively and without premeditation, Clane picked up the telephone. "Operator, I'd like to put a call through to New York please." He gave the number.

Two thousand miles away a phone rang. "Hello?"

"Good evening, Gina."

There was a pause and she caught her breath. "Clane." Her tone was shocked, accusatory, exasperated.

"Could I speak to Siobhan please?"

Gina tutted. "She's sewing her costume."

"I only want a moment."

Gina sighed and he heard the receiver bump down and in the distance her voice shouting: "Siobhan! You're dad's on the phone!" Footsteps approached. "Hello?"

"Hi, honey." An involuntary smile split his face.

"Hi, Dad."

"How are you?"

"Fine. How's New Mexico?"

Clane and his twelve year old daughter spoke on the phone for ten minutes, about her school, her being band leader in the July fourth parade the next day, her friends, life in New York. When the call ended the motel room felt cold and empty. He felt the urge to run out to his car and drive and drive until he reached her. A few days ago he had received the letter from Gina's attorney; she was filing for divorce.

....

Clane awoke with a jolt and sat up in shock. The *basso profundo* crash of thunder shook the ground like an earthquake. Lightning flickered behind the curtains. He breathed a sigh of relief and stood up. The air was stifling with humidity and he was drenched in sweat. He walked in a circle, relishing the cooling breeze as he moved. He pulled aside the curtain and looked out. Torrential rain was hosing down from the sky. The lightning strobed in the background behind the gentle wash of the forecourt floodlights. A million spattering drops frosted the inundated pathway. Rain coursed through the beams of light like a river in the air. A flying insect fluttered against the inside of the windowpane. He returned to his bed and lay back down. He had been dreaming of Japan again. These dreams varied in lucidity and realism; this one had been near the top end of both scales. This was the real reason he had broken his friendship with Jesse Marcel.

The war had ended almost two years earlier, on the fifteenth of August 1945. When the radio message arrived, the crew of USS *Tunny* cheered and applauded. They dashed up onto the bridge and casing, dancing for joy. The captain ordered the torpedo room ceremoniously to unload the tubes. Clane had spent over three years fighting in the Pacific theatre. *Tunny* had been depth charged while preying on ferryboats and coasters in the Bungo Channel. They'd been dived-bombed off the coast of Taiwan and two of Clane's pals had been killed by shrapnel. They'd also sunk a spying trawler with deck gun shells while patrolling the Aleutian Islands off Alaska. The moment the war ended, all these experiences crashed through him and evaporated into a cloud of the harmless past. It was like getting out of jail or drinking a glass of water after a long period of intense thirst. Clane genuinely believed that it was all over. He and his pals could immediately set course for Pearl Harbour and have a beer; then home to New York for apple pie and Guinness... The truth could not have been more different.

USS *Tunny* was directed to join "Operation Blacklist", something none of the crew had ever heard of before. The boat was ordered to set sail directly for Osaka on the Japanese mainland of Honshu. When the submarine had docked the entire compliment were lined up on the wharf and handed a package of new orders and kit. Clane and his pals were to be seconded to the US Military Police. The crew were split up and he never saw some of his pals again. The next few weeks involved the hardest work he had ever done. From dawn till dusk, and sometimes long after, Clane was put in command of a team whose job it was to unload cargo from ships. Boxes of canned food, bags of rice, clothing, medical supplies, water stills, sacks of coal, barrels of oil, wheat, powdered milk, powdered cement and every other commodity imaginable. Once these items were ashore they had to be carefully registered in an inventory and then piled up in warehouses ready to be moved onwards. Ship after ship pulled in, one after the other, and was emptied of its freight. Rows and rows of trucks queued up, driven by other MP's, and Clane's team would have to help stack the goods in the back of the trucks. "You'd think the Japs didn't have any of their own shit." Clane quipped to one of the truck drivers.

"They don't." replied the man with a grave stare.

A month later Clane's team was ordered to stand down for a weekend off, much to their relief. They were all exhausted; their limbs aching, their hands covered in calluses and blisters. On Monday Clane joined the truck driving corps and found himself behind the steering wheel instead of loading boxes into the back. It was the first time he had stepped outside the boundaries of Osaka harbour since his arrival in Japan. He guided his vehicle down the cracked road into the city centre. The autumn rain battled with the windscreen wipers and the wheels jolted in and out of potholes. Very little of the city was left. Crumbling scorched masonry poked out of the ground like rotten teeth. In the suburbs nothing stood at all. Japanese architecture favoured wood as the principle construction material and between the frameworks they used panels of solidified wood pulp, paper literally. This made the buildings very vulnerable to fire. The incendiary bombing by the US air forces had therefore been extremely effective. The surviving residents of Osaka were now living in tents that they had thrown together from any textile they could find; drapes, bedsheets, clothes. Clane had been told to drop his wares off at a distribution point; this was easy to find because a huge crowd of people were milling around it. The point was surrounded by a barbed wire fence and guarded by armed MP's. As Clane broke to a halt the people began chattering with excitement and surging forward. "Get back!" yelled an MP. "Stay back, all of you! There'll be enough for everybody. Wait your turn." Clane and the MP's unloaded the cargo from the back of the truck and the citizens lined up eagerly, holding up their ration books. As soon as they had them they gratefully ran off with their precious groceries, rushing to get them home to their families. Clane had never seen people like these before. They were all emaciated; many didn't have adequate clothing and he could see their ribs protruding. They shivered in the chilly rain. What would happen to them when winter came? They were unwashed; their hair was overgrown and unkempt. The infants sat passively in their mothers' arms, tearstains running down their cheeks. The adults stared with their small black eyes, their faces expressionless and attentive in that unique Japanese way. They maintained their national obsession with honour and dignity, even as their bones pressed against the drum-tight skin of their empty bodies. When he was a small child Clane's grandmother had horrified him with her tales of the Irish famine, but none of her descriptions came close to this modern reality in Japan. However, the worst was yet to come. Clane's supply missions into Osaka eventually progressed to longer distance journeys. He was transferred to a fleet of big haulage trucks and sent out to other cities several hours away. One day he went to Hiroshima.

It took him all morning to get there. Many of the freeways had been bombed to gravel so he had to use smaller roads which themselves were sometimes reduced to mud tracks and his rig got stuck a few times. He entered the city of Hiroshima without even knowing it because there was little left of it to see. He found himself driving along a straight road between what he thought were disused dried up rice paddies. Then he saw some human figures wearing white overalls with a hood and gasmasks over their faces. They were scanning the ground with Geiger tubes. One of the men raised his mask to call out: "Hey buddy! Don't stop; it ain't safe to hang round in this area too long." Sure enough, nobody lived here. The tent cities that he'd seen in Osaka and other places were absent in Hiroshima. No further destruction was possible here. Even the cinders of old buildings had vanished, pulverized in the nuclear fire. As he approached the river he saw a single building, a rotunda with a domed roof. Its walls were cracked and warped, its dome reduced to a frame; but it still stood, defiantly, against all odds and adversity.

The only undamaged hospital in Hiroshima was the Red Cross infirmary at the edge of town. It was here that Clane was heading to drop off medical supplies. It had been greatly expanded to cope with the extra workload; its grounds and carpark now lay beneath rows of tents and Quonset huts. While he was helping the hospital staff unload and store the goods, he got talking to an elderly English doctor. The doctor offered Clane a cup of tea after the job was done and showed him round the hospital. Clane met some of the patients, the residents of Hiroshima. They were mostly women, children and old people who were packed into beds side by side while doctors and nurses, faces tight with stress and exhaustion, attended diligently to them. It was now two months since the bomb had been dropped and many of the victims were still bedridden with third degree burns. Clane saw a man whose left eye had been melted in its socket. "We have a reflex that shuts our eyelids tight when our eyes are exposed to very bright light." explained the doctor. "But that reflex only worked quickly enough in this chap's right eye." Another young woman had a burn right up the top of her forearm and the back of her hand; it had caused her wrist to curl back and lock, and her fingers could hardly move. Some of the patients had come down with what the doctor called "Curie fever". It caused nausea, vomiting and diarrhoea; and it made their hair fall out and their gums bleed. They developed burn-like lesions on their skin and eyes. "Most of these people will recover," said the doctor, "but for how long? In a few years they'll come down with cancers and that'll finish 'em off."

"What causes it?" asked Clane.

"Exposure to particulates made radioactive by the bomb. Grains of dust, ash, cinders. It's everywhere; in the air, the water, the soil. It'll be a good couple of years before anybody can live healthily downtown again. It's become known as 'fallout'. Good job the Gerries never managed to build the bomb!"

Clane sighed. "How could just a single bomb do so much damage?"

"Nuclear fission. That Albert Einstein has a lot to answer for!"

"How many people were killed altogether?"

"Oh, well over a hundred thousand. We're not sure exactly because some of the bodies will never be found..." He looked sadly into Clane's eyes. "Some of them don't even exist. You must understand that the temperature close to the epicentre of the explosion was millions of degrees, comparable with the interior of the sun. Human bodies exposed to that would have just instantly vapourized. Think how hot it feels when you walk outdoors on a warm summer's day... well that sun is over ninety million miles above your head. For those poor folk it descended to two thousand feet!"

Christmas in Osaka was a miserable affair. Some building work had been completed and some of the people rehoused, but for others it was too late. On the morning before Christmas Eve, Clane and a few other MP's had to assist a medical team in digging a row of tents out from under a snowdrift. Four of the people were dead; two old men, a young woman and her baby son. Twelve others had to be rushed to the Red Cross and were given treatment for hypothermia and frostbite. At the harbour Clane and his colleagues set up a makeshift ballroom in an empty warehouse. They strung up some decorations and brought in some tables and chairs. A wireless and gramophone provided music and there was even a delivery of liquor from Pacific Fleet Command. A bar was quickly constructed out of planks of wood and sandbags. A troopship put in from Okinawa and on board were several battalions of the US Marine Corps. The men were hungry for a run ashore and wasted no time in seeking out the ballroom. There they quickly ate into the supply of beers and spirits. The atmosphere of the party became boisterous then rowdy. Singing, laughing and altercations blended into a single raucous din. "Hey, Navy-boy!" asked a drunk corporal who was propping up the bar. "You ever been to Okinawa?"

"No." replied Clane.

"It's quite an island." he slurred and took a gulp from his bottle. "Dames, dames, dames, everywhere! And they're all looking for a fuck!"

"Sounds great." responded Clane, wondering how he could politely extricate himself from this conversation.

The marine grabbed his arm and leaned forward. He lowered his voice; his breath was soured by Budweiser. "I dated some of them, a couple of dozen in fact." He leered and giggled.

Something in his tone alarmed Clane.

"One thing you mainland GI's need to realize about Jap girls... When they say 'no', it usually means 'yes'... You get me? Even if at first they don't like it; afterwards, on reflection, I think they feel grateful... We marines are very persuasive. And command is very keen for us to... fraternize with the natives. Oh yeah, they don't mind one bit... And they've got no time for silly groundless complaints from them."

Clane backed away from him in disgust. *Rape*. It was as if he'd shouted the word at the top of his lungs.

The day after Christmas, Clane put in a request for demobilization. It was turned down. He was livid. He felt an unquenchable burning lust to get out of Japan and home. During the whole three years he'd been in the war he'd naturally missed his home, his wife Gina and their daughter Siobhan; but now this homesickness rose to a shrieking pain. One day he drew his sidearm and considered shooting his own foot in order to get a medical discharge, but his courage failed him. He prayed every day for anything that would take him home; then a few days after New Year, his prayers were answered. ComSubPac decreed that the USS *Tunny* had to be returned to Pearl Harbour for a refit so some of her old crew had to be rounded up, and Clane was amongst them. He was ordered to stand down from all duties in the Military Police and return to the boat. In his anguish Clane had completely forgotten about his old submarine tied up at the end of the quay where they'd left it four months ago. After this mission was complete all the *Tunny*'s personnel were to be sent stateside. What followed was a gentle fortnight's surface cruise across the smooth blue Pacific Ocean and then a plane ride to San Diego, and for Clane another to New York.

His elation at coming home was short-lived. As soon as the hugging and weeping was over Clane found it impossible to settle back in with his family. Something had changed between them and he couldn't work out exactly what. One day in May, Siobhan came to him crying. Her mother had asked her to keep a secret and she couldn't. Clane demanded more information and, over the next hour, she revealed all she knew about "Norman". Clane was numbly calm as he comforted his eleven year old, but as soon as his feelings came back he was struck down by an emotional hijack. The fact that Gina had begun her relationship with "Norman" just two weeks after Clane's heartfelt and sacred return home doubled his torment. It was also no consolation that "Norman" lived in a plush Long Island beach mansion and drove a Maserati. Clane sped as quickly as he could to "Norman's" villa in Amityville and rang the doorbell. As soon as the door opened Clane landed his fist squarely on the man's top lip and walked away. As a final gesture of outrage and contempt, he took a half-dollar piece from his pocket and scratched it along the bonnet of the Maserati parked in the driveway, leaving a long straight gash of clean steel through the immaculate black paintwork. Clane was arrested later in the evening and the police informed him that he had not even assaulted "Norman" at all. The man Clane had punched in the face was actually the butler; luckily his mistaken target chose not to press charges.

1946 was the worst year of Clane's life. Gina ended her affair with "Norman" and she and Clane made a half-hearted and futile attempt to reconcile, but before long he had been forced to move into his own apartment near the docks and became a visiting father to Siobhan. In October his discharge papers came through and his daily commute to the naval yard changed to one at the *New York Times*. He had returned to his old employer; however he was not welcomed back in with open arms. It was abundantly clear that the boss only took him back at all because Clane's war contract forced him to. The source of this hostility was soon revealed, predictably in retrospect. "Norman" was a major shareholder in the paper and had had a word in the boss' ear about a certain ex-Navy Irish pleb-scrawler who could perhaps be dropped as part of a "streamlining exercise". The boss liked Clane and didn't want to do it, but the purse strings had spoken. He did all he could for Clane in transferring him to alternative work, but the best he could offer was a seat on a local rag in a dusty little stop-out in New Mexico called Roswell.

Chapter 2

"It was like a wheeling whirring saucepan lid. And shiny and steely. It must have been a hundred feet across!"

"How high up was it, Mrs Crewe?" Clane scribbled shorthand in his notebook as she spoke.

"I don't know, Mr Quilley. It's hard to tell when something's in the sky, like an aeroplane or something that looks real small."

Clane sighed inwardly. "Then how do you know how big it was, Mrs Crewe?" He was sitting on the verandah drinking iced tea in the shade of the house. Amelia Crewe had turned out to be a far less competent witness than she was a letter writer. Her house was on the limits of Picacho, a barren remote tumbleweed-rolling truck stop on the Seventy, just over the border into Lincoln County. After the interview Clane went to his car to fetch the camera. *Roswell Daily Record* had a dedicated full-time photographer, a man called Tom, but Owen Mollett didn't waste him on flying saucer stories. Clane fiddled with the unfamiliar instrument as he set up the tripod and loaded a magnesium bulb into the flashgun. "Mrs Crewe, could you point at the place where you saw the flying saucer in the sky please?" Clane took the photograph that he knew would never be published, even if somehow his article was. He wasted no time in driving back to Roswell before his July the 4th was completely ruined by extra work. He entered the *RDR* building, dropped the photo slide into an envelope and left it in the pigeonhole outside the darkroom for Tom. Then he headed back out to enjoy the parade. However, while Clane was standing on the sidewalk outside the *RDR* office with his cotton flag, waving it as the parade went past, he heard a voice from the window above. "Quilley! Get up here!" Clane felt no surprise; he knew that Mollett would be in his office as usual. There was not a lot he could say in protest without losing his job. He climbed the stairs and got to work typing up his interview with Amelia Crewe. He was one of only a handful of journalists in the office which normally housed fifty. The room was stiflingly hot and Clane had not yet got used to the New Mexico climate. Amazingly, nowhere in Roswell had air conditioning despite the endless months of heat. The offices at the *New York Times* were all air conditioned even though the appliances were only needed for a couple of weeks a year.

The doorbell rang in the lobby and Clane ignored it. It always rang every hour or so with a delivery or pickup or something; Julia the receptionist handled those. When the phone rang on his desk Clane was surprised to hear her say: "Hey, Clane. I think this is one for you."

"Excuse me, Julia?"

"There's a gentleman here with a...um..." She lowered her voice, "flying saucer-related matter to discuss."

Clane rolled his eyes. Mollett had trained them all concerning Clane's new speciality. "OK, Julia; send him up."

The visitor was a sturdy pastoral cowboy type of young man that one rarely saw in town. "Pardon me for dropping by, sir." he drawled. "We got no phone out at home and I was here in Roswell watching the parade anyhow."

"That's no problem, Mr..."

"Brazel, Mac Brazel."

"So what can I do for you, Mr Brazel?"

"Well, I'd be much obliged if you'd keep this confidential like; my boss didn't want me to talk to you guys."

"Of course."

Brazel lowered his voice in the same way Julia had and took a step closer. "Well, I've been hearing all about these flying saucers like everybody else and... well, I think I saw one the other night. It was this weird moving light in the sky anyhow and... well, yesterday I found something a bit strange."

"What kind of thing?"

Brazel looked down and shifted his feet. "I'd have to show you to explain. I can take you there right now if you like."

"Where is this thing?"

"On the Foster Ranch, just south of Corona."

"What!? That's thirty miles away! Mr Brazel, I don't have time..."

"Ahem!" Owen Mollett cleared his throat. Clane turned round to see his boss standing behind him.

....

Clane wondered if his car would make it. The road was nothing more than a dirt track running along a shallow canyon and the suspension of his Chevrolet strained at every rock and pothole. He was following Mac Brazel's rusty old pick-up truck. The Foster Ranch was an isolated patchwork of prairie and thin dry trees where sheep and cattle roamed in loose clusters. There was a wind-pump and well with a water channel; and a few sheds for storing the animals' grain feed. Brazel pulled up beside one of them. The sun was dropping towards the mountainous western horizon and the daytime heat had eased. Brazel informed him that there was still a moderate walk ahead so Clane brought a flashlight with him; the night falls quickly out in the desert. Brazel led him up a path between some parched piñon trees until they came across an object lying in their way. It took a moment for Clane to recognize it as the body of a cow. He turned to his guide perplexed. "Is this it?"

Brazel looked down at the corpse and nodded grimly. "A prize Hereford. Do you know how much these cost?" He caught Clane's nonplussed gaze. "Look." He crouched down and pointed.

Clane noticed that one of the beast's eyes was missing; also its lower jaw had been stripped of all its flesh, leaving behind clean dry white bone. He sighed. "What am I supposed to be looking at, Mr Brazel?"

"Look how it's been done." replied the ranch hand. "The edges of the wounds are clean and smooth, like it's been operated on by a veterinarian. Look, no blood. In fact I can't see any blood anywhere... And check this; half her tongue is gone. Cut lengthwise right down the middle; straight as a butcher's cleaver... What's more it gets worse." Brazel lifted one of the cow's back legs. "Get a load of this!"

Clane grimaced. "I'd rather not."

Brazel ignored him. "This is really twisted. Look, one teat's gone from her udder; just one. The others are untouched... And come round here and look at her from behind. Her asshole is gone, and so has her... um... ladypart."

"Is that the medical term for it?"

"Mr Quilley, we loose a few animals to natural causes and I see their carcasses real regular. By the time we get to them they're usually half-scavenged. I found this cow yesterday; how come she's still here intact? The hawks and coyotes have left her alone." He leaned down close to the cadaver. "Can't even see any ants crawling on her, and ants ain't normally fussy eaters... It was somewhere in this direction I saw that strange light in the sky." He gestured at the corpse again. "I've heard of this kind of thing on other ranches, but I've never seen it on Foster... What do you think, Mr Quilley?"

Clane gritted his teeth; he had been keeping his temper with difficultly since they'd arrived at the scene of death. "Mr Brazel, it's July the fourth and you've dragged me thirty miles out into the middle of nowhere to show me a dead cow!" He turned around and stormed back down the path.

"Mr Quilley..." Brazel protested.

"I'm a Goddamn news reporter!" he shouted over his shoulder. "And a dead cow is not news!"

Clane drove home though the dusk hissing and muttering to himself. "Mollett, you shit! I'm sick to death of flying saucers!... Get me off this piss-ass assignment or I'll quit. I swear I could care less! I'm off the paper!" When Clane entered Roswell he stopped at a gas station and filled up his tank on the *RDR*'s expenses coupon, the closest he could get to revenge.

....

Over the weekend most of the *Roswell Daily Record*'s staff had at least one day off. The paper only produced a twelve-page Sunday weekly, so they had two days to get their work done for Monday's edition. The exception was of course Owen Mollett who so rarely left his glass-walled cigar-stained haven that it was almost impossible to imagine him outside it. Clane spent an easy Saturday afternoon at the movie theatre where *Black Narcissus* was showing.

The movie was a new release and all the critics were raving about it. It was a stunning Technicolor epic with vertiginous camerawork. The story was a fascinating one about sexually compromised nuns in Tibet. The star was Deborah Kerr and she lacked none of her usual good looks despite being in a habit. Clane left the cinema feeling a bit dizzy and dislocated. The familiar dusty streets of Roswell were temporarily alien after almost two hours of being immersed in the big screen realism of a mountaintop convent in the Himalayas. On Sunday morning he went straight into work from church. As he sat down Marietta was just leaving. "I've got a weird lead." she said. "A phone call from a policeman's wife in Corona. Apparently the army is out there right now. They've closed a couple of roads leading off the 247 highway. Armed roadblocks and everything."

Clane chuckled. "Germans or Russians?"

She frowned in mock reproach. "Clane, this is not the *National Enquirer*!"

He laughed. "Alright, Mari, take care out there."

Two hours later she called Clane's desk. "Clane? It's Marietta. I'm at a box in Corona. I can't get any goodies; the lead was real though. The Gallo Canyon Road and Duchness Road are both sealed off by army checkpoints. I spoke to the soldiers minding them and they aren't saying a word. I got the feeling they don't know either."

"OK."

"I'm going to knock on a few doors and see if anybody's talking. Could you tell the old man for me? I tried to call him direct, but he's on the line."

At 2 PM Marietta called in again, this time from Carizozo. "I've driven all the way south on the Fifty-Four and all the roads to the left are closed too. The same kinds of military cordons at every intersection. In fact it looks like all of western Lincoln County is off limits."

"That's strange, Mari. Something must be going on."

"Yeah; dunno what. Nobody round here seems to know."

"Alright. I'll give the boss your latest."

"I'm coming home now along the Three-Eighty so I'll be able to see how far south the sealed-off zone extends. I did speak to somebody who says they live in Arabela and everything's normal there, so it can't be any further east than that."

"Could this be a plane crash or something?"

"No idea. If it was though somebody from the base would have given us a call."

"Unless it was something hush-hush."

"If so we'd be told to keep shtumm... Oops, there goes my dime. See you soon."

When Clane gave the news to Mollett the latter pondered for a moment and said: "Take a drive down to the base and sniff around."

"Me, Mr Mollett? Why? I'm your flying saucer correspondent, remember?" He couldn't keep the sarcastic jeer out of his voice.

The *RDR*'s editor glared at him. His cheeks flushed; for a moment he looked as if he'd explode, but then the fire died down. He puffed on his cigar and mopped his brow with a handkerchief. "Quilley, if I had anybody better than you available I'd send them instead. Show's how busy we are because that includes almost everybody."

Roswell Army Air Field lay to the south of the city at the end of a long straight road that was just a continuation of the Main Street. It led past a number of arable farms and the waterworks. Unspeakable thoughts of his boss ran through Clane's head; he bashed the steering wheel in fury. The base was bordered by a high barbed wire fence and the gate included a barrier across both lanes of the road. A squad of MP sentries manned the gate. Their white infantry helmets reflected the sunlight; their headgear looking incongruous above their starched working khakis. Clane felt a shiver of familiarity; he had worn uniforms like this. He noticed from the colour of the status board that the base was not in a state of alert. He drove up to the barrier and flashed his press card at the MP. "Clane Quilley, *Roswell Daily Record*."

"Good morning, sir. I'm afraid I can't let you in today."

"What? I'm a reporter."

"I can't let you in, sir."

Clane pointed at the status board. "But you're on normal operations. I'm ex-Navy; I know what that means."

"I can't let you in, sir." the man repeated like a stuck gramaphone.

"Why? What's going on?"

"No comment, sir."

"Perhaps you could tell me what the army is currently doing up near Corona?"

"No comment, sir."

"Do you know yourself?"

"No comment, sir."

Clane paused. "Could you pass a message from me to Lieutenant Haut?"

"No comment... Sir, could you move along please?" The sentry pointed behind Clane's car at a personnel transport truck that was waiting to enter the gate. Clane reversed out into the road and headed back into town. Within minutes of him sitting back down at his desk, the phone rang. "Good afternoon, *Roswell Daily Record*, Clane Quilley speaking."

"Hi, Mr Quilley; this is Mac Brazel. Man, you wouldn't believe..."

Clane slammed down the receiver. He did it instinctively before he could stop himself. He stared at the phone for a few moments, daring and dreading the sound of the bell; but Brazel did not ring back.

....

It was almost midnight. Clane was sitting in his armchair, reading and thinking about going to bed when the doorbell rang. He frowned curiously. His meagre social life in Roswell meant that he very rarely got callers. Hilda Ray was the last person who rung his bell; she had dropped off his photo on Thursday, but she was never up this late. Clane got up and went to the door. In New York he would have peeped through the viewer or used the door chain, but the crime rates in Roswell were much lower so he just flung the door wide. Jesse Marcel stood before him. He smiled. "Hello, Clane."

"H... hello, Jesse." Clane stammered.

"Can I come in?" Marcel was wearing his khakis; they were crumpled and sweat-stained. His face was reddened by the sun as if he'd had a hard day's work outdoors. He was carrying a small cardboard box, and he held it in front of him in his arms as if it were a present. Clane stood aside to let Jesse walk into the motel room. The AAF officer had a peculiar expression on his tanned face; a wistful smile, but also a shocked stunned mien, a thousand yard stare. Marcel placed the box on the table then turned to face him. "I felt compelled to come and see you, Clane. I had to tell you."

"Tell me what?"

There was a long silence. Jesse stared down at the box and tapped it gently, almost affectionately, as if it contained a beloved pet rabbit.

"Can I get you a drink?" asked Clane. "A coffee?"

He shook his head. "You know, Clane; I really should have apologized for our argument."

"Me too." Clane felt no relief this time.

"I know you were in Japan." Jesse looked up at him. "What did you see that I didn't?"

"People starving, freezing, dying... Also dying from the after-effects of the A-bombs... Marines boasting about how they raped girls on Okinawa."

"You're right, Clane. I don't know what that looks like. I should have realized that and handled you more gently."

"Maybe."

"I stand by what I said though. Those bombs saved a million lives, both Japanese and American."

"It would have saved even more if we'd brought in the Russians and let the Japs back down while saving face."

"No, it had to be unconditional surrender." There was no ire in Jesse's tone this time. "If we'd left Hirohito on his throne, by now he'd be reconquering everything we shed so much blood to liberate. We had to destroy the empire, Clane. If we hadn't we'd be counting down to a new Pearl Harbour."

There was a long pause. Clane shrugged. "Who knows what would have happened."

Marcel nodded. "Maybe there are multiple different worlds out there where each and every outcome gets played out. Some scientists are saying that nowadays. Maybe there's a world where the Japs were left in place. We don't live in that world."

"You know, I thought I was going to die on Thursday, Jesse. I thought I was finished. Then I took a second look and saw that I was completely safe. Did I die in another world?... And there was this old Indian..." he trailed off.

"You know something, Clane?" Marcel spoke slowly for emphasis. "I think we might be at one of those great turning points in history, right here and right now. What world we'll be living in, what outcome you and I will play out, I don't know yet."

"What do you mean, Jesse?"

"Something's happened, Clane... Something which means the world will never be the same again." He stood back and pointed at the cardboard box on the table. "Take a look inside the box, Clane."

Clane stepped forward. The expression on Marcel's face and the timbre of his voice unnerved him. He picked up the box. It was the weight he would expect it to be if it were empty. He shook it lightly and heard something very light rattling inside, like pieces of screwed-up paper. The box was not sealed and only the unfastened flaps concealed what lay within. He grasped the edge of one of the flaps to lift it. Then he stopped; a subconscious dread filled him. "What's inside?"

"Pieces of a flying saucer."

Clane wondered if he'd misheard. "Did you say 'pieces of a flying saucer'?"

Marcel nodded. "A rancher found them on his land yesterday. Take a look."

"A rancher?... Was his name Mac Brazel by any chance?"

"Yes. How did you know?"

"Holy shit!" Clane tossed the box back down onto the table. "Mac Brazel is a time-waster! He's a fantasist! He's taken you for a ride too, Jesse!"

"Clane." Marcel pointed again. "Take a look in the box."

"Are you kidding!? No way! I've had my career jeopardized enough for one week by this horsepucky!... I was a respectable journalist! Sure, Jesse, I know that the war has fucked me up; hasn't it fucked us all up? But I've been trying to pull myself back up. I've been trying. I've lost *everything*! My job, my home, my family! I came to New Mexico for a new start, a blank slate! And what do I find? I'm being kicked while I'm on the fucking deck!... And now you're doing it to me as well!"

Marcel paused sadly. Then he stepped forward and picked up the box. "Very well, Clane. I shall take this home to show Vy and Jesse Junior." He tucked the box under his arm and walked out of the motel room.

Chapter 3

The heat in the wheat field was intense. Crickets chirruped intrusively as the farmer led him along one of the tramlines, a furrow where the wheels of the tractors ran as they dusted and harvested the crop. Clane took off his hat and mopped his brow.

"We're almost there." the farmer called over his shoulder. This was not a quiet country field; to his left Clane could see the main road between Roswell and the airbase. The noise of the traffic competed with that of the cricket noise in his ears. There was a clear space ahead in the thigh-high tightly-planted crop and Clane suddenly found himself in a wide-open area where no crop stood. The circular lagoon in the field had been created by the crop being flattened to the ground. The farmer tutted and spat out a wad of chewed tobacco onto the horizontal stalks. "Never seen nuttin' like it in all my born naturals!" he muttered. "Look how sharp it is, like a cookie cutter." Sure enough the edge of the circle was clearly defined; the normal standing crop immediately gave way to the completely flattened lay. The farmer frowned and puffed on his corncob pipe. "I reckon one of them there flyin' saucers done it!"

Clane crouched down. "Looks more like somebody's pushed it to the ground, with a lawn roller perhaps. Mr Lamont, have you seen any strangers hanging around?"

"Nope. Nobody. They just appeared overnight."

"Could be some kids did it?"

"Why in God's name would they do that?"

"You know? Kids larking around."

"Where are their footprints then?"

Clane stood on tiptoes to try and see the other structures. "How many of these circles are there?"

"Five. This big guy and four little bitty ones around it, all evenly spaced. One of the smaller ones has no tramline access so how did they get to it with them their lawn rollers without leavin' a trail through the crop?"

"I think we'll only be able to see this properly from the air."

"Well, Mr Quilley; we should ask the pilots down on the base if they've noticed it. Maybe they'd be obligin' and get us a photograph."

"I think they have higher priorities then to take snapshots for us, Mr Lamont."

"Sheesh!" Lamont shook his head. "It's mighty weird. Yes, siree! These here stalks don't look like they've been trampled. They're bent real neat-like at the growth nodes."

"You still insist flying saucers did this?"

"Darn right! Who else could? Who else *would*?"

"I could ask you the same question. Why would whoever is inside the flying saucers come here all the way from Mars or Venus or wherever, make these circles in the crop and then fly all the way back home without stopping to say hello?"

"I dunno, dammit! I ain't one o' them!"

"I don't think flying saucers did this." said Clane. "There are no flying saucers; they're as real as Santa Claus."

"They *are* real, Mr Quilley. Ain't you heard? One even crashed up near Corona a few days ago."

"What the hell are you talking about?"

"Well you know how the army has been shuttin' off a load o' roads around Corona?..."

"Where did you hear about that?"

"That guy Mac Brazel."

Clane groaned. "Not him again! He's been bullshitting to you too now has he?"

"No, he's been on the radio."

"What!?"

"He was interviewed by Frank Joyce on KGFL. He was on just before you showed up."

"What was he saying?"

"That a flyin' saucer came down on the Foster Ranch and he found the debris; it was all in little bitty pieces in one o' the fields."

Clane took a few photographs and then returned to the car. He decided to nip back down to the base again to see could confirm or deny what Brazel said on the radio show. He approached the MP's at the gate, but just as he was about to pull up at the barrier he had to brake hard to avoid colliding with a large black vehicle that emerged from the exit lane at high speed. He watched in his rear-view mirror as it screeched onto the Main Street and accelerated in the direction of Roswell. Clane turned the car around and followed. He had to speed up considerably to catch the black vehicle, driving much faster than he felt comfortable doing. He hoped he wouldn't meet a cop. His reporter instinct told him that his quarry held a clue. Eventually he caught up with the black vehicle and recognized it as a hearse. On the back was stencilled the words *Ballard Funeral Home- Roswell NM*. When the hearse reached central Roswell it pulled up outside *Browny's*; the driver got out and paced angrily into the bar. By the time Clane joined him he had already polished off his first Bourbon. He turned on his stool as he heard Clane's approach and they recognized each other. "Glenn."

"Mr Quilley." His youthful face smiled awkwardly.

"What was that all about?"

"What do you mean?"

"You've just been driving like there was a hungry bear behind you."

Glenn ground his teeth. "I've just been thrown off the base!"

"I thought you worked there."

"So did I!"

"Why?"

"I dunno!" He glanced at Clane suspiciously. "Mr Quilley, is this on the record?"

Clane chuckled. "I'm a reporter, but I'm also a human being."

The younger man relaxed somewhat. "You know Ballard has the mortician contract for the RAAF?"

"Yes."

"Well I got a call from Lieutenant Jimmy Burton; you know, my pal who I brought in here last week and who always drinks wine?"

"Sure."

"He asked me if I had any child-sized caskets. I mean, that's weird. How many kids are there on the base? Anyway, Jimmy wanted three of them and they needed to be hermetically sealed. He also asked me about how to preserve bodies that had been lying in the desert... Well, I'm totally curious. I've heard these rumours that the army is up to no good on that ranch near Corona. I guessed it must be a plane crash which the government don't want anybody to know about. I asked Jimmy about that, but he wasn't keen to tell me. We only had one of the caskets he wanted in stock so he told me to bring it in; and I called our supplier in Texas to order some more. Then I took the one we did have up to on our shelves up to the base. I dropped the four-foot coffin off at the infirmary and then went to the mess to get a coke. Anyway, this nurse came in, one I've been dating. She ran over and she said: 'Glenn, get out of here! Please! Get out now before you get into trouble!' Next thing I know there's this officer breathing down my neck, telling me to get out.... Telling me to get out of the place where I work!" Glenn's face screwed up. "I've as much right to be there as anybody else! So what if I'm not military? I serve as well!... Besides, I've never seen this guy before. He's not in the 509th, that's for sure. So he escorts me back to my car with this black sergeant major. I say 'escort', but they kept pushing me and cussing at me. Threatening me like I was a piece of dirt."

"What's a negro doing assisting that officer?" asked Clane. "There are no black units based at RAAF and if there were, they wouldn't be mixing with the white guys."

"There's a lot going on the base right now that ain't normal."

Clane drove back to the office to drop off the slides for Tom the photographer, and then he had an idea. He headed next to the Roswell County Courthouse and, as good fortune would have it, caught Hilda Blair Ray at lunch.

"Hi, Clane." She waved at him as she walked down the steps and saw him parked and waiting. She was dressed smartly for the courtroom.

"Hi there, Hilda. Are you busy this afternoon?"

"No, the judge has just adjourned until tomorrow morning."

"I wonder if you'd be able to do me a big favour."

....

Clane had never been in a light aircraft before. He buckled his seatbelt according to Hilda Blair Ray's instructions and she started the engine. It was loud and vibrating; far more obtrusive than a car's engine. Hilda lifted the radio microphone to her lips and spoke to air traffic control. The plane started bumping along the grassy surface of the airfield until it reached the runway. Clane subconsciously grasped the sides of his seat as Hilda opened the throttle and the aircraft leapt forwards. The bumping stopped and the land dropped away beneath their feet. The rooftops of Roswell scrolled below, getting smaller and smaller. "Where is this place?" Hilda had to raise her voice above the engine noise. The propeller was a semicircular blur in the windscreen.

"Just north of the base, a farmer's field."

"OK, I'm going to have to be careful not to fly over the base itself. Get your camera ready; it won't take long to get there." She shifted the yoke a few times and the aircraft banked like a fairground ride. The formation of flattened crop in the farmer's field was very prominent and easy to see. It was a quintuplet of five circles; a central large one and four smaller satellites, perfectly aligned and symmetrical. Hilda began circling and Clane slid back the Perspex side window. The roar of the wind and engine made conversation impossible as Clane trained and focused the camera as well as he could; holding it tightly to avoid dropping it. He flicked the shutter and then closed the window.

"What is that?" asked Hilda.

"The farmer thinks it was done by flying saucers."

She chuckled. "Reminds me of when I went to a museum a couple of years ago. I took a photo of an original Mesa Verde mummy. When I developed it into a slide and showed a friend she thought it was a man from Mars!" She laughed heartily.

"You'd better label that slide carefully, Hilda. Years from now, long after we're dead, somebody might come across your slide and get the wrong idea... Hilda?" He'd had an idea, but wondered if it was fair to ask more of her.

"Yup?"

"How long can we stay up here?"

"We've got enough fuel for a whole hour."

"I was wondering if you could fly me someplace else."

"Sure."

The square grid of the city gave way to the open, pockmarked yellow ochre desert. The highway was a black thread running through it, and the cars and trucks glinted in the sunlight like beads of silver. Hilda consulted her map that was mounted above the instrument panel on a stand. "Where exactly are we going, Clane?"

"I'm not sure. Keep heading towards Corona. You've heard of these rumours about a flying saucer crashing?"

"Yeah, Bernard was telling me it's been all over the radio."

"I just want to have a look."

"You don't believe it do you?" she scoffed.

"No." replied Clane after some hesitation. "But I just want to be sure."

She gave him a quizzical sideways glance. A few minutes later the sun was suddenly darkened as a black shadow loomed over them. Hilda and Clane jolted in shock. "Unidentified light aircraft!" a voice on the radio barked. "Identify yourself! You are entering restricted airspace!" Another aircraft appeared about two hundred feet their left, matching their speed and course precisely. Clane recognized it as a P51 Mustang of the Army Air Force, probably one from the resident Roswell squadrons.

Hilda coolly picked up the microphone. "AAF aircraft, this is KJTFY out of Roswell Civic Airfield. Negative, this is not restricted airspace. We are on a public airway designated by VOR's victor-29478 to 37646. Over."

"Negative, KJTFY. This area is now restricted airspace. You must turn immediately onto a reciprocal course. If you do not comply within two minutes I shall open fire."

Hilda gasped. Clane looked across at the fighter aircraft. The pilot's helmeted head was visible inside the bubble cockpit of his aircraft. His goggled face was turned to look at them. "Hilda, you'd better do what he says." Her knuckles trembled as she rotated the yoke and banked the aircraft. The Mustang escorted them for a few more minutes to make sure they were departing the area; then it soared into the air and zoomed off without another word. "Hilda, I'm so sorry." said Clane. "I'd never have asked you to fly out here if I'd known it would put you in danger."

"It's alright, Clane; it was quite exciting actually; beat's Roswell County Court." she giggled.

"Clearly whatever's going on out at Corona, the government are totally bent on keeping it secret."

She paused. "Do you still think it's not a crashed flying saucer?"

Clane didn't respond.

....

The motel room phone rang within ten minutes of Clane getting home. It was ten PM and he was just boiling the kettle for coffee. "Hello, Clane Quilley?"

"Mr Quilley? It's Glenn Dennis." His voice was low and tremulous.

"Glenn? Are you OK?"

"I need to see you now, Clane. It's really important."

"Sure, at *Browny's*?"

"No. I'm at the old Harold Saloon. We need to be alone."

"OK."

There was something in Glenn's voice that alerted him. The way he suddenly switched to calling Clane by his Christian name was uncharacteristic. He drove to the location, one of the less upmarket establishments to the west of the city. When he first walked in he couldn't see Glenn anywhere until the undertaker called his name. He was tucked away in a dark corner booth hunched over a half-full beer. Clane ordered a drink and then went over to join him.

"Clane, I need you to be a human being and not a reporter."

"Glenn, you know I never write anything unless a subject gives me permission."

"My girlfriend at the base; did I tell you her name this morning?" Clane shook his head.

"Good... I've just been to meet her. She called me and told me to meet her at... It doesn't matter where." His hand trembled as he picked up his glass and he gulped nervously. "She wanted to give me an explanation for what happened earlier. Before she agreed to tell me though, she made me swear on the bible never to tell anybody her name."

"Fair enough, Glenn. Tell you what?"

"She told me..." He shivered and looked around the bar to check that nobody was eavesdropping. "She told me that they did an... autopsy."

"Autopsy? On whom?"

"Not whom... *what*! She drew me a picture. She wouldn't let me keep it, but I've done my own copy." Glenn produced a notepad page folded in two.

Clane took it from him and opened it up. On it Glenn had drawn a pencil outline of a thin humanoid shape with an outsized head. It had large eyes, a slit mouth and a bald scalp.

"She had to make notes for the doctors." continued Glenn. "She said the smell was repulsive. And she's been a nurse for four years so she doesn't gross out easily. Their skin was blackened, as if they'd been burnt; or maybe it was the sun."

"The sun?"

"They'd been lying on the ground out in the desert."

"Near Corona?"

Glenn ignored him. "They were about three and a half feet tall; the size of a little kid. They only had four fingers on each hand, and they had these pads on the fingertips, like suction cups. One of them was dismembered, ripped up like the coyotes got to it; or maybe it was the crash... She was nearly hysterical as she was talking to me. What she was saying was for real, I tell you."

Clane shook his head and blew out his cheeks. "What are they?"

"Men from Mars, Clane." He shrugged. "Those rumours are true. There really has been a flying saucer crash. An aircraft from another world; it's come down just a few miles from where we're sitting. There's life out there, and we've lived to see it." He grinned through his nervousness.

"I'm not sure we will, Glenn."

"What do you mean?"

"The government are keeping it secret at the moment." he gave Glenn a summary of his own experience at the base and his plane flight with Hilda Ray. "Maybe they'll just decide to keep it that way indefinitely."

"They can't for long." retorted Glenn. "Not something like this."

"I'm not so sure."

Glenn turned pale; beads of sweat budded on his forehead. "Clane, you don't suppose this isn't really a man from Mars? What if it's something from Satan?"

Clane chuckled. "Not with the amount I've been praying. If Satan comes near me, I'll rip his balls off!"

Glenn relaxed somewhat in the glow of the older man's confidence. The atmosphere eased. "And why would Satan appear as strange bodies in the desert? You know, it makes sense. Why would God fill the universe with planets and then only put life on Earth?"

"Yeah, I wouldn't be at all surprised if there was life on Mars, Venus and probably all the other planets. Maybe they're reaching out to us because they know deep down that they need the word of Jesus Christ."

The two men ordered another round and talked for a while longer about the theological implications of extraterrestrial life. On the way home Clane pondered about his own thoughts. A part of him still didn't believe it, and that this was all a huge series of coincidences for which there was, literally, a down-to-Earth explanation. However, something strange was definitely going on; nobody doubted it. Everybody in town could feel it. Was it really a flying saucer crash? Was it possible? If so then it wouldn't matter because the government would soon cover it up and everything would go back to normal. Unlike Glenn, Clane had been in the war and had seen many newsworthy things which had never appeared anywhere in the media. The noisy public characters who didn't believe in flying saucers would go on being noisy and their retractors would riposte with equal vehemence; but with the truth denied, what difference did it really make?

....

Clane awake early the following morning. That was unusual for him. On weekdays he almost always rose groggily to his alarm clock rubbing his eyes and cursing the obligation to end his sleep. Today it was still twilight when he opened his eyes. He sat up and looked at his clock: 5.55 AM. He groaned and rolled over onto his side. He closed his eyes, but sleep had slipped from his fingers. After half an hour of fruitless effort he surrendered to wakefulness and got out of bed. The morning sunlight was sifting through the curtains. He drew them back. The sky was vanilla blue with white flecks of herringbone cloud in random patches across the zenith. The sun had yet to clear the buildings on the opposite side of the carpark and the light had that unique shady quality which added brightness to the sky. Clane opened the window and took a deep breath of clean dry air. It smelled of dew and flowers. Birds crossed from one side of the yard to the other like shuttlecocks. He turned back indoors and looked at the calendar on the wall. It was Tuesday the 8th of July 1947.

Clane had a leisurely shower and breakfast, listening to the music stations on the radio; then he drove to work through the usual morning traffic. He arrived dead on time, the same time as everybody else, and chatted to Marietta and Stanley as they ascended the stairs to the office. They formed an orderly queue at the coffee pot and then sat down at their desks, lit up cigarettes and got to work. The office rang with the raindrop staccato of typewriter keys. It took them a few minutes to notice something was wrong. "Hey, guys." piped up Tristan. "The boss isn't in."

They all stood up and looked. Owen Mollett was not sitting in his glass alcove. They all stared at each other with bemused expressions. This was the first time ever that any of them had seen the editor's cubicle empty. Stanley phoned his home to see if he were alright; and when it had rung twenty times he hung up and called the hospital to check Mollett hadn't been admitted. He hadn't. There was nothing more they could do except carry on with their work. Mollett appeared suddenly at eleven o'clock. Everybody stopped and stared at him as he entered the office door. His face was a mask, revealing nothing. "Tristan!" he barked urgently.

"Sir!" responded the junior, standing up straight like a solider.

"Is the telex switched on?"

"Yes it is, sir."

"Good. Everybody hold all pages!... Quilley!" Mollett didn't wait for him to affirm and just strode over to his cubicle. As Clane entered after him the editor was feverishly lighting a cigar.

"Mr Mollett, where were you this morning?" asked Clane.

"At the base."

"The RAAF?"

"Yes, I had a meeting with Lieutenant Walter Haut; you know him?"

"Of course, sir. He's their press officer."

Mollett managed to get his cigar alight and he puffed it a few times until it was burning properly. "I know you resent me, Quilley." He spoke without looking at Clane. "You think I'm putting you down by giving you this flying saucer assignment."

"Don't expect me to deny it!" Clane glared at the boss' sweaty nape.

Mollett turned and met his gaze as pokerfaced as ever. "You might feel differently by the end of today... Go watch the telex; there's something coming through for you. When you get it, do me something for page one, two hundred words or so. We'll go to press as soon as you're through."

"Page one!?"

"You heard me correctly. Get to the telex."

Clane went to the corner of the main office where the telex machine stood. Within a minute or two the light on it blinked to indicate it was receiving a message and the keys began clacking. Line by line, a block of text appeared on a sheet of paper that emerged from the slot. When it was finished the light blinked again and Clane tore the sheet off the roll. He read it, stopped, and read it again. "Wh... what!?" he guffawed to himself. He knocked on the editor's door.

"Come."

"Mr Mollett." He held up the telex printout. "Excuse me, but... what the hell is this!?"

"It's your story; now get to work."

Clane did his job like a good newsman; his fingers and eyes adapting the press release into coherent journalistic prose. His mind was split and the conflicting sides yelled at him through his numbness. By the time Clane had finished, Tristan had already delivered everybody else's copy sheets to the typesetters and so Clane had to take his down himself. He descended the stairs and entered the print shop. The dark, oily room was as hot and noisy as always, and Clane put on a pair of earmuffs at the door. He handed his own sheet to the printing supervisor, a man called Enoch who was clad in filthy overalls. Enoch went over to the typesetter's desk and they conversed in their sign language, the only way possible in the print shop. The gargantuan steel dragons of the presses began rolling and the hot wet sheets of newsprint began piling up as the machine spat out ream after ream of them. The collators separated out the sheets and neatly folded them together, and eventually the finished copies of the *Roswell Daily Record* for July the 8th 1947 filed out along the conveyor. Enoch picked out one of them and handed it to Clane who nodded and smiled in thanks. He took a few more of them with him up to the office, still warm and smelling of ink. He dropped one off in Mollett's cubicle and then walked around the office placing them on people's desks. He saved the last one for

himself. He sat back in his chair and studied the smooth new copy of the familiar newspaper. Its banner was in elaborate Gothic typeface, the name of the paper in the middle and its phone numbers at the side. Below that was a bar with the date, place of publishing and price, eight cents. Then beneath that was his front page article. Its headline was simple, factual and unimaginative: "RAAF Captures Flying Saucer On Ranch in Roswell Region", subtitled: "No Details of Flying Disk Are Revealed."
....

"So what kind of place is Roswell?" asked the man on the other end of the phone in his polished English accent.

"Well..." a dozen things Clane could say flashed through his head. He gave the British journalist a brief, yet accurate and representative description.

"Hmm, sounds like an out-of-the way sort of place, a bit like Devizes." His voice crackled on the transatlantic cable. "Right, Mr Quilley. That's all we need for tomorrow's edition. You must excuse me, it's almost nine PM over here and I'm going to retire for the night." The moment he put down the phone it started ringing again.

"Who was that?" asked Marietta?

"Somebody from *The Times* in London."

"Good heavens! I've just had a guy from Venezuela."

He picked up the phone. "Good afternoon, *Roswell Daily Record*." The office was a mill race of activity. The phones rang and rang like insatiable baby birds. Calls had not only come in from the entire United States, but also Mexico, Europe, Canada, Panama, Australia, Brazil and several other places. The telex rattled with continuous written requests for information. The *RDR* staff had been plundered for their rusty and amateurish language skills. Fortunately a few could speak Spanish and were put on all the calls from central and South America. Somebody was found who could speak French and dealt with *Le Monde* in Paris. Clane's story was flashing all over the world on various newswires. His arm ached from taking notes and his voice was hoarse from shouting on the phone down low-gain connections on the intercontinental cables. Tristan and his trolley had been commandeered full-time to the task of delivering coffee to the people at their desks. Roswell was transformed in the space of a few hours. Everybody was out on the streets, the blocks were gridlocked right up to 9th Street and the police were out in force. A large crowd had gathered outside *RDR*'s offices; their inquisitive and worried voices rose as high as the office windows. Stanley came back from the base; he had tried to call in but the phone lines were continuously engaged. There were more onlookers outside the gates, but the RAAF was admitting nobody and the sentries were mute.

"Quilley!" Mollett beckoned Clane over to his cubicle again. Marietta smiled gratefully when Clane left the phone off the hook as he got up. The *RDR* editor handed him a folder. "Quilley, the Eighth Army Air Force is holding a press conference this evening. I want you and Tom to attend. You're to report to Gen. Roger Ramey."

"Sure, Mr Mollett."

"It's not at the RAAF though; it's at Fort Worth. Take Tom's van and claim everything you want or need on expenses; food, drink, cigarettes..."

"Fort Worth!?"

"Yes, Fort Worth, Texas."

"Sir, do you know how far away Fort Worth is? It's half a day's drive."

Mollett reached into his desk and pulled out an atlas. He flicked through it until he found the right page. "Damn! You're right... We're too late; you'll never get there in time."

"Mr Mollett... Wait a minute! I've got an idea." Clane made a quick phone call and then came back with good news.

Mollett smiled more broadly than Clane had ever seen him do before. "Mr Flying Saucer Correspondent, your time is come."
....

The light aircraft bumped down onto the runway and Hilda Blair Ray eased back on the throttle. Tom breathed again. The *RDR*'s photographer had been manifestly uncomfortable for the entire hour-long flight. He had quietly informed Clane that he disliked flying on the drive to Roswell Civic Airfield. Hilda taxied the plane away from the main terminal at Love Field Airport because it only handled large long-distance airliners. They pulled up beside a small hangar and she cut the engine. They climbed out and Tom unloaded his equipment from the luggage compartment. "Thank you, Hilda!" gushed Clane. "If I win the Pulitzer for this then you'll get a share of the cash prize."

"You're welcome, Clane." She smiled behind her pilots' sunglasses. "I just wish I could wait and fly you back afterwards, but I've got to get home. I'm in court tomorrow first thing."

"That's alright, Hilda. We'll stay overnight and come home tomorrow morning on the Greyhound." They helped Hilda wheel over a bowser so she could refuel the aircraft, then they headed for the hangar. Clane helped by carrying Tom's tripod. He had several cases of his equipment; not only two different cameras, but slides, flashbulbs, tools, cleaning wipes, bottles of chemicals, lenses and everything else he might need. Tom was a demure mole-like man who never socialized with the other RDR staff. His skin was pallid from spending long hours in his darkroom. He was a bachelor and seemed to care about nothing except photography. His only reading material were books and magazines on the subject. Because they were not at a passenger terminal there were no facilities for onward journeys. There was just a gate at the back of the hangar leading onto an empty road bordering the airport. Clane and Tom walked along the road, the afternoon heat weighing heavily on their bodies. Sweat soaked into Clane's trilby hat, and he loosened his collar and tie. The tripod slipped back and forth in his slimy hands. None of the passing drivers stopped to give them a lift. Eventually they came upon a cafe with a payphone and a list of numbers for taxi firms. Ten minutes later they were heading for Fort Worth AAF in a cab.

The taxi dropped them off at the base's main gate. It was very similar to the one at Roswell and they were questioned thoroughly by the sentries. They had their press cards taken away and examined for a few minutes. Then a pair of MP's escorted them inside the compound. They were shown over to a building and their escorts wordlessly held the door open for them. Clane found the cool air-conditioned interior luxurious after the flare of the outdoors. They were given refreshments and then asked to go and sit in a large conference room with wooden chairs around the wall. In the corner there was a steel radiator, off at this time of year of course, beneath a curtained window. The curtain had flowery prints on it and there was a black cloth sash lying loosely on top of the radiator. There was a thin stringy carpet that left the parquet floor at the walls clear. More people joined them, fellow newsmen from other papers. Clane recognized some of them and they chatted, catching up on old times. A door opened at the far end of the room and a high-ranking AAF officer walked in. He was a Brigadier General with a row of shoulder stars and a Persian rug of medal ribbons on the breast of his jacket. His face was severe and moustachioed; to Clane he resembled the actor Clark Gable. "Good afternoon, ladies and gentlemen." he began in a deadpan and official tone. "My name is General Roger Ramey of the Eighth Army Air Force. We will be starting the press conference in twenty minutes. Please take that time to make your preparations." Without another word he returned through the door. Tom got to work. He unfolded his tripod and opened his cases of equipment. With the ease of a complete expert he assembled his camera and flashguns. In the corner of the room an airman emerged from the same door Gen. Ramey had just exited; he was carrying a large cardboard box. He tipped the box upside down and emptied its contents onto the floor in the corner. He returned to the adjacent room without acknowledging the reporters and shut the door. Clane moved closer and saw that the material from the box, now strewn across the parquet floor, was a pile of broken wooden struts, and crumpled and torn metallic foil. He turned to Tom and frowned. "What's going on?"

Tom was all set up in good time before the office door opened and five men marched formally out into the room, led by Gen. Ramey. "Jesse!" Clane gasped aloud.

One of the men was Jesse Marcel. The Major looked up at his name being called and briefly met his friend's eyes before snapping back into professional catalepsy. Behind his military poise, Clane could see that Marcel was in mental turmoil. His eyes were blanks and his cheeks flushed. The row of men were stood at ease and Gen. Ramey stepped forward. "Ladies and gentlemen of the press." he said. "I've invited you here today to give you the real story behind what happened yesterday in relation to the claim that the Roswell Army Air Force had salvaged the remains of a flying saucer. I'm afraid the truth is far more mundane. Maj. Jesse Marcel here," He pointed at Jesse, "made a mistake. What he thought were fragments of a shipwreck from the stars were actually just a high altitude weather balloon. What you see before you," He pointed at the debris on the floor. "are the shattered pieces of just one such balloon. These are the very fragments that Maj. Marcel found. The foil pieces are part of a radar reflector. Warrant Officer Newton will explain."

Another man advanced a pace and addressed the audience. "The General is correct; this is definitely a broken weather balloon. I'm part of the meteorological team here at Fort Worth AAF and we send these up all the time, maybe a few every day. The radar targets are attached because the balloons float very high; too high to see. They tell us wind speeds and directions which is very important for flight operations. This balloon may well be one of ours; it drifted westwards and came down in New Mexico where it was found by the rancher Mac Brazel..." He rambled on for a few more minutes giving technical details. Then it was time for the photo shoot. Ramey directed it. "Maj. Marcel, could you hold the material for the cameras please? You'll need to crouch down to be in their frames... Is the light in here alright for you folks?" Tom clicked away; his flashgun thumped over and over, joined by those of the other photographers until they blended into a flickering drum roll. The stench of burnt magnesium filled the air. Maj. Jesse Marcel squatted down in front of the radiator and the wooden chairs, holding one of the largest pieces of weather balloon in his hands. He managed to force a thin smile as he gazed up at the press gang.

....

Clane entered Mollett's cubicle and handed him his draft. The editor put on his spectacles and read. "Hmm, the article is OK... But 'Roswell Flying Disk turns out to be Army Weather Balloon'? Not a very good title, Quilley. Can you come up with something punchier? With more style? Use a pun or metaphor of some kind." Clane returned to his desk and loaded his typewriter. As always he began with today's date: *Wednesday 9th of July 1947.* After some deliberation he came up with "Gen. Ramey Empties Roswell Saucer." He grinned sardonically at his own wit. "You don't look very happy, Clane." Marietta smiled at him sympathetically.

Clane smiled back and shrugged. "It's just been a very strange week, Mari."

"It has too!"

"I started out totally skeptical. When all this talk of flying saucers began I just wanted it to end. Now it's over I feel almost nostalgic; I miss it."

"Me too. It was certainly exciting."

"Even before the press release from the base yesterday I'd begun to believe that flying saucers might be real and we do share this universe with other beings like us. But it was all a huge mountain made out of a tiny molehill... And it went to my head, Mari; being the *RDR*'s official flying saucer correspondent on the day flying saucers were proven real, in Roswell of all places. I was the man on the spot. I was talking to people from all over the world, right here in Roswell!" His voice faded wistfully.

"And now everything's back to normal." she said. "And it feels so boring! I've faced normality my whole life; why does it seem so unbearable all of a sudden?"

"It could be worse I suppose." Clane was thinking of Jesse Marcel; his heart ached for his friend. The prints of Tom's photographs were lying in a folder on his desk. He picked them up and took them over to the telex. He looked at each one of them at a time as he scanned them in. He hesitated and then pressed the SEND button. He had just added the visual record of Marcel's humiliation to the Associated Press wire. Within a second those photographs could be printed off in every newspaper office in the country. Within a minute they'd be copied to the international wires; then anybody anywhere in the world could press a button on a machine and see a picture of Maj. Jesse Marcel prostrating himself amid the debris of his blunder.

By mid-morning all the day's copy was ready. Tristan was off sick so once again it was Clane who carried the sheaf of typewritten articles down to the printers. He manoeuvred the earmuffs on with one hand as he grasped the papers close to his chest. Enoch made the gesture that meant "hello"; the only part of the print shop's mysterious sign language that Clane had learnt. Clane watched with interest as Enoch and his team got to work, transforming the typewriter text into blocks on the lithographic plates. These were then loaded into the huge machines which began churning like rock-crushers. Chains relayed, rollers rotated and the mechanical behemoths steadily digested their instructions before neatly excreting newspapers.

"STOP!" The voice was audible even above the din of the machines. They all turned and stared. The sight that met their eyes was the last they expected. Owen Mollett, the editor of the *Roswell Daily Record*, stood in the open doorway. He was waving a sheet of paper in his hand. Enoch recovered from his surprise and turned to his team. He drew his hand flat and horizontally beneath his chin and the men fiddled with levers and buttons. The printing machines ground to a halt. The following silence was the deepest and most uncanny Clane Quilley had ever heard. Slowly, one by one, the printers removed their earmuffs. Their faces were grey and ashen in the garish light.

Mollett, not the fittest man in the world, was out of breath from his run downstairs. "Stop the press! Scratch the entire issue!" he puffed. "Quilley! This is just in on the AP wire." He waved the chit. "We're to withdraw the entire story from the Fort Worth press conference."

"Who says?" asked Clane. "Gen. Ramey?"

"No!" Mollett grinned with excitement. "Washington!"

Enoch and the other printers muttered with surprise too.

"This is direct from the White House." confirmed Mollett. "The President is going to address the nation at six PM."

"But... Mr Mollett. This can only mean..."

"That's right, Quilley. The Roswell flying saucer is real."

Chapter 4

Clane entered his motel room and went straight to the phone. After the usual curt and perfunctory exchanges with Gina, his daughter picked up the receiver. "Dad?"

"Hi, honey. Have you got the radio on?"

"Dad, we've got a TV now. Norman got us one..."

"OK, OK; whatever. Is it on?"

"Yeah, but I've got chores to do."

"Never mind that, Siobhan. Just keep the TV on and stay in front of it."

She hesitated. "Why?"

"Wait and see."

"OK, what station?"

"All of them!"

....

"A reminder, ladies and gentlemen, that the President will be addressing the nation at six o'clock this evening; in approximately half an hour's time. He will be speaking on a matter of extreme importance to the United States and the world at large..." Clane switched off his car radio. The streets of Roswell looked normal. Word has not yet got out from the printshop. Perhaps during the last few days people had built up a tolerance to flying saucer stories and so took less notice of breaking ones. Clane had the address of the person he wanted to visit, but had lost the phone number. The house was a boxy mini-mansion near the city limits. He parked beside their white picket fence and rang their two-tone suburban doorbell, checking his watch. The door opened and Dr David Preston stood before him. "Hello..." he said. "It's Mr... er... from the *RDR*?"

"Quilley. Clane Quilley."

"Well, hello, Mr Quilley. What can I do for you?" The dentist took a step back. "If it's more about that root canal fiasco, I'm not your man."

"No, no. It's alright, Dr Preston. I'm not after a story this time. I was just wondering... do you still have a television in your home?"

"Yeah sure; just bought a new set."

"Would it be possible for me to watch it for five minutes?"

Dr Preston gazed at him quizzically, as if he could read his thoughts. "I guess so, if Shirley and the kids don't mind. Is it the address the President's about to give?"

"Yes. I know it's on the radio, but... I'd like to see his face."

Dr Preston frowned. The dentist's clean bald scalp glinted in the sunlight. "Mr Quilley, this isn't something to do with that flying saucer business is it?"

"Erm... I'm not sure." lied Clane. Preston stared at him hard and then stood aside so he could enter the house.

Mrs Shirley Preston was an attractive red-haired woman. She was sitting in the lounge; her forearms still damp from doing the washing up after dinner. Her year-old son James sat on her knee sucking his fingers. He gave Clane a curious look with his wide blue infant eyes. The two older children were sitting on the settee at opposite ends. Anita Preston was fourteen and had ringlets in her hair and a homework book open on her lap. Her ten year old brother David Jr was reading a comic. Both children still had their school clothes on. "This is Mr Quilley from the paper." said Dr Preston. "You remember him?"

The family all gave him a cautious and probing smile of greeting.

"Take a seat, Mr Quilley." said Dr Preston. "Can I get you a beer?"

"Yes please." Clane say down on the only seat available, between the two children. He felt their eyes on each side of his head simultaneously. The lounge was clean and well-furnished with pictures of country scenes on the wall and photographs of family members on the mantelpiece. In the corner stood the television set. Its gleaming square eye stared out at the family from its dark chestnut cabinet propped up on four stout legs. The flicking electrical lightshow from the cathode ray tube inside strobed over the glass convex window onto the sepia, horizontally lined world beyond. Clane turned to Anita's scowling face and grinned, feeling slightly embarrassed. "Mom, can Frieda come over this evening?" Anita asked.

Mrs Preston frowned. "I'm not sure, honey. Frieda's mommy told me she spends too much time round here."

Anita gasped with indignation. "Mom, she only came over once last week."

"Three times, Anita. Monday, Tuesday and Friday."

Clane looked at the clock on the mantelpiece. It said five fifty-five PM.

"Mr Quilley, do you know what the President is going to talk to us about?" asked Shirley Preston.

Clane shrugged awkwardly.

"Mom, can I watch *Hopalong Cassidy* when the President's finished?" piped up, David.

Clane looked away, grateful for a change of subject.

"We'll see, Davy." answered Mrs Preston. "I'm not sure all these westerns are good for a boy your age."

"Aw, come on, Mom. You let me watch newsreels during the war."

Dr Preston came into the lounge and handed Clane a large glass of beer. His face was solemn and apprehensive. He brought in a small wooden chair from the kitchen and sat down by the window.

The clock reached 6 PM and its bell rang. *Bing, bing, bing, bing, bing, bing.* He and Clane exchanged a silent look.

The previous programme was just ending. It had been some light-hearted game show that Clane had never seen before. The credits rolled and jocular theme music played while the studio audience applauded. The screen went blank. Normally a commercial break would now begin, but none did; it was a black, empty glass square. Then a disembodied voice announced from the speakers: *"Ladies and gentlemen, there will now be a change to our scheduled programme. We will shortly be going to a live special broadcast. An address to our nation by the President of the United States."* The picture remained blank for a few more seconds, then it flashed a few times and an image appeared. The scene was instantly recognizable, as was the figure within it. President Harry S Truman sat at his desk in the Oval Office. The fact that he'd chosen this location instead of the more usual White House Press Briefing Room indicated that he had something to say of extraordinary gravity. The frame of the television picture included the twin flags on either side of the desk, the top of the desk and the President himself sitting behind it. Harry Truman looked into the TV camera lens. He licked his lips and grinned briefly with his small teeth. His large brown eyes were magnified slightly by his spectacles. His hair was meagre and neatly styled. *"My fellow Americans."* he began in his Midwestern accent. *"No doubt you are aware of the recent news stories of the past few weeks regarding flying saucers and speculation about what they might or might not be."* He paused and looked down, fiddling with his papers in front of him. *"I have spent long hours in consultation with key members of our defence and intelligence services over this matter, along with the Secretary of Defence, the chairman of the joint Chiefs of Staff and a number of experts in the scientific community. I am now in a position to inform you, the American people, that there is now overwhelming evidence that the United States of America, and the world at large beyond our borders, is being interacted with by an intelligence that is not human and does not originate on planet earth. The exact nature of this intelligence is not currently known, but research into this question is well-advanced. However, let me reassure you that there is no indication that this said intelligence has hostile intentions towards the United States and the human race in general. The aforementioned interaction has been ongoing for many decades and no harm has been done to us so far. If anything, I would comment that it appears we are under neutral, detached observance by this intelligence. I will shortly be making available by executive order an extensive press package containing newly declassified material relating to this subject. This will be free to distribute to all media outlets. I am also establishing, via another executive order, a new government* department, reporting directly to me, to manage this matter; an Office of Extraterrestrial Affairs. I am well aware that the inherent nature of my announcement this evening is worrying and frightening. I understand your feelings, but also have a duty to maintain an environment of calm debate. Therefore I have instructed the Secretary of the Treasury to order the closure of all stock markets until further notice. I have also instructed all state governors that the National Guard will be available to any of them who feel they require its assistance to maintain law and order." The President paused and cleared his throat. He took a sip of water from a glass. "I believe that a similar announcement to the one I am giving now is also being delivered in most of the countries of the world; simultaneously, or within the next few hours due to differences in time zones. I shall now give way to a separate broadcast from the White House Press Briefing Room where the Secretary of Defence, the Secretary of the Treasury and other officials will discuss the various details of what I have just outlined. We are safe, our nation is safe. We will move into this new era together. I believe we all have a right to know, and a need to know. May God bless us and protect us."

The telephone ringing broke them out of their stupor. Dr Preston stood up shakily and walked over to the instrument. "Hello... Yes, we've just seen it... No, Gary, I don't think it's a joke... I don't know; we'll have to wait and see... OK, talk you later." He ended the call. After another minute it was David Jr. who next broke the silence. "Holy shit!"

"Watch your mouth, young man!" His mother's rebuke was wheezy and half-hearted. The phone rang again and nobody answered it. After ten rings it stopped. Clane and the Preston family continued to sit in silence and the emergency TV report continued. The phone rang again; this time it continued to ring for several minutes until eventually Dr Preston got up and answered it. "Hello... What?... Clane Quilley?... Yes." he reached out the receiver to Clane. "It's for you."

Clane stood up, confused, and took the instrument. "Hello?"

"Quilley!" Owen Mollett's voice bellowed in his ear.

"Mr Mollett? How did you know where I am?"

"Never mind that; just get your ass to Washington!"

....

Clane stepped out of the Preston's home. The street was full of people, as if all the residents had come out of their houses. They stood on the sidewalks in knots and bunches, talking animatedly; some of them were arguing. There was a screech of tyres and a car emerged from a driveway. It arced into the road and tore off at high speed. As Clane drove home, the main streets of Roswell were devoid of pedestrians; a few vehicles were driving far too fast. A number of solemn and pale faces peered out from the windows of diners and shops. As he approached his own residential district he had to brake sharply as a station wagon jumped a red light and crossed in front of him. They didn't look at him or give him the customary wave of thanks. On the front lawn of one house, a man stood wearing nothing but a dressing gown and slippers. He cradled a shotgun in his arms and was staring up at the sky. Clane parked in his usual slot and walked up to his motel. He knocked on the neighbouring door and Hilda Blair Ray answered. She was flushed and breathing hard; and her eyes were slightly damp and bloodshot, as if she'd been crying. "Hilda." Clane said. "I'm glad I caught you. Could you...?"

"Clane, I can't fly you anywhere." she interrupted. "I'm leaving right now. I'm heading up to Four Corners to pick up Bernard."

He looked past her into the room and saw two open suitcases on the bed. "Where will you go after that?"

"I don't know. Please excuse me." She shut the door. Clane entered his own room and tried to call Gina and Siobhan, but the operator didn't answer. He reached under his bed and pulled out his own suitcase.

....

The sun was setting as Clane drove up Highway 285. The straight, unblemished road was paced by a row of telegraph wires. He only met a handful of vehicle, all cars, all heading south towards Roswell. Most of them didn't bother to dip their headlights and Clane learnt to shade his eyes as they approached. The landscape changed from flat desert plain to rocky hills. The road became more inclined and at ten PM he entered Albuquerque. This city was much bigger and more bustling than Roswell, with a number of tall buildings and wider streets. Clane had never before been to Albuquerque, but he sensed that the place had weathered the impact better than Roswell. A number of restaurants and bars were still open and people walked normally on the streets at this late hour. The municipal airport lay to the south of the city and when Clane arrived, the gate was chained and padlocked. A painted signboard hung on the gate with the words: *ALL FLIGHTS CANCELLED UNTIL FURTHER NOTICE.* Hand-scrawled underneath in chalk was: *Due to the flying saucer problem.* Clane sighed with relief. It was too late to drive back to Roswell that night so he went to find accommodation. Albuquerque was full up, but he eventually came across a hotel just outside town with a single room free. The owner was a cheery middle-aged Latina who was the first person he'd met who appeared unfazed by the President's flying saucer speech. In fact she was delighted. "You know, I've been seeing these spaceships all my life." she revealed as she led him up the stairs to his room. "I've even met the little men who fly in them. They come for me sometimes and take me away with them. Nobody believed me. My husband even tried to get me committed!" She handed Clane his key. "Maybe now they'll see I was right all along."

....

Clane awoke. He looked at the clock: nine-thirty-three AM; very late for him. The window was open and the curtains swung lightly in the breeze. Fuzzy sunbeams washed through the textile to illuminate the room in pastel shades. He got out of bed, had a shower and then dressed. The aroma from downstairs told him that breakfast was cooking. In the dining room beside the kitchen a radio played in the corner. The programme was a political talk show with two voices he didn't recognize.

Presenter 1: The whole world has changed! Completely and in every way.

Presenter 2: Not really. After all, this show is still on the air. Right across the Land of Enchantment people are listening to us, just like they have on previous shows. All my life people have talked about there being life on Mars and other planets. Damnit, I used to love comic books and magazines about beings from space when I was a kid...

Presenter 1: But, Johnny...

Presenter 2: David, nothing has been revealed that a lot of us didn't suspect anyway. We're human, with God's help we can adapt. You heard the President; these creatures from Mars aren't exactly the monsters I read about in those magazines. They're not about to launch an attack on us. If they wanted to, they could have wiped us out years ago.

Presenter 1: Johnny, I don't think you quite grasp the implications here. What people read in a story is something they do for fun. This is real. I don't agree that most people suspected it anyway. I never met a single person my whole life who took the idea of flying saucers seriously, until last night.

Presenter 2: Come off it, David!

Presenter 1: Let me finish, Johnny... It doesn't matter if a few people had a half-hearted hunch. Our society is still built, from foundations to roof, on the assumption we're on an island. And it's an island where no other land is in sight. Now we're suddenly just one street in a big city.

Presenter 2: Maybe not. We don't know how many of them are out there.

Presenter 1: What effect do you think this is going to have on our institutions? Science and the church. People will want to know why God never mentions the men from Mars in the bible.

Presenter 2: Maybe Mars is where the angels live.

Presenter 1: Or demons!

Presenter 2: *Look, we can speculate all we like, but we just don't know what they are. However, we do know we're not in immediate danger. Hey, let's enjoy the adventure! The universe suddenly just got more interesting; and for once New Mexico is at the heart of it. Nobody can pretend anymore that we're just a backwater where nothing ever happens. Thanks to what happened last week in Roswell, we'll be forever on the map!...*

After breakfast Clane used the hotel payphone to give Owen Mollett the bad news. He smiled to himself as he dialled. "Mr Mollett, good morning." he began cheerily.

"Quilley!" Mollett barked in reply. "I've spoken to my contact in DC and he says you're not there yet!"

"That's right, Mr Mollett. I'm still in Albuquerque. I'm afraid the airport is closed so I won't be able to go to Washington."

Mollett hissed. "Damnit!"

"I know, sir. Rotten luck isn't it?"

He paused. "Never mind, go by road."

"What?"

"Drive, Quilley. There's nothing wrong with your car is there?"

"No, but... *drive* to Washington DC!?"

"Yes. Just stick the gas on expenses as usual."

"But, sir, it's two thousand miles! It'll take me a week!"

"Nonsense! These aren't the days of the wagon trains. My brother did it last year. Stay on the interstates, don't mind your speed, grab naps on the kerb. I reckon you can get there by tomorrow night."

Clane gritted his teeth.

"Did you hear that, Quilley?"

"Yes, sir, but..."

"But what?" Mollett's voice was a threatening growl.

"Mr Mollett... I'm not doing it. I'm not driving all that way for another flying saucer story. I don't care if the President says they're real; I'm through with flying saucers!... Haven't I done my time yet? I want to come home to Roswell, write legal columns and for you to let somebody else take care of this novelty."

"Quilley!" roared the *Roswell Daily Record* editor. "Don't you dare refuse a direct instruction from me! I'll fire you!"

"Then fire me!" Clane heard a voice bellow in reply. "Kick me off the fucking paper, you lard-assed old bastard!" Clane then realized that the voice was his own.

Mollett gasped. There was a volcanic silence. Clane could only hear the pounding of his own heart in the earpiece. "Quilley, please! I need you on this." Mollett's voice was tremulous, pleading. Clane had never heard his boss speak in this tone before and he almost dropped the receiver in surprise. "Quilley, don't you understand? You're not just *my* flying saucer correspondent any more; you're the *world's*. When you arrive in Washington you'll be given a hero's welcome. They're waiting for you! You are the man who brought the world the greatest story of the century! The *RDR* was founded for this moment!... Go to Washington and I'll make you assistant editor! I swear!" Mollett sounded as if he were on the brink of tears.

"Alright, Mr Mollett. I'll go."

"Thank you, Quilley. Thank you!"

....

The first part of Clane's journey was along Interstate Forty, part of the classic old Route 66. The tense atmosphere from which he'd felt a reprive in Albuquerque returned. The road was almost empty apart from police cars and National Guard jeeps. It was like driving on Christmas Day without the festive thoughts, nor the knowledge that things would return to normal within twenty-four hours. The military presence was palpable. He passed grey-painted trucks, staff cars and armoured personnel carriers every few minutes. The blue sky rumbled almost continuously with aircraft engines. Squadrons of Mustangs and Boeings passed overhead as if an air show were in progress. At Tucumcari he was pulled over by a New Mexico state policeman, but at the side of the road stood a squad of soldiers, assault rifles at the ready. The cop asked to see his drivers licence and as soon as he looked at it, his eyebrows rose and his manner transformed. "Clane Quilley? Are you the reporter?"

"Yes."

"Well it's an honour to meet you, sir. I don't know what to make of this flying saucer malarkey, but it's just great that for once, we New Mexicans are in the midst of it..." As with the radio show presenters, state pride overrode any fear he had felt. He shook Clane's hand and then offered to escort him all the way to the border at Glenrio, about twenty miles ahead. Clane waved goodbye to the admiring state trooper and entered Texas. At two PM he reached Amarillo, the first major city he'd seen since leaving Albuquerque. Here the people looked far more alarmed. They stalked the street like guerrillas, loaded down with bags of groceries. Most of them were armed. He once saw a man with a supermarket trolley stacked with boxes, level a pistol at another man who approached him. The second man backed off before any shots were fired. At the main store in the city centre people were piling in and out like the New Year sale. Clearly everybody had decided to stock up on as many commodities as possible in case the Martians invaded. The problem was that Amarillo's retail sphere had limited supplies. At the next block down from the shop, a fight was in progress involving about a dozen people. Clane slowed down and prepared to duck below the dashboard, but fortunately this scuffle did not involve firearms. Men and women merely yelled abuse at each other; pushed, kicked and punched. A posse of patrolmen ran over to break it up. A fire engine whooped by, ignoring the melee, heading for a different emergency.

Clane needed to stop for gasoline, but didn't feel safe in Amarillo, so he headed out of town hoping he'd come across a station in a calmer location. A church stood at the city limits surrounded by a huge crowd of people. There was a crush at the doorway as parishioners struggled to enter the overcrowd building. A man stood on a bench seat nearby shouting manically at the throng. He had an open bible in his hands and appeared to be reading aloud from it. It was open towards the end, about where the Book of Revelations was. Clane came across a Texaco garage at Groom, twenty miles east of Amarillo. The sign above the forecourt said *OPEN*, but nobody was serving. Clane tried the pump and found that it was switched on, so he filled up the car's tank himself. He entered the office to pay, but there was nobody in sight, so he left a few dollars tucked under the till. He charged the tyres and filled the radiator too before he left.

Once he was in Oklahoma the landscape became greener. A few forests could be seen at the side of the road along with some post-dustbowl farms. It was twilight when he reached Oklahoma City. He realized that finding a place to rest and eat was out of the question. The electricity had gone off and the tall buildings downtown were as dark as mountains. Some people had lit bonfires and braziers on the pavements. The place was even more lawless than Amarillo as the world entered its second night knowing that it was not alone in the universe. Clane continued driving eastwards. The blackout continued beyond Oklahoma City. There were a few spots of light, indicating farms that had their own generators, but apart from that Clane's headlights cut into pure darkness. Eventually, after midnight, he saw an intersection and a copse of trees to the right. He left the interstate, parked in the shelter of the trees and cut the engine. Clane had slept in many strange places in the world, including a submarine bunk which he had to share with another sailor on the opposite watch, but at least there he could lie flat. The only way he could do this is the car was to open one of the back doors and lie on the back seat with his legs dangling out. His feet throbbed and tingled from pins and needles. He was hungry, having not eaten since breakfast. He turned from one side to the other, trying different positions. It was humid and sultry outside and mosquitoes whined around his face making him slap himself, with limited success. Eventually he fell into a doze.

Clane woke with a start. It was cooler now and a breeze played across his body. Crickets warbled loudly outside. His eyes were half open and he thought he saw movement. Had a dark shape just silently drifted past the open car door? Had he dreamt it? He sat up and rubbed his eyes. There was indeed something outside the car; a lofty black shadow was standing in front, visible through the windscreen, damped vaguely by the moon and starlight. Adrenalin surged. "Ahh!" Clane yelped in alarm. He leaned over and manically groped the dashboard until he found the switch for the headlights. He squeezed his eyes shut in pain as his night adjusted retinas were overloaded by the pair of electric beams. He squinted as his irises struggled to contract. "You!"

"Hello, Mr Quilley."

Clane rolled onto the back seat and clambered out of the car. He approached the illuminated figure. There was no mistaking the small wizened face, the poncho and broad-brimmed hat. It was the old Indian he'd met near Roswell the previous week.

"I told you we'd meet again." The man grinned playfully.

"How did you get here?" Clane gasped. "This is Oklahoma!"

"Actually we're in eastern Arkansas; you've made more progress than you thought."

"How did you get here!?"

The Indian gave him a quizzical look. "Why don't you ever ask yourself that same question?"

Clane shrugged and there was a long silence. "What do you want with me?"

"Several things. First of all I strongly recommend that you switch off the headlights."

"Why?"

"Just switch off the lights." The stranger said this in a low voice, almost inaudible, but tangible, like infrasound. His small chestnut eyes bored into Clane's. Clane reached in by the driver's seat. The night returned to darkness in an instant. The blackness was more profound now Clane's night vision had gone. "Now what?"

"Now we'll be safe." replied the Indian.

"Safe from what?"

Gunshots rang out. Clane started and crouched behind the chassis while the Indian remained impassive and motionless. More shots followed; they were not close. Clane could see nothing in the direction of the sound. A woman screamed and a man shouted. There were more shots, then silence. A minute later Clane heard voices, those of young men chatting animatedly. The voices got louder; the men were approaching. He saw the red glowing spots of cigarettes being smoked. The flare of a lighter lit up a group of men walking up the sliproad. Clane shrank back further behind the car, holding his breath in case his lungs made enough noise to alert them. The group of men numbered six or seven, walking swiftly, carrying sacks over their shoulders. They came within a dozen feet of the car and walked past without seeing it. The sound of their voices faded with distance and eventually silence returned. "What happened?" sighed Clane.

"Those men just attacked a car on the interstate." replied the Indian. "They killed the driver and his wife to steal the goods they were transporting."

Clane turned and stared at his black outline. "You knew that was going to happen. How did you know?"

"It's hard to explain, Mr Quilley... Those men all think they're about to die and go to hell. Therefore they believe they have nothing to lose by committing that crime."

Clane trembled. The Indian's words unearthed a subconscious dread of his own. "Are... are these really the Last Days?"

"No."

The positivity in the Indian's voice reassured him. "I don't know how you know my name... but what's yours?"

The Indian laughed. "Are you sure you don't already know?"

"What the hell does that mean?... Damnit, man; you say some strange things!"

"Tell me what you think my name is."

"Jeez, I don't know... Flying Buffalo?"

"That's it." He tittered.

"What?"

"That's my name; Flying Buffalo."

"Come on, man; I was just guessing."

"And you guessed right first time, Mr Quilley."

Both men were silent for a minute or two; then Clane said: "I can't believe we just witnessed two people getting cold-bloodedly murdered on a US highway. Is the whole world like this?"

"No." responded Flying Buffalo. "Of course, everywhere is effected to a greater or lesser degree, but some places are worse than others. Some nations have fared much better than the United States. Within the US, there are differences between regions."

"Mr Buffalo, twice now you've saved my life. Twice in as many weeks. I trust your judgement... Is the President telling the truth? Are there flying saucers?"

Flying Buffalo paused. "That's not a question I can answer right now."

Clane sighed. "Oh, Lord! Look, either they're real or they're not."

"Maybe, but that kind of question will have no place in the environment you're about to enter. You will have to get used to a world in what is thought to be real and unreal, is not decided by logic."

"How can reality be decided by anything but logic?"

Flying Buffalo was a silhouette against the starry sky. "It happens all the time." he muttered. Then he said more firmly: "I must go now, Mr Quilley. Good luck!" He backed off into the road and headed in the direction of the highway.

"Wait!" Clane called after him, but Flying Buffalo was out of sight.

....

The cold awoke him. Clane was shivering and slightly damp with dew as he opened his eyes. It was early dawn and he could see the shapes of tree branches against the sky. Low cloud scrolled across his view. The warmth and humidity had passed and the morning was chilly and fresh. Birds were singing in the woods, oblivious to the tumultuous goings on in the human world. He stood up and stretched a few times to loosen his stiff body. He wondered about his second encounter with Flying Buffalo during the night. Had it been a dream? He found the footprints of Indian moccasins around the car, dispelling that possibility. He got into the driver's seat and started the engine. As he turned onto the I-forty he saw a crescent of policemen guarding an empty car, the site of the previous night's murder. The sun rose ahead behind the haze. Flying Buffalo had been telling the truth; he was indeed in Arkansas and before long he reached the great river, the Mississippi. The brown water of the river tumbled and bulged as it passed below the steel framed railway bridges. Across on the far bank was the skyline of the city of Memphis. There was no way to get a car across the river except by a new bridge that was only partly constructed. He had to move aside a wooden barrier and guide his car carefully along a rocky builders' road towards the new bridge. Luckily the deck of the bridge was completed although it was just a bare metal mesh. Clane bumped across the Mississippi and entered Tennessee. His stomach protested with hunger so he went looking for a shop or diner. Central Memphis was virtually a ghost town and Clane only saw one person walking the streets. He came across a suburban supermarket on the far side of the city and pulled into the carpark. The glass doors and windows of the mart were shattered and the fragments were splashed in ever increasing circles around the frame. They glinted like diamonds on the ground. A pile of cardboard boxes was arranged haphazardly on the entrance path and a group of people cautiously searched through them. As Clane watched from the car, a man and a woman emerged from the doorway carrying more boxes. Clane got out and approached them. "Good morning, friends." he said. "Do you have any food?"

The man and woman both moved between Clane and their pile of boxes. They stared at him with grim and fearful expressions. The woman's hair was a mess and her face was stained by old make-up. The man's hand moved to a spot near his jacket pocket where there was a bulge shaped distinctly like a revolver. Other people in the group walked over and stood at his shoulder. "No." said the man.

"Please, sir. I'm really hungry."

"We're *all* hungry!" he hissed between clenched teeth.

"Can't you even spare one thing?"

He paused and then pointed at the doorway. "Take what you want from in there."

"Thank you." Clane entered the supermarket. It was still chilly from the night and there was condensation on the few plate glass windows still intact. There was no electricity and the only light came from those windows. There was a high-pitched squeak and a rat scurried away along an aisle between the shelves. Clane found a loaf of bread, a jar of pickled onions and some powdered soup. He quenched his thirst with a bottle of mineral water, which he also mixed with the soup granules to eat cold from a plastic mixing bowl. He heard a crashing sound from the far end of the shop floor and as he left he saw a boy of about sixteen trying to break into one of the tills.

Clane drove on through the long state of Tennessee, bypassing city after city; Jackson, Nashville, Knoxville, Jefferson City. The sun came out and landscape became more wooded and hilly. He still saw few vehicles apart from police and military cars. He was stopped twice, but was not detained for long. He crossed over into Virginia at lunchtime and the atmosphere changed dramatically. He was amazed to re-enter a world that appeared almost normal. He peeled off the interstate at mid-afternoon and entered the town of Blacksburg. Shops and bars were open; cars queued up at working gas stations. Buses rumbled past on streets that were only slightly less busy than they usually would be. He passed a sports field where there was a ballgame in progress. He stopped at a diner and wolfed down a burger and beer with relief. Everybody around him appeared like they were having an average day, but Clane did overhear the words "flying saucers" from the surrounding hubbub. He passed the sprawling campus of Virginia Tech as he drove back out to the interstate. In the entrance drive a huge outdoor student party was in progress. Clane slowed down and wound down his window to have a closer look. The young people had virtually set up camp in the university's forecourt. Their tutors were nowhere in sight. A gramophone was playing a popular jazz track while some of them danced. All of them were smoking and held a bottle or beer or wine in their hands. A hundred yards further along just inside the perimeter fence Clane saw the colour of skin between the branches of shrubbery. He felt himself blush and instinctively look away as he realized they were people having sex. He couldn't be sure, and didn't want to verify, but he perceived that there were more than two people involved. Back on the I-eighty-one, Clane switched on his car radio and picked up some stations. The airwaves had been dead all the way from Albuquerque to Tennessee, but now he found several programmes broadcasting. As he suspected, they were all focused on the flying saucer subject. After traversing the entire dial, he settled onto a talk show phone-in.

Presenter: *Hello, I believe we have a Mrs Freeman on the line from Baltimore.*

Guest: Yes, hello, Trevor. I'd just like to say I totally disagree with the man who was on the show earlier. How can he possibly say flying saucers pose no threat to air travellers? These are vehicles not listed on air traffic control and they have no heed for our national borders or our airspace...

An hour later Clane passed a small town. Just outside it a crowd of several hundred people were gathered on the summit of a hill. Clane thought they might have gone to watch the sunset, but then noticed that they were all looking up into the sky. Some of them had binoculars and there was even a large telescope on a tripod.

His journey was almost at an end. The interstate fed into the conurbation of Arlington County, the city bustling and brightly lit. Then his way was blocked. A dozen squad cars and a tank were parked across the road. He stopped and was about to reverse in the road and double back to find another route when a policeman held up his hand and walked over. Clane opened the door and stepped out. "Excuse me, sir." said the cop. "Are you Clane Quilley?"

"Yes."

"Could you come with me please?"

Owen Mollett had not been fooling him. Clane was surrounded by reporters as he was escorted to a rather upmarket car. He was so used to being the hunter of news that he was taken aback at suddenly becoming the hunted. He clambered onto the extensive back seat and noticed a man sitting beside him. "You must be Clane Quilley." he declared, and without waiting for an answer held out his hand. "Good evening, I'm Charlie Ross, the White House Press Secretary. It's good to finally meet you." He shook Clane's hand enthusiastically. "Did you have a good journey?"

The previous two days on the road flashed through Clane's head. "Erm... not bad."

"You must be exhausted. I'm sorry we couldn't arrange transport for you from New Mexico. We're taking you to your hotel first."

"Thank you." The car drove along the Washington Boulevard past Arlington National Cemetery. The wrinkled water of the Potomac River glistened in the city lights. They crossed the Arlington Memorial Bridge and there saw the Lincoln Memorial glowing under its night time floodlights. It loomed majestically on its small hill like a marble Parthenon. They passed through a police checkpoint and headed down Independence Avenue. The military presence Clane had noticed throughout his journey climaxed here in the nation's capital. The elegant dual carriageway was devoid of all traffic except jeeps, army trucks and a few lumbering tanks. Clane felt uneasy as he watched the familiar postcard vista of the Washington Monument, the Smithsonian Air Museum and the Vaticanesque dome of the Halls of Congress surrounded by so much battlefield hardware. East of the Capitol things returned to normal.

The car had to wait behind a bus as it banked left onto Second Street. Eventually they pulled up outside a grand neoclassical building, and a man in coattails and a top hat opened the door. "See you in the morning, Mr Quilley." said Charlie Ross. "Sleep well."

Once he was checked in Clane wasted no time in heading for his room. The hotel was the most opulent he had ever stayed at with a green chandelier hanging from its vaulted ceiling. Nineteenth century velvet chairs were arranged like chess pieces on the thick carpet. He took a shower and leapt into the glorious silken bed. He fell asleep instantly.

....

When Clane awoke he remembered no dreams. It took him a few moments to take in his surroundings. He got out of bed; the clock read half past seven. Outside the sky was blue and cloudless. The street was packed with traffic and pedestrians shuttled across the sidewalks. The bedside phone rang and he picked it up. "Mr Quilley? It's Charlie Ross. Are you awake?"

"Yes, sir. I am."

"Good. Get some of that famous Monaco breakfast down you. A car will pick you up from reception at eight-fifteen." Clane's jaw dropped when he saw the car. It was a stretched Rolls Royce. He hesitated to step inside as the porter held the door for him. Was he worthy? He sank into the cool, soft leather seat. To his left was a cabinet on top of which was a silver bucket containing a bottle of costly-looking champagne embedded in a tumulus of ice cubes. A pair of tall crystal glasses stood beside it. "Help yourself to a drink, sir." cooed the chauffeur from the driver's seat about twelve feet in front of him.

"Thanks." Clane unwrapped the foil from the top of the bottle and unscrewed the wire. He had been a wardroom steward at the New York navel yard so he knew the technique of opening champagne without spilling it everywhere. He looked up and was astonished to see that the car was moving. The quality of the Rolls Royce's engineering made its workings almost silent and imperceptible. He sipped the champagne and savoured its sharp taste. He gagged slightly as the bubbles rose up the back of his nose. "Why are there two glasses?" he asked the driver.

"I'm picking up somebody else."

"Who?"

"A..." he glanced down, presumably at some notepaper. "A Mr Robsark."

"Robsark? I've heard that name before. Can't remember where.

"He's some guy on TV or the radio I think." The huge car negotiated the DC traffic with skill until it came to another hotel with revolving doors. A porter came over from the entrance, spoke to the driver and then returned to the doorway. A few minutes later he came back with a man in a black suit who eased himself into the seat beside Clane with mechanical precision. He studied Clane carefully through his clear, rimless spectacles. "Good morning," he said in a nasal alto voice.

"Morning. Clane Quilley." he held out his hand.

"Hector Robsark." He shook Clane's hand and then helped himself to the champagne bottle and the second flute. He sipped the sparkling liquid slowly and thoughtfully. The limousine started moving again.

"We've got fine weather today." said Clane brightly to break the silence.

Robsark slowly turned his head and glared at Clane; his spectacles magnified his eyes. "Actually I think you'll find that the temperature this morning is sixty-eight degrees Fahrenheit. That is almost exactly average for Washington DC at this time of year." His head jerked back to its original position and he continued analyzing the champagne with his taste buds.

Clane opened his mouth to reply, but then closed it again. He shrugged to himself and raised his eyebrows.

The National Press Building was a square concrete box fitted perfectly into the corner of a block east of the Capitol. Neat rows of identical square windows were set into a facade of vertical concrete columns. The Rolls slowed as the driver tried to find a parking place, but this would have been impossible even for a normal-sized car because the kerbs all around the building were packed with media vehicles bumper-to-bumper. TV vans, radio vans, newspaper vans. Some of them had raised collapsible antennas for live location broadcasts. Eventually the limousine double-parked a hundred yards down the road and the two luxury passengers had to unceremoniously crawl out between the front of an NBC truck and the back of a minibus carrying *Washington Post* reporters. Robsark didn't speak to Clane or even look at him as the two men walked up to the National Press Building's entrance. Charlie Ross was waiting outside. He greeted both of them warmly and ushered them into the lobby where they were offered a cup of coffee and once again Clane had his picture taken by reporters. Within a few minutes Ross chivvied them on. "Not a moment to lose, gentlemen; we've got to get you into wardrobe."

"Wardrobe?" Clane frowned.

"Yes, we're going live in twenty minutes."

"What on, television?"

"Of course, Mr Quilley. The nation is waiting to know more about flying saucers."

Robsark snorted loudly through his nose and rolled his eyes.

Ross escorted them to a lift which took them up a few floors. From the lift they headed for a room with large mirrors and chairs.

A pair of young women applied powder to their faces and sprayed their hair; then they took out a clean jacket and tie to wear. When they were considered correctly attired, they were shown to an ante room and told to wait. Clane was feeling less and less comfortable in the presence of his aloof and taciturn companion, so he got up and walked out to the corridor. He spotted Charlie Ross standing in a doorway talking to a sound engineer with earphones on his head. "Excuse me, Mr Ross. Who is that man, the one I'm going on TV with?"

"Why, that's Hector Robsark; haven't you heard of him?"

"I've heard the name somewhere."

Ross chuckled. "That's *the* Hector Robsark! Don't you watch ABC?"

"No, I don't have a TV at home."

Ross gave him a quizzical frown and said in a flat tone: "Oh yeah, you're from New Mexico, aren't you... Jeez! Hector Robsark has a weekly programme on ABC called *The Skeptic Show*. Look." Ross disappeared into the gallery and came back with a pair of new paperback books. This guy is totally against flying saucers; he thinks it's all bullshit. Check it out." Ross handed Clane the books.

Clane flicked through them. One was called *The Flying Saucers are NOT Real* and was dated that year; the other was an older title dated 1944 called *Science vs Stupidity- Why do People believe Nonsense?*

"He's the biggest mouth in the world when it comes to the crew who disbelieve; not just flying saucers, but they're against ghosts, Bigfoot, the Loch Ness Monster... You name it, they don't believe in it."

Clane opened one of the books to the "about the author" page. It had a photo of him and it was definitely the man he had met in the car this morning and was currently waiting to be on television with. "What? This guy is positive flying saucers don't exist?"

"Yeah. We're hoping you two will give us a good debate."

"But how does he explain what the President said?"

Ross was about to reply, but he was interrupted by a woman sticking her head out from the gallery behind them. "We're going live in five! Positions please, gentlemen."

"OK, Mr Quilley; let's get you into the studio."

Clane and Robsark were both led into a room that was greenhouse hot and very brightly lit. Sweat gathered uncomfortably at the collar of the suit Clane had been dressed in. The lights flared blindingly down from brackets on the ceiling. Through the glare, Clane could make out the dusky eyes of TV cameras with a cluster of people moving around them. Electric cables snaked across the floor. In front of the cameras was an enclosure formed by three walls of wooden panels with the logo of the National Broadcasting Company printed on the rear screen. Inside were three armchairs and a small table with three glasses of water. The show's host sat on the middle chair and gestured for his two guests to join him on either side. A studio technician stepped forward and hung a loop of wire around their necks, supporting a microphone connected to a cable that led back into the gloom behind the cameras. "Hello, gentlemen. Tom Watson." The host shook hands with both of them. He was a polished man with thick smooth hair and a handsome profile. "Mr Quilley, ever been on TV before?"

"No, never."

"Right. We're broadcasting live, so no foul language, OK?..." Watson ran through a list of rules and disclaimers. Clane began to feel exposed and vulnerable. He took in the gleaming lenses of the television cameras all focused on him. How many people would be watching him? Hundreds of thousands? Millions?

"Alright, folks!" yelled a disembodied voice from the back of the room, presumably the director. "We're coming out of commercial in twenty seconds. Standby... five... four... three..."

Watson addressed the cameras. "Good afternoon from the National Press Club in Washington DC. I'm Tom Watson. Welcome to today's series of special programmes dedicated to the discussion of what has become known as the 'flying saucer crisis'. As you know, a few days ago an unknown object of intelligent creation came to grief on the surface of the earth. It crashed to the ground in the desert of New Mexico, not far from the city of Roswell. The event was first reported in the local newspaper, the *Roswell Daily Record*, and the reporter who broke the story was the newspaper's official flying saucer correspondent, Clane Quilley. Hello, Mr Quilley."

"Hello." Clane tried to keep the quaver out of his voice. He took a sip of water.

"Is it true that you are the only journalist in the United States specializing full-time in the flying saucer phenomenon?"

A dozen sentences flashed through Clane's head. How he had been made the *RDR*'s flying saucer correspondent only one week ago. How it had been a penalty imposed on him for turning up late at the office. He could have told Watson and the viewers how frustrated he was with his work; how he'd been taken away from stories he wanted to write, in order to cover what he believed, and still partly believed, was a falsehood. Instead he found himself replying: "I believe so."

"How fortunate that you happened to be based near where a flying saucer actually crashed."

"I guess it is." he forced a grin.

"How did this incident reach the news?"

"Well, there had been a multitude of rumours circulating around the area about strange goings on up in the sky. This lasted for a good few days. We knew the Roswell Army Air Force was carrying out a covert operation in a remote area of Lincoln County; they'd sealed off a large area of ranch-land and desert. I made some inquiries at the base and to begin with they said nothing, but then on Tuesday we received a press release from the RAAF stating that a flying disk had crashed and they had salvaged it. The rest you know."

"As we've addressed on these broadcasts before, the speech the President made gives the impression that the government already knew in advance what the Roswell flying disk was; in other words, they've been quietly monitoring these flying saucers for some time already before informing the people."

"Quite possibly."

"Why do you suppose they've decided to come clean to the public now?"

Clane paused. "I couldn't say."

"Thank you, Mr Quilley." Watson turned to his other guest. "As always on this programme, we wish to give you, the viewers, a balanced assessment of all situations by providing a multitude of opinion; in doing so we hope you will all make up your own minds. With this objective we have also invited onto this programme the bestselling author and host of the ABC programme *The Skeptic Show*; he is also chairman of CASRA- the Capital Area Skeptics and Rationalist Association, Hector Robsark. Hello, Mr Robsark."

"*Doctor* Robsark." the second guest corrected.

"Excuse me, *Doctor* Robsark." repeated Watson.

Robsark immediately leaned forward and addressed Clane over the host's lap. "Mr Quilley, is it true that on Tuesday afternoon, a few hours after the 'flying disk' press release, the Army Air Force held a press conference at Fort Worth, Texas?"

"Yes."

"And you attended it, did you not?" Robsark spoke quickly and loudly like a lawyer in court.

"Yes."

"That press conference resulted in the publication of a second press release, later on Tuesday July 8th; what did it say?"

Clane hesitated. He felt a stab of irritation at his fellow guest's manner. "Why don't you tell us, seeing as you already know?"

Robsark faced the front to address the TV audience. "This is a part of the story that the American public has not been told about. The RAAF revealed on Tuesday evening that there was in truth *no flying disk captured at all.*" He spoke slowly for emphasis. "What Maj. Marcel found on that ranch in New Mexico was in fact nothing more than a weather balloon."

"Wait a minute." interjected Clane. "That story was withdrawn. I wrote it myself and..."

"Oh please, Mr Quilley! I know very well what your activities have been all this week; I've researched you thoroughly." He sneered and the studio lights made his teeth glitter. "I know that during the press conference at Fort Worth Maj. Marcel actually showed us the supposed space debris that he found and one can see clearly that it was nothing but a weather balloon... You know this *yourself*! *You* were there! The photographs were published even though your story was withdrawn..."

"It was withdrawn because of a direct communiqué from the office of the President of the United States."

Robsark snorted again in the exact same way he had in the lobby, breathing out loudly through his nose while he rolled his eyes and shook his head. "That is the *real* tragedy. It's not that some junior AAF officer was taken in by balloon fragments, or that a local New Mexican rag is guilty of shoddy and amateurish journalism. It's not even so bad that rioting and disorder has hit large areas of our country causing loss of life and damage to property and infrastructure... The real tragedy is that this debacle was only caused because this flying saucer lunacy has risen to such a level that it's infected the highest office in the land. As I explain in my book *The Flying Saucers are NOT Real...*"

"Alright, Dr Robsark." Watson butted in. "This show is not a commercial break for your book. Mr Quilley, would you like to respond?"

Clane could see by his frown that the presenter disliked Robsark as well. "Mr... Dr Robsark can think what he likes about flying saucers. He may even be right that they don't exist, but he was way out of line with what he said about the *RDR...* I assume he means me personally. I am not guilty of amateurish and shoddy journalism. I did my job to the best of my abilities. This is not a job I enjoyed. As I said, I'm still not completely sure if the President is right or not. As for Maj. Jesse Marcel, he is not some 'junior officer'; he's the intelligence specialist for the 509th bomb group. He's in charge of atomic bombs, for goodness sakes! He's an officer of great expertise, honour and integrity."

"Anybody can be deceived." responded Robsark. "By others or themselves. May I suggest in this case we employ the basic scientific precept of intellectual parsimony, or Occam's Razor? Have you heard of that?"

Watson and Clane shook their heads.

Robsark grinned and tossed his head as if to say *I didn't think so*. "Intellectual parsimony or Occam's Razor is a problem solving method which states that when applying logic to an unknown, always address the most likely possibility first, the one which demands the fewest assumptions. So for example, if your flashlight stops working, try changing the batteries before taking the device in for repairs, because a flat battery is by far the most likely cause of the flashlight's malfunction."

"What's that got to do with flying saucers?" asked Watson.

"Well, let us apply Occam's Razor to this situation. Which is more likely? That an advanced race of creatures from Mars flew down here in a Flash Gordon rocket and ended up crashing into a field in rural New Mexico... *or*, what actually crashed was a weather balloon, made by man, right here on earth; and that a tired and sun-struck military investigator made a human error?" Neither replied so Robsark went on. "Gentlemen, people of America, it is time to put this vacuous baloney behind us and grow up. Belief in supernatural garbage and dim-witted fantasy has been shown once again to be the pernicious pathology that it is..."

"That'll do, Dr Robsark." said Watson. "Let's not forget that this is my show and not yours... I'd like to thank both of you gentlemen for appearing this afternoon; and I'd like to deliver some good news. Just before we went to air, we had word from the White House that there is going to be another press conference tomorrow at Wright Field, Ohio where physical remains of the alleged flying disk will be put on display to a group of selected members of the press. And I'm pleased to inform you gentlemen that both your names are on the invitation list for that group."

"Excellent!" exclaimed Robsark with a victorious grin. "I shall very much enjoy viewing the remains of an old weather balloon, and in doing so taking the opportunity to give the American public and our nation's government a very much-needed lesson in critical thinking."

....

The Rolls Royce came for Clane after breakfast again. He left the hotel in apprehension, not feeling comfortable with the prospect of sharing it once more with Hector Robsark. However, the limousine bypassed the skeptic's hotel and went straight to the National Press Building. A dozen or so people sat on settees in the lobby drinking coffee. Robsark was among them; he must have arrived earlier. He was chatting to some of the others and ignored Clane. After a half hour wait, an Air Force minibus arrived. There was quite a crowd to see them off, other envious journalists as well as members of the public. The bus took them to Andrews Field in Maryland south east of the Capitol. From there they flew to Wright Field in Dayton, Ohio by an AAF DC3 transporter. The short journey was tedious because Robsark did nearly all the talking. He held court on the back seat of both the bus and the plane while the others all faced him and nodded their heads dutifully, occasionally asking obsequious questions that the skeptic easily fielded. "Remember, extraordinary claims require extraordinary explanations." he said. "And the claim that we are being visited by beings from Mars is pretty damned extraordinary... You have no idea how many letters I get from people saying: 'I read your book and you are wrong because I've seen a flying saucer and it's the real thing!' and they'll enclose a blurry photo of some fuzzy blotch that could be anything. That's literally all the evidence there is. Don't you think that if we were being visited by aliens out in space then there'd be some hard evidence? Good photographs? High quality multiple eye-witness sightings? Physical remains? How about a drop of Martian blood?... Why don't they land on the White House lawn and say hello to the President? Don't get me wrong; I'm open-minded. I just don't think we should be so open-minded that our brain falls out!"

His acolytes laughed loudly.

"There is *no* evidence for flying saucers; none. All we have are people with anecdotes; and the plural of anecdote is not data."

Clane sighed with relief as the DC3 descended to the runway and bumped down to land. The transporter taxied a short distance to the terminal and then cut its engines. He followed the other journalists down the sloping cabin aisle and down the gangway onto the sunlit apron. A lieutenant in khaki uniform was waiting to greet them. "Good morning, ladies and gentlemen. Welcome to Wright Field. Please follow me." Without another word he turned around and walked over to one of the airbase's buildings. The posse of newsmen were led down a corridor to a large briefing room with large windows overlooking the interior of a hangar. Airframes and wings filled the view out of them. As they took their place in the rows of seats a colonel entered and addressed from the desk at the front. This man was in his number ones, as if dressed for a special occasion, and Clane had to rein in his military habit to stand to attention and salute him. "Ladies and gentlemen of the press, my name is Col. Elliot Transcope and I'm in command of the Army Air Force Technical Data Section. Our duty is to use science and engineering to work with all the intelligence agencies and units, to acquire and analyze materiel, both enemy and neutral foreign. This press conference has been called in answer to a direct order from the commander-in-chief. It concerns the outcome of a covert recovery operation in New Mexico last week that..." He paused. Perspiration beads broke out on his hairless head. He licked his lips and gave a tremulous sigh. Clane could tell that he was afraid and this unnerved him. Clane had got used to seeing fear in men's eyes from his time in the war. This colonel was middle aged and experienced; it would take a lot to scare him. "Erm... that led to the salvage of some materiel of unknown origin. It is of a type that does not resemble any other kind thought to be made, anywhere." Transcope stuttered slightly, as if unsure of his words. He shrugged. "That is all the information we have at present. The materiel was brought in after being transferred from the Roswell Army Air Field to Fort Worth, Texas. It has been kept under secure storage since then and remains at that status at present. In a moment I'll take you to the laboratory to examine the materiel; but first, any questions?"

"Yes." Hector Robsark raised his hand. "Colonel, if you don't mind, I think we'd find it more interesting to look at one of your new and undamaged weather balloons." He tittered. Only one of the others laughed. Robsark smiled thinly with embarrassment as his joke failed to register. The cluster of reporters had become as alarmed as Clane was at Col. Transcope's gravitas.

Col. Transcope himself gaped at Robsark. He didn't say a word but a series of emotions passed over his face in succession; disbelief, rage, contempt, and finally sadness. He bowed his head and then raised it again. "Please follow me, ladies and gentlemen."

Col. Transcope escorted them along a corridor with windows on both sides, connecting one building to another. At the end was a double door guarded by an armed sentry. He saluted Transcope and greeted him by name, but examined his ID nonetheless. He checked the press passes of all the reporters and ticked their names off from the list he had on a clipboard. Only then did he unlocked the door and allowed them all through. The crowd entered a wide, grey-coloured passage with breeze block walls that smelled of swarf, engine oil and charcoal. At the end was another double door covered in warning signs. Clane didn't have time to read any of these before they slid open electrically, clearly operated from inside.

The room inside was as big and tall as a gymnasium, and was painted completely white including the floor. On the left hand wall was a large slatted steel roller door like the ones on aircraft hangars. A quartet of steel stands had been set up with red plastic tape stretched between them. This cordoned off a passage of the floor between the door through which they had entered and an identical door at the end. "Come in, ladies and gentlemen, quickly." The door slid shut again as soon as they were all inside. "Stay within the barrier please. Do not touch anything outside the barrier! We do have some items you are permitted to handle, which we will bring forward in a few minutes." There were two other men in the room dressed in clean white laboratory coats. A crescent of dark brown fabric mats were laid out on the floor beyond the red tape and on top of these were positioned some silvery objects of various shapes and sizes. Col. Transcope spoke; his voice echoed off the steel walls. "These objects were found on two separate sites in Lincoln County, New Mexico. We believe they appeared there sometime the week before last. They were reported to the RAAF on the fourth of this month. In the days before, a number of people called the police and newspapers to report unusual sights in the sky..." The reporters were lined up against the tape, staring at the objects. Clane pushed his way between two of them and they slowly moved in a line like visitors at a museum. The objects all looked metallic; some were thin sheets like aluminium foil. Many looked smooth and shiny; others crumpled, or even compacted, like the foil balls that Clane used to make as a child. There were also struts of different lengths and thicknesses. Some were square or rectangular in cross section like wood sawn by a carpenter; others were just like conventional I-beams. There was one large circular object about four feet across that looks like a tractor wheel without the tyre. "Come forward please." Transcope gestured to a spot where one of the white coated men had set up a folding table inside the tapes with one of the brown mats draped over it. Lying on its top was a collection of some of the smaller objects. "These, ladies and gentlemen, you may handle, but first permit me to demonstrate." He picked up one of the smooth pieces of foil and folded in half; he folded quarter ways, then eights and again into sixteenths, so that the sheet was crushed into a little package. "Now watch." He smiled mischievously like a stage magician. The pressed foil began to open like a flower. It unfolded itself exactly in reverse of Transcope's action until it was once again a single sheet; and the single sheet stretched taut until all the creases were gone and it was as smooth as it had been in initially. The reporters gasped. "There is more." Colonel Transcope drew a small penknife from his pocket and scored the sheet roughly. "Look how strong it is. I can't cut it." He held up the sheet. Quickly the visible line he'd made with his knife vanished, absorbed like a healing wound on skin. "Come forward and examine these objects, ladies and gentlemen, but make sure you return them to the table afterwards. We have an inventory and they will be counted." he warned. The reporters clustered around the table like party guests at a smorgasbord, waiting for their turned to study the material. Clane picked up one of the I-beams. He was surprised how light it was, no heavier than polystyrene; yet its surface was cold and smooth like steel. It was very precisely shaped, and it struck Clane that none of the debris looks bent or broken or torn in any way. There had been talk of a flying saucer "crashing" yet this was surely not debris from an accident. These items all looked new and undamaged, like spare parts. "Colonel Transcope, what is this material made of?" he asked.

"We don't know." He shrugged. "We have our best chemists working full time to find out. It's some kind of metal, but obviously it presents properties no metal we know of does, like the one's I've shown you... Now this one is especially fascinating." Transcope picked up one of the larger I-beams from a mat just beyond the red tape. "Take a look at this, ladies and gentlemen." He pointed at the inside of the I-beam's vertical. Along the metallic surface were markings, pictograms or motifs of some kind.

"Is that writing?" asked one of the female reporters.

"We don't know." replied Transcope.

"Is it Egyptian Hieroglyphics?"

"Is it Chinese?"

"It's neither." said Transcope. "In fact this inscription does not resemble in any way characters from any known script, past or present."

Clane leaned forward and stared at the mysterious symbols. He glanced over at Hector Robsark. The skeptic was pokerfaced. His mouth was half open, his eyelids drooped; his previous swagger had gone. Clane felt a rush of vindication that made him laugh. "Dr. Robsark." he jeered. "Interesting weather balloon, isn't it?"

Robsark glanced briefly at him and then urgently averted his gaze.

"Ladies and gentlemen." said Col. Transcope in a louder voice. "I'd now like to show you the largest fragment we found; we have it in the separate chamber, through the far door." The reporters trooped after the colonel as he led them towards a set of sliding doors on the far wall identical to the ones through which they had entered.

The second chamber was less well lit than the first and it was not painted. There was some dust on the floor and the smell of hardware and mechanics returned. The room was empty except for a single object placed on top of a collection of forklift pallets. It was a burnished silver coloured object about twenty feet across. It was shaped like an Olympic discus and was featureless except for some darker oblong markings near the top where its regular discus shape was broken into a squat turret with a flat roof about nine feet above the base. "We found this at the second site." said Transcope. "Because of its size we have to move it at night on a flatbed truck."

The reporters spread out around the disk. They move closer to it and touched its hull. To Clane it felt like metal, very smooth and polished, cold; similar to the objects in the first chamber.

"Col. Transcope." piped up one of the male reporters. "Is this a... flying saucer?" His voice dropped off at the end of the sentence as if he felt self-conscious uttering the term.

Transcope took a deep breath. "We've never seen this object fly. We found it lying on the ground."

"Oh come on!"

"Let's just stick to the facts please, sir." The colonel held up his hands in a pacifying gesture.

"What's this?" asked another reporter from the far side of the disk is.

"Ah, now that is very interesting." Col. Transcope rushed over to join him, as if concerned he's fallen behind the group's progress. Clane and the others all moved over as well to see what the first reporter was indicating. There was a gaping cavity in the far side of the disk. It was invisible from the direction they had approached, but very plain to see now. The gap in the hull was a good eight feet across and mostly on the lower half of the object, but it included some of its rim. A cable emerged from the hole and led across the floor to an electrical socket on the wall. The inside was as dark as an unlit cellar. "This is how we found the object." said Transcope. "We don't know why it has this huge hole in the side of it. It doesn't look like damage from the crash." Clane also noticed this, as he had with the loose items he'd seen in the first chamber. The cavity didn't look like a door; there was no mechanism visible, and it was very big and slightly irregular. The sides of the hole were smooth, as if it had been cut open with an oxy-acetylene torch or a power saw. If this had been a normal aircraft involved in a crash, there would have been loose ragged edges to the hole, snapped struts sticking out, ripped flaps of aluminium skin.

"Have a look inside." said Transcope. "I'll switch on the light." He walked over to the wall socket and flipped a switch. Electric light issued from the interior of the unearthly machine. The cavity opened onto a cylindrical cabin that was made of a very different substance to the outside. It was as black as tar and appeared to be a kind of plastic or wax. The light from the portable lantern within was swallowed up by the gloom of the bulkheads. The only features inside the cabin were four structures that looked a bit like small bathtubs about four feet long. These were built into the deck without any visible seams, welds or rivets. They were made of the same the material as the rest of the compartment. Clane laid his hand on the side of the nearest bathtub. It has a slippery and greasy consistency. He lets go with a start and looked at his palm and fingers, but there was no residue on them. There was something strange about the acoustics of the cabin. The voices of the reporters leaning into the hull to look inside didn't sound as they normally would in the compartment that size and of that material. Clane spotted another anomaly. He left the crowd of newsmen around the structure and approached Transcope. "Colonel, how big is the inside cabin?"

"Ten feet three inches across by six-five high."

"Is that small enough to fit inside the exterior?"

Transcope found in confusion. "What do you mean?"

"I was in submarines in the Navy; I know about confined spaces. I'm wondering if a compartment that size might be too big for the exterior hull with the sloping sides."

"Well, it obviously does..." Transcope tailed off as it dawned on him what Clane had said. "You mean... It might be bigger on the inside?... But that's impossible!"

"We've seen a lot of impossible things already. I think you should do the measurements."

Robsark stood at the edge of the group, not wanting to look inside the cabin. His face was now tight and wan, his eyes darting nervously from side to side.

"How does this thing work?" asked another reporter, one who had not spoken so far.

"We don't know, sir." replied Transcope. "There's nothing apparent with any of the fragments that suggests a propulsion system or power plant, at least any kind we're familiar with." Col. Transcope waited patiently for about ten more minutes while the newsmen pored over the enigma. Then he asked for their attention. His apprehensive mien redoubled as he cleared his throat and said: "Ladies and gentlemen of the press, my orders from the Commander-in-chief are to show you all physical evidence of the salvage operation last week. There is more I'm going to reveal, but it's in another part of the Tech Data facility. Please follow me, and stay close. If you get lost in this place it could be a very bad situation."

They walked swiftly down another covered walkway to another windowless building, also guarded by an armed military policeman. This one was different in ambiance. It had linoleum floors and tiled walls; and it smelled of bleach and detergent, similar to a hospital. They passed through more electric doors until they came to a place where Transcope ordered them to dress in white lab jackets and pull elastic overshoes onto their feet. They also donned paper hats and dry-smelling masks over their noses and mouths. His mood became very solemn as they passed through another door and entered a large chamber with a row of heavy metal doors on one side and a window on the other covered by a blackout blind. In the middle of the room were three small caskets on top of gurneys. By the way the ceiling light glinted on them, Clane could see that their top panel was made of glass. "Prepare yourselves, ladies and gentlemen." the colonel warned. The crowd approached the caskets. The first man leaned over to look inside, He jerked back with a yelp, as if he'd touched something hot; one of the women screamed and pressed her back to the wall, panting and gasping. Clane went over and had a look into the nearest casket. "Holy Mary!" he hissed. His heart pounded. For the first time since it had happened, he recalled his late night rendezvous with Glenn Dennis, where he had seen Glenn's crude sketch on a piece of notepaper. He recalled his description, the enormous head, the large eyes and the featureless mouth and scalp. As he'd said, it had four fingers on his hands which had flat flared tips like suction cups. The creature was real; it was lying right in front of him. It was the size Glenn had said too, about three foot six. Its skin was grey, like milky coffee. From a distance it appeared smooth, but when he leaned in close Clane could see scales or a mesh-like texture to it. The body had no external features at all; no nipples or navel, no genitals or hair. It was slightly built with skinny limbs and it also was proportionally smaller than normal. Its child-size feet had no toes; the foot just lead to a rounded-off end without nails. The most remarkable features were its eyes. They were huge, oval-shaped and deep black, without pupils, iris or whites; or else they were just all pupil. Their corneas reflected the light like black billiard balls.

The journalists continue to exclaim for a good few minutes. Col. Transcope stood quietly to one side. Eventually one man yelled at him unashamed: "Colonel! What the hell are these things!?"

"We don't know. They're some kind of biological organism, but they are nothing like anything alive on earth today, nor do they resemble any extinct creature we find in the fossil record. We have our best biologists examining them right now. They have some vague features that resemble primates, fish, even some species of trees, but they can't be fitted anywhere into the taxonomy of life as we know it."

"Are they from Mars?" asked the woman who had screamed.

"We don't know, ma'am. We don't know anything about their origins."

"Are they from Venus?" asked another man. "From Jupiter even?"

"We don't know, sir."

"Are they associated with that thing we saw earlier?"

"Yes, sir. We found them lying on the ground at the second site not far from the debris you saw."

Clane moved to the second body. This one's skin was patchy; some areas were blackened, as if burnt. The third one's left arm and right leg were missing. Scraps of ragged flash hung at the points where the limbs would normally be. Its interior tissue was chocolate brown in colour and there was no blood.

Col. Transcope's tone of voice changed and for the first time he spoke personally. "When I first saw these beings, I reacted exactly as you did."

All the poise Hector Robsark had been working to maintain disintegrated as he moved close to the caskets and gazed inside. His face blanched and his jaw dropped behind his mask, he blinked repeatedly as his eyes perceived the impossible.

"Colonel." asked Clane. "Why are they covered with glass panels?"

"These caskets are hermetically sealed for safety. We're still not sure if these entities are harbouring any kind of harmful infectious agent."

"A disease?"

"Possibly. We are treating them in accordance with barrier biohazard regulations just in case."

"Colonel!" shouted Robsark. He was standing in the corner; his cheeks were now flushed with ire. "Did you make them?"

"I beg your pardon?"

"Did you make these rubber puppets you've got here?"

"What?"

"I asked... whether you made these goddamn mannequins you're try to fool us with!... What you've been fooling American people with, you asshole!"

Transcope sighed. "Please calm yourself, sir."

Robsark swung round and leaned his forehead against the wall. He began whimpering plaintively like a dog. One of the women went over to try and comfort him.

"Colonel, the disk you showed us had those four things inside that looked like bathtubs."

"Yes, we call them 'capsules'; we don't know what their function is."

"Could these creatures have come from inside the disk, and the capsules are intended to house them?"

"It's a possibility. They're about the right size and shape; but we don't know for sure."

Clane paused. "Well there are four capsules, but only three creatures."

Transcope smiled. "I know, I was just coming to that." He addressed the entire group. "Ladies and gentlemen, could you please return to the anteroom now. We have one more place to visit before the completion of the tour."

They went up in a lift one or two floors to another equally windowless storey. After traversing another threshold upon which rolled the electric door, the kind to which they had become accustomed, they entered what looked like a hospital ward. There were several people dressed in doctors' coats and nurses' uniforms mixing medications and writing in card folders. They paid the visitors little attention, as if they'd been expecting them. Ahead was a floor-to-ceiling plate glass panel that split the ward in two. There was no way to pass around the window and the other side of it was completely sealed off. The reporters moved forwards and pressed their faces to the glass with curiosity. Against the far wall was a single hospital bed with the back rest pulled up. The lighting was white and intense, more like an operating theatre than a ward. A man sat beside the bed on a chair. He was wearing what looked like a beekeeper's suit except there was a curtain of clear plastic hanging down to his shoulders instead of a net. He wore a backpack with pipes connected to his headgear like a spacesuit from a science fiction story. Behind him was a long window beyond which there appeared to be some kind of viewing gallery. Several men sat there in ordinary clothes. Lying in the bed was a corpse identical to the ones they had seen a few minutes earlier in the mortuary. It had wires attached to it at various points and these led to sockets on the wall.

By then the reporters must have built up a tolerance for shocks because they only started moderately when the creature in the bed moved. It tilted his head slightly to the right and shifted its spindly arm on the bed sheet covering its lower body. "We didn't realise one of them was alive until after they all arrived here." said Transcope; his own voice was laced with fear. "It... woke up in the middle of the autopsy; scared the shit out of the poor pathologist... We had no idea what to do with it. What does it eat? What does it drink?... It turns out it has some kind of circularity system. It has some organs that are the equivalent to a heart and lungs. It can breathe normal air, but it has no digestive system. It hasn't eaten or drunk a thing, but it doesn't seem to need to..." He smiled warmly. "We've started calling him 'Clyde'... Hey, what's going on!?"

There was a disturbance behind them and they all swung round. Hector Robsark was sprinting towards the ward entrance. Col. Transcope ran after him as he disappeared around the corner. The others trotted along at a slower pace. When Clane caught up, he saw Robsark on his hands and knees beside the electric doors. The expensive five star Washington hotel breakfast he had eaten that morning was now a puddle on the floor in front of him.

....

When the reporters returned to Washington DC they were taken straight to the National Press Club. A news frenzy had broken out. Hector Robsark was driven back to his hotel to recover, but all the others were expected to do a number of interviews describing the morning's tour of Wright Field. The president had announced that he would release the press package the following afternoon. These would, he promised, include photographs and descriptions of everything connected with what was being called "the Roswell incident", but also declassified files on other events related to the flying saucers. Nevertheless, everyone was keen to get a preview from Clane and his colleagues. He repeated his experience at the Ohio air base over and over again in front of TV cameras, radio microphones and journalists with notepads scribbling shorthand. It was nine PM and dark outside when the limousine arrived to return him to the hotel. He was drifting off into a doze on the sumptuous back seat when he awoke with a start and realized that the chauffeur was talking to him. "Pardon?" Clane said. "What was that?"

"I said, it looks like we're being followed, sir." repeated the driver.

Clane shifted himself in the seat and looked out of the rear screen. "That Plymouth behind us."

There was indeed a black Plymouth sedan behind them, keeping a reasonable distance in the same lane; not too close, not too far away. Its speed was steady and matched the limo's perfectly. Its headlights felt like eyes staring at them. "Are you sure it's following us?"

"I took a little detour and they stuck with me all the way."

Clane turned back to face the front. He met the chauffeur's gaze in the rear-view mirror. "Strange. Who are they?"

"Your guess is as good as mine."

"The government?"

"Wouldn't be the first time. I've been driving important folks around for years and plenty of them grow tails."

"It would make sense seeing as what I've been doing today."

The driver nodded. "Flying saucers and all that."

When the limo dropped Clane off, the Plymouth drove past and disappeared into the traffic. Its glasswork was heavily tinted so Clane couldn't see who was inside.

The staff at the hotel treated him like a film star; they all wanted to talk to him. Clane used to wonder what it was like to be a celebrity. Now he was one, he was surprised how he didn't feel very different. Once he was in his bedroom he dialled Siobhan's number, but got no reply.

Chapter 5

The following morning the car picked him up to take him to the White House. The day ahead would be a busy one because the President would be revealing all the classified data on the flying saucers. The world's media were assembled at the White House like fleeing Israelites. Those who couldn't fit into the Press Briefing Room sufficed by staying with their cars and vans, and watching on the closed circuit television link. White House catering had ordered an entire harvest of coffee to keep them sated. The first thing Clane had to do was pick up Hector Robsark. For some reason Clane felt more well-disposed towards the skeptic than he had the previous morning. Despite his pompous attitude, Clane couldn't hold back the wisps of inexplicable pity when he saw the scientist collapsed on the floor of the Wright Field laboratory. The car stopped outside Robsark's hotel and waited, but the skeptic did not emerge at the scheduled time. "He's late." said the driver. "Excuse me, sir; I'll just go in there and hurry him along." He got out of the car and went over to speak to the porters. They conversed for a minute or two, then the driver came back. Clane lowered window. "Sir, it appears Dr Robsark is still in his room. He never came down to breakfast this morning."

"That's strange." said Clane. "Has anybody knocked on his door or phoned him?"

"That's against hotel policy unless the guest specifies an alarm call."

Clane groaned. "But we can't let him sleep all day. I know he was shocked but... Well, can I go up and get him?"

"Dunno."

Clane got out and entered the hotel. He asked at reception and, after explaining that Robsark had an appointment to attend the White House, they agreed to give him access to the room. Clane took the lift up to the eighth floor accompanied by a porter with a key. Clane knocked on the door. "Dr Robsark?... Dr Robsark!" There was no reply. He looked at his watch; eight-twelve AM. "Can you open the door?" he asked the porter.

The porter looked awkward. "You know, I really shouldn't, sir."

"Come on, man. The President is waiting to see him. We need to wake him up... Look, tell your boss I'll accept full responsibility."

The porter raised his eyebrows. "OK." He inserted his key into lock and turned it. Hector Robsark was hanging, suspended vertically in the middle of the room below the chandelier. His face was dark blue and his tongue protruded from his mouth.

"Grab him!" yelled the porter. He and Clane dashed forward and seized the belt of Robsark's pyjamas, holding him up to reduce the pressure from ligature around his neck. With one hand, the porter extracted a penknife from his pocket and reached up feverishly to saw through the noose, which appeared to be made from several neckties bound together. They lowered him gently to the floor and Clane hastily recalled his Navy first aid training while the porter used the bedside telephone to alert reception. "He's got a pulse!" declared Clane. "I think we were just in time." Paramedics arrived and attended to Robsark. The TV presenter regained consciousness and his neurological observations soon became close to normal, but he refused to speak other than to reply to the paramedics' questions about his condition. Clane went with them as they wheeled him out of his room on a stretcher and carried him down the stairwell to the hotel entrance. Robsark raised his head, watching the busy road as he was carried out into the open air to be loaded aboard the ambulance for the trip to the hospital. A large tanker lorry had just turned a corner and was accelerating towards them. Robsark leapt up so quickly nobody had time to react and stop him. They yelled in alarm as the skeptic ran out into the road still dressed in his pyjamas. The truck driver braked, tyres shrieked on tarmac. There was a thump and a penetrating cracking noise. Clane recognized the sound. He had heard it a few years before when a torpedo had rolled over a sailor's leg. It was the sound of breaking bone. Everybody rushed over, including the paramedics, but it was futile. Hector Robsark's head protruded from between two of the lorry's wheels. His eyes were open but blank with a death stare. His skin was ashen and bloodless.

....

The White House was surrounded by a forest of TV and radio transmitters reaching up to the sky as if challenging the Washington Monument. As soon as Clane's car stopped, the journalists mobbed it. A posse of US marshals had to create a cordon simply to allow the driver to open the cars doors. "Mr Quilley!... Mr Quilley!... Mr Quilley!" The newsmen shouted questions at him as he walked up to the White House entrance where Charlie Ross was waiting for him. Even in the light of his newly found social importance Clane was still surprised when Ross escorted him directly to the Oval Office to meet the President. They walked swiftly along the polished spotless shiny-floored corridor from the White House entrance to the West Wing. Paintings and marble statues loomed at Clane from every angle as Ross chivvied him along. The curved interior walls of the Oval Office loomed ahead and Ross knocked on the ornamental door, polished to a mirror-like shine along with all the White House's timber.

"Come in." The famous voice filtered through the wood. Ross opened the door. Two Secret Service bodyguards, dressed in grey suits and sunglasses, stood in front of them. They examined Clane visually for a moment, scanning his body as if their eyes had X-ray vision. Then they moved robotically to the side.

President Harry S Truman was standing in front of the ornate desk studying some papers. He straightened up and turned to face his guests. "Good morning, gentlemen." He looked at Clane. "You must be Clane Quilley. Good to meet you!" He gave Clane's hand a strong politicians' handshake. "Leave us." he said to the bodyguards. They obediently trooped out of the room. Charlie Ross remained, standing to one side. The President walked over to the tall windows of the curved bay overlooking the South Lawn. "I'm sorry to hear about Hector Robsark. He visited me here only last year. I used to enjoy his TV show... I even believed some other things he said in it."

Clane nodded, unsure of what to say in reply.

"Suicide... Oh dear." he grumbled to himself. "There's been a lot of it about, Mr Quilley. More in your part of the country than mine. It can't have been an easy drive up here."

"It wasn't, Mr President."

Truman turned to face him. "I'm afraid to tell you there's been more bad news about Dr Robsark. He wasn't the only one. In fact at about the same time all fifty-eight members of his organization... They locked themselves inside their clubhouse down at Lusby on the bay; and they all downed a big glass of Kool Aid laced with rat poison. It doesn't look like an organized suicide pact; they just seemed to gather together and do the deed spontaneously, like it was some subconscious thing. Why, Mr Quilley?"

Clane shrugged. "I don't know Mr President."

"Strange." Truman looked pensive. "I love life; I really do. Do you know it took me ten years to persuade my wife Bess to marry me?"

"She was worth it I bet though."

Truman laughed. "Definitely, Quilley; definitely!" He became serious. "Charlie, could you go and bring us the packages?"

"Yes, Mr President." Ross left the room leaving Clane alone with the President.

"You know, Mr Quilley; some people perhaps just won't be able to cope with life in the world I'm creating... I checked your record at the War Office. I see you were in Japan after VJ. What did you think of the place after seeing what our A-bombs did?"

Clane gulped. His argument with Jesse Marcel came rushing back to him, as did his memories of those terrible months almost two years ago. Now he was face to face with the man who had ordered Hiroshima and Nagasaki to be destroyed in a way never before known. The debate with Jesse suddenly became less abstract. "It was awful, sir."

"You think what I did was wrong?"

Clane hesitated.

"Answer me, man!" barked the President.

"Yes, Mr President. It was the wrong thing to do."

Truman smiled and sighed. "Thank you for not lying... You see, Quilley. *Everything* I do, and everything I *could* ever do, is wrong. I never knew that until I sat in this office for the first time. All my years in the Senate, then the short luxury of the vice-presidency. Then Roosevelt dropped dead and he dropped me in here." Clane gazed around the Oval Office. It was elegant, clean and well ordered, like everything in the White House. There were carved arches above the door, an oil painting of a sailing ship on the wall, but it looked like a strangely ordinary place. "I can't breathe without hurting people." continued the President. "Every time I blink my eyes, a village burns."

"Is it true, Mr President? Are the flying saucers real?"

Truman frowned. "You saw them yesterday; you know they're real." The President picked up a coffee cup from his desk and took a sip. "The truth of the matter is, what you saw at Wright Field is just the tip of the iceberg. What I announced last week wasn't the real deal; it was just letting people know that a deal exists. The truth is coming today. This new press conference is when the media gets the full picture. I wanted to talk to you because you've become a national spokesman on this issue."

"Not intentionally. Circumstances led me into it."

"Welcome to the club." The president raised an eyebrow. "Quilley, because you're now trusted by the country to tell them the facts about flying saucers, I'm going to need your help in the weeks and months ahead..." He shifted nervously on his feet. "My decision to do this, to reveal... this *disclosure*... the truth about flying saucers, is not without its controversies within the administration especially from the... er... defence element. There are forces at work in this country that I had no idea existed."

"What do you mean, Mr President?"

"Well... what happened last week in New Mexico; it wasn't a one-off. Similar events have occurred before; in fact they seem to be a regular thing. Not just in the United States either. I was briefed by somebody... a person I can't name. They didn't tell me everything. It turns out I only found out about the Roswell incident due to a screw-up at the War Office. I wasn't meant to know about all that..."

"What!?... But you're the President!"

Truman gazed at him sympathetically and sighed. "So what?"

Clane was speechless.

The President poured another cup of coffee from the pot and offered one to Clane. "My decision to address the nation on Wednesday was purely executive... in other words I did it myself. I didn't reveal any more than the basic facts... That was partly for my own safety."

"Safety? Are you in danger, Mr President?"

He paused. "Perhaps... You know what happened to Abraham Lincoln?"

"Of course. He was shot by John Wilkes Booth while sitting in the theatre... Why? Do you think that could happen to you?"

Truman looked hard at him.

"But, Mr President, that was over eighty years ago. Some nutty guy with a pistol wakes up one day and decides to shoot the President; how often does that happen? How likely is it that it will happen again?"

"'Some nutty guy'?... Booth was a very vocal Confederate sympathizer; possibly the equivalent of a communist nowadays. This was at the end of the Civil War and, as he saw it, Lincoln was a monster, the personification of evil. He regarded the President as responsible for all the horrors, destruction and humiliation that his people were suffering... Yet nobody was monitoring him. When he turned up at the Ford's Theatre that night, he was let straight in by the staff."

"Why not? He was an actor. They probably knew him."

"What about the bodyguards?... Not only should they have known him too, as a major security hazard; but they weren't even there. Booth went straight to the staircase leading to the private box. The door was unguarded and unlocked. He simply walked in and opened fire on the back of the President's head... You see, the active role in these kinds of assassinations is not played by the assassin; he could be any old John. The people who actively carry out assassinations are those who have the ability to withdraw the usual security measures at the crucial moment that allow the assassin to move forward and prosecute his target."

Clane's hand trembled as he handled his coffee cup. "Mr President, are you saying there was a conspiracy inside the government to murder Abraham Lincoln?"

"Yes, and that *can* happen again, given the right motivations."

"You mean... *you* could end up like Lincoln?"

"If I'm not careful. If I don't have trusted allies inside the executive structure who can watch my back.

"But why you?"

"Why Lincoln? Like me, he was seen as a heroic war leader, but he also pissed off a few British financiers because of the debts he had taken out over the war, and the fact he wanted to fund the Reconstruction of the South via currency issued direct from the Treasury... Now, I won't even begin to tell you about my monetary policy and the wrath it has generated, but this flying saucer business; it could be even worse..." He broke off as Charlie Ross entered the room pushing a mail trolley on top of which were two dozen rows of stuffed brown envelopes. "Here it is." Truman said brightly in a very different tone of voice. "The media packages as promised. We've entered a new era, gentlemen. Now, I'd like to ask you both how you'd feel if I appointed you, Mr Quilley, to join my Press Office, as an assistant to Charlie here; to handle the flying saucer subject, just temporarily."

"Fine with me!" Ross blurted immediately, looking relieved."

Clane was somewhat taken aback. "I'll... do what I can, Mr. President."

"Good man!" Truman grinned excitedly.

....

"What day the week is this?" asked Clane.

"Erm... Ross looked at the calendar on the wall. "Monday."

"Jeez! All the normal patterns are thrown off. It's like Christmas without the gifts."

"*These* are gifts." Ross patted the packages.

"Everybody's as excited as a kid at Christmas." Clane looked out of the window of the Press Office at the huge crowd of people gathered. Along with the news crews there were ordinary citizens; men and women in work clothes, families having picnics on the public areas of the White House Lawn. "I've looked at the headlines, Charlie. Things are calming down a bit for now. The National Guard still has to run things in some states, but least the electricity and water and stuff are back on. I know the world will never be the same again, but it feels like a new normal is emerging... It beats me really. The skeptic mass suicides were one thing, but most other people believed in flying saucers anyway. You'd think when the President came on TV and confirmed their beliefs; they'd just shrug their shoulders and say: 'Really? I thought so, thanks'."

"Clane, did you ever read anything by Sigmund Freud?"

"Wasn't he that psychologist? The one who said if you dream about a cigar it really means your prick?"

"Among other things, yes. One of his theories was that a nation is kind of similar to a family and that the government symbolises the father. Now, when you're a kid you might well have believed in fairies and Santa and leprechauns; but your dad didn't, did he? As a kid, I bet there was a part of you that was secretly glad he didn't. He kept your world in order. Now imagine being a four year old boy who goes up to his dad and says: 'Daddy, do fairies exist?' and your dad answers: 'Yes son, they're real.' That would screw with your head wouldn't it?"

"What's that got to do with flying saucers?"

"It's one thing to believe privately in flying saucers, and even to be convinced that they're as real as the nose on your face; but to have your beliefs endorsed by this Freudian father figure up here on Capitol Hill is another thing entirely."

There was a knock on the door and an intern stuck his head in. "Mr Ross, Mr Quilley, we're starting in ten minutes."

Clane and Charlie Ross made their way from the Press Office to the Press Briefing Room with the mail trolley. The long chamber was stiflingly hot with all the heat from bodies and electrical equipment to warm it. Every seat was filled and newsmen stood around the walls. They all had their pencils and notepads at the ready. A TV camera stood in the corner ogling them. A radio microphone on a boom hung over them. Clane could hardly believe he was here. His life had been transformed within a single weekend. He wondered if Owen Mollett were watching them. What was he thinking? What about Siobhan? He watched as men and women in maids' and butlers' uniforms moved among the crowd topping up everybody's coffee cups. The mail trolley with the envelopes was placed where everybody could see it in the centre of the dais. Ross spoke into a telephone then approached the podium. He looked at his watch and glanced down the corridor through the open door. He was clearly adept at timing these grand entrances. Clane stood to one side watching. "Ladies and gentlemen of the press." began Ross. "Thank you for gathering here this afternoon. My name is Charlie Ross and I am the Presidential Press Secretary." He gestured at Clane. "I'd like to introduce my new assistant, Clane Quilley; press officer for flying saucer-related affairs. In a mo..."

Clane felt as if every part of his body had been punched at the same time. A blinding flash of light filled his head. The next thing he knew, he was lying on his back on the floor. His ears felt muffled but he heard loud voices around him. He opened his eyes and looked up at the ceiling, but the whole room was shrouded in smoke. "OUT! OUT! Everybody out!" yelled a voice. Hands gripped his limbs like pincers and he felt himself being lifted up. The world wheeled around his head as he was carried along. The ceilings gave way to blue sky and fresh air displaced the smoke. He was laid down on soft grass and slowly his consciousness returned. He sat up. Concerned strangers' faces loomed at his, asking him if he were alright. He raised a hand to his face and it came away covered in blood. Somebody pressed a piece of cloth his brow. "What happened?" he asked.

"Dunno." somebody replied. Their voice was indistinct in Clane's battered, ringing ears. Clane looked back at the White House. Smoke was rising from the West Wing and he could see the flicker of fire in one of the windows.

....

Clane took a seat to the right of the desk. He was told this was where Charlie Ross normally sat. Next to him was Henry Stimson, Secretary of War. Opposite were Secretary to the Treasury, John W Snyder; Secretary of State, George C Marshall and the Attorney General, Tom C Clark. The TV camera was set up, the lights in the Oval Office were all on, making it as bright as possible and two extra TV lights were brought in, shining on the President's chair. Because of excessive lighting the space behind the camera and looked dark, as it had in the TV studio at the National Press Building. A number of military officers stood in the gloom, watching carefully along with other men in dark suits. A man entered the Oval Office; it was Joseph Martin, the Speaker of the House. He dispassionately walked across the room, swiftly, directly and without hesitating, and sat down in the chair behind the desk. He waited patiently while the TV crew finalised their preparations. The director spoke into a telephone headset, waiting for the signal that they were on the air. Martin shuffled a sheaf of papers in front of him. The director raised his hand and Martin nodded. "My fellow Americans." he began. "It is with a heavy heart that I sit before you tonight. Just two years ago, the news was revealed to you that your nation's leader, President Franklin Delano Roosevelt, had passed away during the course of his duties. He was succeeded to office by his Vice President Harry S Truman. President Truman served the United States of America with courage and wisdom during one of her greatest hours of need. His duties have now abruptly and tragically come to an end."

Clane reached up carefully and slowly to adjust dressing on his head wound, aware of how still everybody else was sitting.

"For today, at one-forty PM eastern standard time, President Truman was walking along the corridor here in the White House when there was an explosion. The Secret Service has reported to me that this was a freak accident. A leaking gas pipe caused an accumulation of inflammable gas that ignited just as the President was walking past. The President was killed instantly. Two Secret Service agents were also killed and the White House Press Secretary, Charlie Ross, was seriously injured. I'm pleased to say that he is in hospital and expected to make a full recovery. Obviously we all join together in sending our condolences and prayers to the loved ones of those who perished, in particular the First Lady, Bess Truman, and their children. And we pray for the souls of the departed. A dozen other staff members and guests experienced minor injuries. As you are aware, President Truman never appointed a Vice President; therefore in accordance with the succession directives laid out in the US constitution, the next in line to the presidency after the Vice President is the Speaker of the House. Therefore at two PM this afternoon I swore on the bible in the presence of Judge Matthews of the Supreme Court that I solemnly swear that I will faithfully execute the Office of President of the United States, and in so doing became the thirty-fourth President of the United States. I wish to dedicate my term of office to, and paid tribute to, my predecessor President Harry S Truman. My first actions as President are to continue the good work he did in attending to the current flying saucer crisis. I will establish the Department of Extraterrestrial Affairs exactly as he envisaged it. I will also continue to keep the press up to date on all the emerging new information on this phenomenon. In fact I have just been informed by the Secretary of War that a Navy destroyer on patrol a hundred miles east of Cape Hatteras has detected on radar a large number of unknown flying objects heading towards the eastern seaboard at high speed. I will provide details to the press as soon as possible. In the meantime, I appeal to you all to stay calm, stay hopeful and note that your President has the situation under control. May God bless America. Good night."

After the speech, the people assembled in the Oval Office slowly dispersed. There was little conversation; each was alone with his own thoughts. The TV technicians packed up their equipment. Clane strolled along the corridor towards the Press Briefing Room. The area where the deadly explosion had taken place was cordoned off by a wooden barrier. Beyond it the lights had been broken by the blast and so portable lanterns had been set up. The immaculate White House interior decoration was blackened and withered by the fire. The corpses of the victims had been removed, but the dark red of bloodstains was still discernible from the carbonized background. A diversion had been arranged and so Clane entered the briefing room from a different door to normal. Most of the chairs remained upturned; the podium where Charlie Ross had been standing was blown off its mounting. Something was wrong; Clane could sense it intuitively but he couldn't work out what it was. He ransacked his memory of that afternoon; what was missing? He remembered at the very moment that he heard a voice behind him. He turned round to see the new President standing there. "Mr Quilley? Hello; I've been thinking about the new department and was wondering who should run it. Your name is at the top of my list."

"Me, Mr President; why? I'm not a politician; I'm a journalist."

"Nobody knows more about this business than you. We're dealing with an entirely novel situation here for which we have no precedent, experience or contingency plan. You're the only man on earth ever to study and publish anything on real flying saucers. If you're not qualified for this job then nobody is."

"Well..."

"Think it over." President Martin slapped his shoulder affably and turned away.

Clane hesitated. "Mr President."

"Yes?" He stopped and looked back at him.

"What happened to the trolley?" Clane pointed at the dais.

"What trolley?"

"The one Charlie and I put here, just before the gas explosion. The one with the press packages of flying saucer information."

Martin frowned. "I don't know of any such trolley. I think you're mistaken."

"No, sir. I swear to you, we prepared it just as President Truman told us to."

Martin nodded sympathetically. "Quilley, you took a nasty blow to the head today and I'm not surprised that it's clouded your recollection of the day's events. It's getting late so why don't you head for home now. I'll talk to you in the morning."

Clane slowly walked towards the White House main entrance to where his limo was waiting to take him back to the hotel. He was just about to exit the outer doors when he saw one of the maids standing there looking at him, as if waiting for him. She was an elderly negro with a lined face and streaks of grey running through her black hair. She approached him nervously. "Mr Quilley, may I speak with you a moment?"

"Sure."

"It's about President Truman."

"Of course, he must have been like a friend to you. I'm so sorry..."

"No, you don't understand." Her chestnut eyes trembled with fear. "The West Wing and was all electrified twenty years ago. There *are no* gas pipes where the President was killed!"

....

When Clane got into the limousine, the driver automatically pulled away in the direction of the hotel. He felt intensely vulnerable and precarious, as if he were walking a tightrope. His eyes followed every passing car. He glanced over his shoulder to check they weren't being followed again. "Are you OK, sir?" asked the driver.

"Er... yes."

"You look like there's something bothering you."

"No, no... er... do we have to go back to the hotel?"

"Why, where else do you want to go?"

"How about the railroad station?... And keep that yourself, OK?" He pulled a five dollar bill out of his pocket and slipped over the back of the front seat.

....

Clane travelled overnight. There were no couchettes free so he sat up in the lounge car with his head propped up against the headrest and window. The rumble and rocking motion of the train lulled him to sleep; the boom and roar of a passing train on the opposite track occasionally woke him up. The banshee shrieks of their whistles infected his feverish dreams. The train stopped for an hour or two at a small station he didn't recognize. The loud, boisterous voices of railwaymen on the platform prevented him getting some much-needed slumber. The sky was brightening above the scrolling skyline when they dipped into a tunnel leading under the river into Manhattan. The train ground to a halt on the brightly-lit underground platform of Penn Station. Clane eased his stiff limbs into motion and shook his foggy head. He walked down the platform with the other yawning passengers. There was a commotion ahead on the station concourse. A group of railway staff, helped by several policemen, were talking to a large throng of people. The crowd was only mildly agitated, but Clane sensed something serious was going on. Another small cluster was gathered around a signboard that was standing on an easel at one side of the entrance. It read: *PLEASE NOTE- There is flying saucer activity above NYC at the moment. This is not a cause for alarm. Please remain calm and continue your journey as normal.* It had the emblem of the New York Police Department on it. A week ago Clane would have laughed. He ascended the stairs to street level and merged into the chilly early morning on Seventh Avenue. The concrete mesas of Manhattan's architecture loomed over him, reaching up to a dark blue dawn sky. Clane walked along the pavements towards Herald Square Subway Station. As he reached the Avenue of the Americas he saw a group of a dozen people standing on the street corner looking up at the sky. He joined them and followed their gaze and pointing fingers. There was an object in the sky. It hung above Manhattan like a balloon, greyish black in colour and egg shaped; then again it could have been a disk viewed at an angle. It was hard to tell how big it was, not knowing its distance. Clane had learnt during the long hours he spent on lookout duties on a submarine conning tower that what looks like an oil tanker far off could easily be in reality a fishing boat at much closer range. There were some clouds passing behind the object giving it a maximum distance. Its relative size was roughly that of a bottle cap held at arms length. Clane walked up the avenue towards the subway station. He got the impression, perhaps through a subliminal parallax, that the disk's footprint was somewhere above Harlem, making the objects two or three hundred feet across. People around him were largely unaffected by its presence; they glanced up occasionally with a mild unease as they went about their business. He trotted down the stairs into the subway station and caught a train to Brooklyn. He felt a warm glow as the subway train braked and his local station came into view through the windows. The familiar streets had not changed in the six months since he had last seen them. He smiled to himself as he approached the apartment block where his family lived. For a moment he was afraid that he'd lost the key, but it was still there in his wallet, tucked into a side sleeve. He ascended the lift to the fifth floor and let himself into apartment number forty. "Siobhan!... Gina!" Silence answered loudly. Nobody was in. The flat had a new settee and kitchen table and the new television set stood mute in the corner of the den. The drapes were half open and the shamrock tapestry he had bought Siobhan for her first communion was still on the wall by her bedroom door. The fridge was half full, indicating the home had not been deserted long ago, although the milk was sour and full of curd blobs. Clane walked to the middle of the kitchen and stalled, wondering what to do next. He had rotated in a semicircle before he saw the envelope on the sideboard. It had the word *Dad* written on it. Clane snatched up and ripped it open. *Dear Dad. Mom and I have gone to Norman's house. We thought we should leave the city when the flying saucer business started. Love. Siobhan.* Clane seethed as two emotions collided head on inside his heart. He trembled with internal conflict. Then his eye caught the kitchen window. There was a thin linear speck in the air above Manhattan. It was more distant from here but still recognisable as the object he'd seen when he first arrived in New York.

Clane alighted from the train at Amityville station and marched quickly along the broad straight avenues lined by bungalows, heading for the seafront. He kept his thoughts blank and his pace fast so he would not change his mind. He reached the marina where rows of yachts and sailboats were moored, and turned left along the promenade towards the luxury beach villa belonging to Norman Rockliffe, a successful Wall Street stockbroker with shares in shipping lines, media corporations and supermarket chains. The resprayed Maserati was parked in the driveway and the door bell, which he had pressed the previous year in rage, was before him on the wall by the front door. His arm felt as if it were made of lead as he raised his finger and jabbed it. The door opened and the butler jerked back in alarm as he recognized the visitor. "What you want?"

"No trouble." replied Clane calmly. "I'm sorry for what I did to you; it was a mistake."

"So you've come back to correct it? To flatten the nose of Mr Rockliffe?"

"No, I just want to see my daughter."

"Daddy!" Siobhan's voice yelped from inside. The front door was flung open wide and Clane embraced his twelve year old daughter. Siobhan gave a hyperventilated explanation as she led him inside. The vestibule of the house was oak panelled and nautical in flavour with paintings of ships on the wall and a telescope mounted above the fireplace. "Hello, Mr Quilley." A man's voice spoke from the far end of the room. Clane averted his eyes, as if from a nauseating sight. "Hello, Clane." said Gina. Clane slowly and painfully raised his gaze. He had never set eyes on Norman Rockliffe before; he had not even seen a picture of him. He had always had a mental image in his head of the man who had cuckolded him which was as vivid as a real memory. That make-believe Norman Rockliffe was tall and well-built with smooth tanned skin and shiny white teeth. He had a deep sophisticated voice and thick silky blond hair. His jawline was prominent and straight, his chin protruding and strong. He was arrogant and self-centred; always dressed in the best suits. Coolly dismissive of lesser men and casually irresistible to beautiful women. The real Norman Rockliffe was nothing like that. The man who had stolen his wife was short and badly proportioned with a feeble frame and patchy black hair that was prematurely grey in places. He had a large English nose, sensitive brown eyes and a shy a lopsided smile. He treated Clane as an honoured guest, inviting him into the conservatory facing the beach. He ordered his butler, Jenkins, to fetch them all drinks and Jenkins sulkily obeyed.

Gina had grown her hair long and was now wearing glasses, small readers with tortoiseshell rims. She and Clane spoke neutrally about Siobhan, her progress at school and other matters related to the apartment and finances. When she stepped out to use the bathroom, Norman Rockliffe leaned close and lowered his voice. "Clane... May I call you Clane?"

He shrugged. "That's my name."

"Clane, I want you to know something. Your wife and I are no longer in an intimate relationship of any kind. We're still good friends. She contacted me a few days ago because she had nobody else she could turn to and she needed help." He paused and his pasty white cheeks flushed slightly. "Once we were in love. I wanted us to be together."

"Is that why you got me kicked off *The Times*?"

Norman blushed more deeply. "I'm very sorry. I should never have done that; it was deeply dishonourable."

Clane shrugged again. His animosity for Norman had melted; he almost felt sorry for the man. "That's OK. I'm sorry I scratched your car. I know how alluring Gina can be."

Gina returned to the conservatory. As she walked through the door she froze and gasped. "Look!" She pointed. The weather had changed since Clane had arrived in New York. The clear blue sky was now covered in thin high cloud. A squadron of disk-shaped objects were flying past, more speedily than any aircraft. They were completely silent. Clane, Norman, Gina and Siobhan all got up and ran out onto the patio. "My God!" hissed Clane. "They must be doing four hundred knots!"

"What are they, Clane?" asked Gina in a tremulous voice.

"I don't know, but I saw one floating over midtown a few hours ago."

"Daddy, I'm scared." Siobhan put her arms round him.

Clane counted twenty of the objects in a triangular formation. They disappeared into the distance heading towards the city.

"The President was right." said Norman. "They really are coming."

There was a rolling, rumbling, cracking sound; like thunder coming from the west. "What's that?" asked Gina. "A storm?"

Clane felt his stomach twist in dread. "I don't think so... We had better switch on the TV." They went indoors and Norman switched on his large television set. A special news broadcast was in progress. *"... New York, Los Angeles, Houston. The flying saucer fleet are congregating over all major cities in the United States."* the anchorman announced gravely from behind his desk. *"We're also receiving word from the BBC. Similar collections of these unknown aircraft have gathered above London, also Paris, Madrid... Ladies and gentlemen, it looks as if the whole world is being covered by the strange objects. Where they come from? What they want? Nobody knows."* The picture went blank. Nobody in the room spoke. It lit up again. The reporter was trembling; his professionalism straining. *"Standby for another bulletin... We are receiving word that the vessels flying over New York have released missiles that have caused explosions in the city. The Empire State Building... Jesus Christ!... The Empire State Building has been destroyed... We are receiving word of another attack on Los Angeles..."*

"Oh my God!" muttered Norman. "The aliens are invading."

....

Norman Rockliffe switched off all the lights in his house that night. This is what the TV advised them to do. In the darkness of the night time conservatory, the television screen cast the only illumination. It washed over their wide, frightened faces in flickering, grey glare. They sat in silence, impassively taking in report after report from ABC News. Jenkins had gone home and so they helped themselves to tea and coffee from the kitchen. Some time after midnight, Clane stepped out onto the beach for some fresh air. It was cool and breezy and the crash of the surf was relaxing. He felt no overt fear; he was simply grateful. He muttered a prayer. "Lord, if this really is the end of the world... thank you for bringing me back to my family again." Lights zipped two and fro across the starry sky at high speed. The flying saucers were moving. According to the television they had risen higher and were now moving away from the cities.

"Dad!" Siobhan cried out from inside.

Clane ran back to the conservatory alarmed. It was the first time somebody had raised their voice for hours. "What is it?"

"Somebody's looking for you! It's been on TV!"

"What are you talking about?"

"Here it is again... Shh!"

Clane looked at the TV screen. The newsreader was reciting words of a note that had just been handed to him: *"This just in. The President has put out a call to find Clane Quilley, the new Secretary for Extraterrestrial Affairs who has been missing since yesterday afternoon. His whereabouts are unknown, but he is believed to be somewhere in the New York area. It is vital that he returns to his office as soon as possible. If Secretary Quilley is watching this could*

91

he please call the following telephone number..." Clane grabbed a pencil off the table and began scribbling down the number on the cover of a book as the newsman read it out. He went over to the phone and dialled. It was the White House switchboard. He was transferred to the President immediately. "Quilley!" barked Joseph Martin. "Where the hell are you?"

"Mr President... I'm with my family."

"Oh." His voice softened. "Look, I understand; but... I need you here. America needs you here."

"I can't leave them, Mr President."

There was a long pause. "Bring them with you. Tell me where you are and I'll send some cars to pick you all up."

"Clane?" Gina was standing at his shoulder. "What's going on?"

"Hold the line please, Mr President." Clane explained the content of the call to Gina.

"OK, Clane." she said. "We'll go with you to Washington if needs must."

Siobhan stood up and moved to her mother's shoulder.

"Clane." said Norman. "You don't have to go, you know. The President only appointed you yesterday. You haven't signed any contract yet for your job. You, Gina and Siobhan are welcome to stay here with me."

Clane turned to him. The millionaire looked sad, lonely, almost pleading. "Thanks, Norman, but..." Clane tried to remember why he had fled from Washington in the first place, but couldn't. "I really ought to return to my duties."

....

The sun was rising behind the purple clouds as the two cars approached the District of Columbia on the empty highway from the north. A no-fly zone had been declared above the entire continental United States so they had had to drive the whole way. A light rain began to fall as they passed through the military cordon around the Capitol, more like heavy mist than rain. Clane felt wide awake, even though he'd been unable to sleep on the back seat of the moving staff car. Their military escort peeled away and they parked just outside the White House entrance. Clane stepped out into the dank and chilly morning. He glanced upwards at the overcast, but everything seemed normal. Behind him Gina and Siobhan were also sleepily decamping from their vehicle. An intern came over and offered to take his family to breakfast while Clane was escorted wordlessly by three Marines to the West Wing and the Cabinet Room. A butler held open the tall door and he walked into the high vaulted chamber with the typical White House furnishings and oil paintings on the wall. The suited occupants of the twenty-five or so seats around the oval-shaped table turned to stare at him with a collective piercing frown. At the head of the table sat President

Martin. He was a stocky, craggy-faced black-haired man with sharp eyebrows and these were fully lowered at Clane right now. "Quilley. Why didn't you speak to me last night; before you did a bunk to New York?"

Clane's throat seized up. He shrugged.

"You realize that if you had, I could have arranged for your wife and daughter to be picked up and brought here while you remained in Washington?"

"No, sir... I'm new to this game."

Martin tutted. "It's *not* a game!... Anyway, sit down, Quilley. We need you here for this part of the meeting. We've lost enough time as it is" Clane headed for the sole empty chair at the table. The seat was cold hard leather and forced him to sit in an uncomfortable position. The people around him were all men older than himself with stern and fearful expressions; two were high ranking military officers. The President took a sip of coffee. "Gentlemen, I'd like to begin by taking a moment for my predecessor, Harry S Truman. If he had lived, he would be leading us today in this troubled moment for our country and the world. I know he would have let America and the human race prevail; I pray God I can do as well." Everybody at the table bowed their heads. "And now, Mr Quilley."

"Yes?" Clane answered apprehensively.

"In view of recent developments I'd like to change your title from Secretary of Extraterrestrial Affairs to 'Secretary for Interplanetary War'. Any questions?"

He shook his head. "No, sir."

Martin gestured at a man sitting opposite wearing a black suit like an undertaker. He had a pessimistic down-turned mouth, thin lips and forked eyebrows. "This is Secretary James Forrestal; you will be working closely with him in service to your country. He is the head of another new department established by President Truman, a decision I have also moved forward; the Department of Defence."

Forrestal eyed Clane neutrally; his expression did not change. Clane smiled briefly back at him.

"Secretary Forrestal, give us your latest report on enemy movements?"

James Forrestal spoke in a dispassionate monotone: "The enemy aircraft have all now departed American airspace after the attacks on the Empire State Building in New York, the Broadway Market in Los Angeles and the oil terminals at Houston, Texas. They ascended in altitude at high speed and left the detection ceiling of our ground-based radar. They were accompanied by several hundred other craft which we picked up visually using the telescopes at the US Naval Observatory. They have assembled in a fleet of hundreds more aircraft, some of which carried out attacks on other parts of the world. The entire fleet is now hovering over the area of the mid-Atlantic Ocean at an altitude of approximately one million feet."

"One million feet!? What's that in miles?"

"Just under two hundred, sir."

"They're two hundred miles high!? But isn't that above the earth's atmosphere?"

"Yes, Mr President. They're up in outer space."

POTUS sighed. "So they really are from off this planet... Do they come from Mars?"

"We don't know where they're from."

"Why have they attacked us?"

"We don't know." Forrestal reiterated.

"Creatures from space..." he mused. "Their technology must be way in advance of our own."

"Very likely, sir. These vehicles appear to function very differently to our own aircraft. They have no visible means of aerofoil lift or have any aerostatic buoyancy; no jets, propellers or other devices to produce forward motion."

"It's like they can cancel out gravity... So, what can we do on a practical level?"

There was a long silence. Clane suddenly realized everybody was looking at him. "How should I know?"

"Come on, man!" snapped Martin. "You're the only person on earth to publish material on this subject."

"But that was a news story!"

"President Truman believed in you! So must we. Now tell us what you think."

"Well..." Clane cleared his throat. "We'll need... strong air defences. If the extraterrestrials return for another attack, we must be ready for them. We will also need to prepare for a possible ground invasion... so we'll need the army to be prepared."

"Mr Forrestal?"

"I concur, sir. Unfortunately the bulk of our forces are all still in their wartime formation, in Europe and the Pacific."

"We'll need to pull them back home."

Another man raised his hand.

"Yes, Mr Harriman?"

"Mr President, we can't just 'pull them back home' as you call it. Our military is currently engaged in fulfilling our post-war commitments to our European allies, as well as reconstruction in Japan and the Far East."

"I think, based on the current state of emergency, those plans will have to be shelved for the time being."

"But, sir!" exclaimed Harriman. "This is the aftermath of the war! The only thing currently holding the Soviets from breaching the Iron Curtain are our troops."

"No, the Brits and Free French are there."

"Sir, I really don't recommend..."

"Mr Harriman!" interrupted the President. "Have you gone mad!? Where were you last night?... Thousands of people have just been killed in an attack far greater than Pearl Harbour. It was carried out by an unknown enemy that doesn't even originate on the Earth. I'm well aware of our aftermath role in former theatres of the war, but the world has moved on. Our country is under direct assault from another threat. If we have any hope of defeating that threat we need our armed forces to revert to their primary role; defending the homeland. As for the Soviets, with continuing respect to my predecessor, the Truman Doctrine will have to be shelved, as will the Marshall Plan."

There was a groan from the man in the chair next to the President. Clane recognized him as George Marshall, the Secretary of State.

"Sorry, George, but you must understand the need to prioritize. We'll have to deal with the consequences of our decision afterwards... Mr Vinson, how are things in your office?"

Fred Vinson, the Secretary to the Treasury, responded: "May I suggest that we continue with President Truman's closure of the stock markets. The need to do so is even greater now considering yesterday's attacks."

"Confirmed, Mr Vinson. What about a longer term strategy?"

"I would recommend reconsidering the cancellation of the war-bond programme. The economy is no longer in a position to settle down to the original post-war design. The threat from space is too uncertain."

"Thank you... Mr Stimson?"

....

The Quilley family were given accommodation in Blair House on Pennsylvania Avenue, just across from the White House. This was the private residence where guests of the US President usually stayed. When the meeting had finished Clane crossed over the road to join them. It was now eleven AM, yet the streets of Washington DC were as quiet as midnight. Gina and Siobhan were sat at a table in the dining room fiddling over tea and sandwiches. They were hunched over and fearful, not enjoying their comfortable surroundings or food. "Hi there." Clane called cheerfully.

They looked up at him and smiled. "Hi. How did the meeting go?" asked Gina.

"We made plans. The good news is the aliens have left the Earth. They're still up there, circling round, but there are no indications they're interested in renewing their attack."

"The newspapers say five thousand people were killed in America yesterday." said Siobhan darkly.

"I know." Clane looked down. He changed the subject. "Here, look at this." He took out a piece of paper on which was a circular emblem. The centre had a motif of an eagle clutching a flying saucer in its talons. A circle of golden stars formed a halo around its head. On each side were a few planets of the solar system; Saturn with its rings and Jupiter with its red spot. The central image was surrounded with a blue ring on which were embossed the words: *UNITED STATES OF AMERICA- DEPARTMENT FOR INTERPLANETARY WAR.*

"What's that?" Siobhan asked.

"That's my seal." Clane replied cheerily. "President Martin has made me the first ever US Secretary for Interplanetary War."

"Sounds weird!" exclaimed Siobhan.

"These are weird times."

"Right they are. First President Truman gets killed by a gas explosion, and then the Martians invade. Feels like we're not living in the real world any more."

Clane paused. Something has triggered in his mind at her mention of Truman's accident. There was something very important he knew he should have remembered about the details of that unfortunate event, but he had somehow forgotten.

Chapter 6

Clane knocked on the door of the Oval Office.

"Come!"

He entered the room. "Good morning, Mr President."

"Bah! Is it?" asked Joseph Martin. He was standing at the window with his back turned.

"Something wrong, sir?"

He chuckled ironically. "How long have you been in this job now, Clane?"

"Eight months."

"Perhaps you're learning a bit about how things work on Capitol Hill."

"I reckon it would take me eight centuries to learn that, sir."

Martin laughed. "How right you are!" He turned to face him. "That little shit Dewey gained another forty delegates last night. It looks inevitable that he'll get the Republican nomination and I'll be up against him in the election... I want a second term, Clane. I'd much prefer it if it were Howard Taft; he'd be a pushover... Anyway, any more news from Los Alamos?"

"Nothing; it's not come back."

"Good. Hopefully that's the end of the matter." After delivering his report to the President, Clane left the White House and walked along Constitution Avenue to the Greggory Building. The low row of temporary blocks had been hastily erected during the Great War and it was showing its age. Yet it was where Clane and the Secretary of Defence James Forrestal had their offices. Seeing as they worked so closely together they had been given a joint suite. Clane's colleague looked more troubled than the President as Clane greeted their shared secretary and entered SecDef's room. "Jim, you look awful; what's wrong?" asked Clane.

Forrestal had his head buried in a newspaper. "It's the *Times* again, Clane; your old rag." He forced a grin. "Benjamin Fransky's having a pop at me again."

"The Palestine-Israeli?"

"Never call him that to his face! He's demanding full partition for the Jews. He's sent a protest to the Secretary General of the League of the World comparing me to Adolf Hitler. Says I'll probably start World War III."

"Ooh!" Clane winced.

Forrestal shook his head grimly. "A Jap pilot in a dive bomber makes me feel more amiability than these hacks. Anyways, how did Mr P take your report?"

"He says we can stand down."

"Let's hope it doesn't come back." Clane went to his own office and began typing up his report. A week earlier, a flying saucer had been spotted hovering over the Los Alamos National Laboratory in

New Mexico. A local FBI agent named Guy Hottel filled in an official sightings form. The Signals Security Agency had begun analyzing the radio transmissions the extraterrestrial craft made and worked out that they were communicating with two locations in the universe; the planets Mars and Venus. This was a Martian ship. It was also recognizable because of its shape; Venusian craft had a triangular floorplan. It had been discovered that only Martians had been behind the attacks of the previous year. The ship had cruised slowly above the Laboratory and then shot swiftly back off into space. This caused a security alert. LANL was where the atomic bomb development was underway. The saucer had not been back for over a week, so Clane now hoped it had gone for good. Since the devastating assault on Mars Day the ET's had continued to make incursions into terrestrial airspace, but these had so far been occasional and harmless.

Later in the day he joined Forrestal once again in his office and they discussed the continued redeployment of the Seventh Army Corps back stateside. There had been a vocal protest from several western European leaders, including Konrad Adenaur of Germany; and Queen Juliana of the Netherlands had objected, claiming they were not strong enough to repel a Soviet invasion from the east. Despite Martin's reassurances, Britain under the new Labour government had taken the same line as the USA and brought home its troops to protect their island nation from the extraterrestrial threat. Despite this, things were starting to return to normal after eight months of relative inactivity from the Martians, or at least, once again, another "new normal" had emerged.

Clane looked back at Forrestal as he left his office. He had become good friends with the introverted Defence Secretary. Clane admired how Forrestal worked so hard and was so stalwart in his ideas. How shrewd and adaptable he was to new and unexpected situations; even a threat from beyond the earth did not overwhelm him. Before he closed the door Clane saw his friend pull open the upper right drawer of his desk with a trembling hand. Clane had never told anybody, but he had once looked in that drawer himself. He hadn't been prying; he had simply gone in there one day when Forrestal was over at the White House to get a folder for their secretary. As he pulled the folder out of the drawer, the bottle of pills rolled out from under it. Clane had felt embarrassed when he saw them. He didn't know what the pills were for and didn't stay to look. He felt ashamed for being an unwitting spy against his friend. He put the issue out of his mind for many weeks, but then something happened and he discovered James Forrestal's secret. He was relaxing one evening in his Arlington apartment when the phone rang. He picked it up. "Hello, Clane? It's Josie. Could you please help?" The caller was James Forrestal's wife. She sounded distraught; her voice was tremulous and tearful.

"Sure, Josie. What's up?"

"It's Jim. He's... unwell."

"OK, I'm on my way." When he arrived at the Forrestal's townhouse he found the Defence Secretary lying on his bed in a fit of trembling and weeping. He bawled and yelled, hammering the headboard and tearing at the pillow with his fingernails. "He forgot to take his medication." explained Josie. She showed him the bottle of pills she was holding and Clane recognized it as the bottle he'd seen secreted in his colleague's drawer. Clane had done Navy corpsman training in the war and so knew how to force an unwilling patient to take tablets. He calmed down Forrestal with soothing words and massage to his throat until he helped him swallow one of the pills with a glass of tepid water. Forrestal gradually relaxed and went to sleep. As he left Josie embraced him on the doorstep. "Thanks you, Clane! Thanks you so much."

"That's alright, Josie. Just call me again if you need any more help."

"Sure... Look, I probably don't need to ask you this... but *please* don't tell anybody! Especially the President. Nobody knows.... but Jim has been suffering from bad nerves for some time. It's from the war, and all the aggravation he gets at work."

"Of course not, Josie. It won't go any further. I promise." Forrestal was back at work the next day and he never mentioned the previous evening, although Clane could sense by his demeanour that he knew that Clane knew.

....

The following week Clane was in his office when Forrestal burst in looking agitated. Clane put down his pen. "What's up, Jim?"

"Clane, can you handle the shit here for a few days on your own. I've got to head off."

"Why? What's up?"

Forrestal blushed. "Something's... happened and I've got to go deal with it."

"What's happened, Jim?"

His friend seethed for a few seconds, as if suffering internal conflict. "I... I can't lie to you, Clane." He took a few steps closer to the desk and lowered his voice. "Clane, there's been another crash."

"A crash of what?"

"A... a flying saucer, like at Roswell."

"Where?"

"New Mexico, a place called Aztec, not far from Los Alamos where that saucer was spotted a while ago."

Clane whistled. "And why are you dealing with it and not me? I'd have thought it was more my department."

He shrugged. "Orders from the President."

"Jesus Christ, Jim!... What the hell's going on here!?""

"Clane!" Forrestal put a hand on his arm. "Don't say a word! Please! You're not supposed to know... Now I have to go; I'll be back in a few days." With that, James Forrestal turned and left the office.

Clane picked up the phone in a fury and dialled the White House; he hesitated while it rang, then he put it down again.

....

The plane landed in Albuquerque with a heavy thump. It was the following day after Forrestal's departure and Clane had called in sick that morning. In the arrivals hall Clane bought himself a map of the local area and went to hire himself a car. It was a two hour drive to Aztec, though a typically New Mexican landscape of brush-covered desert and dry stone mesas all baked by a fierce sun. Aztec itself was on Navajo Indian land. It was very Roswell-like on a smaller scale, consisting of straight blocks of wide, dusty roads and low buildings, and lots of trailer parks. The place he was heading for was a few miles outside town. Already the enhanced military presence became obvious. The road was constantly over-flown by aircraft and he met many jeeps on the highway. One of them stopped him, but let him pass immediately when he identified himself. There were a number of unpaved gravel roads leading off to the right and before long he came to one that was closed by a roadblock manned by a pair of rough-looking armed Marines. Clane turned off and approached the barrier. "Sorry, sir." One of the men called from beneath his tin pot helmet. "This is a restricted area."

"Not for me." smiled Clane. "I'm the Secretary for Interplanetary War. You can let me through." He showed them his White House ID.

The Marines studied it and stepped back to confer privately; then they turned back to him. "Sorry, Mr Secretary. We can't allow you access to this site."

Clane feigned a chuckle. "What? Come on, guys. You have a crashed flying saucer in there, don't you? I'm the government official who deals with flying saucer-related matters, now let me through."

"No, sir, we have our orders and..."

"Oh, this is ridiculous." Clane suddenly gunned the accelerator and jerked the steering wheel to the right. The hire car leapt forward and bumped off the track onto the stony verge, which was only of slightly worse quality than the carriageway. He skidded in an arc around the barrier and steadied out again back on the road, ignoring the shouts of the two guards. Then he heard a series of loud cracks from behind him and he felt the car drop down a few inches. There was a grinding sound from the wheels, and the car inexorably slowed and eventually stopped.

"Stand to!... Stand to!"

Clane could see the two sentries running towards him in his rear-view mirror. Their rifles were levelled at their shoulders.

"You are under arrest! Step out of the car now!"

Clane obeyed, holding his hands above his head. He looked down and saw that all four tyres of the car were flat, clearly shot by the Marines. They put handcuffs on him and frogmarched him to a small wooden hut where he was locked inside with only a bench to sit on. He was very hot and thirsty when he heard voices outside about twenty minutes later. The door was flung open and James Forrestal appeared. "Clane! What the heck are you doing here!?"

"I'm doing my job, Jim! The job you and the President are stopping me from doing!... I want to know about the Martian ship, goddammit!"

Forrestal shut the door behind him. The only light came from sun shining through the cracks between the planks of the hut. It cast lines of light on his face. "Listen, Clane!" he hissed. "I'm not going to tell the President you were here! If I did, your life could be in danger, and possibly mine too! I mean that literally!... You don't understand what's going on here! Please, for both our sakes... go back to Washington and shut the fuck up!"
....

It was gone midnight when Clane arrived back in his apartment just across the Potomac from DC. He was dead tired, but he paused before he got undressed and studied himself in the full length wardrobe mirror. He was a man in a suit, with the same face he'd always had; that familiar, recognizable face that he knew so well, the one he associated with his own identity. He'd seen it in his school clothes, in his Navy square rig, in his reporters' outfits. Here that face was attached to a person he never imagined could ever exist, a government official. United States Secretary for Interplanetary War. He shuffled millions of dollars around in his budget. He himself had a five-figure salary. He moved warships, airbases and tank divisions around the globe like chess pieces. How had this happened? How had the man he had always been become what he was today? In truth, he didn't feel particularly different. He certainly didn't have any sense of power. A few hours earlier he'd been shackled and put in a cell like any common drunk off the streets. The world was not what he thought it was, that was for sure. Clane pulled off his governmental jacket, necktie, shirt, trousers, shiny black brogues and went to bed. He fell into a troubled sleep.

He was woken up at six AM by his phone. It was the President. "Quilley! Are you better yet!?"

"Yes, Mr President."

"Good; get your ass to the White House. Have you seen the news yet?"

"No. What's happened?" It didn't take Clane long to find out. A ship had been sunk. SS *Morocco*, a British transatlantic liner, had been on her way from New York to Southampton when she'd been attacked by a Martian flying saucer just a day into her voyage. She had gone down, ironically, just a dozen miles from where RMS *Titanic* had thirty-six years earlier. This time there were plenty of lifeboats, but the ship had sunk so quickly only one had been launched carrying mostly crew. It was the early hours of the morning and almost all the passengers had been in their bunks. There over three thousand of them had drowned. At that time people were just beginning to hope that it was all over and the aliens had gone for good.

....

A few days later the tanks of the Red Army rolled over the borders of East Germany, Romania and Bulgaria. The national forces of Western Europe were powerless to stop them; their lands still exhausted from the war. The President called a meeting at mid-morning and then the ambassador to the USSR was invited to the White House to explain what was going on. "It's for two simple reasons." he said as he sipped tea in a glass mug with a metal holder that he'd brought with him. "We do not believe that the lands formerly occupied by fascists have been completely cleansed of impure ideals. We wish to assist your programme to 'de-Nazify' the West. And also of course, like you, we wish to defend the socialist Motherland against the aggressors from beyond our own planet. Surely we can better do that if we temporarily put our differences aside and unite to repel our common enemy... In fact one of your staunchest allies, Ireland, has already signed a significant bilateral defence treaty with the Soviet Union. We were hoping America would do the same."

The cabinet retired to consider the situation. It was met with mixed feelings.

Chapter 7

Clane entered his office and said good morning to Ellen, the secretary and receptionist. He went straight to his own cubicle while Ellen made his coffee. This was now a routine he rarely noticed. After all, it had been almost a year since he and James Forrestal had confronted each other at Aztec, New Mexico. Before that day, he and Clane always began work by sharing their morning coffee and making small talk; but no longer. Not that they had completely fallen out; indeed they still functioned well together as friendly professional partners, but there was less warmth and intimacy between them. Barriers had been raised and they held each other at arms length. They never once referred to the incident at Aztec. Clane wished they would, and maybe clear the air between them. He suspected that Forrestal wished for the same thing. However Clane had come to accept a lot of home truths during the past twelve months that destroyed many of the comforting illusions he'd previously enjoyed. He'd even made inquiries at the White House about the elderly black maid who had told him she suspected President Truman had been assassinated, but was informed that she had left the previous year and nobody knew where she was. Clane didn't know what was going on; only that something was. There were forces at work he knew nothing about, as the President had told him the day before his death. There was now a third President in the Oval Office; Thomas E Dewey had beaten Joseph Martin in the election the previous year, but why should anything else have changed?

Forrestal knocked on his door; last year he would just have entered straight away. "Hey, Clane!" He looked excited. "You're not going to believe the latest report from the SIA!"

"What's happening, Jim?"

"You know the Naval Observatory has been monitoring Mars' and Venus' radio signatures?"

"Of course."

"Well they've picked up something different... Ever since Mars Day there have been all kinds of encrypted messages that are clearly communications between the planets and their spacecraft. This time though there has been a new signal beam that appears to be specifically intended to be received on Earth. At the same time, something very similar is coming from Venus."

"Yeah, but these are also encrypted, right?"

"No!"

"Really!?... You mean, the aliens are trying to communicate with us?"

"Yup. These transmissions are in a simple binary code that contains a subset which looks like a primer. In other words this is a message designed to be easily decoded into a human language of our choice."

"How long will it take for the SIA guys to crack it?"

"Probably only a couple of weeks."

"Amazing!... the ET's want to parley." The two men carried on their duties with renewed vigour, indeed Forrestal was still crouched at his desk when Clane left at five PM. He was just about to get ready for bed at eleven PM that night when the phone rang. It was Josephine Forrestal again sounding upset. Sure enough, when Clane turned up at their home, his friend James Forrestal was once more in the throes of a nervous seizure. He was sitting on the floor of the bathroom screaming at the top of his voice as if in pain. He had been repeatedly punching himself in the face. His nose and lips were bleeding. "The neighbours can hear him; they've just come round to see what's wrong!" Josie told Clane. "I managed to stall them by saying Jim had stubbed his toe."

Clane entered the bathroom and grabbed his friend's arm to stop his self-harming. Forrestal slapped Clane across the face, forcing him to let go. There was no question of coaxing him to take his pills this time. Suddenly Forrestal got to his feet and seemed to recover slightly. He opened the bathroom cabinet above the washbasin and seized a loose razor blade. Clane just had time to intercept Forrestal's hand before the Secretary of Defence plunged it into his own forearm. Clane yelled with pain as the blade bit into his own fingers, but he managed to disarm his suicidal friend. Josie grabbed her husband's other arm and together they restrained him. There was nothing else they could do except hold him down and wait until he ran out of energy, which took about an hour. Eventually Forrestal collapsed back onto the floor, blubbering and trembling.

Josie helped bandage Clane's gashed hand. "I don't know what to do!"

"Josie, I'm sorry, but we're going to have to call an ambulance."

"If people find out, it will break his heart!" She was only half-protesting now.

"I know, but if we don't get him proper help, he's going to die."

She nodded painfully. "I know." The ambulance pulled up outside the house a few minutes after they'd made the call and a pair of paramedics came in with a stretcher. They secured James Forrestal to it. Josie sat beside him in the back as they took him away to hospital.

....

Clane drove up to Bethesda as soon as the doctors gave permission for visitors. The Walter Reed National Military Medical Centre was square and made of equal sized concrete cubes, as if put together by a giant child's toy building blocks. It was covered in white tiles and dominated in its centre by a tall narrow tower. He entered by the rainbow-shaped driveway and left his car in the carpark. After enquiring at reception he took the lift up to the sixteenth floor of the tower and was faced by a secure locked door not unlike a prison's. He had to wait while another receptionist called inside and a few minutes later a doctor in a white coat and glasses came out and introduced himself as Surgeon Captain Raines. He unlocked the door and led Clane inside. "Technically there are no psychiatric wards for officers." he said as he escorted Clane along the polished shiny-floored corridors. "But of course that's what this is in practice." They stopped by the door to a dormitory and inside a man in his sixties lay on a bed staring at the ceiling. He didn't move or even blink his eyes. "He's been like that since 1918." said Dr Raines in a dispassionate medical tone. "We still have many veterans from the Great War in here."

This ward was different to the other parts of hospitals Clane had been to before. Most of the patients were mobile, and they walked around in green cotton pyjamas and slippers; but they gaped at Clane in astonishment as he walked past, as if he had a green face or three eyes. Nurses and doctors strode purposefully between doorways. The place reeked of sweat, urine and excrement; but on top of that was the usual clinical waft of disinfectant and soap. The two contradictory odours battled against each other in the atmosphere of the ward. Loud voices uttered unintelligible words, echoing from distant chambers. "Admiral Forrestal's condition has improved this week, I'm glad to say. He's gained weight and his anaemia has eased. This is because he's been eating properly again. We're altering his insulin levels to improve his mood and have stopped the amylobarbitone; it's not needed any more... Here he is." The psychiatrist pointed.

At first Clane didn't recognize James Forrestal. They had entered a dayroom and the Secretary for Defence was sitting on a settee at a table by a window. He was hunched over, scribbling furiously in a large leather notebook. Around him the other patients paced up and down, muttered to themselves or sat still watching the television in the opposite corner. Clane walked up to his friend. "Hello, Jim."

Forrestal's face brightened as he looked up. "Clane! Good to see you! Take a seat."

Sitting beside Forrestal, Clane could see that the book the Secretary was writing in was a diary. At the top of the page was printed that day's date: Saturday May the 21st 1949. "The Doc tells me you're on the mend, Jim. Hopefully you'll be able to go home to Josie soon."

"Hope so." He closed the diary and lowered his voice, looking nervously at the other patients. "Listen, Clane. I need to tell you something very important."

"What?"

He looked crestfallen. "I'm afraid I did lie to you. I lied to you a lot. I let you down. I'm so sorry... I've decided to make it up to you. You're a good man and you deserve the whole truth."

"What are you talking about, Jim?"

"The flying saucers! The Martians and Venusians... There's so much more to know; so much we've been told is false."

"Sure, you can tell me if you know more."

"It's all in *here*." Forrestal furtively pushed the diary across the tabletop into Clane's grip. "Take this, read it and get the word out."

"Alright."

A quartet of nurses came into the room to tend to some of their charges and Forrestal made forced small-talk with Clane, suspicious of them. The two men admired the view out of the window which was impressive from that height, the sixteenth floor. The window was made of reinforced glass and was sealed shut by a clasp and padlock. That made sense, Clane surmised, when housing the mentally ill, including people capable of self-harm or suicide, on such a high floor. When visiting hours were over, he bade farewell to his friend and Dr Raines escorted him back to the ward's armoured security entrance. "What's that you've got there?" the doctor asked as they walked, looking down at Forrestal's diary clutched under Clane's arm.

"Something Secretary Forrestal gave me to take home..."

"I'm afraid we can't allow that." he interjected abruptly. "Patients are not permitted to give visitors gifts until they've been vetted by staff. Could I have it please?" His manner was brusque and authoritative. "We'll return it to you on your next visit once we've had it cleared."

Clane handed over the diary, feeling powerless and uncomfortable; for reasons he wasn't certain of.
....

The following day was Sunday and Clane drove back to Bethesda straight after church. The atmosphere of the hospital was transformed. A large fleet of police cars were parked in an arc around the front entrance and uniformed officers stood in the doorway. With them were men in military police armbands and several doctors. Somebody had placed a ladder against the wall of a lower part of the building neighbouring the big tower. Clane recognized Dr Raines as he parked himself, as close as he could. Raines spotted him and walked swiftly over to his car, a grim look on his face. "Secretary Quilley, I'm terribly sorry to bring you this news. Mr Forrestal has passed away."

Clane reeled back as if he'd been punched. His breath caught in his gullet.

"What!?... No!"

"You have my deepest condolences."

"How... how...!?" Clane managed to croak. He felt his head spin and his eyes fill with tears.

"It was an accident that happened late last night. He climbed out of a kitchen window on the ward and leaped to his death. He was killed instantly by his injuries sustained in the fall. There was nothing we could do; I'm sorry."

Clane was still speechless with shock, so Dr Raines took him inside the entrance and into a quiet restroom. He had the receptionist make him a cup of tea. Half and hour later when the doctor came back, Clane had recovered and was more composed. "Doctor, tell me, how did Jim manage to climb out of the window when all your windows are double-plated and locked shut?"

The psychiatrist smiled thinly and blushed. "We don't know, Mr Quilley. That's going to be a part of the coroner's investigation."

"Alright... One more thing; Jim's diary that I handed over to you last night to be checked over before he could give it to me. Could I have it back now please?"

Raines paused and looked nonplussed. "What diary?..."

Chapter 8

Clane awoke with a jolt. He had been dreaming about the war again. He pulled off his eyeshades with a groan and sat up on his sleeping pallet to look around the torpedo room. Maybe it was being back on board a submarine that had triggered the memories. He eased himself off the pallet and nodded to the watch keepers in the compartment. He patted the cold steel flank of a torpedo as he walked through to relieve himself in the head. Then he climbed the ladder to the upper deck and headed for the control room. Yes, this was a submarine, but one unlike any he had ever experienced. The captain was at the conn. "Good morning, Mr Secretary. Did you sleep well?"

"As always, Captain."

"A far cry from old *Tunny*, ain't she?" The two men smiled at each other. Captain George Benson, the commanding officer of USS *Rickover*, had once been known as Lieutenant Benson and he had been the engineering officer of USS *Tunny* during the war; and Clane had known him well. Clane gazed around the control room of USS *Rickover* and marvelled at the lights, dials and consoles that were beyond anything technologically that a sailor during the war could have imagined. "You know something, Mr Secretary." said Benson. "I've done a back-of-an-envelope calculation, and I reckon if we'd had *Rickover* in the Pacific, we could have beaten Japan single handed."

"I can well believe it." *Rickover* was not only far bigger than any other submarine the US Navy had ever produced, she was unique. All submarines before her had had a dual propulsion system; while on the surface they were driven by diesel engines and while dived ran off electric motors powered by batteries. The batteries were charged by the diesels while surfaced. This meant that submarines could not stay dived for very long before having to surface and recharge; no more than a day, depending on how fast they sailed. *Rickover* had a completely different and revolutionary power plant. The atom-splitting reaction that went into the bombs whose devastation Clane had witnessed during the war, had been tempered and tamed into a more drawn out process that generated heat without the explosion. Because it needed no air, this power plant could operate underwater, making it the perfect engine for a submarine. *Rickover* was on her maiden voyage following sea trials, and she had carried Clane right across the Atlantic Ocean in just a single week, averaging eighteen knots, not surfacing once since diving in Long Island Sound. *Tunny* could manage eight knots at her top speed on the electric motors, and this would drain the batteries in an hour. *Rickover* even had the means to purify her own air by extracting oxygen from sea water and scrubbing exhaled carbon dioxide with chemical filters. A new era of submarine warfare had dawned. Clane still wasn't sure how advances in undersea warfare could be of any use when the current threat vector was in the exact opposite direction.

"Conn, sonar. We have a new contact." came a voice on the intercom from the sound room. "Bearing zero-two-six, range eight thousand yards, course three-one-five, speed nine knots."

"Very well. Identify."

"Can detect tonals indicating nuclear power plant."

"Soviet?"

"Yes, sir. It's the *Leninsky Komsomol*."

"Excellent, thank you." Benson turned and addressed Clane. "Our escort into Cork has arrived, Mr Secretary. The Ruskies have sent us their own nuclear-powered prototype."

The klaxon sounded three times. "Surface, surface!" called the chief of the watch and there was a blasting roaring sound as high pressure air rushed into the ballast tanks. Clane felt his ears pop as the pressure hull's atmosphere was equalised with the outside air. *Rickover* started bobbing on the waves. Her long dive was finally over. He was given permission to join the captain on the bridge and he clambered up the long ladder inside the boat's extended fairwater. The cold wet wind of the sea inflated his lungs and sea spray mixed with a light rain dashed his face making him blink. The choppy grey water led away in front of them to the distant shore, an undulating vista of greenish hills partly obscured by mist. Clane could see the outline of the Russian nuclear-powered submarine on the surface a few miles away; the bullet-shaped hull with a short tapering fairwater. The captain spoke through the intercom to the radar operator and then addressed Clane. "I'm glad you're topside right now, Mr Secretary, because we have another escort. The aerial contact is approaching from our two-fifty; about eight thou. That'll put him above the cloud base."

Clane stared at the low damp clouds on the given bearing until he saw a splotch of black sifting through the vapour. "He's descending." He pointed. An object then emerged from the murk. The wisps of mist rolled off its shiny black hull like water. It was the shape of an equilateral triangle and it rotated slowly as it paced the *Rickover*. Captain Benson looked alarmed. "Is it Martian?"

"No, Venusian. Pass me some glasses." Clane took a pair of binoculars off a lookout and scanned the flank of the spaceship.

"I hear the Martians are carrying out false flag attacks with captured enemy craft."

"There have been one or two occasions... Maybe he's just here because of the summit." The black triangular craft pursued the submarine for a few more minutes then shot vertically up into the clouds, accelerating to several hundred knots almost instantaneously as alien spaceships had a habit of doing.

The coastline grew in size and clarity as *Rickover* approached it. The submarine was joined by a pilot boat which guided her along the channel into Cork Harbour. Clane gazed at the land on either side. It was grassy and lush; and there were rows of houses and curved residential streets leading up to the hills lining the inner harbour. Clane could see Cobh and the famous jetty where *Titanic* had picked up some emigrants thirty-eight years ago before on her ill fated trip across the Atlantic to a New York she would never reach. A small motorboat appeared on the submarines port bow. It came to the same course and speed and was full of people waving and cheering. As Clane looked at the swarded shore he suddenly began thinking of his grandparents. "So this is Ireland." he muttered to himself. In 1882 his grandmother and grandfather, Brendan and Colleen Quilley had boarded a ship here bound for New York City knowing full well that they would never see their homeland again. They left from Cobh jetty, each carrying a small suitcase and the clothes on their bodies; nothing more. Colleen wore a silver bracelet, the only piece of jewellery she hadn't had to pawn for the travel costs. Clane was carrying it in his pocket right then and there. All that time ago, Brendan and Colleen would have looked back for one last sight of the same green hills that their grandson was seeing now seventy-two years later. Clane didn't consider himself a sentimental man and so was surprised and embarrassed when he felt tears budding in his eyes. He wiped them away and focused on the passage of the submarine; the terse exchange of orders, the appearance of sailors on the casing ready to handle the docking.

A sizeable crowd was gathered on the wharf as the *Rickover* nudged alongside, guided by a tug boat. Two of them held up a banner with the words: *WELCOME HOME SECRETARY QUILLEY*. Somebody must have already researched his family roots. A huge cheer went up as Clane stepped off the gangway onto the shore. A greeting committee stepped forward including the mayor of Cork, the US and Soviet ambassadors; and the head of the Irish government, the *Taoiseach*, a stern-faced yet friendly man called John Costello. He accompanied Clane up onto a plywood podium where he made a speech. "Ireland is never happier than when one of her lost sons returns. After a long exile from birth in the strange land of America, Clane Quilley has risen to the highest levels in the political structure, from fighting in the war and a career in journalism to taking up arms to defend planet earth from its first external threat..."

The US ambassador was a man Clane had met once at a congressional dinner. His own speech was somewhat shorter and less warm. "Clane Quilley is the first ever US Secretary for Interplanetary War, a title that we all hope will soon change. Two weeks ago we welcomed in the new year of 1950; not just the new year, but a new decade. The world has lived in fear for more than two years. Our internal differences have been forgotten as we faced up to the menace from outer space. We now know that we are not alone in the universe. This knowledge has engendered in us a new comprehension of our common humanity..."

The Soviet ambassador explained in broken English how much he was looking forward to Clane's visit to the USSR zone in Dublin. The mayor of Cork awarded Clane the freedom of the city. Then it was Clane's turn to speak: "Ladies and gentlemen, people of Ireland, this is my first visit to the Emerald Isle..." He related the story of his grandparents' emigration. "... I know that every Irish-American has a dual nationality. You can take the man out of Ireland, but you can never take Ireland out of the man!" The crowd roared at these words.

After the speeches Clane was taken by car into the city of Cork. The streets were narrow and the walls of the buildings were grey stone. A few new year signs were still up as if the Irish were unwilling to let go of their reason for a party. He was booked into the grand suite at the Imperial Hotel. The porter helped him to unpack and showed him how everything in the room worked. Clane was amazed to see that the television set had a colour picture. "Incredible!" he said. "It's like a cinema screen."

"Don't you have colour TV in the states yet, Mr Secretary?" asked the porter.

"Yes, I believe so, but I've not seen it yet. I guess I just don't have time to watch much TV."

When he was alone Clane jumped into the huge bathtub and had a luxurious wash. Thanks to her nuclear reactor, USS *Rickover* had an abundance of fresh hot water, a resource incredibly scare in old *Tunny*; but a stand up spray down in one of the small shower stalls was no substitute for a plunge into the warm soapy depths of the Imperial's bath. He got out after an hour and dressed in a new suit. His wrinkled fingertips made it difficult for him to fasten his tie. As he admired himself in the mirror he was suddenly overcome by the feeling that he was not alone. Then he saw somebody standing behind him in the mirror. A small wizened old man with a Stetson hat and dirty poncho. Flying Buffalo smiled at him. Clane swung round with a yell. There was nobody there; his heart pounded. "Where are you?" he hissed. Then he shouted. "Where are you!?"

There was a knock at the door. Clane went over to answer it. A large man in a grey suit and sunglasses stood there filling up the doorway. "Is everything alright, Mr Secretary? I heard a raised voice."

"Who are you?" demanded Clane

"I'm with the US Secret Service at the embassy; we've been sent over here to make sure everything's okay with you." The man had a pure American accent not an Irish one.

"Well as you can see I'm AOK." He slammed the door in his face. Clane felt the sudden idea to go out; he didn't know why. As soon as the concept came to him, it became a desperate urge. He put on his overcoat and grabbed his room key. He opened the door and headed down the corridor. The Secret Service guard who had knocked just before was standing on one side of the door. When Clane left the room he chased after him. "Wait, Mr Secretary! Where are you going?"

"Out for a walk."

"No! You mustn't."

"What you mean I 'mustn't'?"

"We need to arrange an escort first."

"Why?"

"It's not safe out there."

"What you mean? It's a big city."

"The IRA are active here."

"What? Garbage!" Clane reached the top of the stairs and began to descend; the agent feverishly trotting behind him. "There hasn't been an IRA attack since the war. I know that." As he reached the bottom of the stairs he saw that his way was blocked by a second man, equally big and equally intimidating. "What the...!?"

"Stop, Mr Secretary. Return to your room!" The guard said in a gruff voice.

"What is this!? I want to go for a walk, goddammit! Are you preventing me?"

The agent raised a pacifying hand. "It's hazardous for you to go out alone in Cork, Mr Secretary. If you wish to visit someplace, let us know and we'll make the security arrangements."

Once back in his room, Clane gazed around at the chandeliers, silk sheets on the bed, the marble bathroom. Then he went over to the window and looked out at the street below. People were walking a freely along the pavements; a packed bus rumbled past. "The cage is gold plated." Clane muttered to himself. "But I'm still well and truly behind bars."

He petitioned his bodyguards, saying that he wanted to take a trip to a genuine Irish pub. Of course there were plenty of Irish pubs in New York, tucked into the backstreets of the West Side near the docks where Clane had spent many a long evening. There were some in Boston too, but Clane badly wanted to experience a pub in the old homeland. The agents made few phone calls and an hour later two cars pulled up at the hotel. They drove Clane to a pub with the ironic name of the *Sober Lane Inn*. After the two minute journey, the cars parked outside and Clane went inside accompanied by three bodyguards. Four more stayed in one of the cars outside as backup. The pub was dark and aromatic. It was lined with reddish brown timber and grass green velvet seat cushions. It was half full this early hour and the clientele spoke loudly in their thick brogues. Clane went up to the bar and ordered a pint of Guinness. "Can I get you gentlemen anything?" he smiled.

The three US Secret Service officers shook their heads in unison. "We're on duty." said one.

"Oh come on! A swift pint won't hurt will it? This is proper Irish Guinness, straight out of St James's Gate Brewery and straight into the cellar. This could be your only chance to taste Guinness as it should be." He winked. "Go on!"

The men exchanged glances. "Half a pint only."

Clane spoke to the men about his personal life; Gina, Siobhan, his homes in New York and Roswell. He asked them about their lives. What did they think of Ireland? Did they have families back stateside? How were they coping with the Martian threat? They agreed to a second half of Guinness with little resistance. Their third round was upgraded to pints and they hardly noticed. An hour and a half passed and they were chuckling and speaking informally. Clane then paid a visit to the bathroom. Pub rest rooms in Ireland were almost always upstairs or downstairs in the basement; luckily the *Sober Lane Inn*'s was one of the former. The first time he went upstairs, one of the bodyguards accompanied him. An hour, and another two pints, later he took his time, locking himself in one of the sit-down cubicles. After ten minutes Clane peeked out and, as he had hoped, the agent had got bored with waiting and gone back down to the bar. Clane had to act quickly. He opened the window and climbed out onto the roof of an outhouse; this allowed him to clamber easily down a drainpipe to the beer garden, which was unoccupied on this chilly January afternoon. The back gate opened easily and he found himself in a thin alley. He ran as fast as he could, knowing that he had just minutes before the trio of agents realized that he had absconded and tried to give chase. At the end of the alley he entered a busy shopping street. He slowed down and blended in with the strolling pedestrians, turning up the collar of his jacket and lowering his hat. He wasn't sure where he was going or why; he operated on instinct alone. After walking for half an hour he came to a residential area. The atmosphere of the streets changed. The roads and pavements were cracked, and moss and grass grew through the gaps. They ran in straight square lines around oblong concrete tenement blocks two or three storeys high with shallow roofs. Clane stopped and looked up at one of them. Some of the windows were shattered and streaks of mould ran down the walls from the broken gutter. The smell of dishwater, urine and rotten vegetables wafted from a nearby open downstairs window. He could hear a baby crying in another room. A woman shouted obscenities in a hoarse voice with a strong Hiberno accent. A girl of about seven years old came out of the doorway and walked past him. Her hair was matted and unkempt, her cheeks stained black with grime. She wore no shoes or socks; her toenails were black. She circuited piles of broken glass and dog excrement as she walked down the street. Clane turned his back to shut out the site of such squalor. He was facing a crumbling red brick wall. "Flying Buffalo." he muttered. "Where are you?... What am I doing here?"

....

"Mr Secretary, I am *so* sorry!" The US ambassador to Ireland was almost in tears. "I must apologise unreservedly for the irresponsibility and dereliction of your security detail. They left you alone and unprotected; your life might have been in danger! I have reprimanded them in the strongest possible terms!"

"That's all right, your Excellency." Clane pacified. "Just make sure it never happens again." He half smiled at the men.

The Secret Service bodyguards were all assembled in the hotel lobby. Three of them had grey and unshaven cheeks which indicated a hangover. Even from behind their sunglasses, Clane could feel their baleful eyes glaring at him.

The *Taoiseach*'s coach turned up at five past nine. It was a fairly low key way for a head of government to travel, but that seemed to be the form in Ireland. In the pub the previous day Clane had seen senior members of the Dublin government sharing a beer with simple folk off the street. John Costello opened the passenger door himself and welcomed the Americans aboard. The small motorcade consisted of Costello's coach, a press van and a single patrol car from the *Gardai*, Ireland's national police force. The vehicles pulled away one after the other and drove through the streets of Cork until they reached the main road north. The sun came out and its golden rays shone down onto the fields and forests of the Emerald Isle. As they approached Kilkenny the road rose into a pass between two large beautiful hills. But as they descended the north side Clane's heart sank. The entire northern slope of the hill was stripped bare. The trees had been felled and some remained as crushed logs at the side of a muddy track leading from the main road. "Mr Costello." Clane asked. "What's going on there?"

"Ah!" The Irish leader smiled proudly. "Why don't I show you?" He addressed the driver. "Davy, pull off here would you? I'm going to show Secretary Quilley our future." The coach bumped uncomfortably along the muddy road leading into what was left of the forest. At the foot of the hill, a deep gouge had been sunk into the land swallowing up a quarter of the base of the hill. Among the smooth natural contours of the land it stood out like a cavity in a tooth. At the dusty bottom of the quarry, huge digging machines and transporter trucks moved around like dinosaurs.

"What you digging up here?" asked Clane.

"Oil shale." said Costello. "There's a billion tons of it, stretching right through the country from Clare to the Wicklow mountains. A golden belt of prosperity across the land. When we get to Dublin I'll get my energy minister to show you his prospectus."

"What's wrong with crude oil?"

"The price is getting too high; it's only just below shale refining at the moment. That guy from your part the world has it all worked out; what's his name? Hubbert. There's a limited amount of oil in the ground; it's a fossil fuel, and therefore a finite resource. Sooner or later it will reach a point where all the easy to get at oil is gone and we will have to drill deeper and further until it costs more to extract the oil than any revenue you get from the oil you extract. Then production will peak and decline. At the same time global consumption is rising. There are two and a half billion people in the world today. In 1900 there were only about one-point-eight. That means the population has gone up almost a third in fifty years. And they're living longer and better. They own more technology. There are almost twice as many people with cars in the world as there were 1930. What they going run them on? Also you need fuel to run modern farms; how are we going to feed all those hungry mouths?"

"But, Mr *Taoiseach*. You're surely not planning to strip mine the whole middle of Ireland?"

Costello chuckled. "We don't have to. Davy, drive on." The governmental coach trundled on over the crest of a rise and below them ahead stretched a flat plane of typically Irish pasture land. The difference was that this particular vista also consisted of steel towers emerging from the landscape at regular intervals. These were thin girder work structures about eighty feet high and they stretched into the distance as far as the eye could see. There were also two or three towers of a different kind; black pipes sprouting out the ground with roaring flames at the top. "The shale seam runs deep here." said Costello. "Too deep to mine, but we've found a way of extracting natural gas from the geology which is just as good as the oil. We inject high pressure liquid into the ground to split apart that dense rock layer and that allows the gas bubbles to be released into the well. This hydraulic fracturing process also works on coal beds to extract methane. We plan to expand this process to every viable deposit in the nation; half of the land we estimate. This revolutionary new method will bring Ireland roaring and charging into the 1950s as one of the world's top per-capita net energy exporters. We call if 'fracking'."

....

The USSR Military Globalization Zone was known informally as the "Soviet Pale" and it was almost always called that, even in official contexts. It covered most of County Dublin, basically following the city limits of the city of Dublin. The *Taoiseach*'s motorcade approached the western boundary of the Soviet Pale just before midday and pulled up at the checkpoint outside the suburb of Clondalkin. Everybody had to show their passports or other identification papers to the Red Army police manning the barricades. Heavily armed units were stationed nearby; lookout towers, machine gun positions and a parked tank. Clane had become accustomed to the bilingual signage of Ireland. Everything was both in English and Irish, however the signboard marking the entrance to the Soviet Pale was in English, Irish and Russian with Russian at the top. Even the *Taoiseach* of Ireland was cross examined just like everybody else. The *Gardai* car had to turn back because all law enforcement in the Pale was the jurisdiction of the Russians. This was not an occupation per se, as it was in much of Europe. Ireland had worked out a complex power-sharing system. However Russian influence was everywhere in the Pale. The three language rule of the entrance board applied to every official notice from car parking permits to stop signs. The flag of the Pale, a red banner with a gold star and a golden harp, was seen everywhere. However the parliament of the young republic, the *Oireachtas Eireann*, still sat at Leinster house and was designated the "Irish Capital Zone", an enclave within an enclave.

The ambiance of Clane's tour changed. Now was a time for work to be done, and he was to be a key figure. Ironically the summit was to be hosted in Stoneybatter, a district that had been completely destroyed on Mars Day. During the two and a half years since, a new conference centre had been built where the semidetached houses of the traditional residential district used to stand. It was now being prepared for the upcoming solar system summit. This was the most significant political event since Potsdam; and like Potsdam, Tehran or Yalta, this conference might well end a war.

The venue was not built specifically for this event, but it might as well have been. The Stoneybatter Arena was an elegant art deco grey concrete structure, long and low, only two storeys high. Its main ballroom had a capacity of two thousand. The lights were hemispherical smoked glass rather than the Waterford chandeliers that most official buildings in Ireland had. The interior furnishings were very modern and minimalist. There were numerous smaller chambers surrounding the ballroom and many of these were occupied by the world's media as they prepared themselves for the upcoming fiesta. Every day the ferryboat from Liverpool brought more of them and the airport had never been busier. Other rooms were converted into offices for various officials, the Irish Republic, the UK, prime ministers from various places, the Soviet Union, the League of the World. The US contingent had an entire suite of three rooms. As US Secretary for Interplanetary War, Clane had the largest of these. It had a few collapsible hire desks and bookshelves installed when he first arrived. He began unpacking his three boxes of paperwork that had been delivered from the embassy. The windows of his office overlooked the facade of the building and the Italian style grounds that led up to the north road. On the other side of the road, technicians were working in Phoenix Park setting up a row of floodlights. The enormous green space was the largest in Dublin and was to be commandeered for this event. Clane reached into one of the boxes and pulled out a book. This was a classified title produced by the US Signals Intelligence Agency: *Guide to the Martian and Venusian Languages*. Clane opened it and mumbled to himself as he read out the various phrases. The languages of Mars and Venus had been deciphered by SIA linguists after a direct signal was sent from the planets. They had been studying intercepted communications from the planets since Mars Day, but had failed due to the encryption of the traffic. However their endeavour had been put to the test six months earlier when, for the first time, a message from earth was transmitted to Mars and Venus in the recipients' own languages. Twenty minutes later the Bletchley Park signals laboratory had received replies from both parties indicating that the extraterrestrials had understood perfectly. The grammar of both languages was fairly similar, and quite regular and simple. Clane had been studying his native Irish Gaelic for the last few months and that was far more difficult than learning Martian and Venusian. The vocabulary was also very Spartan; the book contained dictionaries on both tongues, but these were limited to a few thousand words each. Some terms, mostly nouns, were so far untranslated; perhaps referring to concepts that were unique to their home worlds and did not exist on earth.

There were a series of three booming sounds. It took Clane a moment to realise they were coming from the door. The heavy hardwood timber and the door frame exaggerated the sound of rapping knuckles.

"Come in." called Clane.

The door opened steadily, smoothly and silently on it oiled hinges. A head poked around playfully. "Hallo! Anybody in?"

"Yes, me."

"Ah!" A tall thin man came into the room. "You must be Secretary Quilley." He grinned so broadly that it looked as though his cheeks would split. "You're the man I've been looking for." He chuckled. He had an upper class English accent and he spoke in an easygoing sing-song tone. "Gerald Caxton. How do you do."

The two men shook hands. "Clane Quilley. I've seen your name written down somewhere."

"Yes, I'm the new British ambassador to the League of the World. Prime Minister Mosley appointed me last month." He tittered again. "Do you know, some people want the League to go back to its old name of 'United Nations'? I prefer the new name; reminds people that it's not just us now." His watery eyes twinkled and his shiny white teeth glinted. He had tight curly black hair and a neatly trimmed moustache. His nose rose sharply at the tip so that his nostrils pointed forwards. He grinned again for no obvious reason. Then he looked down at Clane's book. "Ah, the languages of our forthcoming guests. Did you know, Mr Secretary, that a professor of linguistics in Oxford has just published a paper claiming that the Martian and Venusian languages have links to ancient Egyptian?" He frowned as he contemplated the fact. "Could this mean that our human ancestors had interactions with extraterrestrials many millennia in the past? Possibly. We don't know how long the civilisations have existed on those planets. Maybe they predate our own by a long time."

"Well, that guy Percival Lowell thought he saw somebody building canals on Mars." Clane leaned back in his chair. Caxton's manner was very intense and a bit smothering. "What were you looking for me about, Mr Caxton?"

"Well, as you may know, I'm on the organizing committee for the summit; and I shall be hosting a preliminary workshop at two PM, and it would be appreciated if you could attend."

"Certainly."

"Goodie! It's in room seven downstairs. And also, don't forget tomorrow is the launch of Athena-One; we're having a television showing in all rooms."

....

The workshop took place around a large conference table in front of a display board with a map of the world pinned on it. About twenty people attended, including the delegates from several countries and the League of the World. Gerald Caxton chaired the meeting and Clane took the floor to lead off the discussion. The subject was an overview of the general political state of the world; to act as a warm up session before the main summit began. As Clane spoke, looking and pointing at the map, he astonished himself with his own surprise at how the world had changed in the last few years. "... As you can see, gentlemen." he said. "The need to defend the planet from Mars has affected the relationship between our nations and as a result the geopolitical landscape. In every sense, the Truman Doctrine and the Marshall Plan of 1947 have been completely forgotten."

General Nicolai Zvegintsov, the commandant of the Soviet Pale, scowled and folded his arms.

"This has led, I think it is fair to say, to the emergence of the Soviet allied nations of continental Europe. We have at least a detente now..."

"De-Nazification!" corrected Zvegintsov in his strong Russian accent. The Red Army general was a stout and hard-faced man who had commanded a tank division during the battle of Stalingrad. "For the rise of socialism has so far only occurred in formally Nazi-occupied territories; why you think that this?"

"To tell, General."

"Because the war did not end in forty-five. It's still going on today. Just this morning our comrades in the Socialist Republic of the Netherlands foiled a plot by a former SS guard to bomb the centre of Amsterdam."

A new voice butted in: "Your sentiments are transparent, General Zvegintsov. We all know the true strategy of your superficial altruism. You don't want to save the world from either the Nazis or Mars. You want to take it for yourself!" The speaker was Yann Avenbois, the delegate from the National Republic of France, called by themselves *France Libre* "Free France". He had fought with the Breton nationalist movement *Gwenn Ha Du* in his youth; and today he was the regional administrator of Brittany. "You have already taken half our country and now you want what is left! Is that not correct, *Monsieur le General*?"

Clane looked to the map admitted to himself that, from a French perspective, it looked like a miserable situation. France had been divided again, for a second time in a decade; this time between the National Republic of France and the Socialist French People's Republic or the SFPR. The latter consisted of all of France north of Leon and La Rochelle, except Brittany; that was a part of the NRF. There was no land corridor linking the two segments of the NRF and coastal ships between the two were regularly harassed by the SFPR's navy. The SFPR had been founded in May of 1948 during the "Red Weekend" in which the French Communist Party staged a coup that overthrew the newly formed Fourth Republic. The USSR had funded and armed the French communists and today the SFPR was a textbook Marxist-Leninist Soviet client state.

General Zvegintsov leaned forward and glared at the defiant Breton. "And you, sir, are a fascist! You should have been put on trial at Nuremberg and hanged!" The NRF was formed by French allies of the nationalist Nazi-backed General Franco and his takeover of Spain at the end of the Spanish Civil War.

Gerald Caxton slammed his hand down on the table. "Alright, gentlemen, that's enough! Let's keep this meeting civil. You can argue all you like down the pub afterwards... Mr Quilley, continue."

Clane went on to precis the rest of the European and global political situation. The crisis in France was repeated over much of the continent. The majority of nations were unified under communist rule. Italy, the Netherlands, parts of Scandinavia. The KKE had won the Greek Civil War, and, thanks to the new unification between Russia and Yugoslavia, the USSR had a major foothold in the Mediterranean. The principle nations resisting this new communist alliance were Spain, the Swedish Union and Britain. Britain under Clement Atlee's Labour government had been as neutral as Ireland to begin with, but following the recent election of Oswald Mosley's National Liberal Party, it looked as though the UK was going to take the same position as Spain and the NRF. Ireland remained the sole neutral arbiter in a Europe that was catastrophically split.

"Is it not true though," said the Russian "that Mr Mosley has permitted the establishment of a Soviet military institution on British territory?"

"Yes." said Caxton. "As part of the Ithaca Treaty, to address the threat from Mars, but in no way does that constitute anything like the Soviet Pale. There will be the licenced use of RAF bases or the refitting of warships in UK docks for instance."

"And as you can see here," continued Clane. "Britain has given up a large chunk of the empire, especially here in Africa where independence movements have taken hold, much of them led by Soviet-backed communist parties. The communist parties in Japan, Australia and New Zealand are also on the rise, thanks to more cash-flow from Soviet missions. Korea is of course a hundred percent communist now."

"What do you mean 'thanks to more cash-flow from the Soviets'?" asked Zvegintsov. "Have you ever considered that socialism is what the people actually want?... Next you'll be blaming us for making the dodo dead." He rolled his eyes.

Benjamin Fransky spoke next. He was the League's ambassador from Palestine-Israel. "It's dismaying how things can change so quickly and so drastically. None of us expected anything like this to happen. Let's face it, if it hadn't been for the Mars question, you Russians would have stayed behind the Iron Curtain where you belong. Imagine how different Western Europe would look today. All the democratic states that were rolled back in forty-five would still be there now."

"Nobody knew back then what was to come, Mr Fransky." said Clane. "It's like expecting medieval Europe to act as if they already knew about the existence of the New World."

"You turned a blind eye!" said Fransky slowly and emphatically. "You looked the other way as the Russians scooped up everything you fought for in the war." He raised his hand to cut off Zvegintsov. "Just a few months after promising to contain them. And for what?

Because you were attacked in an assault that did less damage than a single week of the Blitzkrieg."

Everybody at the table groaned in protest.

"We were all attacked, Mr Fransky. The planet earth was attacked." Caxton gave the PI delegate a stern glare.

"Palestine wasn't!" added Avenbois.

"That's true," said Clane "Palestine, now PI, was spared. However fifty-two cities across the world were bombarded from the air by Martian spacecraft. A hundred and eighty thousand people were killed. I witnessed this myself in New York where a number of craft strafed Manhattan. Los Angeles, London, Paris, and many other cities were targeted. Indeed this conference centre is built upon area devastated by the Martian assault. I'm glad Palestine-Israel has not had that experience; if you did you might understand our trauma."

Fransky flushed. "No, Mr Quilley." He sneered sarcastically. "We only had our people loaded onto a railway carts and shipped off to Auschwitz and Treblinka...."

"Alright, alright, alright!" Caxton's interjected again. "Once again we're drifting off topic and into personal recriminations. Let's remember this is a formal meeting."

Fransky shrugged. "Of course, Mr Caxton. I was merely suggesting that these gentlemen may have made a mistake by allowing the potential threat from Mars to dominate so much of our foreign policies. Remember that following Mars Day there have been only two further attacks by Martian gunships; that transatlantic liner that was sunk in March forty-eight of course; and, last Christmas I believe, a camel train in Mongolia was forced to flee for warning shot." He raised his eyebrows. "Gentlemen, history is naturally shaped by events, but this is the first time ever that history has been shaped merely by what *might* happen. We truly are living in the age of the politics of fear."

After a long silence Caxton's spoke. "Mr Fransky, maybe you're correct, but perhaps the fear in modern politics is well justified. As HG Wells said in what has turned out to be his very prophetic work of fiction, they must have been watching us for a long time before the strike. Mars Day was clearly a demonstration, an act of terrorism. They targeted residential districts, symbolic buildings. It was a message that in a real war of the worlds, we would most certainly be defeated. It is clear that the other planets of our solar system are far more technologically advanced than we are. We have no weapons that can match theirs. If they want us dead, we'll be dead. It's that simple. People have got used to living under the shadow these last few years; it's like the A-bomb."

Everybody at the table became subdued.

"What do they want from us?" asked new speaker.

"Hopefully we'll find the answer to your question on Friday." answered Clane. The meeting cooled down after that and went on for another two hours in a calmer tone, addressing less contentious and more mundane subjects. They closed at five PM and walked down to the river Liffey for a drink at a pub. Zvegintsov came with them; this was one Irish tradition he was willing to respect, although he drank only vodka and never Guinness. A group of off-duty Red Army soldiers were intimidated by his presence so quickly drank up and left; Clane and the others took their table. For a while it was tense because Avenbois and Zvegintsov refused to speak to each other, as did Fransky and Avenbois... and for that matter did Fransky and Zvegintsov. Then a live band began to play, and the mood lightened. All the men hummed along to the *uilleann* pipes and tapped their feet to the rhythm of *bodhran*. Irish dancing girls in traditional dress jigged and reeled back and forth, and soon the whole pub was clapping and singing. Clane got up to buy a round at the bar and Caxton joined him to help him carry the drinks. He leaned on the bar top and ran his finger along the edge of a drip tray. He turned to Clane and said: "Ben Fransky's got a point, don't you think? It has been generally pretty quiet up there since Mars Day?" He stared intensely and gravely into Clane's eyes as if he was saying something highly significant, but didn't want explain what.

After two pints, Clane walked back to Stoneybatter through the dark dank winter evening to do some more work in his study. At eight pm. he left for the entrance and was driven to the famous Gresham Hotel where all the VIP delegates were lodged. He was served dinner and then retired to his room. He was about to undress when there was a knock at the door. He went over and opened it.

"Hello!" The cheesy face of Gerald Caxton loomed in front of him.

"Mr Caxton?"

"Wondered if you fancied a nightcap, old boy." He held up a hip bottle of Jameson whiskey. Clane invited him in cautiously. He felt some discomfort with Caxton as he had in his office earlier. He noticed that Caxton had a large case in his right hand. "What's that, Mr Caxton?"

"Please call me Gerald. May I call you Clane?"

He was standing closer to Clane than was normal for somebody he didn't know. His wide penetrating eyes were fixed on Clane's. For a moment Clane wondered if Caxton were a homosexual attempting to seduce him. "My wife and I enjoy swift drink before bed." Clane pointed out while he fetched two glasses from the bathroom shelf.

"Really? I thought you were separated from her."

Clane frowned. "How did you know that?"

"His Majesty's government furnishes me with information on all the delegates of this event. You know how the game is played,

Clane." He poured out two shots from a bottle. "Your good health, old boy."

"*Slainte Mhaith*." The strawberry taste of the Irish whiskey was totally different from Scotch. As soon as Clane had taken his first sip, Caxton topped up his glass with a generous double. "Easy does it, Gerald. We've got an early start."

"Call yourself a paddy!" joshed Caxton; then he walked over to one of the walls and removed the picture that was hanging there.

"What are you doing, Gerald?"

"Making a screen." Caxton lifted the case onto the table and unfastened its clasp. As soon as it was opened Clane saw instantly that it was a portable movie projector. Tucked into the side pocket was a circular film can.

"What's this?"

"I want to show you something." Caxton unlooped the flex and plugged it into a wall socket; then he fixed the reel to the machine. "Switch the light off would you, old boy?" Clane flicked the switch on the wall and the room was plunged into darkness, save the streetlight sifting through the curtains. Caxton switched on the machine and it cast a square block of light onto the blank wall where the picture had hung; the whirring it made was the only sound. The countdown frames ran down through from ten to one and the film began. It was a silent, grainy home movie with watery colours. It had been shot on a handheld camera on top of a tall building in New York City and the object of the film was the Empire State Building. The tower had just been struck by a projectile of some kind because there was a gaping hole in one of its oblong flanks about two thirds of the way up. Black smoke wafted from the cavity rising and expanding into a cloud over Manhattan. Flames licked at the edge of the gash. A Martian spacecraft hovered a few hundred feet away.

"What's this in aid of?" asked Clane.

"You've seen this movie before?"

"Of course I have; who hasn't? It's been shown on TV endless times. It's the Danlue film."

"Yes, shot by Alfred Danlue on Tuesday, the 15th of July 1947, Mars Day.

Clane felt sorrow rising in him, as he always did when he thought about what happened to New York on Mars Day. "She was the world's tallest building, stood over our town for sixteen years... Why are you showing me this? If you know so much about me, you'll know I'm a New Yorker; so I find this very distressing to watch."

"Apologies, Clane, but it's important that you see this."

"Why? Like I said, I've seen it already."

"Not all of it."

"Eh?"

"You've only seen the first five minutes, that's all that was broadcast on TV and newsreels; the rest was considered unsuitable by the networks. However, Alfred Danlue shot over twelve minutes of footage altogether."

Clane took another gulp of whisky.

"What is the attitude to your work in America, Clane?"

"Well, the Dewey administration has persisted with the same policy as President Martin. My budget has been fixed at the same level. The Department of the Army and Navy are still directed by my military staff committee."

"Is that policy popular?"

Clane shrugged awkwardly. "Not with everybody. I have my opponents on Capitol Hill. There's an entire tendency that wants to reinstate the Truman Doctrine. They're led by this young idiot from California called Richard Nixon."

"What motivates them?"

Clane looked up at him quizzically. "Don't you know? Hasn't your PM Mosley ranted about it enough? They blame me for the Red Flood. Martin cancelled all the communist containment strategies and the world has been left defenceless in the face of Soviet expansionism. Harry S had a whole list of plots to stop it, everything from bribery to subversion to paramilitary war."

"What would the world look like if the original post war package had remained in place?"

Clane chuckled. He experienced a sudden image of Flying Buffalo in his head. "What *would* have happened? That's the same as asking what does not exist."

"It's an interesting thought experiment. Indulge me."

"Well... The Ruskies would have met far more resistance in their move westwards. We had dedicated a huge effort to install democratic governments in Western Europe and provide cash to redevelop them. Also a military force to deter Soviet aggression. I can easily imagine the scenario in which they would never dare even to stray from behind Churchill's Iron Curtain. We'd have a free West Germany, Holland, France, Italy. Franco would probably be replaced by a less belligerent leader in Spain and Mosley wouldn't have been elected in your country. It seems impossible now."

"And the Russians have the A-bomb too."

"I know." Clane said grimly.

"Yes, our commitment to meeting the danger of Martian invasion has cost us dearly. We've allowed communism to take over almost half the world. And, as Ben Fransky said, because of just a single day of attacks. I do sometimes wonder, was it worth it?"

Clane didn't respond.

"Well look at this and you'll wonder no longer." Caxton tapped his shoulder and pointed at the screen. A large chunk of concrete had just fallen off the iconic tower's art deco structure. "It's almost time."

"Are we about to see the collapse?"

"Yes. This is the part considered unsuitable for TV."

Clane braced himself. He'd read many descriptions of the demise of New York's most prominent landmark, but this was going to be the first time he had seen it. It happened very quickly. The spired cap of the tower suddenly dropped down into the rest of the building, pushing out a thick cloud of grey dust. The walls fell outwards like the skin of a peeling banana while a column of darker dust shot upwards from the heart of the gigantic tower. Concrete shanks of the building fell to one side trailing a comet tail of fume behind them. A spherical bubble of particulate expanded larger and larger until it enveloped the cameraman. Clane was trembling; his heart pounding.

"Incredible." Caxton's face leered, his wide eyes were transfixed. The light from the screen glinted on his corneas and illuminated his facial skin in the darkness. "Such power." He looked almost greedy.

A flash of anger passed through Clane's head. "Power that killed people in my hometown!"

Caxton ignored him. "People have been talking about how the impact of the missile and the subsequent fire caused the building to collapse, but that's not what happened."

In the film the dust cloud began to clear and the crosshatch cityscape of Manhattan slowly materialised in the haze. The familiar skyscrapers looked foreign with the huge gap left by the absence of the Empire State Building. "Look, Clane. There's hardly any rubble. You visited the Crater; shouldn't it be piled two hundred feet high with broken masonry? How can a twelve hundred foot skyscraper just vanish into thin air?"

"Does it matter?"

"Very much indeed." In the film, the black disc of the Manhattan gunship was still there. Stationary in the air; calmly surveying its victim like a victorious vulture. "It struck the wall with a projectile." Caxton nodded. "But the destruction of the building involved a totally different process."

"What you mean?"

"A process that can release energy able to dissolve half a million tons of steel and concrete into a cloud of fumes. Maybe it is connected to the technology that drives their spacecraft."

Clane gulped down half his glass of whisky.

Caxton turned and looked at him. Half his face was in shadow, the other half was tinged with the wash of the movie colours. "Interplanetary war?" He quoted "A war is when *two* armies fight each other. Against these visitors there can be no war. The weapon to do what they did to the world's greatest building... What if they unleashed it on a city, a country, a continent? Even the H-bomb is nothing compared to such a destructive force."

Clane nodded. His mouth was numb.

"Clane, have you ever wondered, since 1947, that maybe it would have been better if people simply hadn't found out about the extraterrestrials? In this context, isn't ignorance truly bliss?"

....

Clane was troubled all night by disturbing dreams. Gerald Caxton appeared in many of them. His normally carefree face was scowling. He pointed his finger and snarled: "It's your fault, Clane! It's *all* your fault!" Clane also found himself back at the mouldy tenement block in Cork that he had seen two days previously. This time he couldn't turn away as he watched the people go about their lives in destitution. He woke to his alarm at 7 AM. It was still dark outside and his mouth tasted treacly from the previous night's whisky. From the moment he got out of bed he sensed the party atmosphere. People outside in the streets were whooping and chatting animatedly. The hotel guests talked about nothing else at breakfast; as did his chauffeur who drove him to Stoneybatter. In the ballroom, rows of a dozen television sets were arranged around a huge chamber, all wide screen and colour. By nine AM every seat was full. The only programme was a live broadcast from the Leninsky-Turatam rocket centre in the Kazakh SSR. In a few hours time the Athena-Zvereya-One rocket would launch into earth orbit carrying Major Rodger Murgatroyd, the first man in space. The silver coloured rocket ship stood above the empty desert on its launch pad, quietly waiting to perform its glorious duty. On its flank was embossed both the American and Soviet flags. The Russian built spacecraft had a flared base consisting of four booster rockets that would separate a few minutes into the flight like the first stages of a missile. The TV reporter was Marguerite Higgins, the famous war correspondent. The presence of such a prestigious journalist indicated the significance of the event. A man approached the camera dressed in a spacesuit *sans* helmet. Miss Higgins raised a handheld microphone. "Maj. Murgatroyd, had you feel?"

"Excited." Roger Murgatroyd was an AAF fighter pilot who had seen action in Europe during the war. He was a gentle-voiced middle aged man with greying curly hair and sideburns. "I've enjoyed a good lunch with my Soviet and American colleagues, having a last minute brush up on my Russian. I'd like to thank the Soviet Space Agency, and the American Aeronautical and Space Administration..." He went on to explain how he wished to dedicate his flight to the twelve Americans, eighteen Russians and six people of other nationalities who had died during the development of the international space programme. Then he departed on a bus for the launch pad a few miles away.

The atmosphere among the viewers in the ballroom was tense. The space programme had begun in early 1948 and the first three rockets had all exploded on launch. The first artificial satellite, Terra-One. Has reached orbit in January 1949, and a few months later a piglet called Alexei had survived for forty-eight hours in space before dying of hypoxia. Now, for the first time ever, a human being was about to leave his home planet. The viewers in Stoneybatter were riveted in front of their TV screens, as were people at home and in pubs. The streets of Dublin were as quiet as a Sunday morning, as most were all over the world, as the news reported. Every nation, even in time zones where it was the middle of the night when the launch of the Athena-Zvereya took place, were alert and awake; families were clustered in front of TVs and radios. Groups of students were holding all night parties.

At Leninsky-Turatam, the camera was focused on the rocket. The voices of mission control were audible on the soundtrack. Maj. Murgatroyd was carried up the launch tower on a lift to the top of the craft where the capsule was. A tiny cap on the pinacle of the giant silver tower. The conference delegates leaned forward to the edge of their seats as the countdown began. The launch gantry moved away leaving the rocket standing naked against the bleak landscape. At the one minute mark vapour began to issue from the metallic cylindrical body and the supporting blooms bowed to the side. "Ten... nine... eight..." The launch master counted down the last few seconds. There was a flash of fire from under the rocket nozzle. This rose to a raging inferno and the two hundred ton craft rose from the launch pad, smoothly and steadily as if were hoisted by a crane. A huge cheer broke out in the hall. Joyful voices could be heard on the TV soundtrack too. "Athena-One is on its way!" said Miss Higgins. "Man's first steps into space, on this day Wednesday the 18th of January 1950; a day that will be remembered forever."

"This is an empty gesture."

Clane started and swung round to see Gerald Caxton sitting beside him. He had been so engrossed in the TV coverage that had noticed the Englishman slipping into the seat beside him.

The rocket had three stages once the boosters had been jettisoned. A camera inside the capsule gave the viewer a unique TV experience. The picture was low resolution and monochrome, but one could clearly see Murgatroyd pressing buttons on the control panel with a two foot reaching stick. Telescopes on earth traced the Athena-Zvereya on its journey. The orbital stage reached a fixed altitude after it achieved escape velocity. Murgatroyd was at rest, floating weightless, one hundred and five miles above the earth's surface. He spoke calmly about his feelings and sensations. What the planet earth looked like that such a high level; what microgravity felt like. After ninety minutes the craft had completed an entire celestial circumnavigation and it was time to burn its descent rockets. These slowed the craft to a velocity which allowed it to fall back towards the earth. When it entered the atmosphere it began to heat up from aerofriction. The craft had an insulating shield to keep the interior cool. There were twenty minutes of tension because the TV and radio signals were cut off at the time. Then the craft's parachutes deployed and Maj. Murgatroyd checked in to confirm that he had survived re-entry. The scorched spherical descent stage thumped into the icy ground of the Siberian tundra and the search began for it by aircraft. Another delighted public bellow broke out when, about half an hour later, Soviet Space Agency helicopters reported that the capsule was intact. The aircraft landed and technicians opened the hatch; and a healthy and unhurt first astronaut climbed out and stood beside it waving. A massive celebration broke out all over the world. No extraterrestrial spacecraft were anywhere to be seen around the rocket at any time on its journey.

....

Clane was invited to be interviewed by the BBC. The corporation has set up a studio in one of the first floor offices of the conference centre. The room had been skilfully jury-rigged with cameras and lights. The female presenter sat opposite him on the settee and spoke in an accent similar to Caxton's. "Ladies and gentlemen, we're joined today by the American Secretary for Interplanetary War, Clane Quilley. Welcome Mr Quilley."

"Thank you."

"Interplanetary War? Could that be construed as an inappropriate title, considering the objectives of this summit?"

Clane chuckled. "It's sad your Mr Orwell has just passed away; he would appreciate that."

"How did you end up head of a brand new government department? Unusually you're not a politician."

"Correct. I've never been an elected congressman; I've never even sat on my local council. My background is in journalism. President Truman recruited me to his press staff and President Martin appointed me SecIntWar during the state of emergency following the Mars Day attacks. After his election, President Dewey kept me on."

"I assumed this was because of your report on the Martian spacecraft that crashed in Roswell, New Mexico in 1947."

"Yes, I was the first reporter in the world to cover the extraterrestrial presence. Up until then the earth has existed in ignorance of the fact that outer space is inhabited. I revealed the truth that we are just one among at least three independent civilisations in the universe."

"And thanks to you, we also know what the Martians look like."

"Do we?"

"Yes, you've seen them."

"Not the Martians themselves."

"Well... Yes. Don't you remember? You visited the place where the Martians were being held in captivity... Mr Quilley?"

Clane didn't reply. His head was reeling. The BBC presenter was of course talking about Clane's tour of the facility in the AAF Technical Data Section at Wright Field in July of 1947. There he'd seen the wreckage and the beings captured near Roswell. This was the first time he had thought about it in years. How could he possibly have forgotten? "Er... Sorry, yes. I was taken to see what was found at Roswell along with a handful of other reporters. You must have seen the TV interviews of my experience. Two days later, of course, the world changed for ever."

"Had you forgotten? You looked baffled when I asked."

"Well, you know what it was like when those attacks happened. All of us forgot an awful lot on that day for a very long time; we had to."

The BBC presenter nodded and changed the subject. "Did you see the Athena-One launch earlier?"

"Oh yes, it was magnificent. I've wired my official congratulations to Major Murgatroyd, the first man in space."

"So now we are also a star-faring planet just like Mars and Venus."

"Yes indeed. Hopefully they will be as impressed as we are."

"It's no coincidence that the launch of Athena-One was chosen two days before the summit, is it?"

"Naturally not. It's only fair that before we meet our celestial neighbours we do so on equal terms."

"But we're a long way from being their equals. Definitely we have achieved something great by sending a man up into space, but he only stayed up there for an hour. We can't fly to Mars the way they can fly to earth."

"Not yet, but today's launch is the first step. Our engineers are making more progress every day. Within ten years we will have men on the moon too. Soon after that we will be will be returning the favour by sending our own embassy to Mars and Venus."

The reporter smiled. "I look forward to it. Thank you, Mr Quilley."

....

The sun set over the tree-lined rooftops of Dublin. Its reddish golden glow filtered through the bare winter twigs and television aerials. Venus, the evening star and home to some of their approaching guests, followed the luminous sphere below the horizon. Stars began appearing in the indigo twilight above the city. First the brighter ones, then the others. "Perfect." said Gerald Caxton. "Not the cloud in the sky." By six PM it was completely dark on this January night. The street lights had been left off and the streets were chilled and black. The headlights of Soviet tanks moved among the lighted squares of windows. The sound of marching boots reverberating off the walls as the Red Army were deployed in force. "We had to cut a balance." Caxton explained to the people around him. "We don't want the visitors to come down in the beads of a million gun sights, but at the same time we need to careful. Just three years ago this city was bombarded from space and five hundred and fifty-six Dubliners killed. We have three regiments of mixed cavalry and foot. Should be a nice compromise... Anything, Brodie?"

Sitting a few feet away from Caxton was a man with a radio telephone headset. He was in constant communication with the League of the World's air defence command. "Nothing unusual, Mr Caxton." All commercial flights over Ireland were cancelled this evening. There was a no-fly zone covering the whole of Leinster.

"Could you call Sergeant Borisov and asked him to turn the lights down a bit?"

"How much by?"

"Say sixty percent." The row of floodlights illuminating the area dimmed perceptibly. The hum of the generators powering them reduced slightly in pitch. The warning beacon on top of the Wellington Monument became visible through the glare. It had been hastily installed that morning when somebody suggested that the two hundred foot stone obelisk might be a hazard to their guests. Phoenix Park had been transformed. One of the large green spaces had been fenced off and covered with a metal tiled floor. Lines were painted on it like an airport runway. Beside this workmen had assembled a sloping terrace of spectator seats, similar to those at a sports arena. TV cameras were set up all over the place and reporters from all over the world were making introductory broadcasts in front of them. Clane stomped his feet and rubbed his hands together. His breath condensed in the icy air in front of his face as he stared upwards at the clear heavens, now an inky black pool devoid of stars because of the glare from the lights. "What time did they say they'd be here?" asked Clane.

Caxton scoffed. "God knows. We told them seven PM on the 20th; but maybe they don't understand our clock and calendar."

"Did they acknowledge?"

"Yes, but just with a basic 'received an understood'."

"Mr Caxton!" The communications operative called him. "Aerospace command reports three contacts approaching from the east."

Everyone turned and stared in the direction of the sea, but Clane could see nothing.

"We have a visual!" yelled the communicator. "Unit nine at Dalkey. Three objects approaching from the east, brightly-lit, two are saucers one is a triangle."

"Venusian and Martian!" said Clane, feeling a thrill rise within him. The crowd in the stands gasped and began murmuring with excitement. A trio of white lights rose from above the roof of the conference centre. They brightened and diverged as they approached.

"What speed!" somebody said. "They came in from the radar horizon less than a minute."

There was a stunned silence from the thousands of people watching. The three lights skirted north and arranged themselves into a triangle to the west above the dark unlit park and suburbs of Dublin. Then one of the three increased its brightness until it felt like the area was illuminated by a giant spotlight. The light suddenly dimmed as the focus of its spotlight beam was trained downwards. By now the outline of the saucer-shaped cruiser was discernible in the floodlights. A spotlight from the ground also tracked the craft down. Clane recognized it as Martian, but he had never seen one this close before. The black disc-shaped spacecraft didn't make a single sound until its landing gear lowered with a hiss and a click. Its hull was as polished and smooth as a garnet pebble, without any fixtures or fittings. What looked like a single window was a square crystal jewel on the upper portion. Clane then noticed a very faint musical hum like a bee's nest coming from the craft, so quiet that it was inaudible before. With a penetrating thump, the craft from Mars touched down on the metal runway. Its landing pads skidded briefly then got purchase. The humming reduced in volume but not pitch, until it faded away. There was silence all over the assembled masses. Some exotic animal noises in the distance to their right indicated that the residents of Dublin Zoo were upset by the strange new arrival. There was a cracking noise from the craft and chink of light appeared. An oblong door swung open revealing a glowing aquamarine screen behind it. A set of metal folding steps rolled out and lowered themselves to the ground. There was a deafening whine of shock and exhilaration from the crowd as a humanoid silhouette appeared in front of the screen. One step at a time, the creature from Mars descended from the craft to the ground. Its shiny black boots paused for a moment on the bottom step and then it placed its left foot on to the metal decking. Clane and the others leaned forward in terror and fascination.

The Martian looked like a huge man about six foot five in height. Its arms and legs had prominent muscles pressed against its skin tight white leotard-like garment. On top of the leotard it wore a stiff tunic that resembled leather. The tunic was dark purple with some star-like jewellery embossed on it. The entity's face and forearms were exposed and its skin was grass green. It facial features were also very human and on its head was a bizarre hat that appeared to be made of black fur with streamers of silver foil hanging off it. Everybody jumped as the creature spoke in a booming, imperious voice: "KA JAMBA DOO DOO KEE LO LO OTSHA!"

There was a petrified pause. "Clane, what's it saying?" hissed Caxton.

Clane flicked hastily through the dictionary section of the Martian language guide book. "It says: 'Take me to your leader'." He felt everybody's eyes on him. He waited in case they didn't really mean what he thought they meant; but then Caxton told him: "Go on, Clane! Reply to it!"

Clane forced his body into motion and walked forward until he was ten feet away from the Martian. He felt exposed in the open in front of all those people, lit harshly by the floodlights and the flicker of camera flash. He could see the Martian's eyes on him. They were wide and withering with brown irises. He took one last look at a page in the book and spoke to the creature its own language: "Hello, Mr Ambassador. My name is Clane Quilley. I am the spokesman for this embassy. On behalf of the leaders and citizens of all the nations of my planet, welcome to earth."

Camera bulbs redoubled their flashing in the gloom behind him; they flicked on the Martian's emerald skin. Without changing its neutral facial expression, the being raised its right hand in greeting. "BOO TABBA MOBO EEBIK RA!"

Clane understood immediately and relief washed through system. He turned to the expectant crowd and yelled: "He says he comes in peace!...'I come in peace'!...'I come in peace'!... 'I come in peace'!" The crowd rose like thunder; as if this was the goal of a sports match. The Martian ambassador smiled for the first time.

The Venusian ship landed soon afterwards. It was distinguishable from the Martians' by its shape; it was triangular and looked identical to the craft that had followed the submarine into Cork Harbour. The Venusian ambassador was also humanoid, but was very different in several ways. Its skin was blue and it was far shorter, only about five-foot-three. It had a long white beard and was dressed in a loosely fitting saffron robe. No other beings exited either spaceship. As soon as they had dropped off their passengers, the two vehicles silently rose back into the sky until they had once more become mere points of light. They both joined the third point of light, an object that had remained at a distance; and all three shot vertically up into the sky. Within just a few seconds they'd dimmed to nothing at the zenith.

....

"I guess we'll have to call them 'he'." said Clane.

"They do look masculine; I hope we haven't got that wrong" Caxton raised an eyebrow to Clane. They were in the dining room of the Gresham Hotel on O'Connell Street. Clane was sitting at the table to the right of the Martian ambassador. The rest of the table was taken up with local and international dignitaries. General Zvegintsov was there along with the *Taoiseach*, John Costello and the other summit delegates. Both extraterrestrial VIPs had been checked into the hotel's finest rooms. They had no luggage, but looked around their chambers approvingly. A crowd of curious onlookers were pressed against the windows. Newspaper flashbulbs blinked occasionally like lightning. The Martian was eagerly tucking into his barbecued Guinea fowl and *Paté de Fois Gras* with artichoke hearts, Savoy cabbage and sauté potatoes. He seemed completely adept at handling terrestrial eating utensils. "Is that tasty?" Clane asked him his best Martian.

"Yes, thank you." The ambassador replied. "Earth food and drink is delicious." He picked up his glass and took a long sip of his Argentine Cabernet Sauvignon. He licked his full lips with a red tongue.

The Venusian delegate had yet to speak more than just a brief greeting. He ate in silence with his vanilla blue eyelids drooped. He paused to dab his snowy moustache with a flannel napkin. Waiters arrive for the next course. Then there was desert and after dinner chocolates and brandy. "Oh, sod all this!" said Costello, knocking back his brandy in one gulp. "Let's take these fellers down the pub!"

"Do you think that's a good idea?" Caxton asked fearfully.

"They're not just on earth; they're in Ireland, Mr Caxton. They can't come to Ireland and not visit a pub."

Caxton nodded reluctantly and got down to make the arrangements. The entourage left the Gresham and walked down O'Connell Street. The two extraterrestrials curiously examined the sights around them. The security detail and Red Army guards kept the throng of onlookers at bay. They crossed over the Liffey and entered Temple Bar. Caxton went ahead to try and find a pub which was suitable in terms of security. The Martian had to bow his lofty head to fit under the lower lintel of a small pub on Anglesey Street. The two aliens studied their pints of Guinness carefully before drinking them. The Martian smiled at Clane and nodded his approval. He smoked a cigar with equal gusto.

"What is Mars like?" asked Clane as his charge puffed away.

The alien paused; for the first time he looked nonplussed. "It is a lovely place."

"Does everybody on Mars look like you? Because I once saw one of your people, one of those in the craft crashed at Roswell. He looked very different to you."

The ambassador paused for a long time. "I know who you mean. They live on another part of the planet." He smiled thinly "Excuse me." He walked away to the restroom, accompanied by a secret service agent.

Clane noticed that Caxton had been eavesdropping on his conversation. The Englishman looked nervous and pale.

....

The following day the summit opened. Clane began with the customary TV and radio interviews; then he proceeded to the ballroom for the first session. This time Caxton was not chairing and an elderly English lady did that. She was dressed in a formal black gown like a judge. Clane was a speaking delegate at the event, but he also had to act as extraterrestrial language interpreter. Because of the social the previous night, Clane's Martian was now fairly sharp, but he had yet to converse with the Venusian ambassador. The two non-terrestrial delegates had yet even to acknowledge each other. The moment they were forced to, the meeting burst into a raucous and vitriolic argument of which Clane could only follow a few words. The chairwoman banged her gavel repeatedly on the table. "Gentlemen! Gentlemen! Silence both of you. This is not the place for a slanging match. You will speak one at a time and you will speak calmly and clearly, remembering your speech must be translated into human language. Understood?" Both beings nodded while glowering at each other. They then described their dispute while Clane translated for the rest of the members. It basically ran thus:

Mars: *The reason for Venusian aggression is the result of their defeat in the Metal War. Fourteen thousand earth years ago, Martian prospectors found valuable mineral deposits on the planet you called Ceres. Venus tried to invade and illegally occupy Ceres. They were driven off the planet by the Martian army in a legitimate use of force.*

Venus: *The Martian ambassador is lying. Ceres was not their Martian territory to defend. According to the (untranslatable) Treaty. Ceres' orbit is such that seventy percent of the time it lies within Venusian controlled space. Mars are the invaders, not Venus.*

Mars: *Totally false. Interplanetary law is very clear on the ownership of natural resources' within the solar system. Our prospectors laid claim to the deposit completely lawfully. If Venus had not stolen our rights to mine, we would not have contested the sovereignty of Ceres.*

Venus: *The Martian invaders' response was to attack our orbiting space colonies. A million Venusians died in those assaults.*

The two beings explained in more detail the intricacies of their dispute. They had been a war for all those fourteen millennia since then and a billion of their people had been killed. Benjamin Fransky and the rest of the Palestinian-Israeli contingent appeared genuinely moved by their predicament. "Gentlemen, I'm so sorry." Fransky said. "I know what it's like to experience war, though not one nearly as destructive as yours."

"This is all very well." said the more stoic Zvegintsov. "But why did Mars attack earth? Why did your warships descend onto this planet and bombard our cities killing thousands of people all over the world?"

There was a long pause. "We apologise." said the Martian ambassador dispassionately. "It was a strategic error."

The Venusian scoffed. "They acted impulsively on bad intelligence. They thought we were about to approach you and offer you an alliance."

Clane shook his head. "But we had no idea you even existed."

"We know." said Venus. "When we invented radio wave communication and space transport about twenty thousand earth years ago, we discovered we were not alone in the universe. Before long we and Mars learnt to interact and cooperate, as different nations do on your planet. We soon realized that there was a third planet with intelligent life on it; earth. You were far less technically advanced than Mars and Venus, so we both agreed to leave you alone until you had progressed independently to a comparable level to ourselves. We monitored you carefully, even though we know some of you would see our craft flying in your atmosphere; and even our people on the rare occasions we stepped out onto your surface. But we knew few of you would ever understand what we were. We watched and waited. There was just one problem."

Mars nodded. "Your moon."

"Correct. We investigated your unique satellite. We on Venus have no moon; no airless and lifeless world on which we could extract minerals or conduct scientific experiments that would be impossible on a living planet. Mars has only two very small satellites as well, you call them Phobos and Deimos. We on Venus disagreed with Mars on whether it was ethical to use the moon."

"The moon is not related to your planet!" exclaimed Mars. "It happens to orbit the earth; that's all. You were incapable of reaching it and would not have even noticed, let alone incurred damage, loss or injury had another planet exploited it. However Venus tried to force us to categorise the moon under the same directive that forbade us from making open contact with the earth. We received word from our spies on Venus that elements of their government wanted to breach the isolation directive and make an overt landing, beginning formal interaction with your people. That was a misunderstanding. We chose to maintain the current situation, but then we suffered an accident. One of our vessels crashed on your planet."

"Roswell?" said Clane.

"Yes. We realised that your people now had undeniable proof that we existed. Therefore our analysts concluded that Venus would go ahead with the breach of the isolation directive. We decided there was only one option. Regrettably, we chose a preemptive warning to the earth not to form an alliance with Venus."

"Something we have no intention of offering!" spat the Venusian ambassador.

A hint of red appeared on Mars' green cheeks. He bowed his head "Yes, we know that now; we are very sorry."

"You wished to carry out terrorist attacks against us?" asked Yann Avenbois.

"I have been sent by the Martian government to offer apologies and reparations." A murmur broke out in the room.

"Quiet please!" interjected the chairwoman.

Mars continued. "We will pay compensation in the form of valuable mineral ore, seeing as our money is not exchangeable with yours. This payment will begin the moment your planet reaches a level of technology for which these materials will become suitable. Also both Venus and Mars have now agreed to a new proposal to allow your planet a state of neutrality in the Metal War. We have both pledged not to breach it. It involves returning your moon to your complete and permanent sovereignty. There are valuable resources there which your people can use in the future when you have learnt to cross the gulfs of outer space. In the meantime we will both depart your world. Both Martian and Venusian ships will avoid your planetary system for the foreseeable future. When your planet develops the technology to send spacecraft to Mars and Venus, we ask you not to. We will only communicate with each other on matters of urgency."

The terrestrial delegates all exchanged looks.

The new Dublin Treaty didn't take long to ratify. The total exclusion zone was set at a distance of ten thousand miles beyond the mean orbital distance of the Moon's far pole, and the paperwork was drawn up. The Martian and Venusian signed on the dotted line; their signatures in their peculiar extraterrestrial script, and then all the terrestrial delegates put their names to their copies. Camera bulb flashed as they all warmly shook hands together. Even the Martian and Venusian smiled for the photographers; their green and blue hands clasped. They all went outside and the chairwoman delivered the news to the masses gathered in the park. A deafening cheer went up. Clane looked at Gerald Caxton. The latter was almost weeping. "This is such a relief, Clane; such a relief. It's over... It's finally all over. I wondered if it ever would be. I thought it might be too late."

Clane looked at him curiously. There something strange about the way he had spoken.

Everybody assembled that evening to say farewell to the Martian and Venusian ambassadors. The two beings warmly shook the hands of all the people assembled and then boarded their spacecraft. This time the disk and triangle rose into the air together in formation, until they became a pair of lights shining side by side in recognition of the new accord between their two planets.

As he lay in his bed at the Gresham that night, Clane hoped that their cooperation over the fate of the earth would lead to a warming of relations between the two of them and maybe even an end to their long brutal war. Clane found himself more raptured by the situation than he'd expected. Perhaps that explained Caxton's unusual behaviour.

The following morning Clane was taken to the airport for his journey home to the United States. He flew on one of the new jet engined airliners that were becoming more and more common. They cut the transatlantic flight time down to just nine hours. As he reclined in the first class compartment, Clane had a lot of time to think. The emotion of the previous day had worn off allowing rationality to return. What would the Dublin Treaty mean for his career? Was there a role for the Department of Interplanetary War in a peaceful solar system? How would the end of the Martian threat affect politics here on earth? The plane landed at Washington National Airport with those questions still unanswered in his mind. As he walked down the jetway he was immediately surrounded by Secret Service guards "Sorry, Mr Secretary." One of them said. "We've got a bit of trouble." Clane stepped into a car. As his driver guided them out to the airport car park Clane saw a large crowd of people being held back by the police. Their faces were menacing and they were shouting. Clane couldn't hear the words, but he could read the placards and banners they were carrying: *QUILLEY= TRAITOR!... WAR WITH MARS NOW!... REMEMBER NEW YORK!... KILL QUILLEY!... QUILLEY IS AN APPEASER!... PROTECT EARTH- NUKE MARS!*

Chapter 9

"Looks fake to me."

"Be quiet, young lady." ordered Gina.

"Haven't you got college in the morning, Siobhan?" asked Clane.

His seventeen year old daughter pursed her lips in a recalcitrant manner. "Yeah, so? This is a historical one off."

"You just said it's fake."

"Lori says it is; she reckons it's being filmed in Hollywood."

"That girl's a fool; let's watch." The TV coverage had been running non-stop for three hours now. It was one AM. Clane got two more bottles of beer from the fridge and some Coca Cola for his daughter. The colour TV picture showed a scene in space being filmed from a fixed camera on the Athena-Zvereya-Seven spacecraft. A short distance away was a spider-like eight-legged structure floating in space. A short while ago it had been attached to the spherical command module of the Athena-Zvereya; now it was moving independently, powered by its own rockets. In rotated a few degrees allowing a better view of its bulbous gourd-shaped crew compartment, placed on top of the octagon of the descent stage. Scrolling across the background was the surface of the moon. The American-built Icarus lander drew further and further away as it began its long fall towards its destiny.

"Amazing!" muttered Gina as she sipped her beer. "Who could believe we would one day be sitting here watching people land on the Moon. Seems only a few years ago we got aeroplanes to travel in." Five days earlier the world has held its breath again as the Athena-Zvereya rocket took off from Leninsky-Turatam. It orbited the earth three times and rendezvoused with the unmanned booster rockets that had been launched a few days earlier. This gave the Athena-Zvereya-Seven the extra kick it needed to escape earth orbit and head for the moon. Once in lunar orbit, the Icarus craft detached and headed for the moon carrying astronauts Robert Pelson, Michael McKintock, and Zoya Meishriokova who was also the first woman in space. The fourth crew member, Boris Borodin, remained behind to operate the command module. "He must feel really left out of the party." noted Siobhan.

Clane dropped off into a doze as the TV commentary became repetitive during the uneventful descent of the Icarus. Then Gina jogged him. "Clane, they're about to touchdown."

The camera had shifted to one on board the Icarus. The surface of the moon was a bright battleship grey. It was creased and cracked like an elephant's skin. Features on its surface moved in the picture as the spacecraft moved. The voices of the astronauts speaking to mission control consisted of numbers and times. Their voices were calm and professional as they read out their attitude, speed and the amount of fuel they had left. Clane was unsure of what was going on until the shadow of the Icarus appeared on the bright sun washed surface. Then one of the astronauts said: "Tranquillity Base here, the Icarus has landed." Everybody in the TV studio cheered. An hour later Pelson emerged from the hatch of the craft and descended the ladder. As he placed his boots on the lunar surface he said emphatically. "That's one small step for man, one giant leap for planet earth." Shortly afterwards McKintock and Meishriokova climbed down to join him.

"Honey?"

"Hmm?" Gina had just pushed him awake. He was still sitting in his armchair. Daylight was shining through the curtains. The TV was still on and the three astronauts were still bouncing around the lunar landscape in their white space suits, the low gravity of the moon making them appear to move in slow motion. The American and Soviet flags stood together in front of the Icarus lander.

"It's seven-thirty. Don't you have to work?"

"Erm... yes." Clane showered and brushed his teeth, hoping he didn't smell of the beer he'd drunk. Then he dressed in a suit and went downstairs to greet the Secret Service bodyguards. There were only three assigned to him now; a downgrade from the ten he'd had two years ago after the controversy surrounding the Dublin Treaty. That had died down after a month or so. The extraterrestrials had kept their word and departed; and the human space programme had distracted the public's negative feelings. One of his security detail would accompany Siobhan to college and the other two would stick with Clane. Gina received no protection at all because she and Clane were still legally divorced. Gina kissed him on the cheek as he straightened his tie in the hall mirror. "You look wonderful, honey." she whispered in his ear "I can't believe I ever left you."

He looked tenderly into her eyes.

Clane drove out of the gate of his mansion in Rockville, Maryland. He admired its facade in the rear view mirror of his Cadillac 95 as he accelerated into the road. It was a warm summer day. The USSS escort car closed in behind him. "Will you pick me up later, Dad?" asked Siobhan from the passenger seat beside him.

"I'll be at work, baby. Mom will do it."

"OK"

"Will Lori by a college today?"

"I guess."

Clane tittered. "I wonder if she'll still believe the moon landings are fake now she's seen those guys walking there."

"Probably not; she's a total conspiracy theorist."

"Pah! Conspiracy theorists make me laugh so much." He dropped her outside the gates of Montgomery County College. One of the guards got out of his tail and went with her; then Clane and his two remaining minders headed for the highway to Washington, DC.

The completion of the Pentagon had changed the entire structure of the Capitol community. The five year old Department of Defence needed to be housed in a single office to make it function practically, but the DoD was huge. It included everything from the previous War Office, the reorganised departments of the Army and Navy, the intelligence agencies- the SIA the CSA and ITA. Also the FDPA- Future Developmental Projects Agency and the defence training command. A small suite of offices had been allocated in the Pentagon for the only administration not part of the DoD, the Department of Interplanetary War, Clane's organization. Clane knew very well why this was, long before the President informed him.

As Clane drove into the Pentagon car park, he saw that an impromptu celebration was underway in the forecourt dedicated to the first moon landing. A group of several dozen drunken staffers who looked like they'd been up all night were waving streamers in the air and singing. They called out when they saw him. "Hey, Mr Secretary!" Clane waved. A cluster of reporters were skulking around the south entrance. One of them was carrying a shoulder mounted TV camera; Clane marvelled at the recent advancement in electronics that had revolutionised TV journalism. If only it had been around when he had been a newsmen. As he walked up to the entrance doorway a reporter, a young woman with blonde hair, approached him and asked him for a comment. "Well, I'm delighted I'm sure." he said. "Just like everybody else is. For the first time ever, a man has set foot on a celestial body other than the earth. This day, June 22nd 1952 is a date that will live for ever, not in infamy but in glory." He caught himself wondering if that Roosevelt misquote was appropriate. "It has also sent a message to our friends on Mars and Venus that we intend to assert our rights under the Dublin Treaty. We are not only willing to do so, we are also now perfectly capable."

"What role does your office now play in the future? Do we need a Department of Interplanetary War now there is no threat from Mars anymore?" She gave him a sly half-smile, knowing that she just posed a thorny question.

Clane riposted with a confident chuckle. "Government is nothing if not adaptive. I'm sure our work can be modified to meet the challenges of the new world."

"In what way? Give me an example."

"An example? Well..." One immediately came to mind. He hesitated. He had been planning to issue a formal executive proposal for his latest plan before going public with it. Should he speak about it now? It was, strictly speaking, improper of him to do so, but the nature of his idea was so benign that he couldn't see the President objecting for any reason. Also the TV cameras were on him and he couldn't think of any other good reply. "I intend to contact the authorities on Mars and offer to repatriate the remains of the victims of the Roswell Incident. I don't know what God these people worship, if indeed they worship any God at all; but either way their explorers died on our planet, unknown, alone and far from home. I think Mars would like to conduct a proper funeral for them. Like ourselves, they probably need closure of some kind when this happens."

"Where the bodies being kept?"

"I don't know. The Roswell research project was shelved completely following the Mars Day attacks of July 1947. However, I intend to launch an official investigation which will reveal the current location of the remains. I will then send a message to the Martian ambassador informing him. We will treat the remains with every dignity and honour while we make the arrangements to transport them to their home planet."

Clane went to his office, greeted his staff members and began his Monday morning work. Just before eleven AM the phone rang and his Secretary informed him that the President was on the line. "Mr President?"

"Clane, come to the White House. I need to see you now." The President ended the call without waiting for a reply. Clane slowly put the phone down. He knew he was in trouble, but why? Whatever the reason, keeping the President of the United States waiting wouldn't help his case. Clane had no choice but to stop everything he was doing and head for the White House. However, partly subconsciously, he drove slowly and took a circuitous route north across the Francis Scott Key Bridge through Georgetown and Foggy Bottom. When Thomas E Dewey had first been elected in 1948 Clane had liked him and they'd had a good working relationship; however after he was re-elected the previous year his manner changed as did his policies. Clane first became suspicious when he moved Clane's department out of the old Greggory Building and into the south segment of the Pentagon. Then, as part of his second term reshuffle, he announced that the Department of Interplanetary War would become a subordinate division of the Department of Defence. It would be renamed the US Interplanetary Relations Agency and Clane would be demoted. The paperwork was being processed and the changeover date had been set for the 1st of August. After that Clane would be henceforth called the Undersecretary for Interplanetary Relations at the Department of Defence. Because of his existing contract, his salary would not be reduced, however his budget would be. Four of his staff were being made redundant. The Secretary of Defence, who was currently his equal, would thenceforth become his boss. "Surely you understand, Clane" the President had said. "Dublin has created a very different world. The earth is safe from Martian aggression. You must have realized that your own role in government would therefore have to change. Our focus is going to shift over the next few years. Communism has become a dominant world philosophy, half the world now flies the red flag. They have the bomb too, so we risk destroying the earth ourselves. Nixon has even started calling it a 'cold war'. I'm sorry, but it's no longer the world that needs defending; it's the *free* world."

"What if the Martians change their mind?"

Dewey shrugged. "What if the First Lady changes her mind about cooking me dinner?... Once we start considering 'what-ifs', we spiral down into infinity. We have to deal with the world as it is, and how it probably will be in the forecasted future. I can't waste time with possibilities that show no sign of emerging, especially when they cost the taxpayer fifty-eight million dollars a year."

Clane knew POTUS was right, but still burned from inner resentment.

"There will still be a role for you, Clane." the President soothed. "Just a different one."

That had been back in March; since then things had been much frostier between Clane and the President. He was ushered into the Oval Office as soon as he arrived in the car park. "Jesus!" began Dewey. "How long does it take to drive over here from Dodd for Christ's sake?"

"I left as soon as our telephone conversation had finished." Clane placed the correct amount of sarcastic emphasis on *telephone conversation*. He moved over to a chair.

"Don't sit down!... I needed to speak to you because I wonder what the hell you're playing at!"

"Pardon, sir?"

"I've just come off the pissing phone to Charlie Wilson! He wants me to give him your balls on a skewer!"

"What?"

"Did you do a TV interview this morning at the Pentagon?"

"Why yes, sir."

"And did you announce your Roswell post-mortem repatriation scheme?"

"Yes, sir."

Dewey paused. "Are you not familiar with the correct procedure when it comes to media relations? I assume you are, seeing as you started out as our goddamn press officer!"

"Well... Of course, but..."

"Any new proposals you concoct, I want to hear about them first, from your own lips! Not when I switch on to watch *Capitol* fucking *Sunrise*! You know that!"

Clane gasped. Then he stammered: "But... Mr President, this is just an idea about locating corpses that had been lying around for five years. It's hardly a matter crucial to national security. I know what the correct procedure is; of course I do. But people bend the rules on this all the time. Why, only last week Senator Quinn..."

"I don't give a shit!" roared the President. "It's not your judgement call! You're paid to obey policy not to analyse it."

Clane was dumbfounded. He had never seen President Dewey so angry.

"Right, if you'll excuse me, I have to call SecDef back and get another headache while I spend another half an hour calming him down!... Now get out!"

Clane's cheeks were flushed and glowing like hot coals as he drove back to the Pentagon. He felt humiliated and confused. When he got into his office, his receptionist, an elderly maternal woman, sensed his upset and made him a coffee without him asking. The level of aggravation displayed by the President, as well as Charles Wilson the Secretary of Defence, made no sense. Technically they were correct, but the context made their response a gross overreaction. "It's just four Martians who died five years ago!" Clane shook his head to himself as he sipped his coffee. He thought back to 1947 and the tour he had taken part in at Wright Field. He picked up the phone and dialled a number.

"Hello, Wright Field command."

"Good afternoon this is the Secretary for Interplanetary War. Could you put me through to the head of the Technical Data Section please?"

"One moment, Mr Secretary." A few seconds later a male voice came on the line. "Mr Secretary?"

"Hello, Colonel Bryan. I'm enquiring as to the whereabouts of the Martian casualties from the Roswell Incident. I visited the technical data facility in '47 and was part of the press crew who were given a tour of the situation by Col. Elliot Transcope."

"One moment, sir."

He left Clane on hold. A minute passed, then two, then three, then four. "Come on, man!" muttered Clane.

The phone was picked up. "Hello, Mr Secretary?"

"Colonel?"

"I'm afraid the information you requested is not available."

"What?"

"The cadavers you refer to are no longer present in our medical laboratory."

"So where are they now?"

"I'm afraid we're unaware of the whereabouts of the deceased Martian gentlemen?"

"How is that possible? They were being stored in the Technical Data Section. I saw the bodies of three dead Martians; and a living one who was badly ill. If they're not with you now, where they have they gone?"

"I'm afraid that information is not available."

"But that's ridiculous! Don't you have any records of...?"

"I can't help you any further, Mr Secretary. Good day."

"Don't you hang up on me! I'm the goddamn SecIntWar!" But the line was already silent. A chill ran down his spine. He tried to get back to his usual work, but found it hard to concentrate.

At four PM he left his office and walked to the cafeteria. There was an unusual level of activity. People were running up and down between the Central Command room and other locations. The Pentagon was highly compartmentalised and Clane only had access to his own department and the block's public areas. He stopped a few people and asked what was going on. They just shook their heads and said they didn't know before quickly walking on. In the cafeteria there was a TV set on a wall bracket. Clane flicked through the channels, but every programme looked normal. There were no news bulletins about any untoward sudden events. He went back out into the corridor. A Navy master chief petty officer was walking towards him. He stopped and stared. "Hello, Chief." he grinned "I was hoping to run into you".

"Tommy!"

Clane and his old buddy embraced. Tommy had been one of his torpedomen in *Tunny* during the war and had stayed in the service afterwards. They spent a couple of minutes catching up on old times then Clane asked him: "Tommy, what's all the hassle about here? People are acting like war's broken out again."

"Well..." He looked uncomfortable. "I can't tell you, Clane. You know how is." He smiled thinly.

"Come on, Tommy. It's me, your old weapons chief. You're a master chief yourself now and I'm the SecIntWar. It's not like you leaking it to a guy down the bar."

Tommy looked over his shoulder nervously; then he drew Clane into a corner by a lift door. "Clane." he whispered. "You never heard it from me!... But there's been another crash."

"A plane crash?"

"No, a crash like the one at Roswell."

Clane grasped Tommy's shoulders and pushed him through some double doors into the adjoining stairwell. "Tommy! Tell me everything you know!"

A minute later Clane was hammering on the steel door to the Operations room. A yeoman poked his head out. "Mr Secretary? You're not authorized..."

"Shut up and let me see Mr Wilson!"

Charles Wilson, the Secretary of Defence came to the door. "What do you want, Clane?"

"I want to know when you were going to tell me another saucer's down."

Wilson's eyelids rose and his cheeks flushed.

"Oh yes! I know!"

"How the hell did you find out!?"

"Doesn't matter. I want you to let me in!"

"This doesn't concern you."

"Of course it concerns me, Charlie!" shouted Clane. A pair of Marines drew close. "I'm SecIntWar! An ET spacecraft has crashed, presumably it's from Mars or Venus, that violates the Dublin Treaty!"

"Clane, go back to your office and get on with your work. Stevens! Norton!"

"Don't you tell me the get back to my office like I'm some fucking matelot! I'm the Secretary for Interplanetary War!... You're not my boss yet... Ow!" Clane yowled as the two Marine guards grabbed him by the arms and propelled him away from the door.

....

A phrase Clane first heard in his childhood came to his mind. He couldn't remember who had said it, but he recalled the words precisely: *"Clane, have you ever realised something that you've always known, but didn't* know *you knew it?"* The situation he'd just been through with Charles Wilson was almost identical to what he'd experienced with James Forrestal at Aztec in 1948. He drove down the interstate ninety-five at high speed, so fast that he soon left his law-abiding Secret Service right hand men far behind. Luckily, thanks to the information supplied by Tommy, he knew where it was and it was close by; just an hour and a half's drive. He crossed the Delaware River into New Jersey and headed towards the coast on the roads to Atlantic City. Before he arrived there he turned left and entered the town of Hammonton. He came to a large wooded area. The sun was sinking low and the forest looked dark and shadowy. There was a highway running through the forest, straight as an arrow. He turned off down a narrow lane after a few miles and, sure enough, came across a police roadblock. The two New Jersey troopers had parked their cars laterally across the road and laid out a row of red lanterns. "Sorry, sir. We can't let you through."

"Why not?" asked Clane in a toneless voice.

"There's been a minor brush fire. Nothing serious; the Fire Department are putting it out right now."

Clane could hear the sound of a helicopter in the distance down the road ahead. He could tell by the sound that it was an AAF one.

Clane couldn't sleep that night. He lay in bed staring at the ceiling as Gina snored gently beside him. He once again dusted off memories that he had dumped into the attic of his mind long ago. The way his friend James Forrestal had died three years ago and nobody seemed to understand how it had happened. Clane felt trapped. Something was going on; something was badly wrong, but he didn't know what. He was being lied to, manipulated. How long for? Why? What was the situation really about?

....

No matter what the President and SecDef thought, the public responded warmly to his TV interview the previous morning. Maybe because of the moon landing, people's attention was once more turned upwards. As soon as Clane entered his office, his receptionist brought in an entire in-basket full of letters, telegrams and phone dictations. The people liked the idea of a gesture to the Martians following earth's own adventures into space. It was a welcome change in the public mood since that of two years ago when he was continuously beset with hate mail and death threats. His spirits rose as he flicked through the correspondence. He smiled to himself, reaching out occasionally to pick up his coffee cup. There were about thirty messages in all. The last one in the pile made him pause and sit up: *Dear Mr Secretary. I was pleased to see that you want to send dead bodies of Martians home. There is a man from Mars buried in my local cemetery...* Clane reread the message twice. The sender gave a return address. Clane picked up the phone to call the President, but then hesitated. He put the receiver back down.

....

Clane walked down the dry dusty road. He kept his pace slow so that the old lady walking beside him could keep up. "Not far now, Mr Quilley." she informed him in her strong twang. The heat from the sun was solid and there was no shade. The "city" of Aurora, Texas was even more of a misnomer than Roswell. Clane had driven through it on the highway without even realizing it was there and had to double back after asking directions. Aurora had a population of less than four hundred who lived in a collection of houses that were spaced so far apart that few were in sight of each other. Between them was farmland, bushes and a few lawns, parched yellow by the summer heat, linked by unpaved tracks like the one he was walking on now. They turned a corner and the cemetery came into view. "We're really proud of our little cemetery." said Mrs Cayce. "We take real good care of it." A white metal fence surrounded the graveyard. Inside were the tombstones, all clean and all different shapes and sizes, and arranged in rows. Between them were immaculate baulks of grass. This was lush and green, indicating that it was regularly watered. There were aggressive warning signs by the gate giving a list of numerous everyday activities there were banned inside the cemetery. "It's got bigger over the years." said Mrs Cayce.

"Obviously." added Clane.

"My granddaddy fenced off the north side. The old part got filled up." She sighed mournfully. "We lost a lot of folks in the Civil War; also the spotted fever outbreak. Boll weevils wiped out our cotton

146

plantation. The planters and their men left town before they died."
She crossed herself as they stepped through the gate. Clane
respectfully took off his hat. The sun scorched his scalp, but there
were many large trees with thick foliage dotted all over the
necropolis, providing shade for mourners. Squared flagstone paths
separated the blocks of plots. "It's over here." The elderly lady
hobbled across to a tree with a large overhanging bough. The grave
was like all the others, covered in unblemished turf. The only sign of
its presence was its stone marker. However this marker was smaller
than most of the others and far less well made. It was an oblong of
dark sandstone about two feet high, crudely knapped into a rounded
off top. On the face was no epitaph, but instead a rough pictogram
consisting of two lines in a horizontal V shape and a row of circles
inside.

"This is it?" Clane stared incredulous.

"Yup. Buried here is a man from Mars."

"How did he end up here?"

"He was the pilot of an airship the crashed here a long time ago;
almost sixty years ago, matter of fact. I remember it like it was
yesterday. I know here in Texas we're famous for our tales of
wonder, but I swear this is true. I was just a young girl, thirteen
years old. It was a Monday morning, April 19th 1897. I was woken
by huge boom coming from the north of town. It turns out
something had crashed in Judge Proctor's garden, completely
destroyed all the flowerbeds. It had been flying through the air and
blundered into his wind pump. Pieces of wreckage was scattered
everywhere and the body... This one." She pointed at the grave. "We
buried him here the next day. The minister performed the service.
The man was beat up pretty bad by the crash, but Mr Weems
thought he was not an inhabitant of the earth. And Mr Weems was a
real authority on astronomy... Well, he had a telescope."

"What happened to the debris?"

"Some folk came in from around the county to collect bits of it.
There were some larger chunks. They was picked up by some guys
from Dallas who came here in three wagons."

Mrs Cayce led Clane back through the village and across the
highway to a large flat-looking house. "This is where Judge Proctor
lived, and his well is over there." She pointed to a small
clapperboard outhouse. "Some of the pieces were thrown down the
well, but Mr Oates cleared them out. That's the man we're going to
see now." She knocked on the door and a man answered; he invited
them in. When he was introduced to Clane he didn't shake his hand.
Clane also noticed that Mr Oates had handled the front door very
clumsily. When Clane saw his hands he understood why. Mr Oates's
hands were hideously deformed. He had swellings on his knuckles

that were so huge they made his hands looked like baseball mitts. "What's happened to you?" asked Clane.

"The Doc says it's rheumatoid arthritis." replied Mr Oates. "There ain't no cure. I take pills that make it a bit better sometimes; or I rub in cream for the pain. But I never had it till I moved in here eighteen years ago and started drinking from that well."

"That's the well struck by the airship." added Mrs Cayce. "The one where people dumped some of it afterwards."

Clane returned to Mrs Cayce's house where she dwelt with her husband. Her children and grandchildren were visiting. "Mr Quilley, can you return that man to Mars like you are those others who came down in New Mexico?"

"I'm not sure, Mrs Cayce. First I'd need permission to exhume the grave. Texas has strict rights of sepulchre laws, so to dig up a grave without authorization is a serious offence. That would have to be arranged through the courts. Then I'd need to contact Mars direct and sort out his transport to his home planet... Are we even sure he came from Mars?"

Clane got back into his hire car and returned to Love Field Airport. For the majority of the hour-long drive he was shadowed by a black car with tinted windows.
....

The phone rang on his desk. It was the President of the United States summoning him to the Oval Office. This time President Dewey was in a cheerful mood. "Clane, hello! How are you? Take a seat." Charles Wilson was sitting in another chair nearby; his face was a mask. "Did you have a good weekend in Texas?"

"Yes thank you, Mr President." Clane had told POTUS that he was going to Texas, but lied and said he was going there to visit some friends.

After a few more sentences of small-talk, he asked Clane with a smile on his face: "Clane, have you ever given any thought to your future career?"

"No, not really, Mr President." Something in Dewey's tone; his exaggerated smile, as well as Wilson's detached manner, put him on guard.

"But, Clane! You're an intelligent and experienced man. You're still fairly young. I can imagine a lot of exciting opportunities for you in the next few years."

Clane became annoyed with Dewey's prevarication and also the way he had bought in Wilson to watch the execution; something that Wilson himself looked uncomfortable with. "Mr President." Clane said darkly. "Am I being fired?"

Clane drove home with his mind blank. The house was empty and as soon as he got indoors he went straight to the drinks cabinet and knocked back two bourbons in three minutes flat. He stopped after that; he didn't want Gina and Siobhan to see him drunk when he broke the news. He sat in front of the TV and mindlessly flicked through the channels until he heard her key in the lock. She walked in with her bags of groceries and stopped dead in the doorway. "Clane? What you doing home this time of day?"

He stood up and took a deep breath. "Honey..."

"He's fired you hasn't he?"

Clane stood up.

Tears rose in her eyes. "Oh God, Clane, no!"

"Honey, it'll be alright."

"Why!? Why did he do it!?... That fucking asshole!"

"I don't know." He guffawed sardonically. "The other day he was demoting me, now he's firing me."

Gina pulled a tissue out of her pocket and sobbed into it. Clane came over and embraced her. She blew her nose and became more composed. "Did he give you a golden handshake?"

"More like a brass sucker punch!"

"How much?"

"Twenty-five K."

She brightened. "That's not bad. We may be able to keep the house."

"If I can get work in the area... You see, Dewey offered me a new job as well; he had to really to avoid looking too bad to the rest of the cabinet. Thing is though, it involves moving. I think he's hoping I won't be able to take it."

"Not Roswell!" She snapped

"No, not Roswell... Gina, do you love me for the man. I am, not just because I've been a government official?"

She looked up at him. "Yes, Clane. I always loved you for the man you are."

"Where would you not follow me... apart from Roswell?"

"Why? Where's the new job?"

"Ireland."

"Ireland?"

"The president has offered me a job on the ambassador's staff. It's not much of a salary, but we do get a house thrown in."

She frowned. "We need ask Siobhan." It suddenly struck Clane that his daughter was now virtually an adult. If she wanted to stay in the United States alone, she could. He looked at Gina and realized that she was thinking the same thing. It felt uncomfortable to consider her not living with them. However it turned out that Siobhan was very excited about the idea of moving to Ireland. "It'll be great to be among people who know how to spell my name." she said when she came home from college and they talked to her about it.

"But what about what your friends?" asked Gina with relief.

"Oh phooey to them! They don't give a damn about me; even Lori."

"Ah yes!" smiled Clane. "Lori the conspiracy theorist."

"Yes. Did you know today she told the President Truman was murdered! Insane isn't it, Dad?"

Clane opened his mouth to affirm, but then paused. He shut it again and remained silent.

Chapter 10

Two documents lay on the desk in front of him. One was the morning's *New York Times*, the other a map of the world. The map was colour coded, like the ones he had seen a few years earlier in the same city, yet the bloodstain of communist expansion had not clotted; it continued to flow as if the earth were a haemophiliac. A vast flood of red had covered Africa, swallowing most of the former British and French colonies. South Africa and Rhodesia held out and south and in the west, Senegal, French Sudan, Mauritania, Morocco and Algeria aligned themselves with the National Republic of France. South America as well as the Far East, Australia and New Zealand were marked with red strips indicating possible revolutions in progress. North America remained communist free, as did the Middle East, India and Palestine-Israel. The headline in the *Times* read: *Emergency= Red Bloc Invasion of Iran*. Clane addressed the people in the room. "Ladies and gentlemen, as you are no doubt aware, what we have predicted has happened. The rebellion by the Nadeen Party in Iran has forced Prime Minister Mossadeg to resign. The country is now ruled by the People's Coalition, a democratic leftist popular front. The Red Bloc has sent troops over the northern borders on both sides of the Caspian Sea, after a direct invitation for them by Nadeen socialists. The first column will have reached Tehran by this evening."

There was a murmur of disquiet from the audience.

"Also, spy satellite and aerial reconnaissance data indicate a major naval sortie from Bremerhaven, Flushing, Antwerp, major Red European bases. A number of ships have set sail for the English east coast. Clearly this has alarmed Prime Minister Mosley and he has contacted President Goldwater demanding assistance. He wants American nuclear weapons to be stationed on British soil."

A rumble of consternation rose from the others. "Absolutely not!" said Creeks, an Alabama military attaché. "That would inflame the situation. We can't risk all out war with the Red Bloc."

"And what about Mosley's our own human rights record?" asked McCord, a bespectacled academic from Rhode Island. "His 'state of emergency' is still in effect. He's given himself the same position as Oliver Cromwell and called a halt to general elections. The young Queen Elizabeth the Second is right beside him."

"Let's hope he doesn't cut her head off!" quipped Franklin, the globulous industrialist, facetiously. "Anyway, going back to Iran; is it the end of the world if Iran goes commie? Turkey is commie yet they're very cooperative. Their pipeline deal from Kazakhstan has earned us over a trillion dollars. And the Bloc is far from being united under the socialist banner. Look at that fuss between the USSR and China; it's swallowed up Soviet military resources. I think it's made Chairman Mao think again. He's introducing economic reforms to open up China to the free world. It's ironic that in twenty years China could become the world's greatest capitalist power."

Everybody laughed, welcoming a joke to ease the tension.

"It's too much of a gamble for President Goldwater." said Clane. "This could be a move against entire Middle East. If they seize our oilfields they can hold the world to ransom."

"So what happens now?" asked Creeks.

"The National Security Council is meeting at the moment. We'll have a plan of action soon. The Secretary of State has asked us in Ireland to maintain the situation and keep him informed."

Noise from outside the embassy drew their attention to the streets. Another flash demonstration had broken out at the gates. This time the placards were those of the Irish Communist Party and they looked more focused. A few days earlier an organized protest had broken down when the ICP and *Sinn Fein* contingents started fighting each other. The split between the two groups had been triggered by the discovery of some empty oil drums in a cave at Dingle Bay, County Kerry. *Sinn Fein* had admitted that they had been left there by the IRA after refuelling German U-boats during the war. *Sinn Fein* had refused to apologise for that. The communists had then denounced *Sinn Fein* for their allegiance to the Nazi fascists and their coalition had collapsed.

The meeting broke up and Clane headed for the cafeteria. The large windows in the curved walls overlooked the gates where the communists were demonstrating. Red banners and virulent placards bobbed above the fence. *Gardai* in riot helmets formed a line to hold them back. A brick arced through the air, aimed at the windows of the embassy but it fell short.

Clane then had a meeting with the ambassador. The United States ambassador to the Republic of Ireland was a large Latino called Jose Gutierrez. The Irish ambassadorship was one of the most prestigious jobs in the US Foreign Service and was usually given to an Irish American, and so Gutierrez's appointment had been controversial. Clane headed downstairs to the computer room in the basement. The linoleum white-lit chamber was chilled by fans that cooled the tallboy banks of computers. They whirred and clicked and hummed. Lights blinked on panels and reels of magnetic tape rotated back and forth. "Hi there, Amy." Clane greeted a young woman sitting at the computer console.

"Morning, Clane." she replied in her Dublin accent.

"What's happening here?" He looked at the TV-like monitor. The screen was black with white text, and words and sentences were appearing in boxes.

"Mr Gutierrez asked me to keep an eye on GovMesh."

"What's that?"

"A system that allows me to access information and talk to other people through computers. It's a network that spans the world. Look at this; it's written by somebody at the American embassy in Australia."

Clane read the block text on the screen: *Amy, it's getting late here. I wanna go to bed.*

"Amazing!"

She laughed "What did you expect? This is 1954 you know."

"How are people responding to the situation in Iran?"

She shrugged. "They're ready to do their jobs, but they're scared."

"We all are." said Clane and patted her shoulder.

Clane approached the gate of the embassy accompanied by a *Garda*. Beyond the walls of the embassy compound he could hear the crowd baying with an incoherent rage. "Some *Sinn Fein*-ers have turned up." said the policeman. "It's distracted them. Makes it easier for us to keep path clear at the gate." The heavy steel bars of the gate slid aside and Clane stepped out onto the street feeling unprotected. He looked back. The Irish embassy was a brand new building, a rotunda sticking out between a fork in the road on the south side of Dublin. The traffic had been stopped for the demonstration and a group of *Gardai* escorted him through the crowd. A few of them noticed him and rushed over. "Get out, Yankee!" they yelled. "Yanks out!" One the placards read: *USA- HANDS OFF IRAN!* It had been crudely painted on torn piece of cardboard; prepared in a hurry to meet the new emergency. The remaining protesters were focused in the opposite direction, facing the *Sinn Fein* mob. The two sides grunted and gibbered at each other like beasts at a waterhole.

Dusk was falling and a light rain dampened the air. The streets were slimy with moisture and car headlamps were reflected as lobes and strands of light in puddles. An old blue signboard on a fence announced that he was passing Merrion Square, a large urban park. This sign was trilingual, a hark back to the days of the Soviet Pale. When the Russians had gone home following the Dublin Treaty the authorities had a speedily replaced the existing notices with new ones that were English and Gaelic only. They must have missed this one. He reached Temple Bar and entered *The Windmill Inn* on Crown Street. The pub was half full of students from Trinity College and suited government types, cooling off after work. A group of them called to him and he recognized them as his colleagues from the embassy. He ordered and then joined them at their table. They discussed the new crisis in Iran in jocular terms. One laughed: "The night before they drop the bomb, I want to have a wild party. When they drop it I want to be right underneath it, drunk out my head!" Another said more seriously: "I can't get it through my head, a 'cold war'?" Clane was distracted by a commotion at the bar. A short man in a dark pinstripe suit was complaining to the barman about the pint of Guinness he had just been served. "It's all head and no pint!" the man explained in a harsh American accent. One of Clane's friends leaned forward. "Who's that?"

"No idea." said another. Americans in Dublin were a distinct community centred around the diplomatic mission and several corporate offices. Most of them knew each other, by sight if not by name. The importance of their unrecognition was eventually reprioritized and they resurrected the previous subject. The suited man took a seat at the end of the bar close to their table and sipped disapprovingly on his supposed substandard Guinness. An hour passed and they drank two more points, then Clane's friends bade him farewell and left the pub to join a party at somebody's house. Clane's pint was only half-finished so he remained behind. He drank smoothly for a few minutes, but then felt strange. His right ear was glowing as if a warm breeze was playing on it. He turned his head and noticed that the suited man at the bar was looking at him. Clane swivelled in his seat and faced him. He gasped as recognition clicked. "You!"

Flying Buffalo laughed. "May I join you?"

Clane nodded, unable to speak.

The old Indian reached into his pocket for some money and ordered two more pints of Guinness. He brought them over to the table and sat down opposite. It was definitely him. His small brown eyes, the lined face and cracked voice. The difference was his totally incongruous clothing and neatly coiffured short black hair. "So how are you, Mr Quilley?"

"I..." He cleared his throat. "I ought to be surprised. I would have been once; but for ten years now my surprise tank is empty. I've used it all up. I mean... you're clearly some kind of ghost aren't you?"

Flying Buffalo shook his head. "A ghost can't drink." He sipped his pint and licked the creamy head off his top lip.

Clane paused "What are you?"

"What are *you*?"

"I'm human. You're not."

"Define human. Do you mean an upright walking hairless ape with an extra large brain?"

"I mean an old Indian who doesn't keep appearing in my life in inexplicable ways."

Flying Buffalo chuckled. "So would you consider Karl Dennison human?"

Clane gasped. His heart jumped into his throat and his head wobbled. "How the hell do you know about that!?"

"Answer me. Was Karl Dennison human?"

Clane was trembling. He had not even thought about this subject for many years. His mind was instantly and excruciatingly cast back to his childhood. His sore memories always began with a wedding when he was just ten years old.

"Sit up straight! You'll crease your jacket!" Arthur Quilley had snapped from the seat in front.

"But, Dad, I'm uncomfortable!" moaned Clane.

"I ironed for an hour last night just to make these suits nice!" said Marianne Quilley, Clane's mother. "I'm not having you creasing up yours by slouching!... And put your tie on!"

"It hurts my neck. And we're not there yet; nobody can see me."

Mrs Quilley, turned round in her seat to look at him. "Do it, Clane! You're going to have to wear it all day so you might as well get used to it while we're on the train."

Clane raised his chin and gingerly fastened the top button on his shirt. He then pulled the tie until it closed like a noose around his neck. "Creighton's mom and dad aren't going to make him wear a tie; he told me." Clane muttered.

"We're not Creighton's mom and dad." said Marianne. "We're yours."

"It's not fair!" he choked.

"Well, life isn't fair!" retorted his father without hesitation.

They'd been on the train for an hour now after leaving home at eight in the morning. After rising at dawn to bathe and dress with precision they'd joined other family and friends and bundled down to the Metropolitan Station for the journey. They headed north through the Bronx and Yonkers for the trip to Albany, the hometown of the bride's family. Clane's sister Daisy was sitting to his left and his older brother Mark was leaning against the right-hand window. The wedding was to take place in an ancient stone-walled church in a tiny little village suburb that looked as old as the round green hills that surrounded it. The place was done up with white ribbon and roses and the guests all crowded in chattering and laughing as the organ played ecclesiastical Muzak in the background. Clane and his siblings were hemmed in by mohair-covered backs and low-cut busts; the air stank of perfume, silk, aftershave and flowers. An usher in a morning coat showed them to their seats on the varnished wooden pews. Just before they all sat down their father stopped and turned to them leaning forward with his hands on his knees, his characteristic posture of seriousness. He glanced around him to check nobody else could hear and then whispered: "Listen, you three. Today is a very important day, not just for Karl Dennison and Susannah, but for us. This is a day when we have to behave well and be courteous to our fellow guests, and Karl Dennison's and Susannah's family, and you will all show respect and cooperate fully with proceedings at all times; is that clear?"

Clane and Daisy nodded and Mark shrugged.

Their father glared at Mark, acknowledging his projected unwillingness. His bald pate flushed slightly. "If any of you act out of turn or so much as look at anybody rudely today then I'll make you very, very sorry! Do you understand!?"

Another nod and shrug. "Don't worry, Dad." sneered Mark. "We won't make you look a fool in front of all your snobby frrrriends!" He rolled the "r" of the word like a Scotsman or Italian.

Quilley's eyes bugged at his older son and he bared his teeth: "And one disobliging remark like that from you, my boy, and you can forget Clearwater!... Understood!?" Daisy tittered. This was not the first time that their father had used Mark's upcoming trip to summer camp as a bargaining chip. Mark returned his father's malevolent glare.

"I said is that understood!?" hissed Quilley in a voiceless shout.

"Yes!" spat Mark tonelessly.

Everybody was now sat down. The children all looked unfamiliar in their Sunday bests; they rotated their heads to catch glimpses of each other. Creighton, a boy in the school year below Clane, turned around from several rows ahead and waved to him mouthing some words that Clane couldn't interpret. He pulled up short as his mother gave him a stern snap.

The priest walked round to the front and nodded at the organist. Arthur Quilley straightened his back and smoothed his thick moustache. The strains of *Here Comes the Bride* began and Clane watched as Karl Dennison stood up. Clane couldn't see his face and had never seen him wearing a suit before, but even if he hadn't known that he was the groom Clane would have recognized him. Even on this day his huge mop of brown hair was as unkempt and protruding as always. Clane felt the usual twinge of unease as he always did in Dennison's presence. Susannah marched solemnly down the aisle arm-in-arm with her father and flanked by a group of waif-like bridesmaids whom Clane had never seen before. Susannah's dress was peach in colour and the bodice was crepe, obviously designed to hide, and failing badly at it, the open secret of her now fairly advanced pregnancy. She was a bookish-looking woman with thick glasses and neatly-curled hair, styled with ringlets and bangs; a bit virginal, like a librarian. She stood at the altar next to Dennison and beamed up at him adoringly. He turned his head and smiled back at her, allowing Clane to see his face. His smile was the same one he always used, no different because of this occasion. "In the name of the Father, the Son and the Holy Spirit." began the priest. "AMEN." everybody said in unison. "The grace of our Lord Jesus Christ and the love of God and the fellowship of the Holy Spirit be with you all." "AND ALSO WITH YOU."

The wedding mass lasted for about an hour and a half. Clane quickly lost interest in it and felt himself slip into an ultradian state of consciousness, like he sometimes did at school, as boredom and his early rise that morning caught up with him. His mother had to nudge him several times to stay awake, and to remind him to join in during the hymn singing. The congregation became deeply fervent as the wows and rings were exchanged; a woman in the front row began weeping as quietly as she could, her sniffs echoing off the colonial rafters above. The organ then struck up the Wedding March and the couple paraded out of the church; Clane averted his eyes as they passed in case Dennison looked at him.

The mood of the day then changed from one of reverence to one of jubilation. People trooped out of the church and along the street into Albany chuckling, chatting and grinning. They came to an ornate building made of greyish-brown stone. As they entered the building, men dressed up in bow ties invited them to a grand hall which had been laid out for a banquet with spotless, white tablecloths and rows of immaculately-matched crockery and cutlery. The same men then served them with dinner. The food was delectable, but came in very small portions; this included the slice of the wedding cake Clane was given which was so thin that he could see his hand through it. After dinner the guests were all excused from the table and his mood lightened because as the adults withdrew to a lounge to enjoy alcoholic drinks the children were free to play in the building's grand, carpeted corridors and chambers. Everything was very clean and neat with stainless sofas and armchairs that provided wonderful locations for games of Hide-and-Seek, Forty-Forty, Off-Ground Tig and even soccer, using a rolled up mache of napkins wetted with the dregs of a wine glass, as a ball. The best thing about the reception venue was the tower. Clane had seen it from the outside when they arrived. The centrepiece of the building was a squat, solid tower with a polygonal plan that resembled an observatory. He'd thought at the time how much he'd like to get inside it and climb to the top; now to the delight of the children, they realized that the tower was openly linked to the building's grand hallway and that there were no doors to keep them from exploring it. The top of the tower was accessed from the ground floor by a wide spiral staircase that wound around the walls with a gaping well in the middle; this landed onto a gallery that ran around the inside of the roof and was lit by large, square windows that offered a stunning view of Albany's skyline. A tournament of "Tigget" quickly broke out. This is a game in which two to four participants stand at opposite sides of a large toroidal court, its dimensions defined for example by a playground roundabout, and then run around the court and try to catch the player in front of them, while simultaneously avoiding capture themselves from the player behind them. The object of the game is to catch all the other players, while completely escaping capture themselves, and the one remaining in the designated field-of-play is declared the winner. Under some variations of the rules sudden switches of direction are permitted. The novelty of the location enhanced the enjoyment of the game, with the gallery serving as the field-of-play, and the Tigget match was raucous and thrilling. It only paused when Mark appeared at the top of the stairs. Mark was several years older than Clane and his friends and so straddled that strange demi-monde between childhood and "Grown-Up Land". He was too old to play Tigget, and was allowed a few sips of alcoholic drink with the adults, but not yet entitled to his own glass. "What do you want, Mark?" demanded Clane with a scowl when he saw his brother's crafty smile and noticed that he was carrying a bundle in his arms that seemed to be made of a screwed-up section of tablecloth.

"That's not very nice, Claney." he replied. "I just wanted to come and say hello."

"'Hello'!" said Justin sarcastically. "You've said it so you can go now."

"Yeah!" chimed in Creighton. "Go back to your crumbly mates and kiss Karl's ass, Mark!"

Mark chuckled with mock-affront. "Aw, dude, that's mean; after I brought you all a present and everything." He unwrapped his makeshift parcel and revealed that it was secreting a bottle of white wine.

The hostility of the younger boys transformed instantly to affability and elation.

"Hey, swell!"

"Cool!"

"Yeah! Nice one, Mark!"

"Top man!"

"Thanks, Mark!"

"I want some!" Mark left them to it and headed back down the stairs laughing. Clane and his friends gathered round the bottle in excitement and awe. "How do we open it?" asked Alec.

"We need a corkscrew." said Michael.

"Anybody got a penknife?"

"I have!" piped up Creighton and pulled the device out of his pocket. He fiddled with the array of blades for a while until he'd deployed the corkscrew and sat down by the bottle, the others avidly following his progress. It took about five minutes with lots of false starts, but the cork was eventually extracted from the neck of the bottle, mostly in ground-up pieces. The boys all roared with triumph as Creighton lifted the bottle to his lips and quaffed deeply. "Hey! That's enough, Creighton! Leave some for the rest of us!" The bottle was passed round from hand to hand, each boy drinking as much as he could before the protests of those in the queue ahead cut short his swig. Clane was last in the line and gulped what was left, raising the bottle above his open mouth to catch the last of the drips.

The empty bottle was partly concealed behind a radiator and the Tigget game continued. However after a few minutes it began to break down. Clane started to feel unsteady on his feet and noticed that sounds around him were muted and warped. His vision began to blur and he became dizzy; but at the same time he felt strangely jovial and laughed out loud at his most staid and mundane thoughts and words. Looking around him, he realized that all his companions were similarly afflicted. He recognized the symptoms of drunkenness. This was not the first time in his life he'd become drunk, in fact it was the third. The other two occasions had been during his parents' house-parties when he'd covertly mine-swept the table of all its half-finished glasses when the adult revellers had gone out for a walk. The boys gave up the Tigget game and all collapsed in a heap telling feeble jokes and screeching with helpless mirth at every one of them. Justin became nauseous and vomited behind the radiator near the bottle. After a while Clane stood up and went for a walk around the gallery, clutching the parapet hard to steady himself. It was then that he noticed that something was wrong. He stopped to take a look out of one of the windows and saw that the landscape outside has frozen solid, as still as a photograph. There was a building site next door to the venue and it had been a hive of activity with cranes swinging, cement pouring and bricks being laid; now the cranes were still and the cement looked set in mid-flow. The men working on the site were all as still as waxworks. One was petrified in mid-stride while walking along, another held a brick in one hand a mortar-trowel in the other. Clane rushed to another window and saw that on the neighbouring street exactly the same had happened; the people on the pavements behaved exactly as the builders on the site, and automobiles and horses were immobile. Most peculiar of all, a cloud of black smoke hung in the air above a chimney, like a fly trapped in amber.

"Hey!" Clane yelled. "Get up, guys! Something's wrong!"

"What?" moaned Justin.

"Everything's fine. This is a great place." said Alec, slurring his words.

"No!" replied Clane. "Look out of the window." One by one the boys all clambered to their feet and moved to a window. They all gasped. "What's going on!? Why is everything still!?" Justin started crying.

Clane turned back to face the interior of the tower and saw that something else wasn't right. The sounds from inside the wedding reception venue had gone too. Throughout the party their own activities had been accompanied by the distant background murmur of the adults' conversation in the lounge at the base of the tower;

this was now silent. Clane also noticed that a lot of the colour had faded from their surroundings. The bright green wallpaper of the building had now turned a gloomy forest colour and the signal red trimming on the windowsills was now a kind of maroon. At the same time another strange sound emerged from the silence, a continuous hooting whining sound that seemed to come from all around them. Clane checked his panic by reminding himself that he'd just drunk a large quantity of wine and was probably just experiencing an abnormal type of drunkenness; adults may suffer from this all the time when they drank alcohol and just think nothing of it, waiting for it to pass. "Don't worry!" he voiced his reassuring thoughts to his friends. "We'll be alright! This isn't real. It's just the wine we drank."

"Then how come we can all see the same things?" demanded Justin. "If this was all in our heads..."

"What's up with Creighton?" asked another boy, and all eyes turned. Creighton had not joined in with the exclamations and queries of the others. He was standing bolt upright staring into space as if he were in a trance. His eyes were wide and unblinking and his mouth hung open.

"Creighton, are you OK?" asked Clane.

Then Creighton started walking. He slowly took one step at a time in the direction of the spiral stairway that led down to the ground floor.

"Creighton, where are you going?... Creighton!"

When Creighton reached the top of the staircase he didn't descend; instead he leaned over the banister and swung one of his legs over it so he was straddling the rail. Terror stabbed Clane's heart and everybody trembled and moaned, but the boys were all frozen to the spot and unable to move through fear.

"GET OFF THERE!" bellowed a new voice, a gruff adult voice. They all swung round to see Arthur Quilley scaling up the stairs towards them. Suddenly, as if a switch had been pressed, everything flipped back to normal. The normal colours and sounds returned and the strange hooting noise stopped as if it were on a radio that had just been unplugged. Creighton obviously came out of his trance at the very same moment because his eyes bulged and he screamed with shock as he realized where he was: about to fall off a stair-rail a good hundred feet above the hard marble floor and baize-thin carpet at the base of the tower. He hurled himself in the opposite direction, rolling onto the floor of the gallery just as Quilley reached them. "What the hell is going on!?" Clane's father yelled, but everybody had shrunk back and they were all weeping profusely. Creighton hugged himself as he lay on the floor, groaning and trembling.

Quilley's gaze rotated like a lighthouse, absorbing everything; it came to rest on the radiator where there stood the empty bottle of wine and the puddle of Justin's vomit. His cheeks flushed and his face creased into a bitter frown. Clane looked out of the window; the people on the street outside were moving normally, as were the men and machines on the building site. All the normal sights and sounds of the world had returned. Clane then glanced back at the stairway and saw that more adults were ascending the staircase towards them to see what was going on. Leading them was a man with his wide eyes gleaming in the glow from the windows. It was the groom, Karl Dennison.

It was getting dark and starting to rain as they caught the train back to New York City. For a long time nobody spoke and Clane just watched the raindrops course down the carriage windows, illuminated by the glow of streetlights. Then his father cleared his throat and turned to face him. "Clane, where did you lot get that bottle of wine?"

Mark gave him an almost imperceptible nudge with his foot.

"I don't know." replied Clane quietly.

"I'm going to damn well find out!" snapped Quilley. "Karl Dennison and Susannah's big day almost ended in disaster! Imagine if Creighton had fallen; it would have ruined everything for them! I mean, that's a fine story to tell the grandchildren isn't it!?"

"It might have dampened the spirits of Creighton's mum and dad slightly too." said Mark with a sardonic grimace.

Quilley snorted and shook his head.

"Dad..." Clane had deliberated over whether he should tell them anything on this subject: "Something weird happened up there. We heard this strange noise, everything we could see changed and everything outside froze solid. We all saw it."

"Rubbish!" scoffed his father. "Nothing weird happened at all! You just got sozzled up! There's nothing weird about that!... I hope to God you have the mother of all hangovers in the morning, boy; that'll teach you a lesson!"

Clane's mother sighed and shook her head. "Clane, I was totally mortified by what you did. How could you!? Next time we go to a wedding we'll have to leave you with a babysitter... God alone knows what Karl Dennison thinks of us now!"

Mark tittered too quietly for their parents to hear above the noise of the train. He winked at Clane and grinned.

It was almost a cliché in Clane's household: "What about Karl Dennison?" They almost always referred to him by both his names for some reason, even though he was the only person called Karl that they knew. Clane couldn't remember when Karl Dennison had first come into their lives. He was just there one day. After that he was there almost continuously. He had some connection with Clane's father's work and held some senior position in his office at the Sanitation Department. He was also a qualified mathematics teacher, which had terrible consequences for Clane. He treated Clane's home as his own. Clane's parents began leaving the front door unlocked and Karl Dennison used to walk in through the front door without knocking. He had a bizarre manner. He wouldn't say anything when he walked in and tread very quietly with slow footfalls, almost as if he were tiptoeing. Then he would enter the lounge and say: "Ah!" smiling and raising his eyebrows. Arthur and Marianne Quilley would then stop whatever they were doing, smile extremely broadly back at him and say: "Hello, Karl." Clane always studied his parents carefully when they were with Karl Dennison; whenever he was around their manner always changed considerably. All his father's grouchiness and melancholy would evaporate and so too would his mother's phlegmatic timidity and they would become completely different people. Their faces would take on a rhapsodic smile and they would look at Karl Dennison with starry eyes, an almost childlike adoration. Clane's parents were two very different people, opposites in many ways, but when Karl Dennison was around they behaved exactly the same. And Karl Dennison was in their home a lot, in fact Mark used to joke that their parents should charge him rent. He would visit at least once every evening, not just drop in briefly, but stay for several hours, often sharing their dinner. At weekends he'd be there all day Saturday and Sunday. This was at a time when the Quilleys had just moved into a new area of town and Arthur and Marianne were constantly talking about the need to "fit in" and used other phrases like "circle of friends", "neighbourhood community", "getting in with the crowd" "Residents Association" and "middle classes". Clane didn't know what these terms meant, but he got the gist of it: His parents were doing what the new boys and girls did at his school: making a place for themselves in society. For schoolchildren it meant joining the baseball teams and finding the right kind of kid to sit next to in class; for adults like his mother and father it meant meeting the people who would introduce them to the Bridge circles, joining the Tennis club, finding out how to lie about the price of their apartment, how to conceal the fact that they sent their children to the local church school, and that they didn't have private health insurance. Clane remembered well the night his father came home carrying his embroidered gilt apron, proof that he'd been accepted into the Brooklyn Mason's lodge. He hadn't looked that happy in years; genuinely happy, not the false happiness he showed when he was around Karl Dennison.

Karl Dennison was nothing special to look at. He didn't dress very well for a man of his social standing, which frankly was way above Clane's family's. He always wore faded bush-green corduroy trousers and the thick woollen sweaters that Marianne knitted for him. His shoes were always scuffed and worn and the tread on the soles filed down by use, as Clane could see when Karl Dennison sat in his characteristic posture on the settee: laid back with one of his legs crossed over the knee of the other. He was clean-shaven and didn't wear spectacles. In fact his twenty-twenty vision was one of the many marvels about him that his parents raved about. One of his most striking features was his hair. It was light brown, and thick and heavy, and it stood out from his head evenly in all directions. He probably never brushed it as it was extremely chaotic and scruffy, like a bird's nest. However Karl Dennison's most striking feature of all, by a long shot, was his eyes. For his whole life, whenever Clane recalled Karl Dennison, it was always his eyes that shot to the front of his mind. His eyes were wide and staring, usually the whites were visible all the way around his electric blue irises. They were active and intelligent eyes, perceptive eyes, eyes which drank in information. However at the same time they were strangely lifeless. They were eyes like a corpse's; they looked as if they'd been painted onto his face. When he smiled, which he did a lot of the time, he looked like a waxwork smiling. He was extremely calm and emotionless and never reacted to anything that other people did, like weepy plays or news stories about disasters; he never cried at funerals. However he did laugh, and his laugh was very loud and intrusive. What would happen if, for instance, somebody told a joke which made everybody chuckle mildly in their own way, Karl Dennison would throw back his head, face the ceiling, open his mouth wide and scream: "Hahahahahahaha!" so stridently that he could be heard halfway down the street. His laugh always sounded exactly the same: "Hahahahahahaha!", like a cross between a braying donkey and a chattering monkey. And it always lasted almost exactly the same amount of time: 3.5 to 3.9 seconds; Mark timed it with a stopwatch. As soon as the laugh ended his head would snap back into its upright position like a Roman catapult and his expression would return to normal. While other people would be dabbing their eyes and giving out little hilarity aftershocks, Karl Dennison would look as if he hadn't even laughed at all. Yet this didn't seem to worry anybody; on the contrary Karl Dennison was extremely popular; he had what the Quilleys called a "very wide circle of friends" and at house-parties he was always the centre of attention. What's more, other people at the parties where he went acted in the same perplexing way that the Quilleys did: they wore that same ridiculous and sycophantic smile, had the same glint of devotion in their eyes. Clane watched in amazement as everybody leaned towards him at the dinner table like flowers facing the sun. Mark put it very well when he said: "Karl Dennison can make people act like dogs." Mark was a good artist and he drew caricatures of Karl Dennison walking along the street with a pack of dogs following him, their tails wagging and their tongues hanging out; he gave the dogs human faces that resembled his parents and their acquaintances. Clane chuckled at this, but deep down there was something frightening and sinister about this observation. People did indeed behave in a manner towards Karl Dennison that was very canine: passionately loyal, worshipful and, above all, obedient.

Clane hated Karl Dennison. He hated him more than anybody else in the world, more than the school bullies, more than the most brutal teacher. But the odd thing was: he didn't know why... or at least not at first. He didn't even get upset the night of one party when he saw Karl Dennison kissing his mother in the park and his father kissing Karl Dennison's girlfriend just a couple of dozen yards away. They were very drunk at the time after all, or rather the Quilleys were. Arthur and Marianne often stayed up late with Karl Dennison at weekends, sometimes until long after midnight. Occasionally other friends would join them, like Lizzie, one of Karl Dennison's early girlfriends... one of his *many* girlfriends. They used to put away several bottles of wine during these benders, and although Karl Dennison used to drink as much as they all did, he never seemed to get inebriated. Clane's grandmother had been staying the night of the kiss-swapping and had created a scene when she saw what was going on, but Clane, Mark and Daisy had just shrugged, categorizing the incident as one of the many insoluble mysteries of the adult world. No, Clane hated Karl Dennison besides that, not because of it.

"Clane, your mother and I have been discussing your latest school report." Arthur Quilley had said one evening during dinner. Clane knew trouble was brewing; he'd had a long lecture following the last parents' evening and had never imagined that that would be the end of it. His father thrust a piece of paper in Clane's face covered in a long list of meaningless capital letters and numbers. "What do you have to say about this!?" he demanded. Clane shrugged and his parents exchanged glances, misinterpreting his incomprehension for indifference. "It's not good enough!" Arthur exclaimed. "At this rate you'll fail your exams and be unable to continue your education. Good God, don't you understand!? We want you to go up in the world! We've fought and battled to lift our family from its lowly roots to a higher place. Catherine Sims' sons have both got into Harvard! Do you realize that if you let us down we'll be the first family among our new circle of friends to not have children who went to college! Think what that'll do to our reputation!"

"Your father's right, Clane." chimed in Marianne. "How would I be able to hold my head up at the Women's Institute meetings if you let us down?"

"Math seems to be your weakest subject." said Arthur. "For that reason we've decided that you are to have extra after-school tuition."

"With who?" he asked, but he already knew the answer.

"'Whom' not 'who', and it's with Karl Dennison." The thought of spending time alone with Karl Dennison terrified Clane. To sit in the den, just Karl Dennison and himself, while his family were in other rooms! It gave Clane nightmares. But then something happened that he hadn't expected; he found that he couldn't remember the private maths lessons he had with Karl Dennison. They were a black hole in his mind. He'd recall Karl Dennison turning up in his usual way, then leaving at the end of the evening after his regular socializing with the Quilley elders. Then his parents asked Clane how the lesson went. Clane, thinking quickly, replied: "Oh... very well. I learned a lot." He decided not to look a gift horse in the mouth and just enjoyed the fact that the thoughts he worried about weren't there in his mind. It seemed foolish for him to be worrying about not being worried. He did question this course of action after the lessons had been going on for a couple of months because he noticed that he was developing bruises on his body where he hadn't knocked himself, but his intuition told him to keep quiet. During this period he also had outlandish and horrifying nightmares about monsters growing inside his body and vampires drinking his blood, but he let it pass. As his mother always told him, they were just dreams, not real; and he was now too old to be frightened by them.

However a day came to pass when he almost did ask his mother about his symptoms when one of these regular lacunae lasted all day. It was a day when his parents had both taken Daisy to a special gymkhana and they had asked Karl Dennison to babysit Clane and Mark. He had turned up on time and let himself in because, of course, he had his own key. After that Clane remembered nothing until his parents returned at four PM. It was as if one moment it had been morning and the next afternoon. What was stranger was that Mark commented that he too could remember nothing of that day. That night Clane had one of the worst nightmares of his life. It was daytime and he was alone in the house with Mark and Karl Dennison. He'd been in his bedroom and heard a voice crying and realized that it was Mark, which was so confusing and upsetting because Mark was three years older than Clane and hadn't cried in front of him since they were very small children. The voice came from downstairs. Clane quietly descended the stairs and identified the voice as coming from the lounge. He opened the door and saw Mark and Karl Dennison both standing in the middle of the room, Mark was naked and Karl Dennison was ferociously beating Mark's back and bottom with a belt. But in the midst of this brutality his face was as placid and deadpan as always. Clane woke up at that point and screamed aloud in horror. He almost got up and went to his parents' room, asking if he could sleep in their bed with them, something he hadn't done for years. It had been so vivid and lucid that Clane could hardly believe the self-reassurances he gave himself, repeating his mothers', that it was only a dream and not real.

However there was one incident which Clane did remember very painfully because it revealed the true nature of the relationship Karl Dennison had with his mother and father. One evening it was the Quilleys' turn to host the Bridge circle and a dozen people turned up and settled into the den. Karl Dennison joined them and, as always, was the star of the show. He sat at the head of the table and dealt the cards. Clane, Mark and Daisy stayed in the lounge and read story books. The evening wore on for an hour or two then Clane and Daisy had an argument over the ownership of a comic. After a handful of angry exchanges the door burst open and Arthur charged into the room. "Will you lot be damn-well well quiet!?" he shouted. "Your mother and Karl Dennison have a partnership that's about to break the circle's scoring record! They're on their last trick! So if you two don't pipe down and let them concentrate I'll take those books away and give you knitting brochures instead... OK!?" Clane was in a bad mood after a rotten day at school and his father's antipathy wounded his already thinned skin. A few minutes after Arthur returned to the den Clane followed him. He peeped round the door, taking in the adults all perched on their chairs, facing Karl Dennison at the head of the table. He entered the room and said loudly with a snigger. "Mom, I hear you and Karl are partners. I thought you had more sense than that."

There was a moment's pause. Everybody stopped talking and turned to look at him. Then Karl Dennison leapt out of his chair, crossed the room in a single step, raised his hand and landed a stunning forehand blow across Clane's face. He seized Clane's collar, dragged him out of the den and threw him onto the floor. Clane caught a glimpse of the room as Karl Dennison strode back inside and slammed the door shut. As soon as Clane had recovered his wits he stood up. Stars filled his vision and his head reeled. "What have I done!?" he yelled, but nobody in the room answered. The skin of his face still stung from the impact of Karl Dennison's palm and when he touched his nose he saw blood on his fingers. He stumbled silently to his bedroom and lay quivering on his bed in the darkness, teetering on the border of tears. He had no idea how long he lay there. He lifted his head as he heard cheerful voices in the hallway, including Karl Dennison's trademark cackle. The evening had ended and the guests were going home. The front door shut and Clane heard footsteps in the hallway. His mother was coming up to his room. She knocked on the door: "Clane, can I come in?"

"Yes."

Marianne made an effort to open and close the door as quietly as possible as she came into the room. She switched on the light and then adjusted the dimmer switch so as not to dazzle him. She sat on the bed and took Clane's hand. "Clane, I want you to know that Karl Dennison was very sorry for what happened downstairs earlier. He was very, very sorry."

"Mom, can I stop having math lessons with Karl Dennison?"

She signed tremulously. "No... I'm sorry, Clane; you need them." What haunted Clane for years and years after that evening, what he recalled most about that traumatic moment, was not the pain of the attack, nor the humiliation of being beaten like that publicly in front of his parents' friends; it was the looks on everybody's faces. Firstly Karl Dennison's. Clane had already noticed how he never seemed moved or ruffled emotionally by anything; his only outward expression of feeling was his unearthly laugh. As Karl Dennison attacked and beat Clane, his face was as calm and nonchalant as always, displaying no anger or offence. The other thing that disturbed Clane was the faces of the other adults who witnessed him carry out his attack, even his mother and father. They were equally impassive, but more than just impassive; they were sheepish, slavish and frustrated; as if helpless, trapped in the unbreakable chains of some higher power. That higher power was Karl Dennison. Mixed with that was embarrassment and perhaps the minute twinges enjoyment that is worn by young children in school while a teacher is punishing one of their peers.

Karl Dennison turned up the next day and acted like nothing had happened. If he really was "very, very sorry" for what he'd done then he was hiding it well, and he had clearly only revealed his shame privately to Arthur and Marianne. Clane's tuition with him continued for the rest of the year.

However after the wedding Karl Dennison spent somewhat less time at their home, for which Clane was relieved, even though he was still by normal standards a regular visitor. He and Susannah bought a house just two streets away and Clane couldn't help wondering if maybe this was so that he wouldn't be too far from his precious friends, the Quilley family. It was only after Clane joined the Navy that he completely lost contact with the Dennisons. During the war they moved upstate and lost contact with most people they knew in New York City. However, as recently as while he was in Roswell Clane learned through the grapevine that his parents still had the occasional letter or phone call from Karl Dennison. He was still married to Susannah; indeed they had three children and one grandchild. Clane imagined him meeting Karl Dennison again. Dennison, an elderly man; and Clane younger, bigger and fully-grown. How different it would be!

"The beast never wanders far from the waterhole." Flying Buffalo placed a comforting hand on his arm. "Your family were his sustenance. Why would he keep away?" Warmth spread from his hand into Clane's flesh. "The word 'human' does not have the straightforward meaning that you think it does. You learned that at very young age. The Apache have a word for certain kinds of people. It translates as 'men without souls'. Every tribe has them now and again. They get born and grow up; then we spot them and banish them from the community. They have anatomically normal human bodies; they can speak with a normal voice. They can interact and communicate with their companions, but their behaviour gives them away. Also their eyes. They all have eyes like Karl Dennison's."

"Why are you telling me this?"

"Because you're about to go through something very difficult."

"What?"

"Something for which you will need to be forearmed with knowledge. The 'men without souls', these people... these *things*. Their power comes from humans not recognizing them for what they are. We are disarmed by them because we assume that they too have human feelings. We believe that the forces of conscience, of principle, of guilt, will affect them to. It won't. To know the soulless is to defeat the soulless." He stared emphatically into Clane's eyes. "Never forget that."

. . . .

Clane turned the key in the lock and opened his front door. "Daddy!" shrilled the familiar little voice. Brendan dashed into the hallway and ran up to his father's knee with his arms expectantly held up in front of him. Clane picked up his two year old son and kissed his cheek. "Hey, Bren; you're getting heavy."

"Hi, Clane." Gina waved from the kitchen. "Good day?"

"I've had better." Clane went upstairs to change. It was six PM and the sun was setting over the Wicklow Mountains. He had left the pub an hour earlier when Flying Buffalo disappeared. He had slipped quietly away while Clane was in the toilet. Clane had asked the landlord and a few of the other patrons, but nobody had seen him leave. His empty glass was on the table where he had been sitting, its white dregs trickling down the sides.

Clane came downstairs in his indoor clothes and the family gathered around the table in the dining room. Their house was smaller than the one they had enjoyed in Washington, but it was charming and comfortable. It was on a gated estate in Greystones, about twenty miles south of Dublin by the seaside. The estate was known as "Foreign Town" because it had been built specifically to house the staff of Ireland's diplomatic missions and their families. Siobhan was now nineteen and studied full time at South Dublin College. After dinner they watched TV and amused themselves watching Brendan playing with his teddy bears on the floor before his bedtime. At ten PM Clane and Gina retired and Gina had a bath.

She came back to the bedroom in her dressing gown and collapsed on the bed. "Oh God!" She sighed.

"Still tired?"

"Yes. I don't feel that all well."

"Oh dear, honey." Clane stroked her dark red hair. "You've been feeling run down for a while now."

"Yes. Maybe it's Bren. He takes some looking after."

Clane looked down at his prostrate wife. Concern filled him. He was far more deeply in love with Gina than he had ever been before. Their divorce had proceeded too far to have it annulled, so they simply got married again. It was a quick ceremony at Montgomery County Court, after which the parish priest at St Mary's blessed their wedding. Gina was dressed in a simple blue suit and pillbox hat. Siobhan was the bridesmaid and the family came down from New York to celebrate. This was four weeks before their departure to Ireland. Then, later in the year, Brendan was born at the National Maternity Hospital in Dublin. After that Gina changed. She went into a period of deep depression, interspersed with fits of hysteria. She would break down in tears for no manifest reason; then she'd shout angrily at the top of her voice for equally ephemeral motives. She accused the next door neighbours of spreading slanderous rumours about her. She hallucinated a few times, seeing cats and dogs and even people wandering around the house when there were none there. The doctor had given her a course of tablets which had made her feel better, much to Clane and Siobhan's relief. However she had not regained the weight she had lost during her illness, even though she was now eating and drinking normally. She also lacked energy. It took longer than before to get her out of bed and she had to take frequent rests while doing the housework. She started waking up frequently at night, but still appeared dazed from lack of sleep during the day. "Clane." she said as he laid down beside her on the bed.

"Hmm?"

"My bras don't seem to fit at the moment."

He sat up. "What you mean?"

She pulled back her dressing gown, exposing her bosom. "Is one of my tits bigger than the other?"

He looked down at her breasts. "I'm not sure, I haven't noticed."

"I swear, the left one's got bigger, or the right one's got smaller."

"Maybe it from feeding Brendan."

"I hardly ever have to nowadays though. He's on normal food."

"So he is."

She rolled onto her side and pulled the quilt over her. "Anyway, night night."

"Good night, honey." He bent down and kissed her temple. Clane couldn't sleep. He got up and went downstairs. He made himself a coffee and switched on the TV. There was a late night news programme about a famine that had broken out in eastern Africa due to a long drought. He cringed painfully at the sight of emaciated toddlers and families drinking water from puddles. After an hour, he went back to the bedroom. Sure enough Gina was lying awake, staring at the ceiling. Her bedside lamp was on. "Hey, honey." Clane began as casually as he could. "Have you taken a trip to the doc lately?"

"No."

"Maybe you should."

She rolled over and looked at him. "Why?"

He shrugged and lowered himself into the bed beside her. "Well, you know; just get yourself checked over, as a precaution. Preventative, you know?" They switched out the lights and settled down to sleep, but Clane continue to lie awake. Gina had forgotten, but he hadn't. Her Aunt Jane had exhibited the exact same symptoms as Gina... six months before she died.

Chapter 11

The nine aircraft flew in formation, as if at an air show. Three C-130 transporters with two escort fighters each. They stacked in the low cloud above Clogham Air Base landing one at a time, their repetitive split-second wing-tip flashes blinked slightly out of step, merging into synch then diverging. The rumble of turboprop engines rolled across the airfield, growing steadily louder as the outline of one plane after another settled as slowly as falling leaves between the two lines of runway lights. Because of the curious effects of perspective, the planes seemed to speed up rather than slow down as they braked on the runway, great vortices of rainwater curling from their wingtips. Clane put his fingers in his ears to block out the cacophony of the multiple jets and turboprops. The wind whipped up by the Hercules' propellers poked through his clothing, making him shiver. As soon as the aircraft wheels were chocked and their engines were off, their AAF escort led him and the ambassador from where they were sheltering beside the main hanger and across the apron to the rear of one of the transporters. The smell of aircraft exhaust was overpowering. A group of several dozen British observers joined them, and everywhere there were security police. They formed the perimeter around the aircraft half-levelling their rifles towards the barbed wire fence that marked the edge of the air force base. The raucous yells of the protesters were audible even from hundreds of yards away. They stood in a line, their fingers grasping the wire mesh as if they could tear it with their hands.

"I see those women are out in force." a voice chuckled behind him. Clane jumped and turned round. "Gerald."

"Hello, Clane old boy." Gerald Caxton's teeth gleamed as his broad grin filled Clane's vision. He reached out his hand and Clane shook it.

"What brings you back to Ireland?" asked Clane.

"Well, after the Treaty, the PM thought I deserved a respite so he devised a mellower occupation for me. He appointed me to the Anglo-Irish office in the Ministry of Defence." He rolled his eyes in mock frustration.

"Of course, I remember now seeing your name on paperwork but never quite associated with you."

"I'm not surprised; we last met months ago now. How is that lovely wife of yours? I hear you're remarried."

Thoughts of Gina struck him like a seizure. He had got through his day so far by suppressing them.

"She's... She's not too well. She's been poorly for a few months now. She's having tests at the hospital to find out what's up with her."

Caxton's brow collapsed into a sympathetic grimace. "Well, all the best to you both." he said.

The cargo ramp at the back of the first Hercules transporter slowly lowered like a drawbridge. The aircraft crew moved carefully as they extracted their materiel out of the hold and down the ramp onto the concrete apron. They were laid on pallets; grey fish-shaped projectiles, ten feet or so in length with red tips on the nose. There was nothing obviously unusual that the untrained observer would pick out. They looked like ordinary finned unguided contact fuse bombs. Some were cone shaped; missile warheads. "Tactical nuclear weapons!" grinned Caxton. His face took on an almost greedy look. Clane had last seen that expression on his face in 1950 when he had shown him the uncut Danlue film of the Empire State Building destruction. Clane and the other members of the British and American observer contingent followed the nuclear bombs as they were gingerly wheeled across the airbase towards the arsenal. The special storage area for nuclear weapons was a row of armoured bunkers covered by soil and turf. The covering apparently scrambled thermal emissions that might be picked up by Soviet spy satellites. Afterwards the group moved over to the airbase buildings where the commandant gave them a lecture about the forward deployment of America's nuclear vanguard onto the three US airbases in Ireland. That one, Clogham, right in the centre of Ireland. Burgess in the south; and Glencar in County Sligo in the north. "This is a direct response to the stationing of Soviet SS-20 medium range missiles along the western coast of continental Europe." explained the officer.

After the lecture, Caxton invited Clane to the pub for a drink. They drove out of the base in Caxton's chauffeured saloon. At the entrance to the base, the peace campaigners ran forward to hurl slogans at the passing vehicle. "Damn women!" tutted Caxton. Clane looked out through the tinted pane at the frightened and angry faces of the crowd. Despite Caxton's appellation, only about three quarters of them were female. They were badly-dressed and looked unwashed. Some of them carried small children in their arms, holding them high as if to display them to the occupants of the car and demonstrate the innocence of the lives at risk, as they saw it, because of the stationing of American nuclear weaponry on Irish soil. Caxton made this observation himself when he and Clane arrived at the pub in a village a few miles away. "I think they're trying to guilt trip us." he noted as he sipped from his pint. "Make us feel ashamed that their poor little babies are threatened by our nasty old bombs."

Clane stared down into the meniscus of beer at the top of his glass. He thought back to the destruction, death and injury he had witnessed in Hiroshima after the war. "From what I've seen, they're proposing a negotiated nuclear disarmament with the Bloc. The escalation of our own forces makes things worse."

Caxton snorted. "So we ask the commie nicely if he'll get rid of his nukes, and we promise to do the same?"

"Why not?"

"The Prisoner's Dilemma. Did you ever study Game Theory?"

"Only while watching the World Series on TV." Clane quipped.

Caxton laughed appreciatively. "Here's our dilemma. Suppose we make a deal with the Reds: we remove our nukes while they remove theirs. We both agree, the deal is stuck. Now, what if one of us chooses secretly to betray the other?"

"Why would they do that?"

"Why *wouldn't* they? If one side chooses to betray the other then the worst that can happen is that the other side does the same and both sides keep their bombs and the situation remains unchanged. However, if one side chooses not to betray they have nothing to gain. The best case is that the other side also doesn't in which case both sides are devoid of nukes... but the worst case is that the other side alone betrays and keeps their nukes while you get rid of yours. So logically an agreed mutual disarmament is impossible. We can never be completely sure that the Bloc has kept its side of the bargain and scrapped all his nukes; therefore we can never scrap ours; never, no matter what happens."

Clane shook his head with bemusement. "God I miss the Interplanetary War."

Caxton chuckled ironically. "Ah yes, those pesky Martians. I'd completely forgotten about them."

"Me too. Funny how that always happens."

"And now the honeymoon is over. The removal of our common enemy has reminded us of our worldly differences. This so-called 'Cold War' has begun."

The two men paused. "How can it ever end?" asked Clane.

Caxton leaned forward to bring his face closer to Clane. It was starting to go dark outside and his skin was garishly illuminated by electric lights inside the pub. "It can't!" he hissed. "It can *never* end. It can never be won and never be lost. It can only be maintained; statically and indefinitely."

"Sounds pretty grim." Clane frowned.

"Reality does not take into account our feelings and scruples."

Clane felt irritation at Caxton's words; while he was speaking Clane was still thinking of Japan. "I know what the reality of war is, Gerald."

"Then you, more than anybody else, will understand the necessity of maintenance and containment of an enemy we cannot conquer nor be conquered by... You've seen those weapons today. You know how many more there are, how much bigger they get. The strategic deterrent, on land and submarine based platforms. Balance is the word, Clane. Balance is everything. World peace *is* possible, but it will be totally different in form to how those malodorous subhuman tree-huggers outside the base perceive it. World peace is not the absence of war, but the perfect equilibrium of warlike forces. Did you know that the American coalition had a plan to invade Europe last year? To depose all the Red Bloc regimes over there?"

"It was on the scuttlebutt."

"It was called 'Project Safety Valve'. Highly classified of course. It would begin with an infiltration of intelligence agents and special forces, then a mass amphibious landing, similar to D-Day... It was shelved in November."

"Because of the bomb?"

Caxton shrugged. "Partly."

"Do we need any other reason?"

"Human psychology. Another world war within a decade of the last? Our... consultants advised us against it."

"What consultants are these?"

Caxton shrugged in an embarrassed and evasive way. "Maybe that's a story for another time."

....

Clane and Gerald Caxton shared a car for their trip back to Dublin. The night sky was heavy with cloud and the stars were smothered. The entire route was lined with fracking sites. The flare stacks above the derricks were all burning and the yellow flames cast a punctuated glow across the landscape like a static swarm of fireflies. They were so bright they illuminated the underside of the overcast, making the clouds look as if they had internal lighting. The stack nearest the road shone so brightly it almost made Clane narrow his eyes. Its yellow fire was like something liquid or solid. An extra-large gobbet of flame broke free and rose above the landscape, keeping its shape like a dragon. Clane followed it with his gaze as the car drove past. "Extraordinary!" said Caxton. Clane looked at him. He too was staring at the array of gas flares, stretching off into the horizon. His eyes were wide, the lights of the flares were reflected of the oily sheen of his skin, illuminating the dark caves of his nostrils. His mouth was stretched into a grin and his teeth glittered; greedy, excited, aroused.

"What's extraordinary, Gerald?" asked Clane feeling uncomfortable with Caxton's manner.

"Energy!... Energy is everything!"

"I thought you said balance was everything?"

Caxton laughed through a half-smile. "One is an example of the other, dear boy. Nothing... *nothing* must come between a nation and its supply of energy. Even these fracking arrays are just the cherry on the cake. Oilfields are still what counts, Clane. Good old fashioned sweet light crude. Why else would we be so motivated to save Iran? The Persian rug factories?"

Clane remembered his transatlantic crossing aboard USS *Rickover*. "Oil is not the only energy source today though, Gerald. In years to come the world may well be run off the power of the split atom."

Caxton chuckled sarcastically. "Of course! Atomic power will change the world!... Pah! It has revolutionized submarine warfare and done zilch elsewhere. Why? Because an atomic reactor costs as much to build as twenty oil refineries and no amount of development or mass production will bring that price down more than forty percent. Useable uranium ore will peak within twenty-five years and still nobody knows exactly what to do with the toxic waste. We can make bombs out of it; but there's a production ceiling even on them... No, Clane, it has to be oil. Oil, oil, oil! Right along the line. From beginning to end."

....

Clane had never known what fear was before; he realized that now. USS *Tunny* had been depth-charged three times when he was on board and had been dive-bombed by four aircraft; one of these air attacks had left a close friend dead. He had been terrified beyond anything he'd ever felt before, but that kind of terror had the sugar coating of action and excitement. That fear was fun; this fear was totally different. He sat helplessly and passively in the waiting room beside Gina, clasping her hand in a cast iron monkey grip that she hadn't eased since they'd arrived at the hospital. She stared downwards at her lap, her gaze as motionless as a statue. The staff in the outpatients department at St James' Hospital in Dublin gave nothing away. The receptionist behaved politely and neutrally as she booked Gina in. Doctors and nurses walked to and fro, conferring with each other in relaxed and cheery voices. At one point Clane saw Dr McGuire. He caught his eye and the medic waved and smiled. Was that a good sign? Clane's heart pounded and adrenalin coursed through his bloodstream; but all he could do was sit there and wait. Everything around him was calm and normal. Lucky people moved around him without the axe of worry that hung over his neck. He glared at the clock; the hands were still in the same place they had been when he'd last looked. He cursed under his breath. His legs trembled and his buttocks clenched repeatedly. He looked again at Gina; she hadn't moved. Poor Gina. He felt a surge of love for her. He would have swapped places with her if he could. Every so often the receptionist would call out a name and one of the people in the waiting area would stand up and head off to the consulting rooms. Eventually she called: "Gina Quilley, Dr McGuire will see you now." Clane kept hold of her hand as he stood up. He felt the urge to flee, to drag her away to an intuitive safety. They walked unsteadily over to the doorway and entered the doctor's office. Dr McGuire smiled and gestured to the chairs on the opposite side of his desk. "Hello, Mr and Mrs Quilley. How are you?" He was a kind-looking elderly man with a thick white beard and a sing-song educated Hiberno accent.

"Fine." They both replied in unison. Clane marvelled at the stupidity of his question and of their answer.

The doctor shuffled through his notes. "Mrs Quilley, we have the results back from the biopsy we performed on your left breast; also the X-rays we did..." He cleared his throat and became grave. "I'm afraid we did detect the presence of malignant lobular carcinoma cells in the biopsy, and also the possibility of similar tumours on the X-rays; we'll need to perform further biopsies to confirm this."

"So, I've got cancer?" Gina said in a voice that didn't sound like her own.

"Yes. I'm very sorry. We'll provide all the best treatments we can for you. Oncology has advanced considerably in recent years."

"My Auntie Jane got it and they cut her breast off. Will I have to have the same?"

The doctor gave a very medical pause. "I'm afraid that would not help much at this point, Mrs Quilley. You see, the cancer you have is very fast growing and aggressive, and it has metastasized. The initial tumour has spread into what we call a Stage Four state; this is what has caused the secondary tumours in your lungs and pelvis. In order to manage your case we'll need to provide a continuous course of radio and chemotherapy."

"Will that get rid of it?"

"No. However it will prolong the tumour growth progression."

Gina paused. "How long have I got?"

"Possibly over a year, depending on how well you respond to the treatment. We'll also make sure you have access to all the pain relief and sedative medication you need... I'm very sorry, but that's all we can do."

....

The walk back to the car was dreamlike. Clane could easily imagine that the last few minutes in Dr McGuire's office had not happened and that he'd imagined them. Gina was impassive and robotic. She kept her gaze straight ahead and blank. The stomach churning fear Clane had felt beforehand in the waiting room had evaporated and all that was left was numb calm. Everything that he'd been dreading had come to pass, but now it felt strangely anticlimactic. Gina turned to face him; her expression was as deadpan as his own mental state. "So this is it; I'm going to die... Let's go home. We have to tell Siobhan." Clane and Gina's nineteen year old daughter screamed with anguish when they broke the news. She cried in their arms for half an hour. "Come now." said Gina in a tremulous but authoritative voice. "We all must go to church. We need to pray."

....

"Hail Mary, full of grace, the Lord is with thee. Blessed art thou amongst women, and blessed is the fruit of thy womb, Jesus. Holy Mary, Mother of God, pray for us sinners, now and at the hour of our death. Amen." Clane, Gina and Siobhan recited the prayer as a canon, with Clane speaking aloud the first two lines and his wife and daughter reciting the third in chorus. Siobhan was still snivelling and her words were occasionally muffled as she wiped her nose with a tissue. Gina was as cool and serene as if this were a normal Sunday mass. Clane flicked another bead of his rosary through the gap between his thumb and index finger and they began again: *"Hail Mary, full of grace, the Lord is with thee. Blessed art thou amongst women, and blessed is the fruit of thy womb, Jesus. Holy Mary, Mother of God, pray for us sinners, now and at the hour of our death. Amen."* They prayed the entire Rosary which took them about half an hour; keeling in the pews of their local church in suburban Dublin. Then they stood, crossed themselves and genuflected as they turned and exited the church. Just before they got into the car Gina looked up at the tower of the church. A large bronze crucifix was mounted halfway up. She smiled as she looked at it. "You know, Clane. I really am so lucky. When Our Lord was on the cross nobody offered him any diamorphine sulphate or Valium. He had to suffer! And he was younger than me too." She grinned in contentment and lowered herself into the car. Clane looked up at the sculpture of the dying Jesus. Intangible and nameless thoughts ran through his head.

……......

They dropped into the diplomatic creche on the way home and picked up Brendan. He was sleeping peacefully in his carrycot and didn't stir for the whole journey back to their house. Once indoors Siobhan retired to her bedroom to be alone with her own thoughts. Gina reached into the cot to move Brendan from it to his crib, but before she did so she sat in a chair and held him close to her. She stroked the toddler's hair and he turned his head, mumbling slightly in his sleep. Gina's hair hung down over her face so Clane couldn't see it, but he could hear by her breathing that she was sobbing. "He'll never really get to know me." she faltered. "You must tell him, Clane. Tell him everything about me."

"I will." Clane croaked. It was the first time he had spoken since their prayers in church.

"I've got an idea." She looked up at him and wiped the tears from her eyes. "Do you still have a dictaphone?"

"Yes."

"Could you go and get it." Clane went to his study and opened the drawer where he kept the small audio recorder for taking down verbal notes and discussions. He brought it to his wife. "Clane, I'm going to record some tapes that you must keep safe and play to Bren when he's older."

"OK."

She sat back in her chair, still clutching Brendan in her arms. She switched on the recorder. "Hello, Brendan. You won't know me, but I'm your mommy. I'm sorry I can't be with you now, but if you listen to these tapes, hopefully you will get to know me almost as well as if I was here..." She filled up three entire cassettes before Brendan woke up and she got up to feed him. Clane put the cassettes in his safe and carefully locked it. The family ate dinner as normal, speaking intermittently about trivia. Then Gina went to bed and Clane was alone. He went out for a walk. The sky was pitch black and overcast again; a tepid drizzle was falling. It was a typical evening in Dublin; the city rushed around him as if everything were normal. He walked around the closes and cul-de-sacs of Foreign Town for a while, then went home and got into his car. He drove back to the church where the family had prayed earlier. The dark granite facade was partly-lit by the streetlights and glistened with moisture from the rain. He stepped out of the car and looked up at the crucifix. His hand reached into his pocket and grasped his rosary, but then he stopped. The bronze cast face of Christ was in shadow. He turned away. There was a loose curb stone just behind the place where he had parked. He felt a sudden craving to pick it up and hurl it at the church. He swung round and faced the statue again. "You motherfucker!" he bellowed at the top of his voice. A passer-by stopped and gaped at him. A door opened in a house opposite and somebody came out to see what the commotion was about. Clane got into his car and drove away. He eventually parked in a dark lay-by. He leaned forward on the steering wheel and wept.

....

Clane went back to work the next day. Word got round of course. The ambassador called him to his office and offered him the opportunity to take some time off, but Clane needed his job to keep his mind focused away from the pain. He knew it was the only way to save himself from depression. "I understand, Clane." responded Jose Gutierrez. "Still, if you need to take a break to attend to your wife, go with her to the hospital and things like that; just let me know." Clane worked hard at his desk and went to meeting after meeting. He talked to the press, sent telegrams to China and sometimes went to the computer room downstairs to send a few of the new "E-grams"; these were similar to telegrams or letters except they were transmitted directly from computer to computer over GovMesh and an updated system called "WorldMesh", which made them conveniently fast. He phoned the US Secretary of State, talked business with Shell Oil and politics with Leinster House. There was a huge amount to do following the arrival of the nuclear weapons a few days earlier and the continuing Soviet intervention in Iran. Late the following morning Amy brought him up a printout of replies from the E-grams he'd sent. One of them was from Gerald Caxton: *Hi Clane. Just to let you know I'll be on my way over to Dublin on Thursday for the strat meeting. I heard about your wife's illness. Very sorry; sending you both my best wishes. Let me know if you want to meet up for anything. Gerald.* Clane smiled and folded the paper.

....

The radiotherapy chamber had a normal-looking interior, but its walls were a foot thick. The door opened smoothly on well-oiled hinges, but it must have weighed over a ton and obviously contained lead panels. It reminded Clane of the shielded bulkheads that surround a submarine's nuclear reactor; and it served the same purpose. Filling most of the room was an enormous white-painted machine that looked like a giant pencil-sharpener. Clutched in its maw was a sliding couch with a mattress and pillow. Gina walked over and rested her hand against its metallic flank. "It looks like it's just come down from Mars." she said.

"It's called a 'linac'." said Dr McGuire. "and it's really just a very powerful version of the device we used to take your X-ray pictures. It will emit a narrow beam of ionizing radiation at the primary tumour in your left breast which will kill the malignant cells."

"Will it hurt?"

"No, you won't feel any sensation at all. The only way you'll know the treatment period has begun will be a buzzing noise from the linac."

"Radiation?" Clane said. "But isn't that in itself harmful?"

"Not in this application." replied McGuire in a confident tone. "The beam is very focused and resonant. It targets only a small area of the body and delivers its entire dose in about one minute. Thanks to the tomography images we took of Mrs Quilley we know the dimensions of the tumour exactly and will be able to irradiate it from several angles in order to minimize exterior cell damage."

"Cell damage?" Clane recalled the patients he had seen at the hospital in Hiroshima. "So there are side effects?"

"Yes, but we don't expect them to be serious."

"What are you expecting?" asked Gina.

The oncologist shrugged. "You may experience some temporary skin irritation at the treatment sites, like minor sunburn. You could feel tired and feverish; maybe a little nauseous. Towards the end of the course you may lose some of your hair. Pretty much the same as with your chemotherapy."

Gina didn't reply. She continued to study the clinical behemoth filling the lead chamber.

"So, are you happy for me to book you in for a two-week course?" asked the doctor.

She nodded.

"You will need to attend every day. We can begin next Tuesday."

"Can my husband be with me while it's done?"

"Not here in the chamber, Mrs Quilley. To prevent anybody else getting a radiation dose you'll have to be in here by yourself. The radiotherapists will operate the linac from the control room just outside. But Mr Quilley is welcome to come with you as far as the waiting room."

Gina shuddered.

After their tour of the radiotherapy suite Clane and Gina headed back to the main oncology block to check in for Gina's first chemotherapy session. The clinic was very different to what they'd expected. There were no steel-framed beds with white linen; instead the room was furnished with big armchairs and couches. There were pictures on the walls and a television set in the corner. The patients were all in their regular clothes and they sat around as if they were in a normal lounge. Some were eating meals or drinking cups of tea. A few were reclined back asleep. The only thing out of the ordinary was that all the patients had drip stands next to them with bags of IV fluid. These were mobile stands with wheels on the bottom. As Gina waited to be seen a man walked past her pushing his own IV set along beside him. A kindly nurse introduced herself and gave Gina one of the seats; then she inserted an IV cannula into a vein on the back of her hand. Gina winced slightly from the sting this caused. The nurse then attached a clear plastic tube to the valve on the cannula and inserted the other end into a bag of grey foul-looking liquid. There was a bright yellow warning label on the bag saying: *CAUTION- CYTOTOXIC. Handle with care*. It quickly ran down the tube and entered Gina's hand. For the next two hours they sat there while the IV fluid emptied slowly into Gina's bloodstream. They talked to the other patients, read books and watched TV. It was a very normal afternoon.

"That wasn't so bad." smiled Gina as they drove home afterwards. "I feel the same now as I did before. I've only got to do that once a week. If I just take the two weeks of radiotherapy on top of that... I could get another six months of life! Sounds like a good deal."

"Very!" Clane smiled back at her in the rear-view mirror, just grateful that she was happy.

They arrived back home, made a cup of tea and ate a meal. Gina went to get up afterwards and sighed heavily.

"Are you OK, honey?"

"Yes... Well... I suddenly feel really tired."

Clane helped her into the lounge where she collapsed onto the settee. "Darn it." she said. "I feel like I weigh a thousand tons." A few minutes later she developed a hot flush that caused her skin to glow bright red as if she'd been running. She sweated profusely and Clane opened a window to keep her cool even though it was cold and wet outside. "Clane, I feel sick." she said. Clane just had time to fetch a mixing bowl from the kitchen for her to vomit copiously into. Her meal all came up, one retch at a time until green bile dripped from her lips. Clane called the hospital urgently. "I'm sorry she's not well, Mr Quilley." said the doctor on the other end of the line. "I'm afraid this kind of malaise is a typical side effect. Lots of chemo patients experience it. Don't worry, it she'll be better by tomorrow."

....

Gina had indeed recovered when Clane's alarm went off at seven AM. She had had a difficult night, mostly because of the attack of rampant diarrhoea that struck her down when the nausea had worn off. She had spent most of the evening sitting on the toilet and had to pay frequent visits all through the night. She had been caught short once and had soiled her panties like a little girl. She handled this embarrassing eventuality dispassionately. She simply threw the garment away and took a bath to clean herself up. By morning she was well enough to eat a small breakfast with her husband. Clane kissed her goodbye and got into his car for the short drive into Dublin. The first feeling he had as he pulled out of Foreign Town was relief. He was strangely glad to be alone and away from Gina. A pang of guilt washed through him as he tried to analyze his own emotions towards his wife. This quest became obsessive and he seethed inwardly as he negotiated the morning traffic around Dun Laoghaire. He had still not succeeded when he arrived at the American Embassy. He walked into his office, greeted his secretary and started to tackle his inbox. He focused hard on each document, but images of his wife appeared in his vision and nothing he did could get rid of them.

At eleven AM it was time for the Anglo-Irish strategy meeting, an event held every month. He was on his way along the corridor to the boardroom when he heard a voice behind him that made him jump. "It's a fine morning, Clane."

He swung round. "Gerald... Hello. Sorry, I forgot you were coming. I got your E-gram, but it slipped my mind."

Gerald Caxton gave his characteristic smile. "That's alright; it doesn't surprise me... How is Gina?"

Clane shrugged. "Bearing up; being very brave."

"I'm sure she is... I'm thinking of you both." His face became serious, sympathetic and concerned. "If there's anything I can do, let me know."

"Thank you."

Caxton went over to join the UK contingent. Clane took his seat at the table in the boardroom and exchanged small-talk with the other embassy staff. He opened his briefcase and began shuffling through his papers. All the other attendees arrived and the chairman called them to order. He opened the meeting and introduced the official who would lead off the discussion. It was some young British junior executive from an oil company with thick spectacles and a monotone voice; Clane forgot his name within seconds of being told it. The speaker read from a clipboard, not lifting his gaze, giving an update on the situation in Iran. "...We have been in regular contact with our Tehran offices and so far they report that all operations remain normal. The fields across the country are still at full production and so far the new government has not attempted to interfere with them. However, we don't believe this situation will last. It's the calm before the storm. Mr Mossadeg remains under house arrest and the Nadeen committee are firmly in control. Naturally they're using the Soviet presence as a massive act of bravado to their rivals. It's only a matter of time before our Iranian contract will be up for review..."

Clane looked at the clock and rolled his eyes. The lead-off had been running for over twenty-five minutes.

"...Communism does not behave like other political movements. It's more like cancer. It begins silently and imperceptibly in remote areas of the human world. Then is expands and spreads into debilitating painful lumps, branching out, smaller but still obtrusive and threatening, until it slowly but surely rots the entire globe..."

Clane felt a mental earthquake rising inside him. His vision clouded over and was replaced by an image of Gina lying in bed, hot, sweaty and sickly. He blinked and saw that everybody was looking at him. He must have spoken, or yelled out, and not heard himself. "Are you alright, Mr Quilley?" asked the chairman.

His skin was numb, his head spinning. He stood up. "May I be excused?" he asked, and headed for the door without waiting for a reply. He dashed to the washroom. His breath was rasping in an out of his lungs uncontrollably, his face and neck were burning, his mouth was as dry as a pocket. The parched and inflamed membranes of his throat stuck together making him gag. He turned on the cold tap at the washbasins and dipped his arm into the chill water. He splashed it onto his glowing cheeks and forehead. He gulped manically at the tap as if it were an oasis. He felt a hand touch his shoulder and a soothing voice speak above the sound of running water. "He didn't know, Clane. He didn't know about Gina."

Clane nodded as he dipped his face into the churning basin. He raised his head to see Caxton standing beside him, leaning on the neighbouring sink. Clane dried his head and arms on the roller-towel. "I'm sorry, Gerald. Something inside me just snapped."

Jose Gutierrez burst into the lavatory. "Clane, are you alright?"

He straightened up. "Yes, your Excellency. Apologies for that."

The ambassador smiled and nodded his head. He said gently: "Clane, go home."

"But, sir..."

"No, Clane. I respect the effort you've made; I know you want to keep on working, but you're simply not in a fit state right now. You're wife needs you; you need to stay strong for her as well as yourself. I'm putting you on compassionate leave for as long as is necessary."

....

Clane approached the bar at *The Windmill Inn* and ordered a second pint of Guinness. It was lunchtime and the pub was filling up so he had to wait a while to be served. He returned to his table and sipped from his glass. It was an hour since he'd been ordered off work by the ambassador. He'd only intended to have a quick one before the journey home, but here he was, an hour later, still drinking.

When Gerald Caxton entered the pub he looked over and waved. Clane's heart soared at the sight of his British friend, although he wasn't sure why. In fact it was the first time he'd thought of the Englishman as a friend; and now he did, that sentiment was very powerful. Caxton ordered his own drink and came over to join him. "How are you feeling, Clane?"

He shrugged. "Pretty crap."

"Spalding was deeply sorry when he found out."

"Spalding?"

"The kid doing the lead-off."

"He wasn't to know, Gerald... He used an appropriate metaphor actually." He attempted to chuckle.

"I don't mean to intrude, Clane, but why haven't you gone home?"

Clane looked hard at him. Caxton's eyes were wide and honest, warm and endearing. "I should, shouldn't I? I ought to be at Gina's side, taking care of her... The truth is, I hate seeing her the way she is so much that I need to spend time away from her. She repels me!... Isn't that awful? I've failed her, haven't I? I'm a worthless coward!"

"No, Clane. You're a man with a heart of your own, and you need to take care of yourself as well as her."

"I wish it was me who was sick, Gerald!" Clane blurted. "I wish it was me and not her... She's going to die." He felt his eyes moisten. "The doctor told us... Well, he umm-ed and ah-ed, but eventually gave us the bottom line. There's nothing they can do except slow the tumour growth as much as possible, which means she might last until late next year. And slowing the tumour means she has to undergo treatment that makes her feel like shit. Her hair's going to fall out, she won't be able to eat properly, she'll loose weight... She's going to spend the last year of her life as an invalid." He blinked back his tears and wiped his eyes with a tissue.

"What if she doesn't have the treatment?"

"Then she'll be gone in a couple of months... Last night when she was throwing up, she told me she was considering that option. She said she wanted to be healthy and well during the time she had left and she'd swap quantity for quality by refusing the chemo and radiotherapy."

"What do you want her to do?"

"I don't know!" he sobbed. "I just want her to be better... and I can't have that!"

"What if you could?"

Clane stared at him irritated. "What sort of question is that, Gerald?... If I could, I'd... I'd do anything! *Anything* to have Gina well again."

Caxton's expression became more severe and he spoke more quietly. "You see..." He quickly looked over his shoulder, as if to check their conversation was not being overheard. "I might be able to arrange for Gina... a second opinion."

"What do you mean?"

"I know some doctors who might be able to provide a... er... an improved treatment regimen for her."

"No good, Gerald. She's currently under the oncology department at St James; they're the best in the country."

"That depends. They're certainly the best if you're a regular Voluntary Health Initiative cancer patient; but there are independent health services, offering specialist treatments, that are far superior, I believe. They're not available to everybody though; they're certainly not available on the VHI. They sometimes cost a lot of money, and are therefore exclusive to those with the ability to pay; and in some cases..." He looked over his shoulder again and lowered his voice even further. "...those with the right connections."

He gasped. "Do you mean... you could find Gina a doctor who could get her more time?... More time and fewer side effects?"

He paused and shrugged. "Quite possibly."

"Can you arrange us an appointment?"

"Certainly. I'll do that this afternoon and give you a phone call."

....

"Clane, where are we going?" demanded Gina as she buttoned up her jacket.

"I told you, to the doctors."

"But I'm going not due back at Dr McGuire's till Monday."

"I know, but this is a different doctor." Clane tied his shoelaces and looked out of the window of their house. Their front garden sloped up steeply to the road giving the window a limited view.

"Why do I need to see a different doctor?"

"I'll explain on the way." A dark shape appeared by the gate. "The car's here now. Hurry up!"

Clane pulled the front door shut and they climbed up the steps to street level. "Who's this?" asked Gina. The car was a black Bentley with tinted windows; its engine was ticking over in a deep latent growl. A door opened and Caxton stuck his head out. "Good morning, Mrs Quilley."

"Oh..." she said. "Isn't it...?"

"Gerald Caxton, how do you do. We met briefly last Christmas, at the Leinster House ball."

"Well, hello again, Mr Caxton. Where are you taking us?"

"You shall soon see." He gave his characteristic playful grin. The Bentley was warm, clean and spacious. It smelled nice and had dark leather seats. The chauffeur kept his eyes on the road and never spoke for the entire journey. They drove north around Dublin on the bypass and then onto the fastroad into County Meath. Occasionally Caxton piped up with some jolly remark like: "You'll like it where we're going." or: "This is going to be a happy day for you." Gina and Clane didn't reply. It was a fine morning and the sun was filtered through the darkened windows of the sumptuous car. After an hour and a half they reached Dundalk and turned off the fastroad. They slowed down to negotiate some narrow lanes that ran through grassy pastures and forests that gleamed in the sunshine. Farmhouses punctuated the flat land and in the distance darker hills loomed. Horses raised their heads above the hedges lining the verges. They eventually came to a grand stone mansion with a high barred fence lining the road in front of it. A wooden signboard by the gate said in mock-Gothic writing: *BALLYBINABY HEALTH SPA- Strictly Members Only beyond this Point*. The car pulled up outside the ornate entrance and a young manservant in a tight-fitting tracksuit came forward to greet them. Caxton got out first and spoke to him and then beckoned to Gina and Clane. Gina looked around herself nervously as the servant escorted them inside. Clane could smell cooking and saw a dining room to his left. Dampness and chlorine also filled the air, and they walked past a glass panel behind which was a large swimming pool. The tracksuited man led them up a flight of red carpeted stairs and knocked on a heavy wooden door. A voice bid him to enter and they traipsed though into a large waiting room similar to the one at St James' Hospital except this one had oak panelled walls instead of cracked vinyl paint, Victorian sofas instead of chrome tube chairs and copies of *Country Life* and *Horse and Hound* in the magazine rack instead of *Woman's Weekly* and *Puzzler*. The receptionist wore a strange uniform similar to a French maids' outfit. A door at the other end of the room opened and a thin woman in a white coat emerged and gazed wordlessly at Caxton. "Would you excuse me a moment." he said and followed the woman into the room beyond where he shut the door behind him leaving Clane and Gina alone. The large upstairs windows provided a generous view of the health club's grounds. There was a running track around which people were jogging with baseball caps on their heads and towels wrapped round their necks. At the far end of the grounds was a high military fence topped with a helix of barbed wire. A solider brandishing a rife strolled along beyond it. "What's that?" asked Gina.

"The line between us and Northern Ireland. We must be right at the border here. Past that fence is the United Kingdom."

The door opened; Caxton and the woman appeared. "Mr and Mrs Quilley?" said the woman. "Could you come in please?" She swung her back and returned to the room without waiting to see if they were following. Caxton went and took a seat in the waiting room.

The woman never introduced herself, which was so unusual for a doctor that Clane was taken aback. He assumed she was a doctor because of the white coat, but she wore no name badge, unlike the staff at St James'. Her office was similarly bedecked to the waiting room. It had a couch against one wall, a bookshelf covered by glass doors with a lock and a solid desk in the middle. "Take a seat please." she said in a nasal monotone. Her accent was part English and part Irish. Her face was bony and austere; her nose and chin were pointed. Clane and Gina pulled up chairs and faced her across the red leather desktop. The doctor produced a small bottle of tablets from a drawer and placed it on the desk between them. "There's a six-week course there." she said woodenly.

Clane picked up the bottle. It was an ordinary glass pharmacy bottle with a plastic top. Unusually there was no label on it. The pills inside were ovoid and mat orange in colour. They rattled slightly as he handed the bottle to his wife.

"Take one a day before mealtimes." continued the doctor. "Do not continue with your existing treatment. No chemotherapy; no radiotherapy. Give your oncologist any excuse you can think of, but do *not* tell him you taking this medication." Her voice rose distinctly at the word *not*. Her eyes were blank, blue and lifeless, reminding Clane of his last conversation with Flying Buffalo. "Your discretion is essential. Tell nobody that you have been here and you are on this treatment. Keep the bottle somewhere hidden at home. When the bottle is empty wash it carefully and dispose of it in the household rubbish. By then you should be in complete remission. If for any reason you are not, let Mr Caxton know and he'll refer you back here."

There was a pause. "What... what did you say?" stuttered Gina. "Complete remission!?"

"That is what I said."

"Do you mean I'll be free of the cancer?"

"Yes."

"Then I'll be... cured? I won't die?"

"Correct."

"You're joking!" yelled Clane.

The doctor lowered her brows and turned her cadaver eyes on him. Her expression made manifest her attitude towards jokes.

Gina pointed at the bottle. "What's in these?"

"That information is not for you to know. You must make no inquiries and ask no questions of Mr Caxton, understood?" She stood up and opened the door, indicating that the consultation was over. Clane and Gina stood up and left the room. "Thanks." mumbled Clane. "Thank you." echoed Gina even more quietly.

They did not speak in the car home and even Caxton was subdued for the journey. He dropped them off at their garden gate promising to get in touch again soon and drove off. Gina and Clane entered their home and sat quietly. It was just gone two PM and Siobhan was yet to come home from college. Brendan was still at the diplomatic creche. Gina reached into her handbag and brought out the bottle of orange pills. "I was wondering if I'd dreamed everything that happened this morning." she said quietly. "But here they are. Our experience was genuine."

"But are those?" Clane pointed at the bottle. "Maybe they're just candy. Maybe this is some kind of sick joke."

Gina held the bottle up to eye level and shook it. The pills rattled voluptuously against the glass. She stared at the little orange orbs pensively. "If I was in a position where I had anything to lose, I might be that skeptical."

....

Clane and Gina smiled and swung their arms hand in hand as they walked along the corridor to Dr McGuire's office. The Oncology clinic at St James' Hospital was like another world compared to the first time they'd come here. "Hello, Mr and Mrs Quilley." The doctor greeted them with open arms. "I'm so glad to see you again. After you stopped attending clinic we thought you were a wanderer... That's what we call patients who give up and leave us. But I'm glad you came back because I've good news on the tests we've just done. The cancer is gone... It's amazing! A spontaneous remission. It does happen of course, but it's extremely rare; one in a hundred thousand cases at best. And yours is the first I've heard of in a stage four mammary."

"So I'm cured?" Gina asked rhetorically.

"We don't use that word where cancer is concerned, but off the record... yes, totally."

All three of them beamed with delight.

As they left the clinic Clane stopped to look back into the waiting room. The seats were filled with rows of emaciated grey-faced people. Bare scalps covered in thin vellus hair showed above collars and bony hands clutched appointment cards. Coughing and spluttering filled their air. His joy was dampened somewhat.

....

When they got home Gina took the empty pharmacy bottle and washed it exactly as the mysterious doctor at the health club had instructed. "I feel like I want to keep it as a souvenir." she said. "My little bottle of life."

"We can't." said Clane.

"I know." She tossed it into the kitchen rubbish bin.

Clane went to the phone and dialled.

"Caxton." said a voice on the other end of the line.

"Hello, Gerald." Clane's voice quavered with emotion.

"Clane! Hello! How are you, old boy?"

"Perfect, Gerald. I'm absolutely perfect."

"Is Gina well?"

"Completely better."

"Good... Now be careful what you say, Clane. This is an unsecured line and we must not discuss confidential matters."

"It's alright, Gerald. I just wanted to speak to you and say thank you... I don't know *how* to thank you to be honest."

"That's quite alright, my friend. I'm happy to be of service... Erm... however, there are a couple of things I might need your help with in return."

"For you, Gerard? Anything."

There was a pause. "Right... Have you ever been over to the UK before, Clane?"

"No, never."

"Would you like to?"

"Sure."

"Good, I'm thinking of arranging a visit early next year for some officials from the embassy and I'd like you to be one of them."

"OK... But what do you want me to help you with?"

"That is something I can't talk about over the phone."

"Right." Clane frowned at the cryptic tone in Caxton's voice.

188

Chapter 12

There was a knock at his office door.

"Come... Oh hello, Amy. What can I do for you?"

"Hi, Mr Quilley. I've got your name on the list for a desktop computer."

"Really?"

"Yes, didn't you get the memo?"

"It must have slipped past my attention... OK, what do I have to do?"

"Clear a space."

Clane shifted a pile of folders over to one side to make room on his desk for the computer while Amy wheeled it in on a trolley. It was a square, white box that looked like a cross between a television set and a typewriter. It was rather heavy and he had to help the small woman lift the appliance onto his desk. The legs of the desk creaked but held. Amy skilfully plugged the array of cables into the back of the machine and connected the other ends to the electric socket, the telex and a small grey box called a "modem" that she plugged into the telephone outlet. She flicked a switch and the computer started to hum. Its oblong monitor screen lit up; words, lines and numbers scrolled and flickered across it, all white on a black background. Amy sat in Clane's chair, adept at the operation; her hands dancing over the keyboard like a pair of courting spiders. The keys were familiar to Clane, being arranged in the same formation as a typewriter, but what was happening on the monitor could have been in Greek. There was a slit on the side of the machine rather like a small letterbox into which Amy inserted some flat plastic cards with software stored on them. "I'll never get the hang of this, Amy."

"Actually, Mr Quilley, it's quite easy once you've had a bit of practice. We're starting training sessions this afternoon if you need to attend one."

"You can bet on it!" Amy stayed with him for a while, instructing him in the computer's use; so by the time Clane got to the training session he already had the basics. As his colleague had predicted, the machine was very user friendly. Clane switched it on as soon as he was back in his office and the black monitor screen lit up. The large letters *HP* inside a circle appeared and under them the words: "Hewlett-Packard TXPb-1955". There was a pause as strange digital messages appeared and then what Amy called a "menu"; a list of different functions. Clane used the arrow keys and "enter" to select "word processing" and the screen went blank. He pressed a few keys and white letters appeared on the screen in a similar way they would on a piece of paper in a typewriter feed, except this involved far less pressure; he only had to touch the key lightly for the character to appear. He used the keyboard to write: *My name is Clane Quilley* and then the day's date: *Wednesday April 6th 1955* exactly as he

189

used to begin whatever he did at the *Roswell Daily Record* seven years ago. His eyes began watering; this was like watching TV with his face pressed close to the screen. He then opened up the telex interface control and selected *print*. Spontaneously the telex machine on the other side of the room began whirring and a sheet of paper emerged from the reel. He went over and looked at the paper. His words were reproduced in ink on the paper, instantly and effortlessly. "My goodness!" he muttered aloud to himself. He returned to his desk, grinning excitedly, feeling like a child with a new toy. He accessed the embassy network page and sent an internal memorandum: *Hello, Amy. My trips down to your computer room are over I'm afraid.* A few seconds later a reply popped up on the line below: *Told you so didn't I? Have fun, Mr Quilley!* Clane realized he could also send external E-grams directly from where he was sitting; no more draft slips and deliveries. He could talk to anybody in the world right then and there. It was a godlike sensation. It took about five minutes for the computer to log him onto WorldMesh. A new screen appeared with a menu of twenty options. He selected the E-gram box and typed in the E-gram address of his favourite person: *g.caxton@mod.gov.uk*. He chuckled to himself as he imagined his friend sitting in his office hundreds of miles away in London. Would the signal run through the cables under the Irish Sea or would they be relayed via the communications satellites that constantly orbited the earth? *Hi Gerald. I'm writing to you on my new desktop computer. Hope all is well with you. Looking forward to my trip to England next week. Best wishes. Clane.*

A reply came back an hour later: *Hi Clane. Sorry for the delay in replying, I was at a meeting with the PM. Glad you've joined us in the Promethean ranks of office computer users. Fancy a quick game of chess? If so highlight this word and press F2: "MESHMASTERS". Regards. Gerald.*

Clane did so and a new WorldMesh page opened with an eight-by-eight black and white square grid on it; a virtual chessboard. Lined up in two rows at the top and bottom were small graphics representing the pieces; they were surrounded by a black line so they could be seen when they were on a square of their own colour. A message appeared in a box at the bottom: *Greetings, Clane. This is your chess Nemesis here. Prepare to be checkmated! Gerald.*

Clane replied in the reply space: *Not a chance, Gerald! Let battle commence!* And for the next twenty minutes he played chess with a man two hundred and eighty miles away. Caxton beat him easily.

Afterwards Clane received another E-gram from Caxton announcing that he was coming to Dublin the following evening and, of course, he and Clane made arrangements to get together.

....

It was Gerald Caxton's first ever visit to their home. Gina put on her best dress and applied her makeup. Brendan was sent to bed early and Siobhan went out on the town with her friends and ten pounds of Clane's money in her pocket. Gina had cooked an extravagant meal and Clane had purchased some of the best wine he could find in the city centre's department stores. At seven PM the doorbell rang. Clane straightened his tie in the mirror and went to answer it. "Hello, Gerald!"

Caxton's grin stretched across the doorway. "Good evening, Clane old boy!"

"Come in, Gerald! Come in!"

"Thank you... And hello again, Gina!"

Clane's wife beamed as she shook his hand. "Welcome, Gerald. It's an honour to have you as a guest in our home... Dinner will be ready soon." They had a cheery meal, laughing and joking. They drank two bottles of wine and some after-dinner brandy; then a high-pitched voice was heard calling from upstairs: "Mommy!... Mommy!"

"That's Brendan." said Gina. "Excuse me, gentlemen while I go and attend to him. When she had left, Caxton said: "Clane, what a magnificent evening. I've had a wonderful time. You and Gina are charming hosts... Now, I understand we're at the seaside here. I'd love to see your beach."

"The beach? What now?"

"Yes."

"But, Gerald, it's almost ten o'clock at night."

"Please, Clane. Let's go for a walk on the beach." He remained friendly, but there was something strangely insistent about his tone. So, after calling up to Gina to inform her of their actions, they left the house, walked through the gates of Foreign Town and headed towards the sea. It was a dank and overcast night. The clouds fluoresced with the lights of Dublin. The moisture in the air dampened Clane's eyebrows and lips. Despite his professed lack of familiarity for the area, Caxton seemed to be leading the way. He walked confidently through the streets of Greystones. They strode quickly across the harbour car park and onto the beach. Shingle gave way to sand under their feet and the darkness ahead swallowed them up. The lights of the harbour fell behind them and became dimmer as they kept on walking. Then Caxton suddenly stopped. Clane stopped beside him. It was chilly on this spring night. A gusty breeze blew past them out to sea. The rustle of the surf, invisible in the darkness ahead, surrounded them. A pair of lights shone out of the maritime gloom, a white one surmounting a red one. It was a ship far out at sea heading north along the coast. "It's delightful to see Gina well again, Clane." began Caxton.

"I never stop thinking that, Gerald. I'll never take her for granted again."

"I'm glad to have done that for you, Clane." Even in the black of night, Caxton's toothy grin was visible.

"I've been thinking." Clane recalled the sick people he'd seen in the oncology waiting room during their last visit. "I know you said we couldn't talk about it, but... please, will you just tell me? The medication Gina had, is it going to be available soon to the general public? Think how many millions of lives it could save?"

Caxton paused, his grin widened. "Yes, of course, Clane. I've not heard the latest, but I've no doubt it being prepared for mass-prescription... While we're on the subject of cancer, do you recall that day in the embassy last year when you were sent home? You told me you thought Clarence Spalding gave a good lead-off in the discussion on Iran. You said he used an 'appropriate metaphor', comparing the spread of communism to the spread of cancer. What did you mean?"

"Well... it was more of an image than anything I can put verbally." Once again, as had happened several times before, Clane felt that his friend was saying something with a hidden point behind the basic meaning of his words. "It's the spreading and infecting vision that I had; it's what upset me so much that day, knowing that Gina had it so badly... When the Red Army quit Iran, it felt like a symbol for her own healing process."

"Yes, we were very lucky there, with Iran I mean." He sighed. "If the Nadeens had held onto power there it could have upset the balance."

"Ah, yes, the precious balance." Clane chuckled, mocking him.

Caxton's grin vanished and he became a dark shadow. "The world is like a body and the body has cancer. We can't cure the cancer, it's too late for that; but we can hold it back indefinitely. The earth will never die of it."

"That's good to know."

"But only if we keep on top of it!" Caxton continued emphatically. "It requires our constant vigilance and supervision; acting when needed, influencing at the right times. It's so important, Clane. Do you understand that?"

"Yes, I guess I do." Clane felt unnerved by his tone. "It's like we here on earth have the same problem as they do on Mars and Venus... I wonder how they're getting on up there." He looked upwards at the glowing murk.

"Ah yes, the Martians and Venusians and their twenty thousand year war." Caxton laughed. "What a nightmare that must be for them."

"Yes, but perhaps they've come to a truce now."

"Perhaps... Listen, Clane. You remember I said that I needed your help with something?"

"Yes, and I said I'd be glad to help in any way I can. It's the least I can do."

"Now, what I need you to do is not easy. I'm asking you because I trust you, and because I think you have the intelligence and ability to be of service."

"What do you need me to do?"

"Well, to cut a long story short; I'm British and I feel a lot of loyalty to my nation. I'm aware of how much Britain has done for the world in the past, and how important it is for the present day too. I believe that we in Britain have a better understanding of the dangers confronting the world than most other countries do. It's very frustrating for us because we stand right on the edge of the New Iron Curtain with literally just twenty miles of the Straits of Dover between ourselves and the Red Bloc howitzers. Some other nations get it, interestingly those who also face the commies head on, Spain, Free France, Australia. However many other members of the global community appear to be in blissful ignorance... and I'm afraid to say, nothing personal intended, that your country is the worst offender."

"What do you mean?"

"Don't you remember those cretins at the first strat meeting last year? McCord, the liberal New England moral relativist, the appeaser!... He's typical of so many intellectuals in the States. Peace-loving, mondialistic, compromising, naive. I hear he's still unmarried at the age of fifty; probably a Nancy-boy. Those deviants are all closet communists!"

"Are they?" Clane was surprised to see Caxton so animated.

"Yes!... Do you think the Soviets have plotted to take us by brute force alone? No! They're infiltrating our academic institutions and programming the youth to be on their side!"

"Really?"

"You bet!... And remember Franklin? That fat greedy turd!... He's almost as dangerous as McCord! He doesn't have evil ideals, he has *no* ideals! Which is worse? He'd sell his own grandmother to Satan for a lucrative deal on a pipeline! He'll do anything for anybody who will pay him enough. Remember what he said, how It's OK Turkey has joined the Reds because at least they're selling us their Siberian oil; and 'China is alright really'... That self-centred shitpot!"

"Why's that America's fault?"

Caxton laughed and said more genially: "It's not the direct fault of the American people, Clane; it's just that your nation is run by obtuse decadent fools who don't realize that their lack of courage and insight forfeits the future of mankind."

"I don't think President Goldwater can be included there, Gerald. He's a decent man."

"Goldwater is a Jew." There was such a malign sneer in Caxton's voice when he uttered the word *Jew* that it almost physically chilled the air. There was a long silence. "That's why I need your help, Clane... You're better than them. You can aid us. You can help save the world from the stupidity and weakness of the scum who have floated to the top."

"What can I do? I'm just a diplomatic aide."

"You are in a position to help me clear up some... misunderstandings between Ireland, the United States and ourselves. You remember when we supervised the arrival of those nuclear weapons at Clogham last year?"

Clane nodded.

"Prime Minister Mosley had a discussion with President Goldwater earlier in the year about US weapons also being stationed on British soil. The Irish ambassador was deeply involved; he advised the President from his own contacts in the CSA."

"Did he? I never heard about that?"

"You wouldn't have; it was not revealed publicly... So we don't know right now where this discussion is going to end up. It seems to have stagnated or gone private between the President and Gutierrez. That's a pity because we really *need* to know, Clane! We need to know for the sake of our own national security, but also that of the rest of the free world... That's where you come in."

"I see. You want me to have a word with the ambassador and see if I can persuade him to talk to Mosley again?"

Caxton paused and took a step away. "Not quite.... You see, it won't help if you just speak to him openly, we need to find out what he's thinking secretly... and what he's *saying* secretly to Goldwater."

Clane chuckled. "How can I possibly find that out?"

Caxton stepped towards him again and lowered his voice, even though they were alone on the beach and it was the dead of night. "I know that the ambassador keeps the minutes of his Presidential seminars in the DQ-29 section of the embassy records office. Do you know where that is?"

"Yes, but the documents in that area are classified."

Caxton's grin returned. "I know, but the information in them could help break the deadlock in Anglo-American negotiations over this essential issue. If only we knew what was in them, oh Lord!... You have access to them; you could tell us."

This time it was Clane who took a step back. He trod on a razor shell and it cracked under the heel of his shoe. "Gerald, you're asking me to divulge classified information from the Embassy of the United States! You know I can't do that."

"Come on, Clane. It's not *very* sensitive information as such; it's just... *confidential*. It's the details of a private meeting that by all the standards of international law should not really be private. It's in the interest of the people of the entire world that we know what is in those minutes, Clane. Yes, it means bending the rules a bit, but so what? Most things worth doing brush against the edge of the law... Please, Clane."

"No, Gerald. It would be highly improper of me to do this."

Caxton snorted. "Well, it seems I overestimated you!"

"That's not fair. I'm at the Embassy to do a job and part of that is handling classified material correctly. Ambassador Gutierrez and the State Department trust me to behave in accordance with procedure and it's not right to let them down."

Caxton sighed and said in a much quieter voice: "Fair enough, Clane. I understand... Maybe I was asking too much of you. We'll find somebody else to help us. I just thought you might like to be involved in doing something genuinely helpful to the wellbeing of people; the way that drug was beneficial to Gina. I hoped you might want to be part of the movement to help heal the world of the cancer infecting its body-politic. That's why I thought you more than anybody else would sympathize, that you'd have the sense of gratitude to inspire you to take action... but you're not obliged to. I apologize for bothering you." Caxton turned and began walking back towards the car park.

Clane put his hands in his pockets and ground his teeth together. "Gerald?"

"Yes?" He stopped and looked back.

"I... er... I suppose I could have a quick look for you."

Caxton turned round and walked back. "Thank you, Clane." he said sincerely.

....

The lift descended. Clane felt no fear, just the thrill of transgression. He was excited like a small boy doing something naughty. The bell rang and the doors slid open. He entered the basement filing room the clerk greeted him. "Afternoon, Mr Quilley."

"Hi, Jacob. How's things?"

"Same as always. What's the weather like up there?"

"Sunny, a few showers... Of course, you never see it do you?" They traded a few more pleasantries then Clane asked him to open the door to Section DQ-29. "I need to look up some figures for accounts." he lied.

Jacob knew that Clane was cleared for access so he selected a key from his wall press and led Clane along to the walk-in cupboard. He opened it and Clane entered. Clane pulled open the filing cabinets one at a time, careful to give the impression that he was busy and purposeful. He made random notes in his jotter and shuffled the papers inside folders. He knew that this cupboard was a "no lone zone" where anybody who went in there had to be supervised by somebody else. Sure enough, Jacob the clerk stood in the doorway.

However Clane knew that these regulations were very flexible and he waited patiently, keeping up the act. The phone rang on the clerk's desk. "Oh sod it!... Mr Quilley, are you OK in here by yourself for a minute?"

Clane laughed. "I won't make off with the silver, Jacob."

The clerk laughed and headed for his desk.

Clane took out the cigarette lighter that Caxton had given him and opened the cabinet where the files he needed were kept. He pulled out the correct folder and opened it. He spread the papers on top of the cabinet and held the cigarette lighter above it at a distance of two feet, the focal length. It was not really a cigarette lighter; it was a secret camera. He pressed the button and it clicked. He flipped over the pages and pressed the button again. He repeated the action over and over until he'd photographed the entire contents of the folder. Jacob was still on the phone when he'd finished. Clane closed the door of the cupboard himself and waved to Jacob on his way out, gesturing to indicate that the door needed locking. Jacob looked up from the phone and waved a farewell. Once he was back in his office he sent an E-gram to Caxton: *Hi Gerald. I hope you'll take me to an English pub next week and buy me a good pint of lager. Clane.* This was code; if he'd used the word "bitter" instead of "lager" in the E-gram it would have meant that he'd failed in his mission. Later on after work when he was sitting in a pub it suddenly stuck him: *I'm a spy.* He was so shocked by this thought that he gasped out loud and almost spilled his Guinness. He had never thought of himself as a spy before. Sure, he was covertly passing on secret information to a foreign power, but that wasn't *spying*... was it?

....

The following day Clane received a visitor to his office, a dapper young man named Ludy Sanders who was dressed in a white shirt with a short narrow collar and wore a medallion at his throat instead of a tie. He had short, well-managed hair and a sparse, sculpted beard. "Mr Quilley." he said. "I am the chairman of the Refugee Alliance of British Jews. I've come to formally protest the upcoming US delegation to the United Kingdom. Are you aware that the Mosley regime is in the process of expelling all Jewish people from Britain? We have been stripped of our citizenship and forced to depart the country at Channel and Irish Sea ports."

"Yes, I know." During the previous year Clane had been involved in resettling over fifty thousand Jewish people who had been dumped on the quay at Dublin harbour off charter ferries from Liverpool and Holyhead. They had been given temporary accommodation in a series of centres in Dublin, Cork and Galway. Many had already moved on to stay with relatives in the United States of America, Palestine-Israel and other countries. Some found permanent homes in Ireland independently and Portobello, the main Jewish quarter of Dublin, had doubled in population.

"Are you also aware that Prime Minster Mosley has formally declared war on Israel?"

Clane noticed that the man's medallion had a Star of David on it with some Hebrew letting inside it. "Don't you mean Palestine-Israel?"

The man frowned. "Please refrain from using that name in front of me!"

Clane shrugged. "What do you want from me, Mr Sanders?"

"I ask you to boycott the diplomatic deputation to the United Kingdom. What your government is doing is tantamount to an official endorsement of the fascist regime in Britain and everything it stands for. You are condoning the oppression of Jewish people in Britain and around the world, along with other minorities."

"I'm not!" he protested.

"Yes, you are! By taking part in an official state visit to Mosley's Britain you are making a statement that both the United States and Ireland regard that regime as an accepted member of the international community. I demand that you refuse to take part and declare publicly that the UK is an illegitimate rogue state."

"That's impossible, Mr Sanders. I've already agreed to lead the delegation under direct instructions from Ambassador Gutierrez and our Anglo-Irish liaison officer Gerald Caxton. I realize you have concerns, and I can use this trip as an opportunity to raise those issues with the British authorities."

Sanders sneered: "You mean... sit down with them over tea and biscuits and ask them nicely?"

"No, I mean set up a dialogue to resolve the Mosley government's current conflict with the Jewish community."

"Spoken like a true politician!"

"I'm not a politician!"

"That's a cop-out, Mr Quilley. No way can you by that naive... Forget all that nonsense and tell them you're refusing to go! Please!"

Clane sighed. "No. I'm not at liberty to do that at this stage. My employer, the US State Department, has instructed me to take part as one of my duties to the diplomatic mission and I'm not in a position to refuse."

Sanders stood up and glared at Clane contemptuously. "I know, you're 'just following orders'!... We've heard that one before... You'll regret this." He marched out of the office and slammed the door behind him.

Clane sat back in his chair and groaned. He fingered the hidden camera in his pocket. One of the reasons he had to go to Britain was the arrangements he had made to drop of the camera to Caxton.

Chapter 13

There was a crowd of press photographers and onlookers at Dublin Port to see them off. Once again in typical Irish fashion, Clane travelled from the Embassy to the ferry by coach, sitting on the narrow seats next to his colleagues. The *Taoiseach* and his ministers were lined up at the foot of the gangway to shake their hands and wish them luck. There were protesters there of course. They were congregated behind a phalanx of *Gardai*, their banners bobbing up and down above the black riot helmets of the officers: *APPEARSERS- GO TO HELL... DEATH TO FASCISM... QUILLEY IS A NAZI WHORE... AUSCHWITZ- NEVER AGAIN* were just some of the epithets scrawled on them. The chants were inaudible, but their content could be guessed. Clane could see Ludy Sanders among them; his body clad in an anorak, his face twisted with ire, his mouth wide open in a yell.

The ship was a medium-sized motor yacht. Crossings between the UK and Ireland were traversed by large ferries the size of cruise liners with multiple decks that could carry cars and other vehicles. Giant hatches at the bow and stern allowed motor vehicles to simply "roll on and roll off". However, as a contrast perhaps to Irish informality, the UK government felt that their guests deserved a more exclusive service. Gerald Caxton stood at the top of the gangway to greet the delegation aboard. There were twenty of them, all junior officers from the Embassy, both Irish and American. The yacht cast off and the vessel headed out to sea. Clane stood on the afterdeck, the briny wind ruffling his hair and Dublin faded into the mist behind him. The sun came out and the weather slowly improved during the four-hour crossing to Holyhead. The rest of the delegation were in the lounge with Caxton, enjoying drinks, while Clane went forward and stood on the bow decks, ignoring the wind in his face, waiting for a sight of Britain. The first sign of the approaching shoreline was the approach of a Royal Navy corvette, a new class that Clane didn't recognize. Its light signalled in Morse code *WELCOME- LAY TO MY PORT QUARTER.* The yacht changed course and followed its escort. A large grey hill appeared on the bright blue horizon. Ahead and below it soon appeared a line of low green coastline. There was a squat square lighthouse on the end of a breakwater leading into Holyhead harbour. The naval escort peeled away to the east and the yacht changed course revealing the breakwater to be a very long and curved structure. The town of Holyhead became visible and beyond it, lush green meadows that basked in the spring sunshine. The wind was coming off the land and with it, the scents of trees, flowers, grass and tilled soil. Clane closed his eyes and breathed deeply; the perfume of the earth invigorated him.

The ship docked and the gangplank was secured. There was a far bigger crowd at this end; two or three hundred people covered the wharf, almost all of them waving small Union Jacks wildly. A huge cheer rose from them as Clane and his cohorts stepped down from the vessel. A red carpet was laid out across the concrete quay and a row of people greeted them; one was the mayor of Holyhead, his chain of office polished brightly and glinting in the sunlight. They had strong Welsh accents which Clane had never heard before. Their hosts escorted them through the crowds under an arch of waving red, white and blue flags. They entered a railway station with a high Victorian roof that followed a long curved platform to where it opened up into sunlight. It was cool in the shade of the parapet. More people were standing on the platform with Union Jacks. Suddenly a man leaped forward out of the throng. He was far less well-dressed than the others and was carrying a very different flag. This one had a green and white horizontal field on top of which was a passant red dragon. He bellowed something at the top of his voice in a strange language. Three policemen in traditional trench coats and custodian helmets ran forward and seized him. They dragged him out of the station by his arms. He continued to shout defiantly over his shoulder.

"Sorry about that." said Caxton and goaded the visitors swiftly along the platform.

"Who was that?" asked Clane.

"Nobody." he snapped. "Come along, people. It's almost two PM; our train will be here soon."

Clane looked back at the station entrance. The crowd was acting normally as if nothing had happened. He wasn't certain, but he wondered if the intruder was speaking in Welsh. He was curious about Wales. Not many Americans realized that Wales was a separate country to England within the United Kingdom. It had its own language that was from the Celtic family; this made it related to Irish Gaelic, which Clane had now learnt to speak fluently. The flag the man had waved was known as the *Red Dragon*; it was the flag of Wales, and that was the only time it had been visible the whole time since Clane had landed. This was despite the fact that there had been Union Jacks, the flag of the UK, every square inch of his visual field. He had recently read a book about Wales which said that Wales was a bilingual country where signs and notices were in both the Welsh and English language. However every single written word Clane had seen since he'd entered Wales was in English. He looked up at the wall of the railway station. It was made of red brick and the cement between the bricks was stained black by coal soot. There was a blue painted metal sign that read: *Welcome to Holyhead.* Below it was a patch of brickwork that was clean and the cement was unblemished white. There were two copper nubbins sticking out of the wall as if a second sign had once been mounted beneath the other and it had recently been taken down. Had it once said *Welcome to Holyhead* in Welsh?

It was approaching two PM. There was a clock on the far wall with a second hand and at the very moment the second hand drifted past the top of the hour their train pulled up the platform. It was unlike any other train Clane had seen before. Trains in Ireland were dirty and ungainly diesel or steam locomotives pulling boxy shed-like carriages. This train was a smooth, sleek electric vehicle with a wedge-shaped aerodynamic nose. It glided silently to a halt and the doors slid open with a hiss.

Clane was amazed at the train; he had never travelled so fast over land before. The mountainous landscape of Wales flew past the wide picture windows, yet there was almost no noise or vibration in the cabin. His soft padded seat surrounded and supported him like a mother's arms. Caxton came and sat down beside him. "So, Clane... do you have something for me?"

"Eh?"

"You know..." He winked.

"Oh yes." He reached into his pocket for the lighter-camera.

"Careful!" Caxton hissed and looked around himself. He reached his hand between them and beckoned furtively. Clane placed the device in his palm and Caxton whipped it into his own pocket. "Thank you, Clane." he said, sounding relieved. There was a silence and then Clane started a new subject. He pointed out of the window at the dark green hills. "Are we still in Wales yet or is this England?"

Caxton gave him a withering glare. "This is Britain."

"Yes, but isn't this part of Britain, Wales?"

He rolled his eyes. "If you want to be pedantic, yes."

"So it has its own language?"

"No, it has the same language as the rest of Britain, English." He expanded when he saw Clane's dubious expression. "Alright, it's true that some of the people here speak a regional vernacular amongst themselves. I suppose we can't really stop them doing that. It's not really a problem so long as they don't inflict it on the rest of us. Prime Minister Mosley's 1950 Act of Unity abolished all devolved policies of the four constituent nations, including the by-laws relating to the Welsh language. Welsh has been removed from all officialdom, education and public literature. You won't see it on any road signs for instance. Their flag and national emblems are all outlawed in public places."

"How do the Welsh people feel about that?"

"Oh, they're perfectly happy; they know it makes sense... With a few noisy but ineffectual exceptions."

"Like that man who burst in at the station?"

Caxton groaned. "Yes, a few of them protest every now and again, but it'll get them nowhere. We all have to obey the law... I truly fail to understand people like him, you know. Wales was once a nation, but it was a protuberance, a bubo, a deformed and diseased teratoma festering out of the flank of a land of a greatness, power and purity that the world had never before seen. Wales was *created* for the sole purpose of being conquered by more worthy creeds... Yet through some insipid and sentimental lunacy, a handful of these people still identify with that politico-evolutionary dead end. Why can't they do the sensible thing and just let it die now, quickly and painlessly. Then they can have the privilege and joy of being part of the New Britain."

Clane looked away, out of the window. He studied the majestic grey cliffs of a nearby ridge.

....

The landscape ironed out over the next half an hour and Caxton reluctantly informed Clane that they were now out of Wales and into England. Rolling verdant pasture scrolled past on both sides of the railway; the landscape divided into square or oblong fields marked by hedgerows. Sheep, cattle and horses grazed contentedly, the sun warming their backs. Interspersed were arable fields of chocolate brown soil covered by a sheen of green, newly-planted seedlings. Tractors moved along lanes beside the hedges. A windmill spooled lazily next to a canal. They passed a small village of thatched cottages in the middle of which was a green with a duckpond. A cricket match was in progress; a cluster of men clad in white suits ran around animatedly. He turned his head to follow the spectacle as the train glided past. Clane had had a friend in the Navy who had visited the UK in the mid-1930's and he related to Clane that England wasn't really like Americans imagined it was. He had been wrong, unless what Clane was seeing was a recent revival. The train slowed down to negotiate the curved railways running through a big city of red-bricked factories; Birmingham, Caxton told him. The skyline was a row of soaring chimneys, all pouring out smoke. The yards outside the factories were packed wall to wall with crates, building materials, shipping containers and rows of shiny new cars. "Modern British industry is the envy of the world." said Caxton. "It has brought British people a prosperity they've never before seen. We are covering the country with railways, fastroads, new houses. Everything the nation could ever need. The train accelerated back up to its full line speed. It reentered the English countryside and cut through a forest of ancient oak trees. Caxton resumed his commentary: "As you can see, we take good care of the environment. You hear a lot of talk nowadays about too many trees being cut down, too many fish being caught and animals dying out. Here in the New Britain we look after our natural world." The train crossed a bridge over a fastroad, a big six-lane straight ribbon of concrete. "That's the F-Forty; it runs between London and Birmingham via Oxford. You can drive the whole length of it in just three hours." A short time later the train approached the outskirts of London. The sides of the railway-line became more built up. Towns and villages took up more space between the green areas until they merged into one. A range of enormous skyscrapers appeared in the distance. Because they were on a train Clane and the others had a limited view directly ahead and so Clane only got a good look at them when the train was rolling between their bases. They were hundreds of feet high with walls of clear grey glass; some were tinted green and blue. There were square blocks, rotundas and tapering obelisks. Packed streets underlined them. "Incredible." said Clane. "It reminds me a bit of New York."

"Ah, these buildings are even taller." said Caxton triumphantly. "This is the Edgware-Wembley Development Zone, designed in a single phase by the country's greatest architects." The train began to slow and soon drifted under the blunt arch Victorian roof of St Pancras Station. The grand gallery of the railway terminal had, like much of London, recently been renovated. Clane and his team stepped out onto a shiny marble platform. The Lord Mayor of London led another reception committee of several hundred people, once again with the ubiquitous Union Jacks in their hands. Clane shook so many hands that they felt like the bristles of a rotating chimney brush of flesh. A dozen people were speaking to him at once. He realized now why film stars sometimes backed away from crowds. Some children from a nearby school were also waiting. They were aged seven or eight and had on smart uniforms. The boys had on little suits and felt caps, the girls were clad in white knee-length dresses. They were strictly segregated into two ranks; the boys on the right, the girls on the left. They waved thin plastic flags on cardboard handles.

A fleet of Rolls Royces was waiting to carry Clane's delegation from the station to their next port of call. Clane began to see the sights of London that were familiar to most people from postcards and tourist brochures; the red telephone booths and post boxes, double-decker buses with a large open gap at the back, steps leading to the Underground marked by red circles with blue lines through them. They reached the vast open plaza of Trafalgar Square. He turned to study the Art Deco and neoclassical entrances to the various important buildings. The grandeur was neatly impaled by Nelson's Column. The motorcade turned left into Whitehall and Clane could see the square clock tower of Big Ben ahead. The car suddenly swung to the right and entered the narrow canyon of Downing Street. It was surrounded by a tight-packed crowd of people; policemen, photographers and men in suits. "We're here."

said Caxton and gestured for Clane to exit the car. Clane opened the door and decamped; camera flashbulbs made him blink. He turned and the famous big oblong black monolith stood before him. The metallic number *10* stared at his forehead. The door opened and the policeman standing outside it ushered him in. Clane and his colleagues found themselves in a grand entrance hall with a black and white checked floor. A row of men in black suits were waiting to greet them. One of them came forward and shook Clane's hand. He was a handsome, long-faced man with a sparse moustache and oily black hair. He wore an armband over his suit with a strange emblem, a red oblong centred by a blue circle inside a white circle. A white jagged line, like a bolt of lightening, cut the blue one in two. "Mr Quilley, welcome." said the man

"Hello." said Clane.

"Clane!" Caxton hissed out of the corner of his mouth. "This is the Prime Minister!"

"Oh!... Sorry." He felt himself blush. "Good afternoon, Prime Minister. My name is Clane Quilley and I greet you on behalf of the United States Embassy to the Republic of Ireland."

Oswald Mosley chuckled genially at Clane's awkwardness. "Come in, gentlemen. Let us retire to the William Joyce Drawing Room." They were served tea on bone china cups while sitting around a table in another luxurious classical chamber. Clane and his colleagues sipped their tea and smiled. Mosley did most of the talking. "I'm the longest serving Prime Minister in British history." he announced in his proud aristocratic English accent. "At least, the longest who's only ever won a single election."

The others laughed politely. Clane feigned laughter in unison.

"Unfortunately our state of emergency will have to remain in force for the time being. Yes, Enoch?"

A short, intelligent looking man spoke: "I've always said, Prime Minister, that now is the best time to call a general election."

"That's Mr Powell, the Home Secretary." Caxton whispered in Clane's ear. "Rather like the US Secretary of State."

Powell continued. "The people love you, they love us. The National Liberal Party has done such wonders for this country. The people want to reinforce their existing affection and loyalty by choosing us officially to run this nation, through what some pundits are already called 'the Golden Age'. It is our greatest hour of need, and paradoxically also our greatest hour of plenty."

"True, Enoch." said Mosley. "Eloquently put as always; but with a new war ready to break out at any moment, it's just not feasible." He turned to Clane's party. "Have you gentlemen been to Kent? It's the Garden of England and is now our forward shield against the Reds. Have you seen the New Cinque Ports yet?"

They shook their heads.

"We'll take you there tomorrow... Gerald, can you arrange that?"

"Of course, Prime Minister." said Caxton.

....

They left Number Ten at about six PM and the cars took them to their hotel, the London Ritz. Clane's bedchamber reminded him of the grand hotel in Washington where he'd stayed in 1947, only this one was even more luxurious. He opened his trunk and dug out his evening wear, a black tuxedo and dark blue bowtie. He took a shower, washed his hair in the hotel's own brand shampoo, which came in a gold bottle, and dressed carefully. He stopped to study his reflection in the gilt Georgian mirror. He couldn't believe how much he'd changed in the last decade. He looked like a different person; he even thought differently. He'd recently heard a recording of his own voice and didn't recognize it. His accent had transformed from the downtown Brooklyn dockers' drawl he used to have into a distinctive middle class Leinster brogue. He now spoke fluent Gaelic and attended an Irish language literature reading club every week. He was truly going native. It was getting dark outside when he descended the grand staircase to the Ritz' dining room. He greeted his fellow delegates and took a seat at the table where there was a card with his name printed in copperplate. To his left was a card with *Gerald Caxton* written on it. Next to that was *Celia Caxton*, Gerald's wife. To Clane's right was one that said: *Caroline Dwyer*. Caxton and his wife arrived just as he was being served his aperitif. Celia Caxton was a plain and cheerless woman who hardly said a word all evening. "Gerald." asked Clane. "Who is this?" he pointed at the card.

"You'll soon find out." He gave him a wink with a sly look in his eye. Caroline Dwyer arrived a few minutes later. Clane couldn't help staring at her as she walked over. She was a young woman aged in her twenties and was extraordinarily pretty. She was clad in an expensive-looking dress and huge gold jewellery. She covered the table with her perfume. She was highly sociable and talked in a very friendly and intimate manner to Clane through the whole of dinner; leaning towards him and brushing his forearm with her hand every so often. Maybe it was being remarried to Gina or having another child; but whatever the reason, it took Clane a while to recognize that she was flirting with him. Caxton seemed quite pleased and gave Clane a few encouraging lascivious looks out of the corner of his eye whenever he could. When supper was over they headed to the ballroom where Caroline Dwyer insisted on dancing with Clane. She held herself close to him wrapping her arm around his waist and moving her hand to his beltline. By eleven PM the guests were heading for bed one by one. Clane bid his colleagues goodnight and walked over to the grand staircase. He assumed that this was where he would also say goodnight to his constant companion. He realized that he shouldn't have been as surprised as he was when she tried to accompany him up the stairs. "Where are you going?" he asked.

She shrugged as if finding the question needless. "Why... with you to your room of course."

"No, Caroline! You can't!... We mustn't... Look, I really like you and everything, but I'm a married man."

Her manner changed in an instant. All the sweetness and warmth evaporated. It was as if she were suddenly possessed by the spirit of an entirely different person. She stepped back and sighed in frustration, putting her arms akimbo. "As you wish, but I'm afraid this is highly irregular."

"What is?"

"This situation!" She shoved her alligator skin handbag under her arm and walked off towards the hotel entrance. She gave him one last look over her silky white shoulder and called back: "Tell your friend Gerald that he still owes me the full fee! No discounts, you understand?"

"What on earth are you talking about?" Clane muttered, but she had already gone.

Soon after Clane arrived back in his room there was a knock at the door. Caxton stood there looking annoyed. "Clane, what the hell are you doing? I just saw Miss Dwyer leaving the hotel!"

"Yes. She wanted to come up here with me; I told her not to." He pulled off his tie and loosened his collar.

Caxton gaped. "What!? Why did you do that!?... For goodness sake, Clane, she was yours! Wasn't it obvious?... I hired her especially for you!"

The penny dropped. Clane turned and stared at him. "You mean... that woman was...?" He laughed. "Of course! Why didn't I get it?"

Caxton sighed. "Damnation, Clane! You naive fool!... She's an escort! I paid her to come here tonight for you... Well, I put her on government expenses to be entirely honest."

Clane chuckled. "There are many another words for that kind of woman."

"Oh no, Clane! Miss Dwyer may be a member of the oldest profession, but she's in its very top league. You will never see her standing around on a street corner late at night. She's an elite executive escort who gets paid very handsomely to keep some of the richest and most powerful men in the world company."

Clane became serious again. "Why did you do that, Gerald?"

He shrugged. "It's a standard service provided to all government VIP guests."

"But I'm a married man!"

Gerald stared at him vexed. "So what?"

"What do you mean 'so what?'?... I am a husband to a woman called Gina whom I love and have taken an oath in front of God to

205

cherish and be faithful to! Didn't you consider that before you hooked me up with that little strumpet!?"

Caxton's face turned deadpan before he replied. "So, you were troubled by the *morality* of the issue... You just don't get it do you? What do you think morality is?"

"It's about what's right and wrong."

"'Right and wrong'!?... Clane, you really are the most unsuitable person for the job you do... I bet you believe the drivel you hear at church don't you. 'The meek shall inherit the earth... Those who are first shall be last and those who are last shall be first'... Do you?"

"Yes, I guess I do."

"Then you have one hell of a lot to learn!... Ethics are a curse! Especially Christian ethics, but any kind of ethics... Morality is a trick the weak invented so they could subdue the strong... You are an elitist now. You are part of the establishment. You must cast aside the falsehoods with which your minions have indoctrinated you so they could dominate you... Only when you have freed your mind of them will you be fit to rule."

....

The following morning the cars turned up at the hotel and Gerald Caxton gave them a guided tour of Britain's defences at the New Iron Curtain. They drove into Kent and headed east towards the coast on the F-Twenty fastroad. Three new army bases had been set up that were a permanent home to five infantry brigades. They exercised continuously on the Downs with the RAF and armoured cavalry divisions. The port of Dover had once been the gateway to Europe, but now its cross channel ferries were gone. Its only visitors were merchant ships from far more distant shores. It was a fine clear day and from the top of the famous White Cliffs of Dover Clane could make out the French coast on the horizon; today it was another world. The English Channel in between was swarming with Royal Navy craft. After that they returned to London to watch a military parade; apparently there was one of these in the British capital at least three times a week. There were tens of thousands of people lining the streets for the route of the parade. It reminded Clane of the newsreel footage of the last royal wedding. The route of the march was cleared of traffic. The whole of Fleet Street, The Strand, Trafalgar Square, Whitehall and the roads outside Parliament in Westminster. "Do you really have one of these three times a week?" asked Clane.

"Monday, Wednesday and Friday; without fail." said Caxton. "Today it's the turn of the Somerset Rifles... You're a war veteran aren't you?"

"Yes, US Navy submarines."

"I was a sapper in the Home Guard. That's good; we can stand together in the second rank."

"Why do you say that?"

"The spectators are arranged in order; servicemen at the front row, veterans in the second and the civilians have to go to the back." His mouth sneered at the word *civilians*. "I'm afraid we don't have any berets for the US Navy. Not to worry, you're with me so nobody will ask." They took their places in the crowd on Whitehall beside the Horse Guards entrance. Caxton looked strange with his Home Guard beret on his head. Then Clane saw something very curious. A space was cleared at the front of the pavement on the opposite side of the road and a large van approached and pulled up. It was a windowless vehicle with heavy sidewalls like a black Mariah. The back doors opened a line of a dozen men emerged. Clane laughed aloud in both amusement and confusion when he saw them because they were all dressed in women's nightgowns, as if they were East End drag queens, although their hair and faces were left normal. The nightgowns were all identical; they were bright pink in colour with frills at the sleeves and hems. The men all had one hand raised to chest level in which they held a large white bird's feather, probably from a goose or swan. Every one of their faces was sad. "What's going on over there?" Clane pointed at them.

"They're the conscientious objectors." replied Caxton with a gleam of distaste in his eye. "The so-called 'men' who were too cowardly, too weak and too feeble to fight for their country!" During this last sentence his voice rose to a furious shout. The rest of the onlookers were joining in, jeering and yelling at the men in pink opposite. "Cowards!... Babies!... Chickens!" None of the mob used any swear words, as if they were disciplined and controlled in their fury. The men did not reply. They stood still and voiceless, white feathers in hands. Their faces were mournful and downcast. Then a row of coaches entered Whitehall and parked. Out of them emerged a huge crowd of women, several hundred of them. All we young and slim, their hair was styled and their faces were made up. They wore clean dresses, blouses and skirts. Each one carried a black plastic bag with her. They chattered excitedly as they walked down the street. Despite what Caxton had told him about civilians always standing at the back, these young women took places in the front row. They spread out down the entire row evenly as if they had rehearsed the manoeuvre. When the sound of military band music rose in the distance, Clane realized the role these women had been brought in to play. The column of troops rounded the corner of The Strand and straightened out in double files, pacing steadily to the beat of the music. The band led the way; drummers, cornet players and bell lyre holders. Immediately following the band were the men. Their marching boots were shiny as black glass, their trousers straight as pipes and their olive tunics immaculate. They moved like well-designed automata, synchronized precisely, sucked dry of individuality, devoid of all thought and emotion. Their faces were frozen in military catatonia beneath the blinkering peaks of their caps.

At the sight of the soldiers the spectators went completely berserk. Clane was deafened by their voices. They shrieked, they cheered, they warbled. The women stationed along the front row were the most enraptured. They jumped up and down, screaming in what resembled religious ecstasy. The bags in their hands contained flower petals and they threw these in handfuls onto the street in front of the strutting boots. The column trampled over them as if they weren't there. After the Somerset Rifles had passed on to Parliament Square the crowds did not walk off, knowing in advance that the pageant wasn't over yet. The young women who had arrived on the coaches left their positions and lined up on the north side of the segment opposite to where the conscientious objectors were penned. They then walked past the nightie-clad men in single file. At the point where they faced the men, they threw a single white feather at them and then turned their backs, sometimes with a shrill and contemptuous insult. Then they strutted away with their noses in the air. The rest of the crowd chortled and cat-called in support of the women. The conscientious objectors were still standing where they had been the whole time, silent and impassive. Their faces became even more mournful and a few of them were bowing their heads and crying.

Clane looked at the line of women and then turned to face the side of Caxton's head. "How much did you pay *them*, Gerald?" he growled, but Caxton didn't hear him above the din of the gibbering throng.

....

When the military parade was over the crowd slowly dispersed. The police roadblocks holding back the traffic were removed and cars and buses began traversing Whitehall like water behind a dam being released. Clane and Caxton strolled back to Trafalgar Square and headed under Admiralty Arch. There before them lay The Mall and Buckingham Palace, home of Queen Elizabeth II. The forecourt of the Palace was dominated by the Victoria Memorial, a white marble edifice topped by golden sculptures of angels. "Quite an amazing parade that, wasn't it?" said Caxton.

Clane looked up at him. He hadn't spoken since they'd left Whitehall. "I've never seen anything quite like it."

Caxton guffawed. "Don't you have military parades in the States?"

"Of course, but none quite like these."

"I take it you mean the conshie-bashing." Caxton was amused.

"I don't like seeing men being humiliated... It was an organized ritual wasn't it? Those girls were trained, like cheerleaders."

208

"Clane, if you don't feel pleasure at watching your inferiors and enemies being humiliated then you need to learn how."

Clane stopped walking. "Gerald... Do I really know you?... Here in your own country, you're a different person. Are you for real now or were you for real in Ireland?"

Caxton replied severely: "Both here and in Ireland, I'm the man who saved your wife's life."

Clane felt himself blush. "I hadn't forgotten that, Gerald."

"Then show it by being more open-minded! Give me a chance to prove my point... You've seen just a few of the wonders of Great Britain. Come back for a fortnight and I'll show you some more. But these things have to be paid for; that is always the way. Nothing comes from nothing. The price for Great Britain has been centuries of blood, sweat and tears... You think it's wrong? You think it's hateful? I've told you before, we've achieved these things not in spite of our immorality, but *because* of it. You've been lied to that hate can only destroy and it must be cast aside. No! Hate can be a very creative force."

They walked along by the decorated fence of Buckingham Palace. Fur-hatted Queen's Guardsmen paced up and down inside. A few tourists were staring through the bars at them. Mostly Americans and Japanese, taking photographs of the sights and each other. They walked slowly down Buckingham Palace Road towards Victoria Station enjoying the fresh air and fine weather. The sunny streets were filled with busy-looking people. "You know what?" said Clane. "There's something about the Brits, those that I've seen so far. Everybody looks so happy." He gestured to the pedestrians. "They're all so full of life, so content, so carefree."

"See what I mean?" Caxton elbowed him playfully.

"Do you know, I've not yet seen anybody sick? Everybody's in good health, everybody's vital; brimming with energy."

"Did you also know our crime rate is virtually zero?" Caxton added proudly. "You can walk the darkest streets of London in the middle of the night and be perfectly safe. You could never say that for Dublin, let alone New York."

Clane nodded. "True. There's one thing that's very weird though."

"What's that?"

"Everybody's white... I've not seen a negro or an Asian or anybody else other than white people. Why is that?"

"Would you walk down a street in Kenya or Jamaica and ask: 'How come everybody is black?'."

"No, of course not."

"Then why ask in Britain why everybody is white?... It's peculiar how that question is only ever directed towards white countries, isn't it? Britain has always been a nation of white Aryan people; it has taken our present government to realize that and do something to maintain it."

"I'm just not used to it, Gerald. Where I come from the people are all colours of the rainbow."

"And how the white people of your country have paid for it!"

They walked on a bit further; the stone edifice of Victoria Station towered over them ahead. "Another thing." said Clane. "I've also not seen anybody disabled. Even the old people can walk properly and do everything the young people can. Is nobody is Britain handicapped mentally or physically?"

Caxton grimaced uncomfortably. "Clane... there's a place I'd like to show you. It's not on your official tour itinerary, but I think you need to see it. Shall we go there?"

"Sure, why not?" Clane followed Caxton down a flight of steps at Victoria Station and found himself in the London Underground. Caxton purchased tickets from an office behind a thick-glassed window and they descended a very long escalator down to a platform inside a tube-shaped tunnel. He felt a blast of warm wind from the entrance to a smaller tunnel at one end and a train emerged from the darkness. It hummed to a halt and the doors slid open. The train pulled away and dived into the tunnel. It was exactly like the New York Subway except more claustrophobic. The carriage roofs curved in overhead giving the interior a suffocating atmosphere. At one point on the journey the train was so full of people Clane had to stand; his shoulders, chest and back pressed against other passengers. They had to change trains at one point and walked along passageways and escalators to another platform. He was quite relieved when the train emerged into the sunlight again where its railway ran onto the surface. It eventually pulled to a halt at a station called Cockfosters where it terminated. Caxton led him onto a wide suburban throughfare which he walked along, confident of where he was going. They passed a well-kept cemetery and then came to a modern brick wall; it was vertical and higher than a roof of a house with a roll of barbed wire on the top. It looked out of place in this residential district. Was it a prison? If so it was unusual because he could see the tops of trees reaching above the top of the wall, as if it enclosed a park or forest. A tall chimney was visible behind the trees. The main road ran along beside the wall and eventually they came to an entrance that did look like the gates of a prison. It had a signboard that read: *Barnet Sanatorium*. They had to ring a doorbell at a security door and wait for an answer. "What do you want?" demanded a grumpy voice on the intercom. When the person recognized Caxton through the CCTV camera, he made a transparent attempt to be more polite. He immediately opened the door and invited them in. He was a rough-looking man dressed in white plastic overalls. "Good afternoon, Mr Caxton." he said, bowing slightly. "We weren't expecting you. Is this an inspection, sir?"

"No. I just brought Mr Quilley here from the Irish ambassadorial delegation. I'd like Dr Skarwell to give him a tour of the facility."

"I'll go and fetch him, Mr Caxton sir." While they were waiting, a uniformed guard made them turn out their pockets and walk through a magnetic scanner. Their guide was a bloated, pale-faced old man with thick bushy white eyebrows and eyes that always looked closed. He wore a white coat that bulged at his waistline and a green surgical cap on his head. He shook Clane's hand and greeted him insincerely. "Mr Quilley, how do you do. Dr Lancelot Skarwell, head of this facility. Would you care to follow me?" His voice was low, mechanical and chesty. They passed through another security door and walked swiftly along a corridor. They emerged in a building that was surprising similar to the psychiatric ward at Bethesda hospital where Clane had visited James Forrestal before he died; straight antiseptic corridors with bare cell-like bedrooms. The patients wore plain medical pyjamas and they tottered nervously around the dayroom or lay catatonic on their beds. Many had physical disabilities as well as mental ones. There were men and women with no arms or legs. Some had deformed faces, or lacked eyes or ears. "We have over a thousand residents here." said Skarwell proudly. "They're well looked after. We pride ourselves on the quality of our service."

Clane found his voice. "Is this a hospital?"

Skarwell frowned at him as if surprised at the question. "Not exactly."

"Who are these people?"

"They're the answer to your question, Clane." said Caxton, looking at him hard.

Dr Skarwell then took them to another part of the facility which was full of children. They were playing in a room full of toys and colourful books. On one table a group of them were scrawling on paper in coloured pencils. There was a patio door to the dayroom beyond which was a terrace. There more of them yelled and chattered as they played in a sandpit and on a climbing frame. Nurses walked around supervising them. Skarwell seemed to sense Clane's uneasiness. "It's important to realize that not all our residents are permanent." he said. "A good proportion of these children, and maybe even a few of the adults, will be rehabilitated to the point where they can achieve ASCapS. Then they'll be permitted to leave."

"What's ASCapS?"

"Acceptable Social Capability Standard."

"It means they'll fit in." replied Caxton. "They'll be able to find friends, work, organize their lives properly."

"Also understand and obey conventional social customs." added Skarwell.

"What about those who can't?" asked Clane.

Skarwell and Caxton exchanged a brief glance. "Oh... they'll be well cared for here by us, for the remainder of their natural lives."

"What about their families, their own children..."

"They don't have any children." said Skarwell. "Come with me."

Dr Skarwell escorted them to the Barnet Sanatorium's medical centre. Here there was a fully-fitted surgical suite. "This facility can handle any clinical emergency our residents should suffer. Also every new resident admitted undergoes a procedure rendering them incapable of reproduction."

"What!?" exclaimed Clane.

"Oh don't worry; it's all perfectly humane. We simply give the males a vasoligation, the females a fallopian tubal ligation. They retain normal sexual function. Males and females are allowed to interact; we even have a few couples among the adults." He smiled benevolently.

Clane felt his head spinning. "Is... is all this strictly necessary?"

Skarwell picked up on Clane's tension. He glanced at Caxton again. "I'll leave you two alone for a moment." he said and walked off to talk to one of the clinic's nurses. Caxton placed his hands on Clane's shoulder. "Come on, Clane. Hold it together!... I told you, the greatness we have achieved comes with a price. It always does. If you can't pay the price you will never be great. Part of our drive for greatness is the biological purity and perfection of our people!... Do you understand, Clane?"

"Yes." he lied woodenly. His thoughts were numb.

Caxton patted his shoulders.

Skarwell returned to show them the grounds. There was a large green space of parks and the trees Clane had seen from the road outside. "Look." Skarwell smiled and pointed at some of the adult residents wandering about in the afternoon sunshine. "See how happy they are, Mr Quilley?" In the distance at the corner of the grounds by the wall was a large building, separate from the main facility, out of the roof of which rose the tall chimney that was also visible from outside. It had blank walls without windows. When Clane had first seen the chimney it was inactive; but now a huge thick pall of black smoke belched from its top. It formed a greasy rolling sooty cloud above the rooftops of north London. "What's that?" he asked.

"Oh, that's our incinerator." replied Skarwell in a sing-song tone. "It's where we burn all our rubbish."

"It's a big place; you must produce a lot of rubbish here."

"Tons of it!" Skarwell laughed loudly. "You wouldn't believe the messes we make if you saw them!" He continued to roar with merriment, as if at a hilarious joke.

Clane and Caxton left the Barnet Sanatorium soon afterwards and walked back to the Underground station in silence. Once on the train Caxton turned to his companion. "Clane, I'm going to let you into a secret, something I'd never reveal to my colleagues in government... What you saw back there at the facility, I don't enjoy that element of our nation. I do wish there were another way; I truly do."

Clane paused, staring deep into his eyes. "Why did you show me that, Gerald?"

"Because I believe you are a special person, Clane... You know so little of how this world works, but when you find out, if you learn to integrate that knowledge properly; you could be one of the leaders of a movement that will save the planet. That is why I'm so interested in you, Clane." He chuckled. "Hadn't you noticed that I am priming you? I'm priming you for glory."

"Save the planet from what?"

"Ah, when you know the answer to that, you will indeed be ready, Clane; ready to fulfil your destiny."
....

Clane was due to have dinner at The Ritz again before the end of his tour the following morning, but he couldn't face it. He absconded from the hotel and went to explore London in the twilight. He had a large amount of British pound Sterling as spending money. He could have afforded to buy his own meal at a grand restaurant; but instead he caught the Underground to Kensington and bought a packet of fish and chips from a backstreet takeaway. He ate them sitting on a bench in Hyde Park. He wandered around the London streets as night fell, deep in thought. He stopped at a pub and bought a pint of English bitter. The pub was almost full of laughing drinkers. Many of them were soldiers in utility uniform who took centre stage. Everyone in the pub was looking at them as if they couldn't help it; the soldiers seemed to draw in attention like a magnet. Young men stood gazing at them reverently; young women did the same lustfully. One of the girls was sitting on a trooper's lap. Clane moved over to a table by the open window and sat quietly, sipping his pint and watching the bustle of a London evening go by outside.

"Hey you!" A hard finger poked Clane's shoulder painfully, jerking him out of his daydream. He turned his head to see one of the young soldiers standing over him with a scowling sneer on his face. "Don't you fuckin' ignore us, mate!"

"What are you talking about?" asked Clane.

"I said don't fuckin' ignore us, you fuckin' civvy piss-pot!" The man was badly drunk and slurred his words as he shouted.

"What do you mean 'ignore'!?" protested Clane.

Another somewhat less inebriated soldier with a corporal's chevrons on his uniform came over and put a hand on the first man's shoulder. "Come on, Steve; sit down!"

The first soldier continued to rebuke Clane relentlessly. "I've just come back from fuckin' Upper Volta, you fuckin' Paddy shit arse! I don't expect to be fuckin' disrespected!" He resisted his corporal's hand and took a step closer to Clane. Two more squaddies came over to hold him back.

Clane stood up and backed away towards the window. Clane knew that Upper Volta was a country in West Africa where British troops were currently putting down a communist uprising. "Why do you think I'm going to respect you when you treat me like this, son!?" he demanded.

The second soldier now glared at Clane, obviously just as angry only more controlled. "He's doing this cos you disrespected us, mate."

"I never disrespected anyone!" yelled Clane. "I've just been sitting here drinking!"

"Yeah you did. You sat there with your back turned ignoring us."

"I was just sitting here drinking and minding my own business!"

"Yeah, but you should show us a bit more respect, mate. We've just come back from Upper Volta and we don't expect to be ignored; you get me?"

The pub landlord approached the alcoholic foray and ordered them all to calm down. Eventually the gang of troops went sullenly back to their own table, still grumbling and snarling loudly, and giving Clane dirty looks. Clane finished his pint in one go and left.

He stood outside a dancehall for a while and listened to the music, feeling confused about the environment he was in. He had a painful bruise developing on his shoulder where the trooper had poked him. Everything in London was so clean and functional. The streets were swept, the windows of all the buildings glinted in the streetlights; not a stone was out of place on any kerb. He eventually found himself wandering along Upper Berkley Street when he came across a derelict building. It had once clearly been a magnificent sight, with an arched and turreted facade and some tall high windows, now all glassless. The masonry was blackened; clearly it had been gutted in a major fire. Clane was surprised to see this broken, shattered ruin amidst the polished splendour of London. There were the remains of a doorway in the middle, now boarded up with splintery planks. To one side was an entrance plaque. Clane brushed it with his hand until the soot and dust crumbled away, allowing him to read the name of the lost structure. It was very indistinct, but he was fairly certain of the words: *West London Synagogue.*

Chapter 14

Clane had arrived in the UK feeling curious and adventurous; he left feeling relieved and with a desperate longing to be home in Ireland again. Caxton would not be travelling with them and Clane was quite pleased to get a break from him and his furtive head-messing. He and his team were seen off at the station by a crowd of well-wishers again. The electric train slid through the English and Welsh landscape with satisfying speed, reaching Holyhead by midday. The same yacht was tied up at the wharf waiting to take them back across the sea, and after shaking hands with a few people for the last time he was allowed to board. It set sail and steamed swiftly out into the Irish Sea. Clane dozed on the settee in the lounge as he had not slept well at The Ritz the night before. He awoke to the vibrations of the engines running full astern as the ship backed down into its Dublin Port berth. He stood up and smiled warmly at the skyline of the "world's biggest village" though the portholes. It was raining lightly and low cloud covered the sky.

There was no welcoming committee for the embassy delegation, but there were none of the protesters either. The antifascist mob who had wished them such a fond farewell was not there to greet them in similar tones, for which Clane was grateful. He was disappointed that there were no coaches, feeling as sentimental as he was for Irish traditions; instead the embassy had sent one of their Bentleys. The driver was an American intern, a young man from Arkansas. He smiled as Clane got in the back. "Nice trip, Mr Quilley?"

"I've had better, Danny." he muttered grimly. "Take me straight home, would you? I need to see the wife and kids really badly."

"Sure, Mr Quilley." It was a twenty mile journey to Greystones from the Port so Clane, still tired, settled down on the Bentley's leather back seat to relax and enjoy it. The driver headed down the F- Eleven fastroad to Bray where he turned off and drove through the town to the coastal road. "You've already picked up the shifting temperaments of County Dublin traffic, Danny." Clane noted.

"Should have by now, Mr Quilley. Been over here a year now."

"That's quite a while for a youngster. How old are you?"

"Twenty-one. I'm hoping to study political science and history at Yale if I can get a good enough report here."

"You'll do fine, Danny.... And if you can't get in, remember at least the dean will hire you to drive him through the terrible Connecticut freeway network." They both laughed at Clane's joke. They were approaching the junction just before the turn off to Foreign Town when the driver slowed suddenly. "Damn!"

"What's up?" Clane looked and saw a stationary saloon car positioned lengthwise across the road, completely blocking it, as if it had skidded into that position. Two people were standing beside the car looking helpless and on the pavement a women with a pram was talking to them. Danny stopped the car and wound down the window. "You broken down?"

The woman reached down into the pram to pick up her baby. When she lifted it up Clane saw that it was not a baby at all; it was an assault rifle. She levelled it at the front of Clane's car. The car exploded with light and noise. Auto-glass flew everywhere. Danny was jerked to the right, flailing against his seatbelt, his blood spraying all over the interior, including into Clane's eyes, which were already dazzled by the muzzle flash of the rifle. Then everything went quiet. "GET OUT!... GET OUT!... GET OUT!" a voice yelled. Clane couldn't move. He blinked the young man's blood out of his vision. The woman was now training her weapon at him. The two men by the car had drawn pistols and were doing the same. "GET OUT, I said!" One of the men shouted. After another moment of pause that felt like an hour, the second man thrust his weapon inside his inner jacket pocket and approached the back door of the car where Clane was sitting. He opened it and grasped Clane's collar, pulling him hard out of the door. Clane tumbled onto the cold tarmac. "Get on your feet!" Both men seized Clane's jacket and hoisted him up into a semi-standing position. They propelled him with kicks and punches towards the boot of their car. He reached out his hands to try and stop them, but his muscles were still paralyzed by shock. They lifted him by his ankles and forced him into the boot. They slammed the lid shut and Clane heard the engine start. The vehicle jerked into motion and he rolled painfully against the side of the boot interior. It was impossible to know how long the journey lasted. Clane was still in a semi-conscious stupor. The car rocked and rolled on its suspension, braking and accelerating. Eventually it stopped and the engine cut out. For the first time Clane's emotions pushed through the shock. He felt cold, sharp terror. Was he about to die? Had they taken him to a quiet country lane to shoot him? The boot opened; sunlight flooded in blinding him. Somebody reached down and covered his head in a black cotton sack that smelled of shoe polish and he was lifted out of the boot and dragged along somewhere. He sensed from the echoes of sounds that he was being taken indoors. The bag was removed and his vision assailed by stimuli. He was in a room that looked like a kitchen. There was a wooden table and a sideboard with a hob and kettle. There was mess everywhere, cans of food, cutlery and piles of newspapers. One of the men secured handcuffs around his wrists and got a length of heavy chain. He looped it around the handcuff chain and threw both ends over a rail stretching from wall to wall just under the ceiling. Then all three of them tugged on the chain and Clane felt his arms jerk upwards. The cuffs bit into his wrists as they took his weight. "AAAH!" He roared in pain as he was lifted up off the floor. His hands felt as if they would be ripped off and his feet dangled free. "I thought the fat pig would break it!" he heard the woman sneer. They must have attached the other end of the chain to something because all three of them approached him with large pairs of scissors and began cutting his clothes. They tore and slashed at his shirt, his trousers and underwear until he was hanging completely naked. He felt incredibly vulnerable. He bellowed with fright as he expected them to take the scissors to his body and mutilate him. Instead they put down the scissors and picked up long bamboo canes. He screamed as they began striking his skin with the sticks. All the time they shrieked abuse at him: "FILTHY NAZI PIG!... FASCIST SHIT!... FUCKING CAPITALIST LACKEY!... RAT!... RACIST TURD!... MISOGYNIST!... RAPIST!... SEXIST CUNT!... HOMOPHOBE!... ANTISEMITE!... IMPERIALIST SCUM!..." After a period of time in which the instant of agony stretched into eternity, Clane suddenly felt the tension in his arms and wrists disappear. The world wheeled round his head and he was suddenly lying on the hard stone floor. They lifted him up and dragged him towards a dark doorway. They removed his handcuffs, shoved him through it and slammed the door. He heard a key turn in the lock. He was in a bare cupboard without enough room to lie down properly. He curled up on the floor. He heard himself panting and weeping, his consciousness detached from his body. His hands burned with pins and needles, his skin felt as if it had been peeled off. A strong lavatorial stench filled his nostrils and he realized he had wet and fouled himself. He fell unconscious.

When he came to it took him a few minutes to remember where he was. He thought for a moment he was at home in bed; then he wondered why it was so dark. Then the truth flooded back like a hammer blow. His eyes were adjusted to the dark enough for him to see slightly from a chink of light leaking in through a crack under the door. Was it sunlight or electric light? What time of day or night was it? He had a pounding headache. He tried to swallow and moaned with pain; the mucous membranes of his mouth and throat were completely desiccated. He longed for a drink. There was no alternative but to ask his captors. He groaned as he forced his aching body into motion and rolled onto all fours. Doing so sapped so much of his energy that he almost collapsed again. He rapped on the door with his knuckles. There was no reply. He tried again and again for a few minutes. Eventually he heard footsteps approaching. "It's awake!" he heard one of the men's voices say. "The pig is awake!" He heard laughter in the distance. "What do you want, pig?"

"Water." Clane choked and dissolved into a fit of coughing.

"Water?... Are you thirsty?"

Clane nodded his head as if the man outside could see him.

"Do you think the people starving to death in Abyssinia right now are thirsty?... EH!?" he kicked the door. "What do you reckon, pig!?" he yelled in fury. "After draining their reservoirs growing cash crops for the corporations owned by your masters whose arses you kiss... do you think they just *might* be a little bit THIRSTY!?... What do you think!?... ANSWER ME!"

"Dunno!" Clane groaned.

The man laughed bitterly. "You *didn't* know?... Well you fucking do now!" He gave the door another slam with his foot and walked off.

"Please!" rasped Clane.

....

At one point that he couldn't remember, Clane fell unconscious again. For some reason, he had a long and detailed dream about the landing of the beings from Mars and Venus five years earlier. He relived the entire experience, only this time it was different. He couldn't see the faces of the Martian and Venusian. He then felt his eyes flooded with bright white light. A lovely female figure was filling his mouth with water. He thought that he must be dead and this was an angel. He then regained a bit more consciousness and realized he was still lying on the floor of the cupboard, but the door was open. Sunlight from a nearby window cascaded in. The woman who had been beating him with a stick earlier was now cradling his head and holding a glass of water to his mouth. "You're softened up enough now, Clane." she said. She beamed benevolently. Then she and her two male companions lifted him out of the cupboard and carried him up a flight of stairs. At the top was a bathroom. They lowered him into a tub of warm water. At first this stung against his sensitive skin, but soon the heat flowed into his muscles and bones refreshing and healing his body. He looked up at his three captors and felt a rush of affection, almost like he used to feel for his parents when he was a child, as they gazed caringly down at his body. After the bath they applied ointment and bandages to his wounds, then they dressed him in a baggy black jersey and corduroys, slightly too big for him. After that they helped him back down the stairs to the kitchen and he sat at the table where they made him a cup of coffee and cooked him some beans on toast. This he wolfed down in ecstasy; it was the most delicious food he had ever tasted.

One of the men put a pile of books on the table. He was a dark haired man in his early thirties with small round glasses and a goatee beard. He was dressed in denims and a black polar-neck. "Are you feeling better now, Clane?"

Clane nodded.

"Good." They all sat down. "We should introduce ourselves. I'm John." He pointed at the other man, a fat-faced youth with thick fuzzy hair and a beard that was an inverted goatee. It covered the sides of his face and beneath his chin, but left his mouth and top lip clear. "This is Chris." He pointed at the woman, a thin young blonde with a broad smile wearing a sheepskin jacket. "And this is Maisey." Chris and Maisey greeted Clane warmly. They all had English accents; they were well-spoken and sounded intelligent.

"Why am I here?" asked Clane.

"This will become clear before long." replied John. "We have a special visitor coming to see you soon. He will explain everything. First of all we need to have a discussion... Have you ever thought what a terrible place the world is?"

Clane almost laughed. A doorstep preacher had once said that to him a few years ago, before he'd slammed the door in his face.

"It's horrific, Clane! At least it is for the majority of the people on Earth. There is poverty, disease, famine, slave labour, war, torture, imprisonment and misery from cradle to grave, usually an early grave. The destruction of the natural world; killing animals, cutting down trees, poisoning rivers, poisoning the sea... Don't you think that's terrible?"

Clane nodded.

"Why is this happening do you think?"

"I don't know."

"We do." John answered emphatically. "Through all of history, the world has consisted of an oppressed majority under the control of a privileged minority. In modern society that is the industrial working class, the *proletariat*, being oppressed by the capitalist ruling class, the *bourgeoisie*. All of history emerges out of this class struggle. The ruling class steal the economic capital of the working class, making themselves more and more wealthy, while the working class becomes poorer and poorer. The solution is for a dictatorship of the proletariat over the means of production that will build a planned economy in which all wealth will be shared equally in a classless society."

"From each according to his abilities, to each according to his needs." quoted Maisey.

"Half the world has already embarked on this quest." continued John. "Everybody else is just a stubborn intransigent digging in their heels."

Clane didn't reply.

"You've picked the wrong side in this struggle, Clane." John spoke calmly and without malice. "You've given yourself over to the bourgeoisie; the side of injustice, counter-revolution and destruction. You're a citizen of the most monstrous bourgeois democratic capitalist state the world had ever seen. You choose to serve the privileged capitalist class who wallow in luxury while their employees struggle to put food in their children's mouths. You have even committed the ultimate betrayal. You have travelled to the fascist heartland of Britain to legitimize the murderous Mosley regime. This gives the signal that both the United States and the

Irish Republic are allied to that reactionary hellhole. Before that they were two of the last few moderate democracies left in the world. This makes *you* an extremely dangerous man... But you can change."

Clane nodded mindlessly.

"We are going to help you change." John pointed at the pile of books in front of him. "We've brought you these books to read. I want you to read them all. It'll be a steep learning curve for you, but you'll have our non-stop tuition. We'll sit with you and discuss them as you work your way through them.

Clane looked down at the pile. There were about twenty books of various sizes. To his surprise he recognized the one on the top. It was *The Communist Manifesto* by Karl Marx and Friedrich Engels. He pointed. "I've read that."

"Have you? When?"

"At school."

John raised his eyebrows with amusement. "Really? Maybe the American education system is not as bad as I thought... In that case we'll move straight on to the second one."

For the next hour or two Clane read aloud *What is to be Done* and the *State and Revolution* by VI Lenin. John stopped him every so often to question him about one aspect of the text or another. Chris and Maisey also added comments and questions. Then they moved on *The Quotes of Chairman Mao*, and then to the other books by authors he'd never heard of. People named Gyorgy Lukacs, Fidel Castro, Harold Laski, Rosa Luxemburg and Harpal Brar. It was beginning to get dark and he felt himself becoming drowsy. John immediately picked up on his mood and they cooked him another meal. This time he was allowed to sleep on a bed in a room upstairs; however the door was still locked.

....

He spent the entire following day reading. He didn't retain anything he read longer than it took him to discuss the points with his three captors. He was like a sentient typewriter. Would they kill him if they thought they were failing to indoctrinate him? This worried Clane and he worked hard to try and superficially understand the literature so he could put on a good act. John, Chris and Maisey were patient and gentle with him, but persistent. At no point did Clane ask if he could stop reading because he knew what the answer would be. They didn't carry weapons inside the house, but their rifles and pistols were arranged on the sideboard where they could be grabbed easily if needed. He had no idea where he was. The kitchen windows looked out only onto a garden surrounded by bushes and hedges. His bedroom window was shuttered from the outside and the bathroom window was frosted. He was not permitted access to any other areas. He could hear no sounds outside other than birdsong and the bleating of sheep. From this he concluded he was in a remote rural locale. On the morning of his third day in captivity... or was it his fourth? Time seemed to work differently where he was... he was served breakfast as usual and told that he was about to receive a special visitor. There was no ceremony to mark the arrival of this visitor. "Oh, he's here." said Chris casually when the sound of a car engine could be heard outside. He went to the door and he could hear voices. A new voice joined Chris' that was not completely unfamiliar. Clane recognized the newcomer as soon as he entered the kitchen. The smart shirt and medallion had gone and had been replaced with a ploughman's jacket and pullover. His hair had grown somewhat and his beard was not as neat. "Hello again, Clane." he said.

Clane's jaw dropped. "Sanders!"

Ludy Sanders slowly walked over to the table and took a seat beside him. His face was stern, but not hostile. "I tried to reason with you, Clane. I told you again and again what you already knew. You could have made a stand! You could have said no!... If so, you wouldn't be here right now."

Clane stared down at the table.

"Clane, there's only one reason you're still alive at this moment... It's because I know that your jaunt over in Blighty was a bit disillusioning; wasn't it?"

"How do you know that?"

"I have my... 'contacts'... over the water who keep me informed. I know that evil shit-fuck Gerald Caxton has been giving you all the soft-soap, but it didn't completely work. I know he took you visit the Barnet Sanatorium. What did you think of it?"

Clane thought back. "It was just a prison for people who'd committed no crime."

Sanders smiled. "Bravo, Clane... but in reality it's far more than that... Look, I've brought something to show you." He pulled a card folder out of his jacket and handed it to Clane.

Clane opened it and saw a ream of photographic prints inside. They were grainy and badly exposed, but could still be made out. He started flicking through them. They showed what looked like piles of dead bodies lying on a floor. Shot after shot depicting hundreds of them, lying as unceremoniously as animal carcasses in a butchers' shop. "What is this?"

"These were taken inside Barnet Sanatorium by a comrade of ours who managed to infiltrate the place by posing as a member of staff. These are the bodies of people deliberately murdered within those walls. Men, women and children. They are killed by lethal injection and their bodies are cremated on the site... Clane, that place is a human slaughterhouse."

Clane put down the photographs, his hand trembling.

"How do you feel now?"

"Bad." he muttered.

"The pain of the uncomfortable truth we all have to face." said Sanders with some sympathy.

"I just wish..."

"What?... What do you wish?"

"I..."

BOOM!... At that moment there was the sound of shattering glass behind Clane's left shoulder and a deafening explosion, all the louder because it was in a confined space. Clane's eardrums ached from a pressure wave. The room was engulfed almost instantly in a cloud of grey smoke that made everything invisible. The next moment Clane squeezed his eyes shut as his corneas caught fire. He inhaled and his lungs exploded into coughing fit. He collapsed to the floor. The sound of gunfire broke out; almost inaudibly in his battered ears. There were a few bursts of rapid fire bullets, then silence. He felt hands grabbing him and lifting him up to his feet again, this time voices yelled at him that sounded distorted as if from facemasks. He walked in the direction his new captors pushed him, unable to see or hear a thing, struggling to breathe. The dark blur became a brighter blur and he realized he was outside. He was bundled into a vehicle with a large horizontal floor surface inside, like a van. He rolled onto his back and opened his eyes. A number of human figures loomed over him, men in black overalls and hoods; their faces were covered in gas masks. He passed out.

....

He awoke suddenly, sat up and looked around him. He was lying in a hospital bed in a small room. A window to his right overlooked flat rooftop. It was raining hard outside. To his left was a chair in which Gerald Caxton sat. He had been reading a newspaper and looked up. "Ah, Clane. You're awake, old boy. Good." He flashed his usual wide grin.

Clane realized that somehow he was not surprised that Caxton was there. "Gerald! Where am I?"

"You're in the Cashel Medical Centre, County Tipperary. It's five-thirty in the afternoon and you're perfectly safe."

Clane looked down at his body. Some additional dressings had been applied, including a large bandage on his head. His left arm was immobilized on a splint. He held it up and looked at it.

"When we brought you in you had a dislocated wrist." explained Caxton. "Luckily that's as serious as your injuries go."

"What happened?"

"You were rescued by the *Garda*'s elite Special Response Unit. They stormed the house where you were being held; it's in a little place called Clareen. They killed the three terrorists who took you hostage on Friday morning. Ludovico Sanders survived and has been taken into custody."

"What about Danny?"

"I'm afraid your driver Daniel Barnes was killed in the shootout at Greystones." Caxton delivered this news deadpan, as if he were revealing that Clane had lost a forty cent bet on a horse race.

Clane gasped. "Oh God, no!... He was just a kid. He was heading up to Yale... This is all my fault."

Caxton stood up. "Your family are waiting outside. I think they'd like to see you." He opened the door and went out. A moment later Gina and Siobhan burst in squealing with relief and excitement. They embraced him where he lay. Gina popped out and came back with Brendan who also looked pleased to see his father, even if he was too young to understand what had been going on.

....

Clane was allowed home from hospital the following morning; however he was soon after called into the *Garda* headquarters by Phoenix Park for a long debriefing. The ubiquitous Gerald Caxton accompanied him. He winced as the anti-terrorist detectives forced him to relive the painful memories of the previous few days. They told him the details of the plot to kidnap him and hold him hostage. The perpetrators were the WRA- the Workers' Revolutionary Army. They were a small underground Marxist-Leninist movement made up of former Trinity College students. They had become a splinter paramilitary faction of the Irish Communist Party that was sometimes discussed at embassy security meetings. They had not been thought of as a significant threat, previously. The WRA guerrillas' ultimate aim was to brainwash him into publicly denouncing the government in a propaganda film. After that he was to be shot. Clane screwed up his face as he heard this news. After he left the *Garda* command centre he opted for the traditional Irish therapy and headed for Temple Bar. Of course Caxton went with him. "We got the information out of Ludovico Sanders." said Caxton as they sat together in *The Windmill Inn.*

"What? You mean he spilt the beans just like that?"

"Well, he... fell off his chair a few times during the interview." Caxton raised an eyebrow.

Clane stared back. "You mean you tortured him!?"

"He was the mastermind behind the conspiracy to take you hostage and murder you. We've always known he was an ICP fellow traveller; he makes no secret of that. Now we know he was also a member of the WRA and was one of their top activists. He was the leader of the cell which abducted you... We did him a lot less harm than his people did you."

"All the same, Gerald... We're supposed to be a civilized nation."

"We're a civilized nation at war!... You don't win wars by being Mr Nice Guy. Our enemy has lowered the rules of engagement, not us. The only way we can defeat them now is by fighting them on their level."

Clane shrugged and changed the subject. "Nobody mentioned the photographs Sanders showed me."

"What photographs?"

Clane described them.

"They're fake." replied Caxton immediately, shifting his chair to one side and sipping quietly on his pint. "He probably got some of his comrades to strip off and lie on the floor of a barn."

"Are you sure?"

Caxton turned his head back and gazed at him with disapproval. "Clane, if you believe the word of a filthy terrorist Kike pinko over mine, then I have some tickets to a seaside holiday in Kansas you might be interested in."

Chapter 15

The following winter was very mild and wet, even by Irish standards. Gales ravaged the entire country and there was widespread damage across the west coast. Roads, railways and houses from Donegal to Kerry were washed away in tidal surges, flooded rivers and storm force Atlantic winds. A leading climatologist and prominent figure in the new ecological movement was interviewed on a television talk show claiming that the global climate was changing because of the increase in atmospheric carbon dioxide levels caused by industry. He called for an immediate decrease in the burning of oil, gas and coal. An old woman in the studio audience disagreed and said she remembered such winters long ago when she was a young girl and there was far less industry. A heated debate ensued which of course the viewers found entertaining. After Christmas the weather eased much to everybody's relief.

Clane came home one afternoon from a hard day at the embassy. He parked on the street and walked down the long row of steep steps leading down to the front door. He looked up and marvelled at the rare sight of blue sky. He opened the front door and his family were waiting in the hallway. "Clane." Gina smiled. "We've got a surprise for you!" She opened the door to the lounge and the furniture had been rearranged. In the far corner was a new table on top of which was a computer.

"Hey wow!" Clane walked in and looked at it. "Where did you get this?"

"CCI's."

"Was it expensive?"

"Thirty-four pounds, and the table cost a pound and twelve shillings."

"Gee-whiz! That's not bad. Amy told me the ones at work cost almost a hundred a piece."

"It was in a sale, besides those are probably special office computers. This is a *personal* computer." she replied grandly.

Siobhan had wasted no time getting the personal computer up and running. It was much smaller and lighter than the first computer Clane had had in his office the previous year, yet it was clearly far more advanced. It consisted of an oblong case about two feet by one and a monitor that was separate and connected by a cable. The cathode ray tube monitor stood on top of the base unit and had a ten inch screen. The keyboard was also a separate module. "What's this?" Clane pointed to a small oval box sitting to one side of the keyboard connected to it via a cable.

"It's called a 'mouse' and it's a new way of operating computers." Siobhan showed him how it moved a cursor on the monitor screen; a much improved user interface. The graphics were better too; higher resolution and in colour.

"Goodness me." said Clane. "I can't believe how quickly these things are advancing. I'll insist Amy throws out my old contraption and replaces it with one of these for my office... Here, let me have a go!"

"We've connected its modem to the phone socket." said Gina. "That means we can access WorldMesh... right here in our home!"

Clane experimented by locating his E-gram service and logging in. It worked. At the top of the list was one from Caxton. "Ah, Gerald is in Ireland and wants to know if he can pop round tonight."

"Naturally!" bubbled Gina. Brendan had walked into the room and looked up at his mother. "Brendan. The man who saved Mommy's life is coming to see us again!"

....

Caxton cheesed up on their doorstep at 7 PM again, as he had the previous year, presenting a bottle of wine he had brought for the dinner. Gina embraced him warmly. They ate dinner; this time Brendan was old enough to sit at the table. After dinner Caxton innocently suggested that he and Clane take a walk on the beach again. Clane agreed apprehensively. They walked onto the sand in silence. Even though it was January this time and not April, the night was brighter and clearer. A glowing moon hung over them and stars twinkled in the black sky. "Gerald, are you going to suggest that I get you any more secret information; because if so I really don't want to... You've done so much for me and my family, you know I realize that; but I feel I've repaid you now."

Caxton visibly smiled in the moonlight. "Oh don't worry, Clane. I wasn't going to suggest that. In fact Prime Minister Mosley asked me to pass on his thanks and appreciations for last year's endeavour. It has provided a valuable insight into your country's nuclear ambitions towards Ireland."

Clane nodded.

"No, I have a far higher destiny in mind for you... How are you these days anyway?"

"Well... could be better."

"You're still having nightmares?"

He nodded. "Gina says my mood has changed. She bought that computer today to try and cheer me up."

"It's hardly surprising, old boy. You went through a highly traumatic ordeal at the hands of those Red vermin... How's your wrist?"

Clane raised his left arm and clenched his fist. "Still a bit stiff. It aches sometimes too. The doc says it might never completely get better."

"I'm sorry to hear that."

"Well, could be worse; at least I'm right-handed." They both laughed.

"Now." said Caxton. "What I have in mind for you is an important new role in the years ahead. I can't tell you too much right now, but the time is coming soon when I will be able to."

Clane glanced at him curiously. "That's not the first time you've said something like that, that you're 'priming' me. What do you mean?"

"Ah, if only you knew, Clane." Caxton put his hands in his jacket pocket and tossed his head around in a cheery manner.

"Gerald, you're the best friend I've got; you saved Gina's life... but I do wish you'd stop talking in riddles and start answering questions straight."

Caxton stopped walking and became serious. "I can't. Not yet... Ask me no more questions. The answers will come in due course. Rest assured the future will be very advantageous for you."

"But in which..." Clane cut off. He suddenly noticed a fast moving point of light among the stars. It outshone them all, gleaming like a spark in a chimney. "Here, what's that?"

"It's a meteor." Caxton responded evasively. "Come on, Clane. Let's get back to the house. I have to go back to my hotel." He began walking swiftly back towards the car park.

Clane stayed put. "It's not a meteor. It's moving in an arc. Here, Gerald, look."

"No, thank you." he snapped. "Come along, Clane..."

"It's getting brighter!" The glowing bright light appeared to be getting closer. It began to display a distinct structure, an orange luminous egg-shape. "My God!"

"Clane!" shouted Caxton. He ran up and grabbed Clane's shoulder. "Turn your back! Don't look!"

"What do you mean don't look!?" Clane shrugged his grip away. "It's a flying saucer!"

"No, it's not! It's a weather balloon!... Clane, come away!" Caxton tried once again to manhandle him.

Clane felt a twinge of irritation. "Get your hands off me, Gerald! I'll look at something if I want to!"

Caxton started back, surprised at his friend's show of defiance. "Please, Clane! Don't look at it!"

"It's not Martian... or Venusian. What the hell is it?"

The egg-shaped object changed course and suddenly shot off southwards along the coast at enormous speed. Clane turned and ran for the carpark. "Come on, Gerald. We have to report this!"

"No, Clane!" Caxton took off after him.

Clane was out of breath by the time he arrived at the gateway to his house. Caxton was pounding up beside him puffing and panting.

Both men stopped and leaned on the gatepost to regain their breath. "They're back."

"No, they're not!" insisted Caxton.

"They're breaking the Dublin Treaty... if that is them and not somebody else. If it's somebody else we're in even bigger trouble. Gerald, I have to report this." He began descending the steps to his front door.

"Clane!" Caxton called after him in a tone of desperation.

He stopped and looked back.

Caxton was sweating from the exertion, his clothes ruffled. His normally tidy hair was sticking out like a spider's legs, silhouetted by the streetlight. His normally smiling mouth was a circle framing his gritted teeth. His chest still heaved from the run. His huge forward-facing nostrils were red-rimmed. "Clane, please! I'm begging you!... Forget you saw what you just did on the beach?"

"Why!?"

"I can't tell you."

For the first time, Clane felt genuine contempt for Caxton. "Not good enough!" He opened his front door and stepped inside. A moment later he heard the engine of Caxton's car as his friend departed.

Clane made himself a cup of coffee and retrieved his embassy phone book from the desk drawer on his study. After making some inquiries with the switchboard he soon got hold of the phone number for the current Undersecretary for Interplanetary Relations at the Department of Defence; he couldn't even remember the name of his successor. He dialled the number, but it just rang and rang endlessly. Clane checked the clock; it was six PM Washington time; the office would probably be empty. He wondered what to do next and then had the idea of using the new computer. He went downstairs, took a seat at the keyboard and called up WorldMesh. The WorldMesh reader was a sophisticated function that allowed the user to search all the millions of different pages on the global network by inserting simple search terms into a box. Clane typed "FLYING SAUCER" and pressed *Enter*. After just as few seconds a list of hundreds of different references appeared. He clicked a meshboard near the top of the list named wmn.flyingsaucers.co.us. A brightly coloured and well-designed meshpage formed on the monitor screen. It had the words at the top: *Have YOU seen an MFO?* Clane wondered what that meant. He scrolled down and saw that he had been reading the banner of a forum. He decided to write something on it. He had to use his embassy E-gram to register an account. He couldn't think of a new handle, so he chose to use his own name in his username: *Clane_Quilley1*. He pressed reply on the title thread and typed: *Yes. I just saw one off the coast of County Wicklow, Ireland. Also, what does "MFO" stand for?* He pressed post and the message immediately appeared on the bottom of the thread. He had to wait a while to get a reply. He kept checking back and just before midnight somebody called *Science_Robot* posted underneath his: *Thanks for the report. MFO stands for "Mysterious Flying Object". Not all MFO's are saucers. By the way, you're not THE Clane Quilley, the former interplanetary war expert, surely?*

Clane immediately replied: *Yes I am. I'm currently working at the US Embassy to Ireland.*

Science_Robot came back within two minutes: *Well, it's an honour to have you on our forum, if you're not having a joke with us.*

Clane added more information: *Thanks. It really is me; promise. I don't think the craft I saw was Martian or Venusian. It was from somewhere else.*

It *took Science_Robot* half an hour to respond. These WorldMesh forums were not the same as live chat, more like organized E-grams: *A lot of MFO's do not come from Mars or Venus. This is controversial within the MFOlogical community, but some say there are no Martians or Venusians at all.*

Clane frowned. *What do you mean "none at all?"* Clane waited twenty minutes for his correspondent to reply, but he didn't. So he posted a few goodnight pleasantries for the anonymous person who could have been anywhere in the world, then he shut the computer down and went to bed.

....

Clane woke up in the morning and had breakfast with Gina and his children. He was just about to leave for work when there was a loud knock at the door. It was a pair of uniformed *Gardai*. "Clane Quilley?" One of them asked.

"Yes?"

"We're detaining you under Section Nineteen of the US Ambassadorial Charter. You are not obliged to say anything unless you wish to do so, but whatever you say will be taken down in writing and may be given in evidence. Because of your status of diplomatic immunity, we are *detaining* you and not arresting you. Do you understand?"

Clane paused. His heart thudded, his head spun. "Yes, but..."

Gina and Siobhan came to the door. "What's going on, Clane?"

"I don't know."

They escorted him to a *Garda* car, never taking their hands off his shoulders. Clane moved instinctively, wondering if he were still dreaming. Behind him Brendan was crying, but he didn't look back.

They drove him into Dublin to the headquarters where he had been debriefed following his abduction the previous year. He was checked in, had his fingerprints taken and was made to empty his pockets. Despite several statements from the officers that he was

229

"not under arrest", he certainly felt as if he was. He sat in a cell for an hour, his mind blank. Then two suited men arrived from the US Diplomatic Security Agency and arrested him properly. He was taken to the embassy and placed into the detention centre there. As he was marched through the corridors his colleagues all looked at him in surprise.

Jose Gutierrez was waiting for him in the office. Sitting beside him was a man in a US Marshal's uniform. "Clane Quilley." he said calmly but formally. "We're repatriating you to the United States as soon as possible in the diplomatic bag."

"Your Excellency... What the hell is going on here?"

"Evidence has come to light that you conspired with a foreign government to commit an act of espionage on these premises in contravention of Article Eighteen of the US Code 793- Gathering, transmitting or losing defence information."

"What!?... When!?"

"Some time in April of 1955."

It all fell into place. The documents he had copied for Caxton just before his visit to the UK. "But, Mr Gutierrez... that was just a couple of photographs... It was just to aid Anglo-American relations... He saved my wife's life! I owed him!"

"Owed who?" asked the marshal.

Clane opened his mouth to answer, but then common sense told him to close it. "I need to see a lawyer." he muttered quietly.

Gutierrez looked at him with sadness and sympathy. "Of course, Clane. We'll arrange it."

....

Clane was permitted to call home. Gina sounded more annoyed than worried. "It must be a mistake, Clane. I'm sure they'll release you eventually. They'd better soon or there'll be trouble!" He was treated well by the embassy staff. They made him cups of coffee in the detention suite until the marshal came back and placed a handcuff on his right wrist and the other on his own left wrist. Then he was taken to a car which drove him to the airport. When his flight was ready to take off he was escorted on board before any of the other passengers and sat in a seat at the back in the middle, away from the windows. When they came aboard, his fellow travellers looked at him curiously and slightly fearfully. The aircraft started moving and eventually took off. Clane was not allowed to wander freely and remained shackled to the marshal the whole time. Even when he went to the bathroom the stern-faced escort stood in the doorway while he used the toilet. The flight gave him time to cool down and think. Almost a year goes by and he hears nothing; he was certain that he'd got away with it and there would be no repercussions. Now here he was, under arrest, heading back stateside to an uncertain future. Espionage was a very serious crime that could possibly lead to the death penalty; however he knew enough about the government to realize that his offence was comparatively minor. He was a fairly harmless spy, as spies go. Sure, he would certainly be fired and that would be a shame, but he would not receive a major criminal change. He was glad he had said what he had to Caxton on the beach the night before... "Gerald!" he hissed aloud.

"Pardon?" The US Marshal turned to him.

"Er... nothing." The marshal's attention turned back to his in-flight magazine, but Clane's mind was churning. Nothing happens for ten months; and then the morning after he meets with Caxton he suddenly he gets arrested. Was that a coincidence? Did Caxton tip them off? Would he do a dreadful thing like that? Why would he do that? As these thoughts shuffled around his brain Clane suddenly realized something: He didn't actually like Gerald Caxton very much. He never had. His friendship with him was completely founded on gratitude. Was all this something to do with the flying saucer, or *MFO*, Clane had spotted on the beach? Caxton's behaviour during that experience was very odd indeed. It was as if he knew what it was straight away but didn't want Clane to find out.

It was dark when the aircraft touched down at Dulles Airport and Clane was handed over to the custody of the FBI.

....

Clane's lawyer was a short bulky man with a puffball of white hair surrounding his head. His name was Ricky Brulloglio; a name that made him sound like a Mafia brief, Clane thought with a smile. During their consultation in a private room, he spent a lot of time talking on his roamphone, as if he wanted to demonstrate his sophistication from the fact that he owned one. He stood up at one point and said, glancing at the warder: "Sorry, Mac. I don't have a very good signal in here. Can you speak up?" Eventually he put the device back in his pocket and was ready to talk to his client. "You know, Mr Quilley, I wouldn't worry too much. You passed on information with classifications of merely Restricted to Confidential. Nothing even on the level of your own security clearance and you only did it once. What's more you shared it with the UK, which is very different to passing it on to the communist Bloc. You received no payment from your contact and have no ideological motives... You're not exactly Julius Rosenburg are you?... What's more you were in a state of severe psychological tension following your kidnapping..."

"Actually I did the spying about a week before the kidnapping."

"They don't need to know that." He winked. "They've only managed to time your act to the nearest calendar month."

Clane nodded imperceptibly.

"What's more I understand your wife had cancer at the time."

"Yes."

"And did your employers offer you any counselling?"

"No."

"Didn't they!?" Brulloglio gaped in mock horror. "Well, what do they expect? I'm sorry, but if the State Department can't be bothered to care for the psychological wellbeing of their overseas diplomatic servicemen then they have only themselves to blame."

Clane smiled. He liked the easy confidence and good humour of the lawyer.

"Fear not, Mr Quilley. You're going to walk; I can virtually guarantee it... Now, I'm off to the office to write up your bail application and I'll be back in a couple of days." He nodded to the warder.

Clane was escorted back to his cell. He had been at the Logansport Federal Correction Centre in Indiana for two weeks now. He was being kept in isolation because of the nature of his charge, yet the prison regime was not exceptionally restrictive, at least for as long as he was a remand inmate. He found it far easer than Navy boot camp in fact. Gina and Siobhan were allowed to visit him in an open room where they could hold hands; no glass windows and telephone handsets. His cell was about ten feet by six and he was allowed books to read. The food was reasonable and he had access to an outdoor exercise yard in which he spent an hour in the mornings and afternoons.

....

The following day Gerald Caxton came to visit him. Clane entered the visitors' suite to see him casually sitting at a table smoking a Gauloise. He grinned broadly in his characteristic way. "Hello, Clane old boy. How are you?"

Clane felt his anger bite. However, his instinctive respect for his friend once again blocked his tongue from voicing his thoughts. "I'm in prison, Gerald; can't you see?"

"I had noticed."

Clane sat down opposite him. "Gerald... how did they find out? Did you blab on me?"

Caxton sighed apologetically. "If I did, Clane, it was to protect you."

"Protect me?... From what?"

"People less understanding than I. It's all connected with the MFO we witnessed on the beach and your attempt to publicize it on that WorldMesh forum."

"How did you know about that?"

"Never mind how I know." He leaned forward and stared at Clane intensely. "You don't understand, Clane! You don't understand what is truly at stake here and how important your role in it is!... I may well have saved your life by getting you arrested."

Clane stood up. "I'm tired of your word games, Gerald. You've ruined my career! You've forced me to leave Ireland!..."

"Clane, wait!" Caxton seized his wrist.

Clane slowly sat back down.

"I've come with good news. The charges against you are about to be dropped. You'll be released within forty-eight hours."

"How do you know that?"

"I have my... 'confidants' within the judiciary."

Clane paused. "That's great."

"What will you do then though? You know State is going to sack you for sure."

"I know."

"So you'll be out of work. Got any ideas for a new occupation?"

He shook his head.

"Good, because I have a job for you."

"What kind of job?"

"The job I've been preparing you for over the years."

Clane became intrigued despite himself. "You've said that before. Has the time come?"

"I think so."

"Tell me what it's about."

"Not yet." He grinned furtively. "When you're free."

....

Caxton was right, two days later Brulloglio turned up beaming all over his face. The government had decided not to prosecute Clane for his misdemeanour. He was informed that he'd undergo disciplinary action at the State Department, but this was just a formality. Regretfully they would have no choice but to terminate his employment. His clothes and belongings were all returned to him and the gate slid to one side revealing the horizon in front of him. Gina, Siobhan and Brendan all came to the jail to meet Clane as he was released. They embraced as the gate closed behind him.

New York City had changed enormously in the years since he'd last seen it. During his time in Washington and Ireland he had stayed in touch with his family, but it had always been a case of them visiting him; not the other way round. Many new skyscrapers had been thrown up, including Earth Tower that now dominated Manhattan. It cut the sky in two from the western side of Fifth Avenue, built on the spot formerly occupied by the Empire State Building until its destruction by the forces of Mars in 1947. It soared to over one and a half thousand feet above the streets; its oblong plan stylishly segueing into a rotunda topped with a done and pinnacle. However New York's changes only appeared to affect its higher levels, anything below the second storey was the same. However, there was another difference Clane detected that was decidedly pedestrian. He passed a mobile soup kitchen on the corner outside a department store, in the very shadow of Earth Tower. It consisted of a parked truck with a window. Inside were church volunteers handing out disposable cardboard bowls of soup to a line of hungry people. There was fear on their faces, and on those of the people passing by. They may have been wondering how long it would be before they would be in that queue. A few months ago the stock market had crashed and unemployment was rising sharply. Several major companies had downsized radically. There was even talk of a "new Great Depression." Clane could remember the old one from his youth and how his uncles and aunts all lost their jobs and had to visit his home for meals. When Clane had finished craning his neck up at Earth Tower, Gina and the children went home while he nipped over to Hell's Kitchen and, sure enough, tucked into a narrow gap between a pair of crumbling warehouses on West Fiftieth Street, was *O'Grady's Inn*. Tony the landlord recognized him immediately. "Haven't seen you in a while, Clane." he noted as he poured him a pint of Guinness without asking. He spoke as if Clane had been away on vacation for a week or two, although it had actually been eight years. Clane looked over and waved at the pub regulars; mostly old men from the docks who still spoke in rough Connacht accents. After a happy reunion over a pint or three, Clane went to the subway and caught a train home to Brooklyn.

Clane's mother and father lived in an apartment off Prospect Avenue, just a ten minute walk from his own home. Their quest to rise into the gentry had ultimately failed and their home was a modest affair. Arthur and Marianne Quilley were now almost seventy years old yet neither had yet retired. Arthur was still busy laying down some poison in a kitchen at the railway terminal while Marianne was returning from the nearby school where she worked as a lunch lady. As Clane walked up the street her face brightened. "Clane!"

"Hi, Mom." he smiled back. They embraced on the sidewalk. The apartment had not changed since his last visit, other than photographs of Brendan on the mantelpiece along with Siobhan. Marianne cooked a meal while Clane had a cup of tea and they waited for Arthur Quilley to come home. Clane's father greeted him less warmly than his mother as he walked through the door. "So, you've lost another job, have you, son?" He scowled and threw his jacket down on the arm of a chair.

"Well I'm not going back to jail, Dad. I thought you'd be pleased."

Arthur gasped. "What the hell were you thinking of!? Spying for an enemy nation!"

Clane bit his tongue. He couldn't tell his father about Gina's cancer.

"It wasn't quite like that... but I'm sorry, Dad."

Arthur tutted and sat down at the table.

"How's work, Dad?" asked Clane, taking the opportunity to change the subject.

He shrugged. "As depression-proof as ever. There'll always be critters that need exterminating."

"What was it today?"

"Rats. Big ones! They've taken over the entire fuckin' railroad station."

"Arthur!" His wife frowned at the profanity. She was setting plates of food down on the table.

He glanced up at her apologetically. "They've definitely grown over the years. Boy, one of them was a foot long if he was an inch!"

"I saw Earth Tower today. I took Gina and the kids downtown."

"Not the same as the old ESB. I wish they'd just rebuilt it... Still, it was quite a good career move for you, eh?" He chuckled, not unkindly.

"What do you mean?"

"The pesky little green men in their flying saucers."

"I guess so."

The three of them all fell silent and looked at each other.

"It's weird." said Marianne. "I think about creatures from Mars and how strange that sounds, how they only existed in the movies and comic books, how unimaginable it was before they came here for real.... and then I get surprised that I think of them as so normal. I swear I'd even forgotten all about them. It's like they're a part of our past, like the war. In fact, we hardly ever hear about them on TV or in the papers these days... Sometimes I can't believe it even happened."

Clane and his father exchanged a look. They had both been thinking the same thing.

....

"Clane Quilley." said the chairman woodenly. "It is the decision of this tribunal that you be discharged from the United States Foreign Service. If you wish to appeal against this decision then you have twenty-eight days to submit a pledge. You will be awarded a severance pay package within three working days. You will now be escorted off these premises." He banged his gavel down and two marshals entered the room to lead Clane out as if he were a dangerous criminal. At the front door they turned away without a word and Clane stepped out into the warm sunshine carrying a cardboard box of his personal effects. He walked out of the gate of the Harry S Truman Building and headed up Virginia Avenue feeling nonchalant. He went to the station and caught a train back to New York. He arrived at his apartment at ten PM. Gina, Siobhan and Brendan were in bed. He fired up the personal computer and logged into his E-gram account. Along with a dozen messages from the State Department formalizing his dismissal was one from Gerald Caxton. *Hi Clane. How did it go today? Gerald.*

Clane chuckled bitterly. "Don't you know?" He typed out a reply: *Hi Gerald. Been fired. Clane.*

Caxton must have been at his own computer because a response came back within minutes: *That's a shame, Clane, but it was inevitable. Have you given any more thought to my proposal?*

Clane had indeed, all the way home on the train. *What have I got to lose? OK, Gerald, I'll do it. But I don't know anything about it yet. Tell me about it.*

The reply came back so quickly it made Clane wonder if Caxton had already written it before he had sent his own message. *Not here and now.*

Chapter 16

Clane was given an appointment for an interview the following week. He received a letter in the mail from an organization called Florenti Inc. It was neatly printed on expensive paper with the coloured letterhead at the top. Enclosed was an airline ticket to Atlanta, Georgia where the company had its headquarters. Clane quickly located Florenti's extensive and upmarket Meshboard. He clicked the "about" tab: *Florenti Inc. was established in 1919 and quickly became one of America's largest and most trusted defence contractors... provides management and technical services... development of high technology and weapons countermeasures on land, air and sea...* Clane then remembered seeing Florenti's logo on equipment used in USS *Tunny* during the war. *Florenti's personnel have made enormous and proud contributions to our nation's safety and progress... Our clients include the AASA, the Department of Defence, the US Coast Guard, the SIA, the CSA...* Clane raised his eyebrows at the mention of the three-letter intelligence agencies. What was he getting involved with?

....

Clane waited for the day of his appointment with a mixture of excitement, curiosity and trepidation. Then he dressed in his best suit, took the subway LaGuardia Field and caught his flight to Atlanta. The sky was cloudy and as the jet-propelled airliner descended, Clane felt his apprehension grow. He grasped the arms of his window seat as the grey ocean of water vapour came closer. The plane dived straight into it and the sun vanished. The wing tips of the aircraft constituted the edge of the world. The miasma below thinned and features became visible; green fields, forests, roads, buildings. The runway slid into view below the fuselage and with a penetrating thud, the plane landed. He exited the plane down a jet-way and made his way to the airport entrance. Heavy rain was falling; cold Southern winter drops pattered on the awning above the drop-off point. He wondered how he would continue his journey until he saw a man in a suit holding up a signboard that read *CLANE QUILLEY*. The chauffeur escorted him to a large saloon car and drove steadily out into the rain-washed streets of the city. Their destination was in a suburb of Atlanta. The corporate headquarters of Florenti Inc. was a four storey oblong block of red ochre stone with gold tinted windows. In the gloomy damp weather it looked like a block of dark copper. The driver parked outside the front entrance and led him inside. Clane had been to many job interviews and always he had to wait beforehand, but not this time. He was offered a cup of coffee by a smartly-dressed female secretary and then shown immediately into a wide-windowed minimalist office. A large bearded man in a grey suit gestured to the seat opposite and introduced himself as the company's personnel officer. The discussion that followed was very atypical. He didn't ask Clane any questions about himself; why he wanted the job, what he thought he could bring to Florenti Inc. He acted as if the decision to employ Clane had already been made by higher powers and his role was simply to orientate the new member of staff. He presented thick reams of paperwork and explained they were legal documents for him to sign; they were related to classified material. "Secrecy is essential!" he told Clane several times. Clane read through as much of them as he could. The print was almost too small to see and was full of words like "aforementioned" and "notwithstanding". Clane's jaw dropped when he saw the salary; this was the highest paid job he'd ever had except when he was SecIntWar. At the end of the interview the two men shook hands and Clane was driven back to the airport.

He took a taxi home from LaGuardia, seething with excitement and happiness. Their route took them past the Macys department store and Clane saw that it was still open. He asked the driver to stop and wait while he quickly went inside and bought a bottle of champagne from the chilled cabinet. It was gone ten PM when he got home. Gina and Siobhan were getting ready for bed; Brendan had been asleep for a couple of hours. "Hi Clane, how did it go?" asked Gina.

Clane said nothing and just smiled. He removed the bottle from the Macys shopping bag and held it up.

"Holy Mary!... How much did that cost!?"

"Eleven-eighty."

"Dear Lord, Clane! We can't afford that!"

He winked. "We can now."

She paused. "What?"

"I got the job, Gina; and it's fifteen hundred bucks a year."

She gasped and jumped to her feet. "Clane!" She embraced him. Siobhan did the same.

"What's happening?" came a voice from behind them. Brendan was walking into the lounge dressed in his pyjamas and holding a teddy bear. "Hi, Daddy."

Clane picked him up and kissed his cheek. "You're daddy just got a new job, son." He addressed them all. "And there's more... Do you guys ever find the Big Apple a bit cold and dreary?"

"All the time." groaned Gina.

"Yeah, especially this time of year." added Siobhan.

"How would you like to move to Las Vegas?"

Their faces brightened again. "Really!?"

"What's Las Vegas?" asked Brendan.

"Son, it's a city in the middle of a golden desert where the sun shines from dawn to dusk every day and gold coins fill every pocket."

"We're going to Las Vegas!" bubbled Siobhan.

"Florenti have an office there; that's where I'll be working... Now, get some glasses out before this Champers warms up. We need to celebrate!" He popped the cork and poured out a generous portion into some glasses, jerking back as the foam overflowed onto the table. Even Brendan was allowed a small splash in a plastic beaker. They toasted Clane's success and their future. "What is your new job exactly?" asked Gina.

Clane paused and frowned. "You know... I'm not sure. I never asked."

....

It took six weeks to make the arrangements. Florenti Inc. provided accommodation for the entire family at a large spacious house in Boulder City, Nevada; a town a few miles from Las Vegas. The Quilleys flew out to look at the place before they moved and the family were delighted with it. Siobhan was about to enrol at the University of Pennsylvania and so would not be there long, but Gina and Brendan were overjoyed with their new home. Their last days in New York were sumptuous because Clane's new wages were backdated to the day he signed the contract in Atlanta and payments started on the first of March. They ate and drank whatever they liked; and spent evenings at the movies and theatres. On the day of the move, they packed all their belongings into boxes that were picked up by rental trucks. Then they walked solemnly towards the Subway station, looking around themselves at the familiar streets of Brooklyn for the last time. Arthur, Marianne and Gina's parents and sister were all there to see them off. There was a subdued farewell before they boarded the train to LaGuardia Field airport.

Clane was given another two weeks to settle in when he arrived in Las Vegas. He and the family spent that time exploring the area and becoming acclimatized to the high desert sunshine which even in the spring was baking hot. They walked together down The Strip and Freemont Street, marvelling at the illuminated casinos and hotels with walls of coloured glass. They walked over the top of the Hoover Dam and hiked through Red Rock Canyon. After that Clane finally received a starting date at the local Florenti Inc. facility which was on the western side of McCarran Field, the city's principle airport. Clane got up early with the usual thrill that came with starting a new job. He dressed as well as the scorching day allowed and got into his car, a new Chrysler provided by the company. He hummed and whistled as he negotiated the morning traffic on the expressway into Las Vegas. He turned right into a dusty and undeveloped neighbourhood west of the airport and approached Haven Street. Strangely enough, he could see no large buildings at all. There was nothing but the perimeter fence of McCarran with a few rusty warehouses behind it. The tailfins of aircraft poked up in the background like trees. He drove up and down Haven Street three times before stopping at a gatehouse to ask directions. "Excuse me." he called to a security guard. "Can you tell me where Florenti Inc. is?"

The man slowly walked over to the car. "I'm not familiar with that name, sir."

"But I have the address here; 5400 Haven Street."

The man pointed. "That's the next gate along."

"No, I've already been past that; it's just a parking lot."

"That's 5400 Haven Street; I promise you." Clane turned the car around and slowly approached the next gate along, shaking his head in bemusement. He drove up to the gatehouse. Unlike the last security guard he had spoken to, the two men inside were armed. "Can I help you, sir?" one asked as he stopped the car.

"I'm looking for Florenti Inc." Clane felt stupid as he spoke.

"Can I see your authorization, please?"

Clane handed the man the letter of instructions that had arrived in the post a few days earlier.

"Thank you, sir. Park over on the left block and proceed on foot to check-in."

Clane mumbled a confused word of thanks and obeyed. The car park was one of the largest he had ever been in and he found his way by following other people who had just parked. There were no signs or direction arrows. Just a footway leading to a low white building that looked far too small for such a big car park. It turned out this was a small private air terminal. Clane looked around for somebody who appeared to be in charge. A suited receptionist was sitting at a desk in the corner and Clane went up to him. "Excuse me. I'm new to this place and I think I've been sent here by mistake. I'm due to start work with Florenti Inc."

The man glanced at his letter. "No, there's no mistake, sir. Take a seat and wait to be called to board."

"Board? What do you mean?"

"Take a seat please, sir." the man repeated. The seats in the departure lounge were almost all full of people, mostly in casual dress. They spoke to each other a lot less than people normally did, as if they were all mutual strangers. After half an hour the loudspeaker announced: "Could all passengers please proceed to the gate for boarding." Everybody around Clane stood up immediately as if they'd been expecting the announcement. He did the only thing he could and copied them. They walked from the lounge out of a door on the opposite side to the car park entrance and out onto the sunlit airport apron. The roar of jets and the smell of kerosene filled the atmosphere around them. The passengers walked in a disciplined file towards a white painted airliner, a Boeing 397. The aircraft had no livery except a for a full length red cheatline. He climbed up the stairway into the cabin. There was no smiling stewardess to welcome him aboard. The cabin crew were all male and dressed in flight suits; and they were as taciturn as his fellow passengers. He managed to get a seat by a window and buckled himself in; his hands shaking. There were no announcements from the flight crew; the plane simply started its engines and trundled out of the small terminal onto the taxiway. Clane leaned to his side to see as much as possible out of the window as the aircraft reached the end of the runway and spooled up before lifting off and ascending above the city. It climbed more steeply than any passenger aircraft he'd been in before and he grasped the arms of his chair. A few minutes after takeoff the plane banked to the right and headed north into the desert. Clane was surprised to find that it began to descend almost immediately after steadying on course. He knew what lay beneath them because it had become the location of some infamy in the media; it was the Nevada Proving Grounds where atomic bomb tests had been carried out during the last few years. There were still regular spots in newspapers and on television expressing concern for radioactive contamination, and how mushroom clouds from nuclear detonations could be seen in the sky from Las Vegas. Why was this aircraft flying here; descending as if it intended to land? There were no airfields in this region, only empty desert and a few disused mines. He heard the sound of the landing gear being lowered; surely it wasn't possible... but then a runway scrolled into view below and the unmarked Boeing 397 struck the ground. The runway was full-sized and paved, and in the distance Clane could see large hangars and other buildings. He was at a full-sized airbase where one simply shouldn't be. It was only twenty-five minutes since they'd taken off from McCarran. In fact this was the biggest airbase he had ever been on; it dwarfed even the wartime one on Tinian Island. It took the aircraft almost as long to taxi from the runway to the stands as it had to fly from Las Vegas. Its buildings were some of the biggest he'd ever seen and he stared at them as the plane glided slowly up to the terminal. The doors were opened and the passengers deplaned via a jetway, politely standing aside to let fellow flyers into the aisles. Clane walked down the jetway into a large but low-ceilinged hallway which was chilly with overactive air conditioning. There was an inquiry desk manned by men in military fatigues and when he showed his letter they immediately presented him with an ID badge to wear. It had a photograph of him on it that he didn't remember having been taken. He also had to turn out his pockets and leave all his belongings in a deposit box before passing through an airport-style metal detector. One of the men barked. "Clane Quilley! Follow me!" It was an order, not a request.

The man walked fast down a long breezeblock passageway without any decorations or paintwork. He strode so quickly Clane almost had to jog to keep up with him. Clane noticed that although the man's clothing was standard GI fatigues there were no flashes or regimental patches on his sleeves; no insignia at all in fact. They reached a door and the man knocked. A voice bid them entry, and the man opened the door and turned away without even looking inside. Clane entered a fairly non-descript medium-sized office with a window overlooking the distant mountains. Behind the desk was Gerald Caxton. "Clane! Good morning, old boy! Welcome aboard."

"Gerald... where am I?" muttered Clane as he took a seat opposite his friend.

"It has no official name. It's built beside Groom Lake in what was going to be designated Area 51 of the Department of Energy Test Site, but they never formalized it."

"But... I had no idea there was an airbase here, especially not one this size! This must be the biggest the AAF has!"

"This is not an AAF facility, Clane, or any other part of the DoD; and the reason you had no idea an airbase was here is because this outfit is highly classified. Its very existence is completely unacknowledged. You won't find it marked on any maps and it's not listed in any government inventory... Take seriously that paperwork you signed; in fact I'll have some more for you in a minute. This is a research and development centre for all the latest aviation projects the United States and its contractors are working on... and that's just *the start* of what they do here."

Clane gasped and leaned back in his chair. "My God!"

Caxton leaned forward and stared at him intently; his flared nostrils widened. "Clane, I'm afraid I have a few more surprises in store for you."

....

Caxton produced more documents for Clane to sign and then he led Clane out of the building to a large bus. When Clane stepped aboard he saw that the windows had been covered with black screens making it impossible to see outside. A black curtain was drawn across the interior behind the driver's seat to block the view out of the front. The vehicle started moving. He and Caxton were the only passengers. The bus rocked back and forth on its suspension; it went up and down some steep hills. The interior was hot and stuffy. Clane began to feel distinctly queasy, as he used to in the control room of USS *Tunny* when the boat was surfaced in bad weather. After about quarter of an hour the bus stopped, the curtains were drawn back and Clane was allowed to disembark. He rolled slightly on his feet as he stepped down to the parched and stony ground. He was in a wide flat-bottomed valley with steep sides and the secret base was nowhere to be seen. A typical Nevadan dry lake bed stretched away to the west. Creosote bushes and yucca plants were the only vegetation, scattered away into the distance, evenly spaced. "This way, Clane." Caxton beckoned him. They walked towards what looked like a large metal hut on the side of the sloping edge of the valley, but when the automatic door slid open Clane could see that it was the entrance to an underground structure. Inside, a steel lined corridor led into the interior of the hill. It was modern, clean and well air conditioned. The passage ended in a set of double doors. Two armed guards stood on each side of it who checked their ID's. Caxton reached for the button to open them electrically, then hesitated. He turned and faced his friend. "Listen, Clane. You've had a lot of upsets and shocks these past few years, but none of them will come close to what you're about to see... I have to show you everything; there is no way to ease you in gently. Please prepare yourself."

Clane nodded, his mouth dry.

Caxton jabbed the button and the door slid aside with a quiet hum. They passed through a second set of security doors and inside was a white-painted room with metallic walls. There were futuristic-looking electronic instruments placed on benches against the sides. In the centre of the room were a row of large glass cabinets, some the size of whole rooms. "Do you recognize these things?" asked Caxton.

"Yes." Clane approached the nearest glass wall and pressed his hands to it; by touch he could tell that the material was not glass, it was more like plastic. Inside was a burnished silver chunky disk-shaped object about twenty feet across. In the neighbouring enclosures were smaller fragments of a similar substance. "These are the debris pieces I saw at Wright Field in July 1947."

"They were moved here in 1951 when this institution opened."

"What about the Martians who were inside it?"

"Ah yes, the *Martians*." Caxton tittered. "Follow me." He walked to a second door at the far end of the chamber and it slid open. In the next space were four transparent caskets. Icicles on the inside surface indicated that the interiors were very cold. Clane looked inside and saw the same strange cadavers he had been shown in the mortuary at the Technical Data Section nine years earlier. "The fourth one died in the end." explained Caxton. "The medical team tried to keep it alive, but it only lasted another month after your visit. We've cryo-preserved all the bodies in these pods."

"I wanted to get them repatriated to Mars." Clane said sadly.

"I know."

"President Dewey wasn't too happy about it."

"I know." Caxton repeated. He stepped closer to Clane and looked into his eyes. "The thing is... these creatures don't come from Mars."

"What?"

"They're not from Mars."

"Are they Venusians then?"

"No... We don't know where they come from."

Clane shook his head. "Eh?... What do you mean?"

Caxton paused. "What I'm going to show you next is the most disturbing part of this story. I ask you to keep control of yourself and not react straight away... And also, don't pass judgement on me for what I've done." Gerald Caxton walked to a door on the right hand wall. He and Clane passed through an anteroom and airlock, and then out into another corridor. They walked for a hundred yards or so. There were large double doors every twenty yards or so along the left hand wall and one pair of them was open. They stopped and looked in at a large concrete floored chamber with a sloping far wall. The room was filled by a black craft that Clane immediately recognized as a Martian cruiser. It was the same model flown by the ambassador from Mars that had landed in Dublin in 1950. "What's that doing here, Gerald?"

Caxton didn't respond; he just walked on down the corridor. Ahead was another open door and somebody was speaking loudly inside the chamber. Their voice echoed through the doorway into the corridor. Soon Clane was close enough to hear their words: "KA JAMBA DOO DOO KEE LO LO OTSHA!" He remembered well enough to recognize it as the Martian language. The doorway came into view and within Clane saw another Martian disc identical to the first one, and strutting up and down in front of it was the Martian ambassador whom he had met in Dublin at the summit. He watched as this green-faced, six-foot-five humanoid walked up and down beside the vehicle in its white leotard and black boots. "BOO TABBA MOBO EEBIK RA!" It yelled. There were a group of people standing to one side watching.

"We've resumed rehearsals." Caxton whispered to Clane. "A time is coming when we'll probably need to do this for real again."

Suddenly the Martian ambassador stopped walking and put its hands on its hips. It groaned with frustration and then shouted in perfect English: "I can't believe I spent two years at the Royal Academy just to recite this gibberish!" It then walked over to a washbasin, switched on the tap and began rinsing its face in the water. Green makeup flowed between its fingers.

"Come on, Joe!" retorted one of the people watching. "You know you're being paid more than Lawrence Oliver."

"I don't care!" the ambassador gurgled through the dripping water. "Olivier has a filmography! This not professional! I can't even put it on my CV!" It rubbed its face in a towel and then looked up.

Clane gasped.

The Martian ambassador had washed all the green tone off his skin and what lay underneath was the completely normal chocolate brown features of a negro. He smiled when he saw Clane. "Good morning, Mr Quilley! We meet again." He walked over holding out his hand. "When was it, six years ago? We had a great time in Dublin didn't we? That was a fantastic pub you took us too." His accent was British with a touch of Caribbean.

"Clane, may I introduce Joseph Marceille. He played the part of the Martian ambassador at the Dublin Summit."

Clane shook his hand mindlessly. "But... but... you're human."

Marceille raised his eyebrows and grinned sardonically. "Well, the civil rights movement in your country has certainly made progress if you accept that fact, Mr Quilley."

"Would you like to meet the ambassador for Venus?" Caxton asked Clane. "He's standing over there... Mr Foster!"

Clane looked across and saw a shorter man with blue paint on his face. He was just pulling off his long white false beard.

Clane backed out into the corridor. Caxton followed, putting a hand on his arm. "Clane, breathe!... Remember! Don't react!"

"What the fuck is going on!?" bellowed Clane.

"It's all a ruse, Clane. It's a charade... There *are* no Martians or Venusians. We invented them. We employed actors to play them. We built phoney spacecraft for them for them to fly around in; we even constructed languages for them to speak."

The underground corridor was spinning around Clane's head. He was puffing and panting but still felt short of breath. He fell to the floor, feeling his body go numb. Just before he passed out he heard Caxton's voice yelling: "Medic!"

He came to on a gurney in a windowless first aid room. Caxton was sitting at his side, waiting for him to awaken like he had in Ireland after Clane's kidnapping. Caxton smiled affectionately. "Clane, hello. Are you feeling better now?" A doctor came in and checked his observations. He gave Clane a drink of water and after a few minutes he allowed him to stand up. Clane slowly limped over to a bench and sat quietly, sipping his water. Caxton sat down beside him with a concerned look on his face. "Clane, I really do owe you an apology."

Clane slowly raised his gaze and met Caxton's. "I was Secretary for Interplanetary War." he croaked quietly.

"And you did a spectacular job, Clane. You truly did." Caxton rubbed Clane's forearm.

"The Dublin Summit... It was in every newspaper on Earth. Every TV screen. Fleets of ships and brigades of troops moved across the world because of the Martian threat. Billions of dollars spent... Are you saying none of it even existed?"

Caxton looked down awkwardly.

"I can't quite grasp this... It's just not possible. Do you know what it meant when Athena-Zvereya landed on the moon? The whole world rose in a moment of joy when we became the third space-faring planet in the solar system..."

"Ah yes, about the moon..." said Caxton. "Are you up to walking again, Clane? There's one more thing I have to show you."

....

Gerald Caxton escorted Clane back out above ground. Night was falling and the sun was sinking behind the hills on the other side of the valley. A jeep was parked near the entrance to the underground base and they got into it. It got darker and darker as Caxton drove along a well-paved road leading up the valley. "You see now why Dewey objected so strongly to your plan to return the creatures' bodies to Mars?"

Clane nodded, still finding it hard to form words.

"Dewey didn't know everything of course, but... higher powers persuaded him to convey our annoyance at your inadvertent blunder."

"The President didn't know?"

"No. US Presidents generally are very low down on the tree of knowledge." It was completely dark. Stars spattered across the sky in a number and clarity never seen in the cities. There was a half moon low in the sky. Caxton slowed the jeep down and turned left. By the moon and starlight Clane could see they were driving into a car park. On the far side there appeared to be a row of towers or masts of some kind. Clane got out and wrapped his arms around his body; the temperature was dropping sharply. "Wait here; I'll be right back." said Caxton. He wandered off in the direction of a small building a dozen yards away. Clane exclaimed in shock and shielded his eyes as the whole scene burst into blinding light. When his irises adjusted he saw that the whole area was lit by giant floodlights like a sports stadium. The lights shone down from the tops of the masts. Caxton came out of a hut and a little way away from it were other single-floor buildings. A few hundred yards beyond those there were a set of structures that were instantly recognizable; they were some of the most famous objects in the world. The gourd-shaped eight-legged arachnoid AASA Athena lunar excursion module and the moon buggy used by the Athena, and previously before the Cold War the Athena-Zvereya, astronauts. Close to them was a flagpole atop which hung the Stars and Stripes. Clane walked forward across the floodlit terrain. He almost tripped over a small railway line running in front of him. It looked to him like a camera dolly track from a film studio. The natural desert terrain gave way abruptly to a synthetic dusty gravel surface into which his shoes cast deep footprints. There were grey rocks of various sizes scattered randomly across the landscape. He kicked one of them and found it was incredibly light, as if made of papier-mâché or fibreglass. He reached the centrepiece of the scene and stopped beside the American flag. "What's this for, Gerald?"

"We're about to start shooting Athena Nineteen. It's due to launch in a few weeks. Some of the footage can be pre-produced and some will have to be filmed live."

"You mean the new moon shot?"

"Yes, the twelfth... Obviously we don't include Athena Thirteen because that was the one where they had the accident and had to come home early."

"I don't get it... This looks exactly like what we see on TV and in those photos; the ones from the moon."

"This *is* what you *think* you're seeing from the moon, Clane."

Clane leaned forward and frowned. "You mean... we... didn't go... to..."

"The moon? No."

He shook his head. "You're lying!... This is just a mock up!... You're LYING!"

Caxton walked over to the lunar roving vehicle and lowered himself into the driver's seat. He ran his hand over the steering handle. "I'm *not* lying to you now, Clane. I'm being completely honest with you for the first time ever."

Clane looked up at the Athena lander towering over them. "No!" he mumbled.

"Lies are Damocles' sword, Clane."

"Lies are... lies..." he mumbled.

Caxton chuckled kindly. "Come here and sit down. I don't want you conking out on us again."

Clane stumbled over to the rover, shuffling through the simulated moon dust. He lowered himself onto the uncomfortable metal seat of the vehicle.

"Remember last year when you visited Britain?"

Clane nodded.

"I showed you our nation, what it had achieved. I'm proud of Britain, but I'm also proud of the world. The great developed nations of the globe were all inspired by Britain and the other European powers, and that includes the United States. I explained how the beauty, glory and ingenuity of Western civilization come with a price. Most people never understand that. They're sheltered from the truth. They enjoy the benefits of Western civilization without ever understanding the foundations on which it is constructed... I envy them." He sighed and turned to stare hard at Clane. "And now so do you."

"What does this all mean, Gerald?... Those Martians and..."

"It's your fault, Clane... It's *all* your fault." Caxton's tone was quiet and without ire.

"My fault? What are you talking about?"

"Your news report into the crash at Roswell. You shouldn't have said anything. You know we wanted to keep it quiet, don't you?"

Clane nodded.

"You stopped us. You should have written nothing... I mean 'RAAF captures Flying Disk'... Jesus!" He slammed his fist against the chassis of the rover.

"But they exist... flying saucers exist."

"Yes."

"But they're not from Mars or Venus. The whole Mars and Venus thing was a... sham?... Shit!" He leaned forward and put his hands over his face as he reminded himself. "No! It's not possible."

"It's perfectly possible."

"Why did you do it!?"

"After your news story came out the whole information situation got out of our control. We had to take drastic action to regain that control. We decided to misinform the world. We led you all to believe that there were civilizations on Mars and Venus fighting an interplanetary war, straight out of a science fiction comic. We just made it appear real. And you, Clane, played your part perfectly... as did Mr Marceille and Mr Foster back there, the men from Mars and Venus."

"No. It's too big a deceit."

As Josef Goebbels said: "The bigger the lie, the more likely it is people will believe it."

"But it changed the world!" Clane spoke with difficulty; his mouth was getting dry.

"It did so more than you know, Clane. The entire world is different to how we intended it to be because of what you did."

"Who's 'we'?"

Caxton sighed. "We're an international alliance of men with power and wealth who are concerned for the future of the world. We want to do something positive and proactive to build a better world for everybody; grasping opportunities for advancement and safeguarding against dangers."

Clane turned and looked at him. "By deceiving the world on such a vast scale?"

Caxton tittered. "Do you want some water to drink?"

Clane nodded.

Caxton got down from the lunar rover and walked over to one of the buildings, leaving a trail of spoors in the grey sand. "The dressers and grips work here during the day to get the set ready for the night time shoots. They need a lot of water in this climate... They'll be annoyed with all these footprints we've left. They'll have to get the rakes out." He came back with two bottles of spring water. He carried on talking as Clane gulped from his. "You have no idea how this world works. It's an understandable position, my friend. Very few people do. Just look at the things around you, the technological wonders that make our lives easier and more enjoyable in a thousand different ways!... What's more the speed of that advancement is ironically down to your spanner in the works. We foresaw the leap forward of the last decade, but we planned to spread it out over half a century or so... And there is a foundation of deceit underlying it all, and few people know. Of the minority who have discovered that, few speak out. Almost none even contemplate it... But what happens if you take that away, Clane? How you thought of that? What would become of the world if we took away the deception and tried to maintain civilization with total transparency?... The same thing that would happen if you took away the foundations of a house... Crash! A pile of rubble."

Clane lowered the bottle and wiped his lips. "You know I stayed up all night with my family watching the moon landings. I met my friends the next day and their faces were shining. Nobody talked about anything else for days. We all remembered the War; we wept after Pearl Harbour was struck... but a few years later we all unite in joy at the achievement of landing a man on the moon." He shook his head. "But it was all a fraud. Nobody has ever walked on the moon."

Caxton sighed in a slightly embarrassed and awkward tone. "Well... not exactly."

"What? Are you now telling me men *have* walked on the moon?"

"Erm... yes and no."

"Is this another of your riddles, Gerald? If so I'm not in the mood for it!"

Caxton paused. "Clane, can I take you out to dinner tonight?"
....

They returned to the jeep and Caxton drove him back to the underground facility which Caxton said was simply called "S4". They returned to one of the chambers with the sloping roof where the disks were stored and Caxton pressed a button on the doorframe. There was a grumbling of mechanics and the far sloping wall began to swing upwards. Cold night air flooded in and Clane realized that this was the outer door of a hangar. "The hangar doors are invisible from the outside; they're textured to look like normal patches of desert ground." said Caxton. A man approached them and smiled. He was dressed in a flight suit, unmarked as was standard for this institution. "This is Lieutenant Stephens." said Caxton. "He'll be our pilot for this evening."

"Step aboard please, gentlemen. Make yourselves comfortable inside the disk." said Lt. Stephens and directed them over to the open doorway of the craft. Clane ascended the steps he had seen the actor Joseph Marceille descend in Dublin in 1950. The screen which had cast the aquamarine light at Marceille's back was an electric one made of neon tubes; switched off this time. Behind it was a circular plain metal cabin with three seats facing inwards. One of them had a control panel in front of it with a pair of joysticks and Lt. Stephen sat in that one. Caxton and Clane took the other two. Clane was interested and excited despite himself. He wondered what it would feel like to fly in one of these aircraft. "Gerald, if this thing is not from Mars, where did it come from?"

"Earth." replied Caxton deadpan. "We built it here."

He looked around. There were no windows and the only light came from completely normal looking electric bulbs. "There are no seatbelts on these chairs."

"You don't need them."

Lt. Stephens put on what looked like a pair of tinted skiing goggles with a wire connecting them to the control panel. The panel itself was very unusual; it was just a sheet of black glass on which images projected like a TV screen. The pilot touched the glass and the image changed, as if he were pressing buttons. There was a similar black pane mounted on the bulkhead in front of them. A noise began; a musical buzzing like a beehive. It came from below the deck and rose steadily in volume, remaining at a fixed pitch. Clane had heard it once before; in Dublin on the eve of the interplanetary summit, as the ambassadorial craft came in to land at Phoenix Park. A few minutes passed. Lt. Stephens fiddled with the controls every so often. Moving the joystick and pressing the glass. "When are we taking off?" asked Clane.

"Five minutes ago." Caxton replied, looking amused.

"What?... But I never felt a thing!"

"Look." Caxton leaned over and touched the vertical pane on the bulkhead and a picture appeared on it, clearer than any from a TV. It showed bluish brown land below and black sky above. "This is the view outside." The arc of the earth's curvature was perceptible which meant their disk-shaped aircraft had to be very high.

"Jesus!... How does this thing work?"

"Gravity. It is powered by the gravitational force; the same one that keeps your feet on the ground. The earth produces a gravitational field naturally because of its sheer size. This vehicle does it artificially."

"Good Lord!"

"You never felt any movement because you're inside a generated gravitational field; it's a kind of bubble, separated from the rest of the world. As a result you feel no inertia from our relative motion to the world outside the field. The same effect shields us against the harmful radiation from outer space."

"Where are we flying to?"

Caxton adjusted the view on the screen until a glowing semicircle came into view.

"That's the moon."

"That's where we're flying."

"But... You're kidding me."

Over the following hour the image of the moon on the viewing screen became bigger and bigger. Clane started to have doubts; this was surely just a simulation. That's why he felt no movement. The images of the viewing screen could have been a closed circuit TV feed. The disk was still parked in the hangar at the underground base in Nevada. That's why they didn't fit windows to the vehicle. This was just another of Caxton's mental pranks. Nevertheless, the picture of the moon continued to grow. It became a crescent instead of half-phase, resembling the TV coverage of the Athena missions. Clane chuckled inwardly and quietly hummed the popular song *Fly me to the Moon* by Kaye Ballard. The surface of the moon became bigger and bigger; Clane could pick out craters and other surface features. Some of them looked very different to the ones he'd seen during the televised lunar landings. They were square and cylindrical in shape; more like artificial structures. The vehicle appeared to be heading for them. The pilot became more active, spending more time altering the controls. Then the volume of the buzzing sound dropped. "Right, we're there."

"On the moon?" asked Clane with a half smile.

"Yes... Don't you believe me?"

"No."

"Lieutenant Stephens; could you switch off the field completely, please?" The buzzing reduced again until it vanished altogether. Clane suddenly felt his body become very light, as if it was being held up by invisible hooks. He stood up in alarm and inadvertently jumped a few inches into the air. He felt as if he were underwater. "What's happening to me!?"

"Don't worry, Clane. You're just experiencing lunar gravity. It's a sixth that of the earth."

He laughed. "It reminds me of escape training at subschool!" The door to the disk opened and the steps extended. Clane stumbled awkwardly over to the door and half-fell half-swam out of the vehicle. Sure enough, the disk was now in a different location. It was obviously a hangar, but it was bigger and painted a lighter colour. He and Caxton bounced down a carpeted corridor to where a red warning sign said: *Normal gravity zone begins here*. After that Clane began to feel less and less buoyant until after about fifty yards he was walking normally. Caxton anticipated his question. "This part of the facility has its own artificial gravity generators; larger versions of the one on the disk."

"Where are we?"

"Spaceviews!"

"What's that?"

Caxton didn't respond and just pointed. Ahead was a doorway above which was an illuminated signboard which had on it the word *Spaceviews*. An elderly man in a tuxedo jacket stood beside it and bowed as they approached. "Welcome to Spaceviews, gentlemen. A table for two?"

Through the door the everyday and the outlandish combined in perfect symmetry. Spaceviews was a classic upmarket restaurant. It was vast in extent with several hundred tables, some of which were on terraces above the main floor. It had a pink carpeted floor, oil paintings on the walls and a dais on which a string quartet and pianist were quietly playing. White-coated waiters slalomed skilfully between tables with silver trays of food. One side of the restaurant was a vast floor-to-ceiling window overlooking the dry grey landscape of the moon. The sky above was pure unadulterated black. "I'm not sure I can afford this." said Clane, checking his wallet. "Also, we're a bit underdressed. Everybody else is in eveningwear."

"Don't worry; we look fine. And the bill will be on Florenti's expenses."

"Thanks." he muttered. He looked around at the other diners. They were mostly men with just a minority women; probably less than ten percent. They looked like the same kind of well-to-do urbanites that one might find in the posh eateries on Fifth Avenue. On a table a dozen feet away a group of Germans were laughing and chattering loudly in their own language. They'd clearly been there a while and there were a few half-full wine bottles between them.

A waiter brought them menus and they scanned the pages of neat copperplate print. "The chef recommends the Dover sole." said Caxton.

"I like the look of the blue cheese cutlet." Clane frowned to himself. "Wow... I'm sitting here on the moon wondering what dish to choose... on the *moon*! This is surreal... Am I really on the moon, Gerald?"

"Yes. In fact that steak is part of a special range they do called "Ambrosia" which has a variety of preparations. The flavour is unique to Spaceviews. You won't find meat like that in any other restaurant.... Shall we have white or red wine?"

Clane looked out of the window. "Where's the Earth?"

"You can't see it from here. We're on the dark side of the moon..." He raised his brow. "Well the *far* side, the side facing away from the Earth... I don't know why it's called 'dark'; because it's hidden from Earth I suppose. We have several structures here. We have to put them on the dark side so all those meddling astronomers on Earth can't see us." The waiter returned and took their orders. Clane got up to go to the toilet. The restaurant bathroom was as sumptuous as the rest of the place. It had marble bowls and urinals, gilded toiletry dispensers and smelled as sweet as a perfume shop. He heard a group of men addressing the urinals speaking what sounded like Russian. Were they Soviets? If so what were they doing there? On his way back Clane took a different route and came across a strange decorative figure in the middle of the room, a polished stone pyramid about six feet high, the same shape as the full-sized ones in Egypt. This one however had a separated capstone and an eye carved on it. This was a familiar motif to Clane and he withdrew a dollar bill from his wallet to check; and sure enough, it was a three dimensional reproduction of the Reverse of the Great Seal of the United States. "Why is this here?" he mumbled to himself. When he got back to his table, Caxton was tasting the wine. "Enjoying yourself, Clane?" he asked.

"Well... yes. Still a bit overawed."

Caxton chuckled affectionately.

"I mean... We've flown to the goddamn moon! That's a journey people have been fantasizing about for thousands of years... and we did it! We flew here in just two hours."

"That's just a taster of what our organization is capable of."

"What I don't get is why people are still flying into space on rockets... Unless all space missions are concocted by you... Are they?"

"No. The orbital missions are all real, going right back to Athena-Zvereya One. Only the moon ones are faked."

"And did you have this gravitational technology back then?"

"Oh yes."

"Then why is the AASA not using it?"

"They don't know about it."

Clane guffawed. "Are you serious?"

Clane grinned at him. "Deadly."

"But... but that's like inventing sailing ships and telling Columbus to cross the Atlantic on a log raft... A rocket! A big noisy dangerous thing a hundred feet high! A massive, expensive thing costing ten million dollars... that chugs laboriously just a hundred miles up with a payload smaller than a truck's... Don't you see? The vehicles you have make rockets as obsolete as horse buggies!"

"We're well aware of that, Clane."

"And the danger. Remember that time a few years ago when that rocket blew up at Leninsky-Turatam? Was it fifty or a hundred people who were killed? All those volatile fuels that it just takes one spark to ignite!... And... Holy shit, this isn't just about space! We don't even need aeroplanes any more!... We don't even need cars and roads for Christ's sake!... What kind of fuel does your disk use to generate its field?"

"It requires an initial electrical current to begin the process, but once running it is self sustaining. The field is itself a source of the energy it uses."

Clane's jaw dropped. "But that means... it means... energy that is free and limitless!... My God!... It could transform the world!

Forever!... I can't even begin to imagine..." His mind suddenly recalled the slum tenement blocks he had seen in Cork in 1950. "Gerald!... This will end poverty! A free and limitless supply of energy! Nobody ever need be hungry or thirsty or homeless again."

"Clane." Caxton interjected quietly.

"Look at what's on TV at the moment, Gerald. How many millions of people are dying right now in Abyssinia? Why? Because they've had no rain for a decade.

"Clane."

"With these machines they don't need rain. They can get water from the oceans, filter out the salt and pump it inland to wherever they want it, to irrigate their farms, for no cost at all."

"Clane."

"And what about in America, Gerald? How many old people die every winter because they can't afford to heat their homes. Homes run on what? Gas! Coal!... While all this time energy exists that will save their lives."

"Clane."

Clane recalled the fracking operations he's observed in the Irish countryside. "And we won't need to cut down forests anymore. No more oil slicks at sea killing birds and baby seals..."

"Clane! Stop!" He held his hands up to cut him off.

"But come on, Gerald; when are we going to see this gear released for public development?"

"Never."

There was a long silence. "Gerald... what?..."

The waiters arrived with their starter course. When they'd gone, Caxton leaned forward on the table and looked hard into Clane's eyes. "Listen to me, Clane. This technology can never be declassified. The public are never going to have access to it."

"Why not?" he croaked.

"Why not?... Well, why don't I turn that question on its head and ask you: Why should they? How can we tell them?"

"Easily." Clane was frowning in disbelief. "We just announce it... easily."

"Easily?... Right, so you plan to knock on the door of the chairman of Royal Dutch Shell and say: 'Good morning. I've just come to tell you your services are no longer required'. Just like that?"

Clane nodded.

"And what's he going to say: 'Alright, no problem. You still need oil to make candles! That's a good idea, Shell Candles! They're pretty colours! They smell nice! They won't stain your wallpaper! There'll be a smart dollar on that!'?" Caxton's face became annoyed and exasperated in his sarcasm; as if he were explaining something very obvious that Clane was foolish not to consider. "You don't get it, do you, Clane?... Oil is not the biggest industry in the world; it *is* industry! It is the lifeblood and the lubricant of civilization! Take that away and what happens? The world order as we know it will descend into chaos! The West will fall into mediocrity! India and China will dominate the globe with their huge populations and vast resources!... Energy needs to be rationed and distributed strategically in order to maintain a stable human world."

Clane poked at his Waldorf salad with a silver fork. "How long have you had these disks?"

"The disk we travelled in was built specially for the Mars and Venus stagecraft, but we've been developing the gravitational field generators for about sixty years. The Nazi's built a working prototype in 1940. We gained a lot of technology after the war when we sequestered their scientists via Operation Paperclip. We were already well advanced independently at the time; probably less than a decade behind them. We've been secretly salvaging extraterrestrial craft since late last century and we've been back-engineering them ever since. They use some kind of gravity control system too. We've also kept a close eye on our own geniuses, like Nikola Tesla, Thomas Townsend Brown, George Piggott and many others. They discovered the path to this technology themselves. That's why we classified their work."

"So we could have started moving towards a world of free energy before this century even began."

Caxton shrugged and took a gulp of wine. "In a fantasy world, Clane. Not in real life."

"In those days most people didn't even use oil. Coal was the primary fossil fuel." Clane started at him balefully. "And you can't exactly come clean now can you? How would you dig yourself out of that hole? 'Sorry, you starving Abyssinians. We forgot to tell you we had the means to save millions of your people's lives... Well we didn't exactly *forget*, we just *decided* not to tell you. Sorry, freezing pensioners in Montana! Sorry, dead whales!'."

"Sarcasm suits me better than you, Clane." Caxton laughed in an eerily similar way to Karl Dennison. Like Dennison, afterwards he flashed to seriousness in an instant. "This is what I mean when I say that our world is built upon an essential and inevitable foundation of lies... And it goes deeper even than that! You know what? However shocked you are by what you've just found out, there are secrets even deeper and more explosive. Lies aren't just a political necessity; they're a law of physics. Deceit is built into the very fabric of the universe." He waved his fork and swallowed a garlic mushroom. "You see, Clane; this is where *you* come in personally. It is because of you that the world has become what it is today. Time and space are not what they might appear to be. Time does not run in a straight line, from past through present to future. It is more like a maze, a labyrinth of passageways and tunnels leading all over the place; splitting off and joining up in many different forms. And since July the 8th 1947, the universe we're currently experiencing has gone down a blind alley into a swamp of confusion that my people never intended." He continued harshly: "We are not meant to be here, Clane; and it's all down to you!... That's why you're here now; to clean up the mess you made. You have to, and it can only be you who does it. It's *karma*, a natural law of reality. If you don't do it yourself, the universe can never get back on course."

The waiters returned with their main courses and Clane instinctively waited for them to leave. "What's this, Gerald; a science lesson now?"

Caxton chuckled again. "I know, it's difficult to understand; but it's not really necessary for you to understand everything; just enough to fulfil your destiny. All you need to know are the basics, and there's a part of you that already does."

"There's not I assure you."

"Yes there is. For example, I know that for the past few years you have been having intermittent contact with a... er... certain Red Indian gentleman."

Clane gaped. "Flying Buffalo!?"

"Is that what you call him?"

"How the hell do you know about that!?"

"It doesn't matter how I know... I could never explain it to you anyway."

"But... I know nothing about him... except that he's not an ordinary man."

"No, he is certainly not. He is a part of... how do I put this in plain words for you?... He is a manifestation of the deviant creation."

"What the hell does that mean?"

"Oh dear." Caxton blushed and rubbed his cheeks. He laughed in an agitated manner. "It means he is what you might call an angel... God, I hate that word! It's so loaded and misleading, but I can't think of a more comprehensive term."

Clane raised an eyebrow and sipped his wine. "Then he hasn't earned his wings yet."

Caxton laughed loudly. "I know, you've had a wonderful life haven't you?... Your Redskin friend is interfering directly into the physical plain of the universe. That is highly unusual. He is part of the forces of chaos trying to ruin the order our tendency has been building with such care and dedication for countless centuries. He is using you to destroy our world."

"You've lost me again, Gerald."

Caxton shook his head, cackling with ironic and frustrated merriment. "Excuse me a moment." He got up and headed for the toilets.

Clane sat back and gazed around him; the wine had gone to his head slightly. His attention turned to the nearby table where the Germans were. A waiter was serving them all a creamy dessert. Suddenly he stumbled slightly and dropped his product. "AAAAAAARRRGHHHH!" One of the Germans let out a deafening roar of fury, so loud it made the chandeliers rattle. He jumped to his feet and yelled at the waiter: "*Dummkopf Schweinhund!*... You've ruined my jacket!"

"I'm terribly sorry, sir." said the waiter, dabbing the man's lapels with a napkin.

"Take your hands off me!" The German continued to berate the waiter in a booming staccato rage until the servant had walked off with his head bowed and his face red. The German continued to grumble, wiping his jacket furiously as he retook his seat. He was a middle aged man with thick black hair neatly parted on one side. He had a dour face, made for scowling; and a small neat toothbrush moustache. Clane stared at him and blinked. He stared at him again, the cogs of recognition fighting against the gears of disbelief. Before he could stop himself, he had got up and walked over to the table. He approached the German. "Excuse me."

"*Ja?*"

"Are you Adolf Hitler?"

"*Jawohl.* Who is asking?"

"CLANE!" Caxton seized Clane's collar and jerked him back. "What are you doing, man!?"

"I was... That's Adolf Hitler!..."

"Come here!" Caxton frogmarched his friend through the restaurant to the toilets. Once inside he found a corner that was empty of people. "Clane!" he seethed. "What were you thinking of!?"

This time Clane's anger hit a critical mass. "What was I thinking of!?... I'll tell you, Gerald! I just met a man who's supposed to be dead! A mass murderer! I just saw a man who I've been told shot himself in Berlin at the end of the war!"

"You fool!" Caxton hissed. His face was red and his white teeth gritted. His nostrils flared like a mad bull's. "You've still got the mind of a slave!"

"Oh fuck off, Gerald!" Clane yelled. "I'm tired of your tricks! You bring me somewhere you say is the moon, but is probably just some fake studio like your moon set! You talk garbage to me about time and space and oil! And now you're harbouring the world's most evil man!" Clane gasped, panting for breath.

"Have you finished?" Caxton asked him in a calmer voice.

Clane walked over to a washbasin and splashed his face with water from the tap.

Caxton sighed. "You know, there's one thing you've never asked me. One question I was almost certain you would ask first."

"What's that?" Clane dried his face on a muslin towel.

"The Empire State Building."

Clane swung round in horror. Somehow the tone in which Caxton said those words revealed everything.

"Yes, Clane! We did that!"

"No!"

"We destroyed the tallest building in the world with a weapon we devised from the technology that brought you to the moon."

Clane opened his mouth. It took a moment for him to form the words. "W... why?"

"To make the Mars-Venus scenario credible. To make the people take it seriously. They had to be shocked and awed. That's human nature. If we hadn't taken out the Empire State Building we wouldn't have been able to use the scenario to fill in the pothole you made with your stupid newspaper story!" He sneered. "The Empire State Building was *your* doing, Clane. *You* destroyed that tower. *You* killed those people."

Clane stared at Caxton, not knowing what to think. "Take me home!" he choked. "I quit. I'll never work for you again."

Caxton took a step towards him in a threatening manner. "Yes you will, Clane!"

"No!... I won't!"

"Yes you *will*!... Listen to me, Clane. You know the medication we gave Gina to heal her cancer? We also have poisons that can bring it back!... We'll give them to her, Clane... Or maybe even Siobhan too. Or Brendan. Would you like that?"

Clane shook his head idiotically.

"Then continue to work for me... You will continue to work for me until I say otherwise!"

....

It was about six AM when the unmarked white airliner touched down at McCarran Field. Despite not having slept all night, Clane felt awake and alert as he got into his car and drove out onto the highway to Boulder City. As he opened his front door Gina and Siobhan jumped up. "Clane!... You've been out all night. Where have you been?" demanded his wife.

"To the moon and back." he replied deadpan.

She laughed, missing his serious tone and obviously relieved. She embraced him. "God almighty, Clane! I called the police. I'd better give them a ring and tell them you're home safe. What kind of job have you taken on that means you have to spend all night away from home?"

"I think it's just a one off, Gina. First day and all."

"I hope so."

Chapter 17

"Mr Quilley. Ready in five." the director called down on his earpiece from the gallery. Clane adjusted the tie on his suit. In front of him was a camera that allowed the remote studio to see him while a TV screen next to it allowed him to see the people he was talking to all those hundreds of miles away. He listened quietly to the proceedings for the first twenty minutes and waited for his moment. The host of the show in Florida introduced him: "And now we shall have on the show the well-known flying saucer pundit, all the way from Las Vegas, Clane Quilley. Welcome to *Mystery Nights*, Mr Quilley."

"Good evening." Clane replied. "It's good to be on the show."

"What are your own views on Jean Shah's experience?"

"Well, I've listened carefully to what Mrs Shah has told us and it sounds very typical of the so-called 'alien abduction' phenomenon. This is an unusual psychological condition caused by a sleep disorder known as hpynogogia. The sufferer wakes up, but is unable to move. They look around them and see strange creatures in the bedroom with them..."

"Mr Quilley!" objected the other guest from the Florida studio. "Perhaps you weren't listening properly. I was not asleep when this happened to me. Also I was not in my bedroom. These beings took me aboard their spacecraft. They levitated me into the air and performed a medical examination on me."

"I heard you correctly, Mrs Shah, and I assure you I've heard hundreds and hundreds of similar stories. The human brain, including its memory, can play tricks on us. There are no such things as aliens and no such things as flying saucers, MFO's or whatever you want to call them. They're a fantasy caused by human limitations of accurate cognition and the evolutionary emergence of folklore."

"Mr Quilley." said the host. "Are you not one of the people who most promoted the idea of flying saucers? You yourself wrote one of the first serious articles about them in the *Roswell Daily Record* of July the 8th 1947."

"Yes, and that was very much to my discredit. I'm not saying I can't be fooled too, and I was. My own cognition failed in deeper ways than anybody else's. It took me ten years to realize that."

Jean Shah looked frustrated and crestfallen at Clane's words.

"Thank you very much." said the host. "That was Clane Quilley by video link from Las Vegas, Nevada."

Clane ripped out his earphones, exited the video booth and walked out of the KLAS TV centre without saying a word to anybody. It was his third TV spot that month and he was getting used to them. He was emotionally neutral, as always when he was interviewed on TV or radio. He always kept it short and basic; he went in, said his piece and left.

He walked north up Las Vegas Boulevard towards the downtown area. It was a fresh spring day, milder than usual. He came across a cafe and nipped in for a coffee. The cafe had WorldMesh access and so he booked a computer and called up his own website wmn.clanequilleymfo.co.us. His Meshboard's homepage included a photograph of himself with a quizzical and slightly patronizing frown on his face. He clicked the "About" tab: *Clane Quilley is a former journalist who specialized in MFO research. He used to believe in MFO's and even generated an MFO scare in 1947, but as time passed he soon realized that MFO's can almost always easily be explained as natural phenomena like aircraft, atmospheric conditions and astronomical objects. This led him to become one of the world's greatest MFO skeptics. He makes regular appearances in the media...* Clane chuckled to himself ironically. He opened up his E-grams and ran though his standard barrage of hate mail: *How much are they paying you?... Fucking government shill!... You're full of shit, buddy. MFO's are real. I've seen them many times... Stick your stupid crap rational explanations up your ass!...* He ended his session, paid at the counter and headed back out into the street. His roamphone beeped in his pocket. He took it out to see that a text message had arrived from an unknown number. *I NEED TO SEE YOU NOW. MEET ME IN REESE PARK. FB.* Clane grinned.

He was sitting on a bench between two baseball diamonds examining his roamphone. He was dressed in the usual Las Vegas attire; cream slacks, a trilby and sunglasses. He scowled as he saw Clane approach. Clane had never seen such an expression on his face. "Mr Quilley." he said.

"Flying Buffalo... or should I call you Gabriel?" He sat down on the bench beside him.

"What the hell do you think you're doing, Mr Quilley?"

"What I have to, to keep my family alive."

"You're an agent of disinformation! You're collaborating with the forces of deception! In doing so, you jeopardize the future of the entire world."

"So should I let Caxton murder my wife and children?... Maybe you don't have families up there." He pointed at the sky. "So you don't know what it feels like."

"You'd be surprised." His face and voice softened slightly, taking on their more customary form. "For instance, one thing I do know is that as you uttered those words a seven year old boy named Hasn died. He lived with his parents, Axhmat and Wibbut in Sekhota, Abyssinia. They loved him very much. He was very good at school and his parents hoped he'd grow up to be a doctor. Right now they're weeping. He died of hunger and thirst because his country has suffered a famine for over eight years... Mr Quilley, I have an awareness of pain and death that you couldn't begin to comprehend."

"I tried to explain that to Caxton."

"You tried to explain that to Gerald Caxton?" asked Flying Buffalo sardonically. "You mean appeal to his sense of right and wrong, or his compassion?... Have you not looked into his eyes?"

"Yes."

"And what do you see?"

Clane paused and gulped. "Nothing."

"That is a very good answer."

"He's like Karl Dennison."

"He is indeed... Mr Quilley, you cannot ally yourself with him."

"And if I don't? Gina and the kids die. I'm her husband and their father! I cannot let that happen."

The old Indian hesitated. "You have to find a way out of this quandary."

"How?"

He winked. "You'll think of something."

They both watched as a home run sailed over the netting and struck the top of a tree. The batting team roared with triumph. "You know Caxton thinks we've both ruined the world."

Flying Buffalo laughed. "He's scared because we're healing the world he and his people have ruined."

"Who are they? Why do they have the Reverse Seal as their logo?"

"Other way round, Mr Quilley. "Why is the US Reverse Seal based on their logo?... It's not something I can explain."

"Now you're talking like he does."

Flying Buffalo stood up. "Think laterally, Mr Quilley. If you were somebody else behind this embargo on the truth about MFO's, how would *you* maintain it?... We'll talk later, if all goes well." He walked off.

Clane sat there for a long time, watching hardballs arc through the air. Players cheered and shouted.

Chapter 18

The day came. It was Monday September the 10th 1957; a year and a half since Clane had gone to work for Gerald Caxton in Nevada, and six months since his last meeting with Flying Buffalo. It had been Labour Day; Brendan was due to start school in a couple of weeks and Siobhan was on vacation from college so Clane suggested taking a trip. They opted for the Crater Lake National Park in Oregon. They booked themselves into a lodge and drove up there to enjoy a week of hiking, bird watching and swimming in one of the most beautiful places Clane had ever seen. At the end of the week, Clane took a deep breath and got his family together. He told them he had a surprise for them and then he drove them up a long winding road high into the mountains above the great blue lake until they came to a small log cabin miles from anywhere. "What's this?" asked Gina.

"Your home for the next few days. I hired it."

"*Our* home, Dad? Not yours?" asked Siobhan. "What about you?"

"I can't stay. I have to go off to work." He forced a smile.

Gina and Siobhan frowned at him in unison. Brendan was running around, excitedly exploring the cabin. "What's going on, Clane?" Gina asked.

"I can't tell you... Do you trust me?"

"Yes."

"Then will you do this without me telling you why? Please! It's very important... Just for now. The answers will come in a few days."

They hesitated, exchanged looks and then nodded at him.

"Great." He sighed with relief. "So, just stay here and enjoy the mountain. Keep away from the towns. Take the batteries out of your roamphones. Have a stroll, have a barbecue, have some beers. The cabin is stocked up with ample food and drink... but promise me you'll stay here!... Until I come and fetch you. Agreed?"

"OK."

He drove back to Las Vegas and took one of the white airliners to the anonymous base. He worked mostly from home these days, sewing discord on MFO Mesh forums, posting half-truths under an assumed identity; but every fortnight or so Caxton would summon him to the S4 facility for a meeting to discuss tactics for increasing confusion, blunting rational thought and therefore protecting the truth about MFO's from being exposed. He felt much calmer than he expected as he boarded the mysterious Boeing 397, which he had just found out was codenamed "Janet". He'd slept well the previous night and experienced only a minor frisson of discomfort. One way or another, this would be the last time he ever took this flight. He was surprised he didn't feel more apprehension; instead he felt completely fatalistic. "Do with me as you will." he muttered to God, partly as a prayer. Meetings with Caxton always followed the same routine. They began in the evening. Clane would take a "Janet" flight to the base and then he and Caxton would fly in a disk to Spaceviews on the moon for dinner. Clane enjoyed the good food despite everything. He usually chose from the Ambrosia collection which were very tasty meat dishes. They would polish off a couple of bottles of wine with some cigars and after-dinner brandies. Occasionally they would share a table with other guests. These sometimes included some very famous people such as David Rockefeller, the actress Marilyn Monroe, Premier Nikita Khrushchev of the Soviet Union and Eamon de Valera, the new *Taoiseach* of Ireland. It was strange because nobody treated the celebrities as VIP's. In any restaurant on earth they'd be plagued by a swarm of admirers and autograph hunters, but here they were just normal guests; or rather all the guests were VIP's so there were no ordinary people to throw them into relief. Once or twice Adolf Hitler came over to join them. He was polite and friendly, but a little aloof. He also had weird habits like spending five minutes or so very focused on folding his napkin so it was in the correct pattern, and getting very up tight if he couldn't do it. Clane feigned the part of Caxton's affable assistant who had come to terms with his predicament and decided just to lie back and enjoy it. This wasn't a difficult attitude to put on; after all he was leading an enviable lifestyle. He was being paid a very sumptuous salary for doing very little work and living like a king twice a month. After dinner he stayed overnight on the moon in Spaceviews' adjoining five-star hotel. In order to completely disarm any suspicion Caxton might have, Clane started sleeping with the escorts they hired for him. This he felt very uncomfortable about, but he knew it was necessary to put Caxton off his guard. Of course he found it impossible not to enjoy the sex, especially as the women his boss selected for him were all very pleasant indeed to look at and talk to. Afterwards however he thought of Gina and felt guilty.

....

In the morning, September the 11th, he and Caxton walked down to the space dock where the saucers were parked. Clane was getting quite adept in the lunar gravity section and took his seat on the saucer with ease. The pilot fired up the gravity engine and they flew back down to Earth. Clane watched the pilot very carefully. He had been studying what they did intensely for the last few months, but this was his last chance to learn so he paid extra attention. When they reached S4, Clane went to his office and did some work on his computer there. It was a highly sophisticated machine with a flat, thin monitor a bit like the flying disk screens, far more modern than anything on sale in the outside world. Then he went to the refectory for lunch. He timed his lunch hour very carefully to overlap with Lt.

Gordon Stephens, the man who had been their disk pilot on the first day Caxton had taken him up in one. Since then Clane and Lt. Stephens had become good friends. They had a lot in common; Stephens had been a Navy flyer in the War and he also lived in Nevada. He had a family in Carson City and Clane had driven up to visit him in the summer. This was strictly against regulations; S4 staff were forbidden from fraternizing with each other in their private lives. Nevertheless Clane had persuaded Stephens to meet him for a beer and grill at Incline Village, a lovely place on the shores of Lake Tahoe. They knocked back quite a number of beers and ate heartily. They joked and laughed and shared details of their lives. Stephens seemed to like Clane a lot. For Clane it was different; he was dispassionately grooming Stephens. This was not easy because Clane knew he was not a duplicitous person by nature, but he forced himself with a rod of iron. As a result, Stephens had divulged invaluable information during the weeks and months of their friendship. This was helped by the fact that internal security at S4 was surprisingly lax. This was probably because anybody who wasn't already at an extremely high level of secrecy initiation wouldn't get through the door anyway. There were many areas Clane still was not permitted to enter, but nobody objected to him wandering free all over the first and second level.

"Hi, Clane." Stephens waved as he walked in and joined the queue at the dispensing machine. When he'd taken his meal he joined Clane at his table.

"How's it going, Gordy?" Clane asked him.

"Bah!" He pointed down at his cook-chill meal. "I wish they'd get some proper chow in."

"Catering staff add to the number of people needing security clearance." Clane shrugged.

"Guess so. Trust a bubblehead to make that observation." He took a bite of a sausage roll.

"How are Jane and the kids?"

"Jane's in a bit of a gripey mood right now. I guess she had her heart set on that Mercedes. How's Gina?"

"Fine. We just got back from Disneyland." He had deliberately lied to Stephens about his vacation. He knew there was a slight chance Stephens would mention it to Caxton and a remote possibility that Caxton had been monitoring Clane's trip to Crater Lake; and would then realize Clane was up to something, but he just had to take that chance. It put Gina and his children at too much risk for every extra person who knew where they were to within a hundred miles. "Gordy, I was wondering if you'd do me a favour after lunch."

"Sure, if I can."

"I need your technical expertise in my office. One of the electric sockets has gone dead. I could call engineering, but you know how long they take to get out of their cubbyholes."

"No problem, Clane."

After their meal Clane and Stephens walked along the corridor and down in the lift to the second level. They continued to make casual conversation as they went along the corridor towards Clane's office. Clane was saturated with adrenalin and his heart was pounding; this was difficult to hide. Every step along the corridor felt like an electric shock. Once in the office Stephens bent down to have a look at the socket in question. Clane picked a Scotchtape dispenser up off his desk and brought it down hard on the back of his friend's head. Stephens fell to the carpeted floor, groaning and holding his crown. Clane struck him again, and then a third time. He lay silently on the floor as if dead... maybe he was dead. "Sorry, Gordy. There's no other way." Clane whispered. He reached down to the pilot's belt and searched for the orange key-ring he always carried with him. He pulled it hard, ripping the waist of Stephens' flight suit as he wrenched it free. He then pushed Stephens' still unconscious form behind a filing cabinet, then Clane headed for the door. He wiped the sweat off his face and forced himself to catch his breath; then he opened the door. He shut the door carefully behind him and then walked back along the corridor to the lift. He let his arms swing and whistled to himself casually in case anybody saw him.

The S4 facility was completely underground and consisted of seven levels on top of one another with Seven being the deepest. The lift opened at each level onto lift bays with security gates and Clane had no idea what was below him. Clane's office was on Level Two and he took the lift up to level One. This level was built into the slope at the edge of the dry lake bed and it consisted of a single corridor with the refectory, workshops and offices on one side, the laboratories to the left where the Roswell artefacts were kept, and the passageway leading to the saucer hangars to the right. Clane ducked into a workshop and grabbed a battery-powered electric drill. He then went to the nearest hangar and peeked round the doorway to make sure there was nobody about. Then he went up to the saucer-shaped craft and opened the hatch. Once inside he removed the inspection cover over the engines and got to work. A few weeks earlier Clane had displayed enough fake curiosity that Stephens had agreed to show him the engines of the disks, what he called "reproduction vehicles". He was an engineer as well as a pilot and explained in detail how they worked. The gravity field was generated by a very powerful electrical circuit running through a toroid accelerator containing a very high pressure vapour of mercury. It was a model created by Nazi scientists just before the end of the war and was secretly appropriated by the United States, along with the individuals who had invented it. Clane could easily see the accelerator inside the engines; it looked like a huge metal doughnut surrounded by electromagnets and wires. He put the bit of the stolen tool against the side of the vapour canister and began to drill. He had to be very careful because the casing of the accelerator was precisely three eighths of an inch thick. He got the idea from a memory of something that happened during the sea trials of USS *Tunny* in 1942. Four young sailors had come up with the bright idea of drilling through the fuel flasks on all of the boat's Mark 14 torpedoes. This was just before a live-fire exercise off San Diego. They drilled holes almost all the way through the flasks, but not quite. They left a thin layer to prevent the hydrogen peroxide fuel from leaking out before the weapon was launched. However after launch the motor started and pressure in the flask would rise sharply to the point where the hole gave way and blew apart, causing the torpedo's motor to shut down and the weapon sink. The sailors took bets on how far each torpedo would get before it failed. It was a reckless thing to do. The torpedo fuel flasks could have given way inside the boat causing an explosion or the leakage of the poisonous fuel into the atmosphere. Also the torpedoes were very expensive and their loss would cost the Navy over a million dollars. The men were all court-martialled and got two years in the Portsmouth brig followed by a dishonourable discharge. Clane was furious with them and happily acted as a witness against them. He got a Captain's Table himself for dereliction of duty. As Chief Torpedoman he was accountable for the misdemeanours of his crew. If it hadn't been for the war he'd have been sent back to general service for sure. Now, as he drilled away at the gravity generator, he silently thanked those young idiots for giving him the idea that could possiblly save the world. Stephens had explained that the pressure of the mercury inside the accelerator was over four kilobars; very high even at idle, but it would rise a dozen fold to fifty kilobars once the generator was started up. Clane finished drilling the hole, replaced the inspection cover and then ran out into the corridor. He did the same to the next disk and then a third one. There were six working disks at S4, each with a hangar of their own. Clane drilled holes in the engines of five of them. When he reached the last one, he threw the drill onto the floor and pressed the button that opened the hangar door. An alarm sounded. Clane ran over to the disk and jumped inside it. He shut the hatch behind himself and quickly sat down in the pilot's seat. This was a much bigger craft than the one he and Caxton used to travel in to Spaceviews. It contained twenty seats and was over a hundred feet in diameter. The pilot sat in a separate cubicle at the edge of the main cabin. He could hear the alarm continuing to blare outside the hull. Somebody by now would know things were amiss. Maybe Stephens had come round and raised the alarm; Clane hoped so. He had to act quickly. He had never flown one of the disks before but he and Stephens had talked about the instruments and controls at great length. It all began when they were chatting about Stephen's missions during the war and he had said to Clane: "These damn disks are so different to a standard fixed-winged aeroplane; they're more like a helo. I used to fly ASW helos off of *Yorktown* during Korea." "In what way?" Clane had responded; and within a few hours he had the basics of the disk's operation out of Stephens. Every time he and Caxton flew to the moon, he would watch the pilot carefully, memorizing every touch on the screen, every tilt of the joysticks. In his imagination he rehearsed the moves himself until he was flying disks in his dreams every night. Clane inserted Gordon Stephens' key into the ignition slot and turned it. Sure enough, the control panel lit up and the buzzing noise of the engines began. Clane placed the pilots' goggles over his face and was amazed. Stephens had described the experience to him, so he knew what to expect, but he was impressed by how clear the image was from the exterior camera on the apex of the saucer above him. It was in three dimensions and gave an all round view with as good a resolution as the naked eye. He saw that a number of people were now standing in the hangar staring at the disk, no doubt realizing that this was an unauthorized launch. By the lighting Clane could tell that the hangar door was completely open. The hangars at S4 were directly behind the steep sides of the valley near the flat dry lakebed. The slope of the doors matched the contours of the land and they were covered with a material that resembled the surrounding ground. This camouflaged them against spy satellites.

One of the people ran over to the door and pressed the button to close the hanger. "Oh no you don't!" said Clane and moved the joystick to one side. Although the view changed he felt no motion as he travelled upwards within the gravitational bubble. However he heard a crashing noise and the disk stopped. He had hit the roof of the hangar. He eased the joystick down a bit and the disk moved away from the wall towards the door. It jolted again as it passed through; the door must have started to close again. Suddenly he was outside and desert sunlight filled his vision. He pulled the other joystick to one side and the craft headed upwards and increased speed. The side of the valley and the dry lakebed concealing the invisible military fortress lay beneath his view. He felt slightly vertiginous even though he knew he was inside the craft and was only seeing the image of a camera. Already the other hangar doors were opening as the staff in the base prepared the other disks to give chase. Clane thanked God he had thought of the idea of sabotaging the other vehicles. He turned his head and the camera topside copied his movement. He faced forward and thumbed the slider on the right hand joystick to increase thrust. The craft leaped like a stung goat, accelerating at a rate that would crush anybody in a normal aircraft. Using the instruments on the glass screen he steadied the craft on a course due east and ascended to fifteen thousand feet. His speed was over five hundred knots. "Washington, here I come!" He laughed out loud, exhilarated at his own audacity and its success.

There was a blip on the panel indicating an incoming radio message: "Clane!... Clane!... What the hell are you up to!?" came the voice of Gerald Caxton over the loudspeaker.

Clane toggled the microphone: "I'm going to blow your cover, Gerald. I'm going to show everybody what you've been doing in your slimy little lair."

"Clane!... Come back now. I *command* you!"

"No way, asshole!... And don't bother trying to follow me; you'll find the other craft are in no condition to fly."

"I know; you blithered up their engines, you loathsome cad!... Listen to me, come back now or we'll kill Gina and your children! We'll rip them limb from limb in front of you! You understand!?"

"You'll never find them in time, Gerald. They're perfectly safe. In a few hours it will be too late for you to do anything."

"Damn you, Clane! Damn and blast you!... You bastard!" Caxton was shouting at the top of his voice.

"Have a nice day, Gerald. See you on TV!" Clane switched off the radio.

The disk was now flying at six hundred and fifty knots, faster than any aircraft. Clane could have increased speed much further, but he didn't want to over-test his amateur and unproven antigravity disk piloting skills. It was a balancing act. He knew he needed to travel quickly so he could complete his mission before his enemy had time to stop him, but he couldn't risk crashing his vehicle. The landscape below changed. The navigation system traced his route. Clane was pleased with his progress; he was already over Utah and the salt flats gleamed in the sunshine like snow. Twenty minutes later he had crossed Colorado and the Rocky Mountains and the green and yellow patchwork of the Great Plains stretched out beneath him between huge woolly clouds. The radio blipped; it was Caxton again. "Clane! Listen to me carefully. We have deployed three saucers from another airbase to intercept you."

"What do you mean? You have these craft on other bases?"

"Yes, several... They are armed with directed energy weapons, just like those that brought down the Empire State Building. Now, turn back before I order them to reduce your stolen disk to iron filings!... DO IT!"

Clane pressed the tab that activated the search radar. A dial appeared on the glass with a line sweeping round it, just like on conventional radar displays. A large number of blips covered the screen; obviously other aircraft. There were three approaching form the northeast that were moving faster than the others. Caxton had not been bluffing.

"Surrender now, Clane! Surrender or die!"

Clane felt a chill run through him as he remembered the Danlue film of the Empire State Building being destroyed. He turned the vehicle southwest and pulled forward on the throttle; he had to risk a higher speed and open the range between himself and the three interceptors. His airspeed readout shot up, one thousand knots, one thousand five hundred, two thousand... The three enemy disks kept on coming; either they were more powerful craft than his own or the pilots, being more expert, were able to fly at higher speeds. They were now just twenty miles behind him and closing. Caxton's manic yell continued to slate him from the loudspeaker like a frenzied street preacher. "You're doomed, Clane! Doomed!... You fool! You had it all! After we kill you we'll kill your family! You're all doomed!" Clane grabbed the left hand joystick and jerked the disk into an evasion manoeuvre. Stephens, along with other naval and AAF aviators over the years, had told him that when they're attacked with a homing missile they carry out a series of very tight turns to try and confuse the missile's seeker. It might work against this kind of "direct energy" weapon or it might not, but Clane had to try something. He saw a flash of light in his eyes and a deafening bang in his ears. The sound of the engines suddenly stopped and the goggles went dark. Clane ripped them off his head, but the cabin lights were also off. He was in total darkness... but not silence. He could hear the sound of wind whistling outside the hull. At that moment the bulkhead closed on his head like a vice and he was knocked out.

Clane came round slowly. His head ached. Sticky metallic-tasting liquid dripped into his mouth; blood. He raised his tingling hand and felt the gash on his head. It was no longer dark in the cabin. There were a few small red lights glowing on the overhead. They were probably battery powered emergency lights like the battle lanterns on his submarines. He climbed to his feet and reeled back into a sitting position; his head was spinning. He crawled across to the control panel; it was completely blank. "Damn!" he thumped it with his fist. He tried to stand up again; this time he succeeded. He had no idea where he was; the camera screens wouldn't work and the goggles were as dead as normal skiing goggles. The floor was slightly tilted as if the craft had settled on a slope. He walked over to the sidewall and placed his ear against it. He could hear no sound outside, but he thought that the metal was unnaturally cold. He went over to the hatch. Without power the door stud wouldn't activate the latch servo motors, but there was an emergency lever to open it manually. He was about to pull it, but then stopped. Maybe it wasn't a good idea until he knew more about where he was. The coldness of the hull was not entirely unfamiliar; it was what the outside of *Tunny* had felt like... when they were dived at test depth. Could he be underwater? Had the disk crashed into a river or lake... or the sea? He had been accelerating steadily during his brief dogfight with Caxton's interceptors. He must have travelled a long way, perhaps as far as the Gulf of Mexico. If he were underwater then the good news was that it would make him harder to locate. No doubt Caxton would still be hunting him. Probably his disks were circling overhead right now, no doubt triggering a few MFO sightings that would drive the forums crazy. Probably his online antagonists would be posting photos on his own threads right now to rub his nose in it, Clane thought with a wry half-smile. However, the atmosphere inside the cabin would not last forever, even though this larger craft had far more space. *Tunny* could stay dived for about two days, depending on how much battery power they used up. However any longer than that and even with a fully-charged battery it would still mean they had to surface, because the air on board became too foul to breathe and the crew risked suffocation. He knew that the S4 disks had an air purification system built in, but they needed power to run them. Clane pulled off the engine inspection cover. The workings of the craft looked normal. Whatever kind of weapon had struck the disk it had obviously not reduced it to dust; it had given him a glancing blow. Clane knew he was wasting his time; he didn't know enough about this unusual engine to even begin repairs, even if they were possible. He really needed Gordon Stephens here. He once again felt a pang of remorse for what he did to the man who considered him a friend. Could there have been another way? Could he have persuaded Stephens to join him in his theft of the disk? Then he'd have had a trained pilot and engineer with him and he wouldn't be stuck in this predicament. Was this God's punishment for killing or injuring Stephens? With that depressing thought in his head he sat back down in the pilot's cubicle and wiped his head wound on his sleeve. He wondered for a moment if the crippling of his craft might simply be an electronic problem. The weapon that brought him down might have missed, but caused an electromagnetic pulse. This is what sometimes happened to computers. Once his PC at home had crashed when Gina had switched on the vacuum cleaner beside it. In such eventualities he found he could restore its function simply by restarting it. Maybe he could get the disk working by putting in Stephens's key again. He tried it and to his surprise and relief he succeeded. The buzzing sound began and the main lights switched back on. The control panel lit up and when Clane put on the goggles he could see through the exterior camera again. It was a good job he had not opened the hatch. He was indeed underwater. There was quite a lot of sunlight outside which meant he couldn't be very deep, probably less than a hundred feet he estimated, from his memory of *Tunny*'s periscope, depending on water clarity. There was a grey muddy bottom visible on which the disk was resting; one end slightly raised. As he watched a fish swam past. He recalled Stephens telling him that these craft could operate underwater too, in fact there was a whole subdivision of MFOlogy concerned with so-called "MSO's", Mysterious Submerged Objects. If the MSO's used the same propulsion system as these "reproduction vehicles" then why should the latter also not be able to traverse the depths? He grasped the joysticks and placed his thumb on the throttle slider. The disk rose up from the seabed amidst a cloud of silt. As he travelled upwards he soon saw the surface above him. He was about to punch through it into the air, but then stopped just a few feet below it. If Caxton's heavies were up there now, if he popped up out of the water they'd attack him again and he'd be back to square one, or even minus a few squares and dead. However, the camera was mounted on the top of the craft and therefore he could sneak a peek above the water without exposing the entire craft, possibly preventing him from being detected. Clane laughed at the appropriateness; it was like being on a submarine raising its periscope. The surface wash broke and the camera cleared. He was beneath a blue expanse of water and above the sky was sunny and clear. There was land in the distance, low green and grey. He thought he saw movement in the air and quickly ducked the disk back down again. He was pleased to see that while the camera was above the surface the navigation computer had updated, perhaps by taking a sextant shot of the sun or picking up a signal from an orientation satellite. He was indeed under the sea. He was ten miles south of the Louisiana coastline, near the Mississippi Delta. He stopped the craft for a moment and took off the goggles. He'd had an idea: Why not do the entire journey submerged? It depended on how fast he could travel underwater. Such a voyage would take over a week aboard *Tunny* which could only sustain eighteen knots. He didn't have a week. Caxton would right now be searching for Gina, Siobhan and Brendan, and despite his precautions he might still find them.

Clane turned the craft south and opened up the thrust. He saw the speedometer creep up, sixty knots... seventy... eighty. Then he slowed down, realizing that at such speeds in shallow water the disk might create a displacement hump on the surface, or even a wake. He needed to find deeper water before sailing at high speed. He looked and the chart and saw that there was a deep water channel leading off the continental shelf along the direction of the Mississippi outflow. He sailed towards it along the muddy bottom at thirty knots and as soon as it shelved he dipped downwards with the seabed, accelerating to over a hundred knots in just a minute. Pretty soon he was at two hundred. This would have been beyond the capability of any submarine imaginable. The drag from the seawater would rip the craft to pieces at half that speed. The gravitational field must create some kind of laminar flow around the vehicle letting it displace water without any friction. The speed peaked at three hundred and fifty knots, as fast as a jet aeroplane. It was pitch dark outside at his current depth of two thousand feet so he took off the goggles and sailed by instruments. He crossed the Gulf of Mexico in just two hours and entered the Florida Straits between the Keys and Cuba. He used the vehicle's small toilet; the smaller ones didn't have them so that was a reason to be glad he chose the large disk. He was hungry and thirsty, but there was no food or water aboard; he'd just have to hold out. He turned north and followed the coast of Florida upwards into the Atlantic Ocean. He decided to come up to the surface to verify the navigation again, seeing as he'd travelled over a thousand miles by dead reckoning. As soon as the turret broke the surface he heard a voice on the radio. It was Caxton: "Clane... Clane?... Are you there?" He was quieter and calmer now. Clane reached for the microphone button, but then stopped. Caxton might use anything he transmitted to direction-find him and send in the killer disks again. "Clane, do you really think you'll get away with this?... I feel really betrayed you know. I thought we were friends! I even saved Gina's life!... I was about to give you everything you know. The entire operation would one day pass over to you... Think of all that power! More power and wealth than you could imagine in your wildest dreams!" His tone was jeering. "You're one of us now whether you like it or not. You're a god like us!... Remember Spaceviews? What gorgeous dinners we had up there on the moon eh? You were particularly fond of those Ambrosia steaks, weren't you? Do you know where those steaks come from? Remember me telling you how it was a brand of meat that you couldn't find in any other restaurant?... Yes? Well, do you want to know why that is? Because it is *human flesh*!"

Clane stepped back and gulped. He felt a wave of nausea.

"Oh yes! I bet you feel sick, don't you?... So you would if you were an ordinary person! You're a cannibal! A savage!... Or are you? Maybe you're just a god! God has the right to eat His people... Come on! Join us, Clane! Join us!"

Clane dived deep again but came up an hour later when east of the Carolinas. Caxton was still talking. He must have been keeping up a continuous monologue. There was no way he could know if Clane was listening or not... But then again, he knew about Flying Buffalo. Was he watching Clane via a sixth sense? The thought sent a line of sweat down his nape.

"Clane! Listen!... We have your wife and children in custody right now. We've found them, Clane. Did you really think you could hide them from us?" He laughed like a Hollywood vampire.

Clane leapt up from the pilot's chair in terror. "No!" He felt tears in his eyes.

"They're imprisoned right here at S4. We're going to kill them, Clane. We're going to kill them slowly and painfully. Do you want me to tell you what my team are going to do to them?... When they scream, I'll hold the mic right beside them so you can hear it!"

Clane was panting and gasping, his heart throbbed against his ribs.

"There's only one way you can save their lives, Clane! Give it up now!... Tell us where you are and surrender!"

With a trembling hand he reached for the microphone and held his finger over the button. Then he stopped. "He hasn't said *where* he found them?... Why wouldn't he tell me? Why wouldn't he brag by telling me where my hiding place for them was?" Clane said aloud. Then he laughed; his fear and sorrow evaporated instantaneously. "He's bluffing!... Fuck you, Caxton!" Clane jabbed the throttle and the disk sounded for the depths again at full speed.

At five PM Clane's stolen antigravity disk entered Chesapeake Bay. He was almost at his destination. It was safe now to fly the rest of the way above the surface. He would probably be detected by the enemy when he left the water, but they were unlikely to catch him in time. All he had to do was get to Washington and it would all be over. Caxton would be able to do nothing about it; a *fait accompli.* He burst out of the calm waters of the river estuary and levelled off at a thousand feet. He pointed his nose northwest and bolted towards the American capitol. No doubt he was making massive noise for AAF homeland defence radar. There could even be missiles coming his way soon, but the gravitational field around the craft would neutralize any conventional weapon. As for Caxton's forces; they were probably still looking for him in the Gulf. Even though they would now detect him for sure, they would not be able to get there in time to stop him. He saw bright streaks of light as missiles and AAA rounds flew into the air. They detonated harmlessly against the gravity wall around the disk. Washington DC appeared ahead, the Potomac River was a blue snake running through the grey, white and green of the city. The postcard images became recognizable and he headed for the White House. A large helicopter was just taking off from the lawn as he approached. No doubt it was Marine One. They knew he was coming and were evacuating the President. The helicopter was departing the North Lawn so he opted for the South Lawn. He slowly lowered the craft down onto the grass and cut the engines. A squad of US Marines were in a line formation between him and the building. Clane knew he risked being shot, but he had to go out. It was essential that the people saw him and he got the chance to speak to them. Earlier on he had noticed a second hatchway, a trapdoor in the roof of the vehicle. He decided to use that. He pulled that latch and there was a momentary hiss, and he felt his ears pop as the internal pressure equalized with the outside. He held up his hands. "Don't shoot!" he yelled. "Don't shoot! I mean you no harm!" He lifted his head until he could see out. The Marines were the only people in sight. To one side he saw the tail end of a crowd of people as they ran away.

The Marines seemed to relax slightly when they saw him. "Who are you?" their commander shouted.

"My name is Clane Quilley. You can bring the President back because I'm not going to hurt him or anybody else. This vehicle is harmless... Please, I need to speak to the press. I have a matter of the utmost urgency that I need to make public."

Chapter 19

Clane stayed sitting on the brim of the trapdoor. He remembered enough about journalism to know that it was a good photo spot. Judging by the number of TV camera lenses ogling him and flashbulbs flickering on the lawn around the disk, he was probably right. However he opened up the main hatch and allowed people to come in and inspect the craft. He removed the inspection cover on the engine. It was gone nine PM and night had fallen. He'd been talking to the reporters non-stop since they arrived. Some people had passed him some food and water. Quite a large crowd of onlookers had turned up to watch now they knew there was no danger. The radio had been silent. He longed to contact Gina and the children, but he dared not in case Caxton was listening in and got there first.

"So, Mr Quilley." one of the newsmen called up to him. "Are you saying that the entire interplanetary war was a sham?"

"Yes." Clane answered him via a megaphone that somebody had handed up to him earlier. "And they destroyed the Empire State Building to make it look real."

"Who's they?" a woman asked.

"This group of people I was involved with. They made me go on TV and lie! Ask anybody who's into MFO's and they'll tell you. I was one of the most notorious skeptics; but it was all an act."

A White House usher appeared and looked up at Clane. "Mr Quilley, the President would like to speak to you immediately, sir." Clane came down from the trapdoor and exited the craft. Curious eyes followed him as he left with the usher for the West Wing to the left.

The Oval Office had different furniture since the last time he'd been there in 1952. Different Presidents liked to decorate their place of work according to their own tastes and used a selection from a pool of items. The room was packed with people, some in suits and some in military uniforms. President Barry Goldwater, the thirty-fifth President of the United States, was a year into his second term. He was a calm-faced middle-aged man with prematurely grey hair, formerly a long-term senator from Arizona. His analytic eyes were filtered by spectacles with thick black frames beneath his high hairless forehead.

"You wanted to see me, Mr President?" said Clane.

"I've just been watching you on TV, Mr Quilley. You're on every channel."

Clane nodded, unsure of whether this was a compliment. Goldwater's voice was cold and logical.

"I've always known what you've proven to me, Mr Quilley. I've known it for a long time. During my days in the Senate after the Dublin Treaty, I made enquiries into the items at the Tech Data

Section in Wright Field. They brushed me off like they did you. I heard rumours that the evidence would be released some time soon, but it never was. I kept pestering my good friend, and current Secretary of Defence, Curtis LeMay, for him to arrange access to the laboratories there. He eventually gave me Holy Hell and told me never even to mention it again."

"Mr President, the items at Wright Field are real, but they've been moved from there. In 1951 the entire research project was transferred to an air base in Nevada. The laboratory is underground and called "S4"; it is part of a larger network."

"Is that at Nellis field?"

"No, north of Nellis at Groom Lake; it's sited in Area 51 of the old Department of Energy reservation."

"We have no air base there." put in a man in an AAF Colonel's uniform.

"It's there! I promise you. Go and have a look if you don't believe me."

"Well it seems that a number of TV and newspaper reporters are doing just that right now." said the President. "Thanks to you."

"Tell them to be careful!" said Clane. "That place is dangerous. They have aircraft like the one I came here in. I managed to disable the other ones at S4 before I stole it, but there are more still active that came from somewhere else; and they're up there now."

The President leaned back in his chair behind the Oval Office desk. "Well, I'd like to ask Defence Secretary LeMay what he thinks of this, but I can't. He's disappeared... You see, a lot has happened while you were sitting on top of that flying saucer preaching to the world. Not only has my SecDef vanished, but so have all the Joint Chiefs of Staff, my civilian secretaries of the branches and a dozen flag ranking officers and counting. At the same time there is disorder breaking out all over the country and I've had to suspend *Habeas Corpus*. That means nationwide martial law. I hear other countries are in a similar condition. WorldMesh is down; all international airline flights are grounded. It's looking bad, Mr Quilley."

Clane recalled the chaos following President Truman's initial announcement in 1947. "Do you blame me for this, Mr President?"

Goldwater frowned. "Does it matter right now?... The sudden defection of these officials at the very moment you pop up on the lawn can only mean one thing."

Everybody in the room shifted their feet nervously.

"Somebody is going to try and stage a coup."

"What can we do, Mr President?" asked one of the suits standing to the right of the desk.

"We will operate through an adapted chain of command. Deputies are taking control of units as we speak. The nation is ready to defend itself against the traitors."

"Mr President." said Clane. "I don't think it is."

All eyes turned to look at him.

"Do you presume your judgement on the condition of our armed defences stands above our own?" asked an admiral indignantly.

"Listen to me!" said Clane. "The people who have vanished have probably done so because they're involved with the same cabal that is running the secret base in Area 51... Tell me, Mr President. Is the chairman of Florenti Inc. available right now?"

"No." said Goldwater. "There are reports out that he also has vanished."

"Thought so. The aircraft they have cannot be harmed by our weapons. Look how easily I flew right through the intense defensive anti-aircraft measures of our nation's capitol. Missiles and triple-A rounds made not the slightest dent because of the gravitational shield cast around the craft by the generator. I doubt if a nuclear blast could penetrate that. The people who are about to stage this coup have these machines. If we're going to beat them we're going to have to devise a new method, otherwise we might as well just throw rocks at them."

"Is it true what you said on TV earlier?" asked the President. "They wiped out the Empire State Building with this technology?"

"Yes. Just think what they could to our tanks, our warships, our bombers."

There was silence in the room.

They took a break for some coffee and fresh air. While he was in the Oval Office ante room sipping from his cup there was a commotion in the corridor. A Secret Service agent was standing in the doorway blocking entry to somebody outside. "No, Ma'am. You cannot come in here!"

"I must speak to Clane Quilley!" yelled a female voice.

Clane walked over. He saw a small woman struggling ineffectively to push her way past the burly USSS guard.

"Wait a moment. I'll come out." Clane ducked under the outstretched arm of the agent and came face to face with a woman wearing a white laboratory coat. She wore thick spectacles and her light brown hair was tied loosely in a straggly ponytail. "Who are you and what do you want?"

"I'm Dr Jenny Bulstrode. I'm the professor of mechanical engineering at GWU. I know you're looking for a way to counter the threat from similar vehicles to the one you flew here in."

"How do you know that?"

"It's obvious... Now, I can build you a weapon that can destroy those saucers! In fact I've already got a prototype."

"Are you serious?"

"Please! Come to my laboratory and I'll show you."

"One moment." Clane went back inside and asked the President. "Well, I guess we've got nothing to lose from you checking it out. You're not much use to us here." said Goldwater bitterly. He turned away from Clane with a contemptuous snort.

....

They needed a Secret Service escort for what was usually an easy drive over the beltway and up the Seven to the Ashburn Tech campus of George Washington University. Dr Bulstrode drove steadily behind the black USSS cruiser. The streetlights were all off and broken cloud floated over the dark city. Stars gleamed in between them and red lights flickered on the black outlines of buildings as the police and National Guard struggled to maintain order. The population had panicked again, just like they had in 1947; only this time there was no catharsis of interplanetary invaders, real or fake, to organize and unite them. The enemy this time was real and internal. Clane had worked out why the President was so annoyed with him. Clane had blurted out everything to the press after his spectacular entry into Washington. Would it have been better if he'd held back on certain details? He hadn't revealed every fact to them. In fact at one point President Goldwater had mentioned how there were also stories of rioting in the Soviet Union and that Premier Khrushchev was not answering the red phone. Clane was about to yell: "That's because he's one of them! I met him in a restaurant on the moon." when he thought better of it and held his tongue.

They drove into the deserted university and Dr Bulstrode showed Clane and the agents to her laboratory. The back-up generator was running and the light flicked on in the room. Clane saw a sea of screws, nuts, bolts, drills, lathes, saws, wires, batteries and other paraphernalia. Dr Bulstrode herself, being flesh and blood, looked completely out of place. "Over here." she called out enthusiastically. In the corner she'd set up a pair of polystyrene blocks with wire carefully wrapped round them. She placed a spanner on top of a small stool between the two blocks and started fiddling with knobs and dials on a control box. "Now, stand back!" she warned. The machine started humming. For a moment nothing happened. Then the spanner started rising into the air as if pulled by an invisible wire. Clane blinked and looked again; it was still there, about a foot off the top of the stool. Smoke started to come off the spanner, as if it were made of dry ice. Then there was a flash of light and the metal started dissolving in front of his eyes into a dark fume. It resembled a soluble tablet dropped into water. After a few minutes there was nothing there at all. What had been the spanner was now a foggy haze that filled the room, making Clane cough slightly. "What do you think?" asked Dr Bulstrode.

"What did you do to it?"

"I made it go 'poof!'." she said. "It's done by allowing two electromagnetic fields to interfere in a certain way. If you get the frequency, amplitude and wavelength just right, it releases energy in the interference zone."

"Releases energy from where?"

"I don't know, but I've proved it works. What happened to that wrench happens to objects spontaneously. It's like some of the strange forces we see in nature. You know when a tornado flies through a barnyard and bits of hay get embedded in intact glass window panes... Look, there's no time to talk over the nuts and bolts stuff right now. We need to start building more of these before the saucers arrive!"

"Will it work against them?"

"Yes, because it's not effected by gravitational fields. There's no escape from this energy; even if you're in a bunker a hundred feet underground. It's like a magic bullet. I knew they'd used this on the ESB as soon as I saw the newsreels. I've written a book about it; look." She threw a large hardback book onto one of the benches. It had on its cover one of the most famous photographs of the Empire State Building being destroyed and the title: *Where did the Tower Go?*"

....

Clane and Dr Jenny Bulstrode drove back to DC to instruct the Army Corps of Engineers. They quickly improvised some telegraph equipment and DoE cables to construct the directed energy weapons. Caxton had provided a vital clue in his taunting of Clane over the radio. The saucers could be reduced to "iron filings" if the fields were arranged just right. The Corps set the transmitters up on top of hills in four locations; Arlington, Aspen Hill, Alexandria and Largo. "Be very careful." warned Dr Bulstrode. "If you focus the fields at any location inside Washington you could pulverize a city block!" The Corpsman she addressed looked ashen, still not believing that this arrangement of wires could do anything other than provide an unusual landscape decoration. All they could do now was wait for Caxton to make his move. Clane lay on a bench in an Army Corps of Engineers tent in Arlington, sleeping in shallow snatches. He thought a lot about Gina and his children. Were they safe?... Considering the circumstances they were probably in the safest place in the world. Not only were they in a location where Caxton was highly unlikely to find them, but they were away from the lawless terror of the cities. He longed to contact them, or even go and see them, but he couldn't risk it; not until the threat was removed.

As dawn was breaking loud voices rose. Clane awoke with a jolt. The capital's air detection radar had picked up a trio of contacts heading inwards from the west. They were at five thousand feet and moving very fast, over a thousand knots. "Those are no planes." The radar operator's voice said over the radio.

"Alert! Alert!" ordered the Corps commander and the soldiers all jumped to their feet, as did Dr Bulstrode. The professor helped the team rotate the transmitter to focus on the targets and follow them, coordinating with the post on Aspen Hill, getting the angle just right.

Clane's roamphone rang. Caxton's number appeared on the display. He answered it. "What do you want, Gerald?"

"We're coming to get you, Clane!" his former friend's voice jeered. "You can't stop us! Your bombs and bullets are all futile against us! We're going to obliterate Washington!... It's all your fault for what you did! You made this attack necessary!"

Clane ended the call. He looked up at the dark western sky and could make out a row of three dots just below the clouds.

"NOW!" yelled Dr Bulstrode. There was a humming noise from the wires. "Watch the angle! Up a degree!... Aspen, you're too far to the east!" The dots in the sky changed. A halo of vapour appeared around them, like jelly around frog spawn. They began to descend sharply; the descent turned into a plummet. They left a trail of vapour as they fell. Like the pieces of the Empire State Building, nothing remained of the reproduction vehicles to hit the ground.

Clane's roamphone rang again. "DAMN YOU, CLANE... DAMN YOU!... MAY YOU DIE IN AGONY, YOU BASTARD!" Clane was disappointed that Caxton himself had not been aboard any of those disks.

Everybody was cheering and whooping. Dr Bulstrode ran over and gave Clane a rib-cracking hug of joy. Over the raucous clamour of voices, Clane only just heard the text tone on his roam. It was a brief message from Caxton: *IT'S NOT OVER YET, CLANE. GC.*

Two hours later more radar contacts appeared. This time they were to the east over the Atlantic Ocean. They were travelling at over two thousand knots and there were hundreds of them. A US Navy warship patrolling off Norfolk, Virginia got a visual sighting of them. They were both disks and triangles. "Oh no." muttered Dr Bulstrode. "How can we possibly beam all of them? It was hard enough just bringing down three." There was a sorrowful silence among the crowd as they watched the vehicles approach on the radar repeater. Then the contacts started to disappear. The ship radioed them to announce that the enemy flying vessels were all dropping out of the sky like dead flies. They were impacting the water a few miles from the warship and sinking. The water there was very deep and the ships sonar heard the hulls imploding under the enormous water pressure as they reached the lowest layers of the ocean. "What the hell!?" murmured Clane. Then his roamphone rang. He answered it. "Hello?"

"Goddammit! It's not easy writing computer viruses when you've got a pounding headache!"

Clane recognized the voice. "Gordy!" He laughed.

"You owe me at least two beers, pal!" answered Gordon Stephens.

"I owe you a barrel!... I'm so sorry about that."

"If you'd asked me nicely for the key I'd probably have given it to you, Clane. I was trying to work out how I could take out those craft; and then I realized that if I attacked them electronically I could do it, because they're one hundred percent computer controlled. When I saw what you'd done I knew those creeps would have to break cover and go for a governmental take-over so I inserted a small 'update' into their software." They laughed together while the others all cheered again.

Clane returned to Washington and entered the Oval Office. "What now?" President Goldwater asked.

Clane looked around at the military officers with smart uniforms and medal ribbons across their chests. They also stared at him expectantly. There was no doubt the President was addressing him. "Well... Mr President. I advise that you go for Area 51. Finish off the scumbags while they're down."

Goldwater nodded at the Army general to his right and the man immediately dashed from the room.

....

Clane sat in the back seat of a jeep. He wore a broad-brimmed sunhat to protect his head from the blazing Nevada sunshine and he gulped from a water bottle every few minutes. His vehicle was driving behind a long column of tanks, armoured personnel carriers and lorries heading south on Highway 375, a principle route through the desert in Lincoln County north of Las Vegas. They passed a tiny settlement called Rachel, just a collection of trailers and a small diner called *Pat & Joe's*; Clane had never heard of the place. They passed a junction where there was a black mailbox, just a boxy structure mounted on a pillar; it looked strange in the middle of nowhere. When they came to another junction the column turned right. There were over a hundred tanks from the US Army North and the Nevada National Guard and Clane's jeep was at the rear so he saw the tanks moving down the new road from a side angle a mile or so before he reached it himself. The road they turned off on was unpaved and the tracks of the armoured vehicles kicked up a massive thick cloud of dust that must have been visible for miles. The road ran as straight as a ruler directly towards the distant mountains to the east, one of the few arteries that linked the covert installation with the outside world. After half an hour they approached the mountains and the road turned sharply into a high pass. There was no fence or gate to stop them entering the unnamed secret base, just a pair or signboards on the verges of the road saying: *WARNING- RESTRICTED AREA. NO TRESPASSING BEYOND THIS POINT. PHOTOGRAPHY OF THIS AREA IS STRICTLY PROHIBITED.* A pair of unmarked pickup trucks was parked down a side road on the crest of a hill overlooking the perimeter. Clane had learned that these were run by private civilian security guards provided by Florenti Inc. The drivers of the vehicles did not move. They sat in their seats dumbstruck, watching helplessly as the armoured cavalry force rumbled past. The column carried on up into the twisting bends of the pass and went past the guardhouse used by the Florenti troopers. As they crossed the top of the pass they had a clear view beyond of the Area 51 secret base. It looked very familiar to Clane because of the views he had had of it at a high altitude as he came into land on the Janet airliners. As they descended to ground level and came close to the facility a squadron of aircraft flew overhead and left behind a trail of opening parachutes. The paratroopers drifted down like dandelion seeds. Their landing was timed perfectly with the arrival of the army at the base's buildings. The jeeps full of observers hung back for their own safety as the infantry units dashed forward and entered the base buildings. A number of the vehicles headed along the road to S4. There were two hours of confused action then Clane saw rows of people being escorted from the buildings with their hands on their heads. A senior officer approached the observer group. "They all surrendered immediately. These are merely low-level contractor employees. We're continuing the search of the facility, but this will take some time. The installation is far bigger than it looks. There are multiple underground levels, as well as the S4 facility and other outreach locations. Some of the sectors of the facility we cannot enter right now. They might contain unknown dangers and will need specialist intervention. We've even discovered what looks like a long-distance underground railway system and we're not sure where it leads."

"Colonel." said Clane. "Have you found Gerald Caxton yet?"

"There's no sign of him, Mr Quilley."

....

Social unrest continued unabated. The day after he returned from monitoring the invasion of Area 51, President Goldwater assigned Clane a new task. Clane drove with his police escort to an address in urban Virginia and banged on the front door. "Mr Lomell, are you in?"

An upstairs window opened and a frightened face appeared. "Who's there?"

"Ah, hello, Mr Lomell." Clane looked up at him. "I've been sent by President Goldwater to ask you to return to work."

"Why should I?" The man was holding a shotgun and he pointed its barrel out of the window.

"Because the country needs you."

"Me? Why?"

"Because you're the general manager of the Bremo Bluff Power Station. This provides electricity to the entire capitol area. The area has been blacked out for two weeks. We need your services to restore electrical power to the region."

"I'm afraid I have to stay here and look after my family, sir." replied Lomell. "There are vicious punks roaming the streets right now, or hadn't you noticed?"

"I know, but why can't you take them with you?"

"Because they need food and water."

"The government has a supply which they will provide you with. You'll also be paid a hazardous duty bonus for your effort."

"How will we get there?"

"There's a police cruiser waiting here right now to drive you."

"What about my staff? I can't run the power station without them?"

"Give us their names and addresses and we'll bring them to you. They'll receive the same bonus you will."

Lomell agreed and within two days the Bremo Bluff Power Station was running again. Clane moved on to other essential utility providers, the gas and water companies, the hospitals, the sanitation operatives. Slowly, but surely, the infrastructure began to be restored. That was the first step to creating an atmosphere in which the general public could gradually calm down. "A new normal will emerge" became one of Goldwater's formulas; it wasn't quite original.

A number of people were arrested by the FBI as suspects, mostly because of the witness testimony Clane had submitted of his trips to the restaurant on the moon. David Rockefeller had vanished in the exodus, but Marilyn Monroe had not. She was taken from her home and questioned for a number of days, but she insisted she knew nothing and was released. It would be necessary to send a rocket up to the moon to verify the presence of Spaceviews. It was likely, given the technology possessed by the cabal, that they had establishments on other heavenly bodies too, but this line of inquiry would have to wait. The first priority was to humanity's own planet. Once the electricity was back on, televisions could be switched on again, Computers would work and WorldMesh could be reestablished. On the thirtieth of September, just three weeks after Clane had landed his stolen disk on the White House Lawn, the President addressed the nation from the Oval Office. His speech was televised on every channel and streamed live on all WorldMesh video boards: *"My fellow Americans. People of planet Earth."* began President Goldwater. *"The time of greatest need is upon our country and our planet. It was only a short time ago that revelations emerged that forced us to confront the fact that almost everything we took for granted about our world, in every field of human experience, past and present, our politics and our history, even our very place in God's universe, was a pretence, a* Wizard of Oz *curtain pulled over reality to blind us from the truth. At the moment there are no answers to the obvious questions; ones that you are all asking as much as I do: If the world I thought was real is fake, then what is real instead?... I don't know. Nobody knows. These answers will come eventually. We must be patient. At the moment we must simply concentrate on keeping calm, keeping strong and working to rebuild our world. The immediate threat of retaliatory global destruction is over, mostly thanks to heroes such as Clane Quilley, Gordon Stephens and Dr Jenny Bulstrode, as well as the brave men of the armed services. As I speak, turmoil reigns across much of the world. In Europe especially, governments have collapsed and society itself as dissolved into chaos. Millions have died. Here in the Unites States of America we have taken the first steps to restoring our civilization. It is my hope that we will lead by example and beat a path for other nations to follow. The danger is not yet over. The criminal conspiracy that had managed to infect the entire globe with its poisonous tentacles has been exposed, but its masterminds are still at large. The search goes on to track down our enemy and deal them a* coup-de-grace *so that their threat to our human world is stamped out forever. Until then, we must maintain the situation. Stand tall, take care of one another. A day will come when we will have a proper society again, and maybe one which is an improvement on what we had before; liberated as it will be from this evil underground empire, one so arrogant in its power that it even placed its secret symbol on the Great Seal of our nation. I don't know the future, but I cherish hope. We need hope. Let us not allow doubts to deflect us from our path. People of America, people of the world. I bid you goodnight. And a good future. God bless us all."*

....

Clane returned to Las Vegas the next morning on the first airline flight to start running again after the crisis. He was treated as a celebrity and given a seat in first class. The captain came back to talk to him. "If these flying saucers can be mass-produced, will that put me out of a job?" he asked.

Clane shrugged. "I don't know."

"Hope not. Either way, I'll miss these normal aircraft." When Clane landed at McCarran, he walked over to the Janet terminal where he'd left his car and drove home. He went to his desk and took his revolver from the drawer. He loaded every chamber and then returned to the car. He headed north towards Oregon. The roads were all deserted except for military vehicles which paid him no heed. He reached Crater Lake National Park by mid afternoon. The weather was hot and sunny and the forest beautiful as he scaled the narrow lanes leading up into the mountains. Leafy shadows swept across the windscreen of his car. He pulled into the glade where the log cabin was and parked. The door to the cabin was open. He got out. "Gina?... Siobhan?"

There was no sound except the twittering of birds in the woods. He went into the little house. There was nobody inside, but he could see it had recently been occupied. Then he heard a piercing scream some distance away. He recognized the voice immediately. "BRENDAN!" He dived into the woods and sprinted in the direction of the scream. Brendan screamed again. Clane tore through bushes and hurdled fallen logs. He drew the pistol from his pocket. If Caxton were harming his son in any way then within two minutes Caxton would be dead; of this Clane had no doubt at all. Brendan screamed a third time just as Clane burst out of the woods into a clearing with a river running through it. Brendan was standing in the river up to his chest a few feet from Siobhan who was splashing water at him. He shrieked in amusement and tossed water back at her. Both were wearing swimsuits. Gina was sitting by the river bank on a picnic blanket reading a book. There was an open basket on the blanket and a half-finished bottle of Coca Cola. His wife looked up at him. "Clane!" she smiled.

"Daddy!" called out Brendan.

Gina jumped up and came towards him. "How was work?... What's wrong, honey?"

Clane was puffing and panting uncontrollably. As the sight of his family sunk in he began weeping the same way. He sheepishly made the revolver safe and slid it back into his pocket.

When Clane had recovered the family returned to the log cabin together. "Do you really have no idea what's been going on?" Clane asked.

"Well, the TV's not working, and you said we shouldn't use our roams." said Siobhan. "Are you going to tell us what all this is about?"

"Good Lord, where do I start?"

Clane, Gina and Siobhan cooked a barbecue as night fell and the woodland crickets serenaded them. It took him that long to explain. They listened unperturbed. Just as he was climbing into bed he received a roamtext: *NICE WORK, MR Q. MEET ME IN PRAGUE. FB.* "Prague?" Clane frowned.

"What's up?" asked Gina.

"I've just had a text from an angel."

"Ha ha!" She chuckled drowsily, snuggled down in her sleeping bag and switched off her lamp.

....

Getting to Prague would not be easy, but if Clane had learned anything from Flying Buffalo, it was that where there's a will there's a way. Transatlantic air traffic was still grounded and there was a minimal continental service in Europe. Most airports were still closed. He had to go online and explore some of the darker regions of WorldMesh where, along with the drug dealers, hit men and prostitutes, he found some chartered pilots with somewhat dubious claims of being properly licensed. He had to pay over a hundred and fifty dollars for the journey and meet his pilot at a rural airfield in Maryland. The aircraft was an ancient DC3 with rust on its skin. The pilot wore a uniform and greeted him professionally, obviously making an attempt to appear legal. Clane strapped himself into a rickety seat in the cabin and prayed as the pilot revved up the badly tuned engines. His ears were muffled and his bottom tingling as he got out to stretch his legs when they came in to land on one of the islands of the Azores. It was three AM and pitch dark. The pilot refuelled quickly, chatting furtively to the airfield staff and looking over his shoulder as if he expected the police to arrive. Then they were up in the sky again for the second leg of the flight. Clane wanted to feel relieved when the pilot called back to tell him that they were about to come in to land at Prague, but found it difficult when he remembered that there would be a return journey. One of the perks of such an overpriced flight was that the pilot would wait at the airport to take him home again afterwards. It was a gloomy wet lunchtime as the plane touched down at Ruzyne Airport. The plane didn't bother with the terminal. It pulled up at a corner of the apron and some people who didn't look like airline employees dragged a staircase over to the door.

The airport buildings were deserted and Clane walked straight through passport control and customs without seeing a soul. His celestial friend was standing outside the main entrance. Flying Buffalo was wearing a dirty duffle coat and deerstalker. He carried a large rucksack on his back and walked steadily along the middle of the tarmac road into the city from the airport. There was no public transport or vehicles available and so they had to walk to their destination; one which the old Indian refused to reveal to Clane when he asked. The picturesque old city in the heart of Czechoslovakia was silent and still. Piles of rubbish cluttered the street. The people were all as badly dressed as Flying Buffalo and they shuffled unsteadily between the tall ornate terraces searching through the piles of refuse or climbing through the broken windows of shops. "This is terrible, Flying Buffalo. It's far worse than '47. Has the whole world gone like this?"

"Most of it. The Middle East has coped slightly better, perhaps because Islam has the concept of alien beings, the *Djinn.* By comparison Christianity is decidedly thin on them."

"But Czechoslovakia is... was.... a communist country."

"The doctrine of Marx and Lenin is even less explanatory on the worlds beyond."

Clane nodded grimly as he watched a thin old woman roasting an animal over an open fire on the pavement; it looked like a cat.

Flying Buffalo continued. "You know, the shamans of the Cree nation of the US Canadian border have an interesting view on the weevil grubs that live inside groundnuts. When people break open the nuts, the grubs die. The shamans say that they die of shock. They've spent their entire lives inside that little nut and so assume that the interior of the nut is the entire universe and there is nothing beyond it. Then what they thought was the whole universe splits open and the grub sees how much more exists beyond what they thought did... and their mind can't cope with it, so they expire on the spot."

"And we humans are like those grubs?"

Flying Buffalo gave him a sideways glance. "Humbling isn't it."

They crossed one of the bridges over the river Vltava and came across a roadblock of broken furniture manned by men with guns and other home-made weapons. They closed ranks as Clane and Flying Buffalo approached. "What's going on?" hissed Clane.

"This barrier marks the edge of the territory of one of the warlords that rule over Prague at the moment."

"Will the hurt us?"

"Not so long as we pay the toll to pass through."

"I don't have any money."

"It's not money they want." The Indian put down his rucksack and opened it. He pulled out a bottle of vodka. He spoke to the men in what sounded like the Czech language and a conversation ensued. Flying Buffalo handed the men three bottles of the spirit and then they pulled aside part of the barricade and stood back to let him and Clane pass. Clane chuckled. "Vodka made in Heaven."

"Literally!" Flying Buffalo smiled. They continued east through Prague until they came across a white wall running along one side of a street. They walked along it until they came to a gate and then went in. They found themselves in a huge cemetery with rows and rows of large grave stones running between long twisting paths. There were tall trees everywhere between the grave plots. Flying Buffalo picked up his pace. "Hurry, Clane! We need to get undercover in time."

"In time for what?"

He didn't reply. They marched quickly towards the centre of the huge necropolis until they came to a circular marble patio on the junction of four paths. In the middle of it was a stone table, like a church altar. Flying Buffalo looked around himself to make sure nobody was watching then he walked over to a large crypt and wrenched back one of the stone panels. "Get in."

"What? That's a grave!"

"Get in." he repeated in the same low forceful tone he used when he'd met Clane in 1947. Clane got down on his hands and knees and crawled into the dark granite enclosure. It smelled dry and mouldy. He hoped there weren't bones in it. The ground under his hands was hard and covered in grit. Flying Buffalo crawled in afterwards and pulled the stone back. They were not completely shut it; there was a small crack on the side facing the patio. "Are you going to tell me what the hell you're doing bringing me in here!?" Clane hissed.

"I've brought you to see something."

"See what?"

"Something you need to see."

Clane rolled his eyes and shook his head.

....

Clane's left wrist was painful. It had never completely recovered from the injury he'd suffered with it during his kidnapping three years before, but all it had been was slightly stiff. Now it was aching badly. Clane had fallen asleep on the stone slabs of the crypt floor. Soon after entering the grave he had eventually plucked up courage to stretch out and his limbs and didn't encounter any piles of solid corporeal matter. He was very tired, having flown all night without sleeping properly on the very uncomfortable plane, and so eventually he failed to resist his drowsiness. A few hours had passed and it was now much darker than it had been earlier. Through the crack outside he could see that most of the sunlight had faded. The cloud had cleared somewhat and stars peeked through. Prague was as dark as a forest, not a single bulb shone from any window in the city. "It's almost time." Flying Buffalo was squatting beside him on the floor. "I want you to wear this." He produced something that Clane couldn't see. When he felt it in his hands he could tell it was some kind of strap that felt and smelled like leather.

"What is it?" Clane asked.

"A gag. Tie it round your head, covering your mouth."

"Why?"

"You need to remain silent. That is absolutely essential; your life depends on it."

"Can't I just stay silent of my own accord?"

In the gloom Flying Buffalo shook his silhouetted head.

Clane put the gag on, leaving it slightly loose.

"Look out of the crack, but be careful not to get too close. You must not be seen." Clane shifted over and placed his eye close to the crack to get a better view. The patio crossroads was about a hundred feet away. There seemed to be some kind of movement there, as if people were walking back and forth; or maybe it was just foxes or rabbits. Then he saw a flicker of light; just the flare of a small flame, but it was dazzling against his night-weary eyes. The flame dimmed slightly and then brightened again. This time it continued to brighten until it became clear that somebody had ignited a brazier, just in front of the altar. The whole scene was illuminated by the light of the flame. Long and undulating shadows weaved back and forth across the rows of tombs. The stone structures gleamed like polished brass. Whoever had lit the brazier quickly departed; Clane saw his or her back vanish into the darkness. Then he heard the sound of voices in the distance. There were multiple voices, male and female. They seemed to be speaking rhythmically and in unison, as if reciting a poem together. The sound came from all around Clane and Flying Buffalo. A procession of people entered the patio, approaching from all four pathways, in groups of three or four in single file. They were the ones who had been speaking and now their words were audible, but were not of a language Clane understood or recognized. All the people were wearing long black cowls that covered their entire bodies except their hands and feet. They had the hoods fully draped over their heads obscuring their faces. Clane wondered how they could even see where they were going. They continued their monotone chant and they spread out in a circle around the brazier and stone table. Clane counted them; there were thirteen people in the circle. They threw back their hoods and exposed their heads. Clane frowned and moved closer to the crack; Flying Buffalo held him back by his shoulder. Some of the people in the strange coven he instantly and easily recognized. To his left was the Queen of England, Elizabeth II. Her black hair was tied back neatly in a bun. David Rockefeller was there, next to the Queen, as well as several other faces Clane knew while their names escaped him. Although they were very famous and some were on Goldwater's missing list. He was so taken aback by seeing these household names in such unexpected circumstances that it took him a moment to notice that one of the men was Gerald Caxton. Despite his bizarre vestment there was no mistaking his dark eyes, snub nose and wide mouth. Their chorus then settled down into the rhythmic repetition of a single phrase: "RAZ-BALOOTA!... RAZ-BALOOTA!... RAZ-BALOOTA!... RAZ-BALOOTA!..." Then, in a single motion they all reached up and undid the clasps on their cowls; these fell to the floor revealing that they were all naked underneath. Their skin glowed orange in the firelight. Then Clane saw the sight that would haunt him for the rest of his life. The fleshy white bodies of the people in the circle expanded and mutated, in just the space of about two seconds, into what looked like a cross between a lizard and a human. They grew about a foot taller in the process and small tails sprouted from the base of their backs. Their faces were thrust forwards; scaly snouts morphed out of their noses and mouths. Their eyes became large, yellow slits like a snake's.

Flying Buffalo's hand was over Clane's mouth before his scream of shock had time to press against the gag. Clane couldn't tear his gaze away, as if he were hypnotized by whatever black magic this ritual was conjuring up. Then another group of people emerged from the darkness beyond the fire to the right. They were children, aged between five and eight; all naked. They held hands and moved forward in a row, about ten of them. At that moment the fire itself began to change. The natural random shapes of the flames began to shape-shift into an organized form...

....

Clane's hands were shaking as he tried to force his key into the front door of his house in Las Vegas. Gina heard him scraping at the lock and opened the door before he had succeeded. "Hi, honey. You're back! Where have you been?"

"Prague."

"Prague in Czechoslovakia?"

"Yes."

"Well, there's good news; the electricity is back on..." She broke off as she saw the expression on his face.

Clane looked at his children. "Siobhan, could you take Brendan for a little walk in the park?"

His daughter looked up at him and nodded, understanding. When they were alone he told Gina what he'd seen. Gina went to the kitchen and poured herself a large glass of wine. "Clane, are you sure you didn't imagine all this?"

"In the morning when we climbed out of the tomb, there were still people washing the blood off the altar... It's like, they were doing it as if they were used to it. As if they were no different to the guys who cut the grass or prune the bushes. They didn't even give us a second look."

She sat beside him and took a long gulp from her glass. "You know what? Deep down I always knew there was something wrong about Gerald. It was not anything I could name; just a niggling sense... The thing is he saved my life."

"Not for your benefit, but for his own."

"I know... And how many millions of other people have died because that medicine is not available."

Clane smiled. "It will be soon. It'll be available in every hospital in the world... Along with a lot of other wonders... That's the good thing that's come out of this."

Chapter 20

It was midday and the heat from the tropical summer sun was almost unbearable. Clane's brow showered into the sunhat that blocked out the glare. Beside him stood Gordon Stephens with his head wrapped in a turban, not unlike the traditional headgear of the local men standing in nearby. He had a bald patch on his scalp. The hair had never grown back on the spot where he'd had his operation to repair the skull fracture and remove the subdural haematoma... that had cost Clane three barrels of beer. He accepted his providence with goodwill, calling it his "sunroof". Dr Jenny Bulstrode was clad in knee-length brown trousers and a legionnaire's hat. They all waited.

Adigala was a town that had suffered more than any other from the decade-long drought that had devastated the region. Its mud-brick buildings rose out of featureless, desiccated land. To one side ran a low undulating ditch that showed where the river used to flow. The soil was gone, turned into dust as surely as if by one of Dr Bulstrode's machines. It blew over the rocky plain in clumps and dust devils. A cluster of about two hundred people stood in disorganized groups. The men wore white gowns beneath their turbans and the women had on multicoloured dresses. They were all thin and malnourished; yet they smiled and chattered optimistically. The monotonous panorama was broken by the large circular depression in front of them. It had been dug a few weeks ago by a team of excavators and it was lined with waterproof cement. The mouth of the pipe was about three feet in diameter and yawned like a python over the edge of the pit. The pipeline itself stretched away to the east as far as the eye could see. It was a very unusual pipeline though because it wasn't built in a straight line. It undulated like a snake in regular meanders, as if imitating the natural course of a river. Near the spot where the pipeline ended stood a thin man dressed in an elaborately decorated tunic and hat. He had brown skin, black curly hair and a similar beard. He was making a speech in the native Amharic language, using a loudspeaker run off a portable generator. There was a round of applause from the crowd as the man finished his speech. Then he turned and gestured at Clane. "Mr Quilley, can you come and talk here?" he asked in broken English.

Clane stepped forward and took the microphone from the Emperor of Abyssinia. "Thank you very much." He squinted at the crowd, trying to filter out the glare from the sun off the ground. "Your Imperial Majesty, people of Abyssinia. I can't speak your language; I'm sorry. I hope you can all understand me."

The people smiled politely, but didn't affirm.

"Your country has suffered terribly these last few years. Over a million of your compatriots have died. All the time this was going on, while the world watched in sympathy with you, a malicious conspiracy was underway that kept secret the means to prevent all those deaths. On this day, June the fifth 1958, we will finally see a real sign that this conspiracy and secrecy has ended. In a few minutes water will emerge from this pipeline that will fill this reservoir. You can use this water to drink, cleanse and irrigate your land. When the water is used up it will be filled again, and again, and again, in a supply that is virtually infinite. The water that is about to emerge comes from the sea, but it is not salty. The salt and other harmful impurities have been removed from it at the new desalination plant at the other end of the pipeline at the Gulf of Tadjoura in Djibouti. The means to desalinate seawater has been known for many centuries, but to do it on a practical scale was impossible because of the energy needed that came from fossil fuels and was very restricted and had to be paid for. This desalination plant runs off a Digby Carrousel, a machine invented in Canada in 1915 by Jemima Digby and immediately classified top secret. It desalinates the seawater for almost no money at all. The fresh water then travels along this pipeline without any pumps. It can even flow uphill. It uses the water's own internal energy discovered by the Austrian forester Viktor Schauberger in 1930 and... you guessed it! Immediately classified top secret. This new irrigation system is just the first of a whole array of them that will be built all the way along the east coast of Africa. It will turn this parched wasteland into a new Garden of Eden. It means that hunger and thirst will never return to your continent again!"

The few people who understood clapped; then those who didn't followed their cue.

Then a rumbling sound rose from the pipe. Like an approaching storm it started, as just a whisper and increasing to a thundering roar. Then a torrent of the cleanest clearest water burst out of its maw; drops of it glittering like diamonds in the sunlight. It crashed into the bottom of the new reservoir and formed a pool, swirling and bubbling deliciously. The crowd of people leapt in the air with delight. They ran down the hard packed bowl of the pond and jumped into the water fully clothed. They splashed around like children, whooping and singing for joy. The women all had large clay pitchers which they dipped into the expanding lake and filled them to the brim. They then passed them up the slope to where a row of children waited with cups and beakers. The whole population of the village gulped and swigged the water blissfully.

Clane, Gordon Stephens and Dr Jenny Bulstrode watched them, laughing and smiling with them. Clane eventually noticed that there was one man who remained calm and didn't join in with the celebrations. He stood behind them, out of their field of view. He was wearing the same local fashion as the other men, but when

Clane walked closer to him he recognized him as Flying Buffalo. "Hello, Mr Quilley."

"Hello, Flying Buffalo. It's good to see you again."

"Have you forgiven me for Prague?"

"It didn't take me long to realize that there was nothing to forgive. What did you do except show me what already exists? Caxton was wrong. We don't need lies to keep our world going. Think how much worse it would be if people *didn't* know."

"Your quest is not over yet, Mr Quilley. Gerald Caxton is still out there, along with all the others. They have not yet given up. At some point soon, they will attack again."

"I know... And we're ready for them!"

The old Indian smiled affectionately and admiringly. He turned his head and studied the horizon. "As for me, my work here is done."

There was a pause. "I'm never going to see you again, am I?" As Clane spoke those words a terrible wave of sorrow and loneliness spread through him.

"You might, Mr Quilley. A time could come when I'll have to reach out to you again, maybe sooner than you think."

"I'll miss you... I'll never forget you."

"I shall always be with you, Mr Quilley; even if you can't see me. Remember that."

"Put in a good word for me with the Boss, would you?"

Flying Buffalo chuckled and shook his head. "For a man like you, anything I could say would be superfluous... Goodbye, Clane. All the best to you." He reached out his hand.

Clane shook it, curiously taken aback by how Flying Buffalo had used his Christian name for the first time.

Clane watched as Flying Buffalo walked away across the desert, exactly as Clane had seen him do when they'd first met outside Roswell in July of 1947. The old Indian eventually crested a gentle rise and dipped down over the other side out of sight. Clane was suddenly seized by a compulsion and ran. He ran after Flying Buffalo as fast as he could. He reached the top of the rise and looked down over the other side. Flying Buffalo was gone. Empty desert stretched away into the distance. Then Clane noticed a large rock with a flat top. There as something lying in the middle of its horizontal surface. He picked it up. It was an American groundnut; a very odd thing to find here in the heart of eastern Africa. He cracked it between his fingers and it fell open. The flesh of the fruit parted neatly and poking out of a hole in it was a white weevil grub. It swung its top segments back and forth like a worm, exposed to the world for the first time. It dropped from the nut and landed on the ground between Clane's feet. Clane expected it to die on the baking hot hard earth, but it didn't. It crawled energetically away. It seemed possessed by a spirit of determination and adventure. Clane followed its brave sojourn with his eyes until it reached a nearby tuft of grass and disappeared from view. He looked again at the groundnut in his hand. "Right." he said to himself. "Just watch what we can do with this planet!"

The End

If you enjoyed this book you might be interested in these websites:

http://www.paradigmresearchgroup.org/
http://www.richplanet.net/
http://www.ufotruthmagazine.co.uk/
http://www.disclosureproject.org/
http://www.exopoliticsgb.com/
http://www.exopolitics.org.uk/
http://www.stantonfriedman.com/
http://www.citizenhearing.org/
http://richarddolanpress.com/
http://www.checktheevidence.com/cms/
http://hpanwo.blogspot.co.uk/

Ben Emlyn-Jones' second novel *Rockall* is available free to read online at:
http://hpanwo-bb.blogspot.co.uk/2009/02/rockall-chapter-1.html

Ben Emlyn-Jones' first novel *Evan's Land* is available via private sale in limited numbers. Please email the publisher at:
bennyjay74@gmx.co.uk

Lightning Source UK Ltd.
Milton Keynes UK
UKOW06f1241020916

282047UK00017B/384/P